Jane Doe Seventeen

by K Lynn Gardner
Cover by Kory Sunday

Jane Doe Seventeen

Dedication

This book is for my mother, who gave me the courage to publish this book, and for my father, who taught me to love reading. For Kory and Alexi, who are my everything, and in remembrance of Mr. Thunderheart, for being my soulmate. And of course, for the drinking club with a book problem, who inspired me to finish this book.

Special thanks to the movie, *Dream House*, because it gave me the inspiration to begin writing this book.

Monday 9:03pm

Shannon stood on the escalator, her cell phone to her ear, as she descended through the center of the massive marketplace, which was essentially a combination department store and grocery store. The second story with its furniture, home goods, clothing and much more disappeared from view as the first floor opened up around her and a very different range of products came into view. Chips, baby food and pet supplies were off to the right, the beer and soda aisle was straight ahead and the frozen food section began to her left.

"I'm probably gonna lose you soon, Honey. I'm headed downstairs and the reception isn't good in some parts of the store. Want me to get you anything?" There was a pause. "OK, I'll be home in about 15 minutes."

Arriving at the bottom, she stepped gracefully forward through the drink aisle where she loaded a four-pack of Starbucks, Frappuccino, Mocha into her shopping basket and then continued on to the pharmacy in the front, right corner of the massive store.

A sweet, elderly man was backing up in one of the store's electronic scooter-carts. Shannon found it quite comical that the cart was making that beep-beep sound like commercial trucks do when backing up.

The man said, "If I run over anyone, just tell me." winking and smiling at her.

She smiled back and walked passed him to grab some antacid from the shelf and add it to her basket. She selected assorted berries because she couldn't stand the regular ones; too chalky. Reviewing her mental grocery list brought the realization that she still needed some vanilla lip balm and wanted to look at the barrettes just two aisles over.

Shannon Medford was a slender young woman in her early thirties. She was barely 5'5" with dark, auburn hair that framed her oval face in curls. She had dark eyes, and across her high cheek bones was a sprinkling of freckles, which her mother informed her at a young age, were angel kisses.

She found the lip balm and then pondered over the wide variety of hair accessories. Most of them would never work in her thick, unruly hair, but she found one barrette that looked strong enough without feeling too heavy. Both items went into her basket and then she checked her watch. It was 9:18pm and it would be getting pretty dark outside. September nights were still nice, but the sun set a lot earlier so she took her basket of goodies and went back up the escalator to the self-check-out station on the second floor.

Four check-out stations framed in a large square area just in front of the entry/exit. Only two were in use; one by a young lady that looked like a college kid wearing a red university sweatshirt, and the other by a man in jeans, work boots and a dirty T-shirt. The man was buying a six-pack of beer. Shannon guessed he had probably earned that beer by working on some construction site all day.

At the third register, she passed each item over the glass where the red laser lights performed their magic and registered a price on the screen. She placed her items into a plastic bag, and then swiped her debit card to complete the transaction. Her receipt crept silently from the tiny printer as she gathered up the flimsy bag and put it inside of a second bag for strength. She snagged the receipt and headed out the exit.

The store was built on a hill so that both the east and west entrances opened to an upper and lower ground level. Shannon exited at the high end, to the east and weaved her way through the rows of parked cars heading diagonally toward the sidewalk. Once there she turned right and headed south toward her home. She lived just southeast of the center of the city in one of the historic districts, and the grocery store was only two and a half blocks north of the turn-of-the-century Victorian home she shared with her husband, Andrew.

She walked under the light of the full moon, accompanied by a few stars peeking out behind gathering clouds. The air was cool and felt refreshing after a hot, September day. When she arrived at the corner, the crosswalk sign displayed the little illuminated man in his perpetual walking position. She checked for cars, out of habit, and crossed the street. Stepping up onto the opposite sidewalk she heard someone else crossing behind her. A lot of people walked and biked around the neighborhood year-round. She looked back and found no one there. She surveyed the entire intersection in search of another pedestrian but the cross walks were all empty. 'My imagination', she thought.

She continued on toward home taking notice of the strange, concrete building on her right. It was some kind of post-modern, two-story architecture firm made of grey concrete slabs. The lower level was a half-basement with huge windows at ground level, and a wide set of steps led up to the first floor. If you drove by it during the day, you would hardly notice it through the tall trees and bushes growing in the wide grassy area between the sidewalk and the building. Walking by, however, allowed time to see everything inside beyond the huge window panes. Tonight, the building was dark and empty, and the trees and bushes made it a little creepy.

As she passed by the far end of the building, she thought she saw someone step back into the shadows; probably a homeless man looking for a good place to crash for the night.

A brick wall running the property line separated the stark, concrete building from another architecture firm who's building could not be anymore the opposite of its strange, cold neighbor. This was a historic building set farther back and separated from the street by a parking lot. The brick wall, which stood about five feet high and matched the building, enclosed the entire property and was disrupted only by a cast iron gate that controlled access to the parking lot. The bricks were varying shades of red and orange-brown, and definitely original to the structure.

Shannon had walked this way many times before, but had never seen anyone entering or exiting, in spite of the cars in the lot, which was dark and empty now.

The next building on her right was a huge garden and nursery that consumed the remainder of the block. From the sidewalk, the building was a two-story stone, structure that reminded her of a castle. The high, second story windows covered with wooden shutters, and the appearance of the building was softened by strategically placed Lamb's Ear, African Violets and English Lavender as ground cover. What really set the atmosphere were the years and years of healthy, Ivy growth climbing the stone walls.

The vast parking lot took up the remaining space at the south side of the building. Tonight, it was closed off by two, large wrought iron gates normally open during business hours. She observed the expansiveness of the empty parking lot through the decorative iron bars. Unseen was the outdoor nursery on the opposite side of the building. It was enclosed by chain link fence with privacy slats. She and her husband, Andrew, had purchased a tree there for the front yard when they first moved into their house five years ago.

She remembered browsing through a large maze of trees, shrubs, potted plants, and every kind of flower she could imagine. She pictured it now; devoid of people and dark with the moonlight casting shadows along the narrow pathways, and wondered if stray cats or other animals ever took refuge in the man-made forest at night.

She heard footsteps again and turned to see a man walking about a half of a block behind her. Was it the man she had seen lurking next to the architecture building? He didn't really look homeless, but all she could make out was his dark clothing. She continued on, picking up the pace a little and arrived at the next cross street which lacked a traffic light regulating foot traffic. After waiting for three cars to pass, she looked over her shoulder and saw the man was moving closer. "Not a big deal", she told herself, "lots of people walk in our neighborhood all the time." Only tonight, there really wasn't anyone else around.

Shannon stepped into the cross walk and the moon slipped behind a cloud, bringing the darkness closer. She didn't want to look like a scared idiot by running across the street, but she did pick up the pace.

It seemed that the man did the same and was closing the distance, now only a few yards behind her. She hopped up onto the adjacent sidewalk and listened to his footsteps coming closer.

This was her block, and it was the darkest stretch of sidewalk leading up to her house. "Sixth house on the right", she used to tell people when giving directions. The first house was a corner house facing north with a tall, wooden fence that ran parallel to the sidewalk.

She thought there might be an above-ground, portable pool in the back yard because she could always hear water running and some kind of mechanical pump noise. The trees along the sidewalk were tall and old, and the branches reached over to meet with the trees behind the fence; intertwining to create a canopy over the sidewalk.

Where the tall fence ended, a strange alleyway led back between two houses and turned to the left. She thought it might be access to one of the houses on the parallel street behind hers. She had never been down the alley way to check but had always been curious. Tonight, it just seemed like the perfect place for a stranger to drag someone off the street.

Shannon felt the hair rise on the back of her neck. It was silly, but she felt like someone was breathing right behind her. 'Screw it!' she thought, 'I'm gonna create a little distance between me and this guy'. She quickened her pace again, moving into a jog and her coffee and other goodies began rustling up and down in the plastic grocery bag.

She felt stupid and knew she would end up breaking something or losing the coffee through a busted bag. Her feeling of stupidity quickly transformed into anxiety tainted by a splash of fear as she heard his footsteps again quicken to match hers. A shot of adrenaline exploded out into every limb of her body, as her heart began pounding in her chest and ears!

She broke into a full run and felt the grocery bag slam against the back of her leg. She swung her arm forward and then back behind her as hard as she could, releasing the bag and hoping it connect with the man and slow him down. She didn't look back. She ran as fast as she could. Her house was not far ahead but she could hear him getting closer! She could feel him right behind her! She remembered her front gate was not only latched, but also secured by a chain and carabineers to keep the neighborhood kids from easily opening it. She and Andrew had two large, loving dogs, but not everyone appreciated the American Pit Bull Terrier, so the chain as a precaution, not to keep the dogs in but to keep the kids out.

Shannon began screaming Andrew's name, hoping he and the dogs would come outside and scare the man away. She was out of breath and her voice sounded foreign to her ears. Only two houses away and she was screaming as loudly as possible hoping to get anyone's attention.

She reached the driveway, signaling the beginning of her property and peeked over her right shoulder to see the man reaching for her! The motion-activated porch light caught her eye and she heard her front door open.

It all seemed to happen in slow motion, Murphy and Molly came tearing out of the house barking and growling! A hand connected with her shoulder! She heard Andrew call her name. She looked back again, shrugging her shoulder away from the man. Her left foot caught the sidewalk and her body twisted sideways. She felt her left elbow strike the hard concrete, followed by her hip, and her knees scrapped against the chain link gate just before her left shoulder smacked the ground. A sharp, bright pain exploded in her head.

* * * * *

Shannon opened her eyes to find Andrew kneeling beside her in the opening of the gate. Murphy and Molly were running back and forth along the fence line barking. "Where is he?" she blurted the question with urgency in her voice.

"Who?" Andrew asked. "There's no one here. Honey, what the hell happened?"

She tried to look around. Her neck was stiff and her head ached. "What happened? Where did he go? The man who was following me? Didn't you see him?" Each question came so quickly Andrew had no time to respond.

"Don't move, honey, try to relax." Andrew calmed her as the darkness of the street was broken by the red flashing lights of an ambulance.

Shannon tried to sit up but a wave of nausea came over her and her ears began ringing. Her vision was darkening around the edges and she leaned against Andrew, putting her head on his shoulder. A paramedic came over and squatted down next to her. "Are you OK, Ma'am?" He gently took her wrist and began measuring her pulse.

Andrew filled him in, "She took a nasty fall here in front of the house, I think she was running from something. I am concerned she might have a concussion."

"I don't have a concussion! A man was chasing me! How did you not see him?" Shannon's fear was turning to anger. Why was no one concerned about the man who tried to attack her?

"I'd like you to come to the hospital and just let a doctor check you out. You *could* have a concussion or even a neck injury. It would be best to play it safe, and your husband can follow us and meet you there." The young paramedic plead his case calmly and rationally.

"That's a good idea." Andrew agreed.

She let out a heavy sigh and tears began to well up in her eyes. She was so tired and the adrenaline had worn off. She relented and allowed the paramedic to gently lay her back while his partner brought a brace to secure her neck. The two of them went to work getting her onto the portable gurney and moving her into the ambulance.

Monday 11:48pm

Andrew turned the car into the long, narrow driveway and pulled all the way back to park behind the house. Shannon was exhausted and just wanted to climb into bed. She knew tomorrow morning would come too early, and to make matters worse she had no coffee. Andrew walked around the car and opened the door for her. He took her hand with his and it felt warm and strong enveloping hers. She swung her feet out onto the ground and he gently scooped her out of the car with his other arm around her shoulder. She heard the car door close behind her and began ambling toward the back door of the house.

"Hold on." Andrew said.

"I'm fine." She said in a tired, indignant voice. But that was the last of her protesting. He caught up to her and she nestled her head into his shoulder as they walked to the back door together. The motion light stabbed bright rays of light over the back porch while he fiddled with his keys. Once the door was open, he let her go inside and the darkness of the hallway swallowed her up while he stayed back to lock the door.

The long hallway led to the bedroom in the very front of the house with windows that looked out onto the porch. It was really meant to be a family room, but would suffice while they were building a master bedroom upstairs. She was met halfway by the very excited Murphy and Molly, waiting and whining behind the baby gate. It didn't ever matter how long she was gone, five minutes or five days, they always acted like she had been gone forever. She set the gate aside and the dogs circled her closely as she continued on to the bedroom. They made it their business to sniff out all of the interesting hospital smells. It was especially bad when she came home after encountering another dog. She couldn't even move because they were so interested in capturing every detail their noses could catalog!

Shannon dragged herself, with dogs in tow, into the bedroom, pulled the covers back and collapsed onto the bed. Andrew came in behind her and directed the dogs to go lay on their own beds. Murphy and Molly slinked off defeatedly and he closed the door behind them.

He crossed to the bed and gently removed Shannon's shoes. She unbuttoned her jeans and gingerly pushed them past her bruised hip and Andrew took over, gently pulling them over her scratched and bruised knees. When she struggled to sit up and he took her hand to help and slipped her T-shirt over her head as she held her arms up like a helpless child. Andrew bent down and kissed her forehead, then her cheek, and her neck as he reached around and unhooked her bra. He slipped the straps down her shoulders and arms and threw the bra on the bench with the rest of her clothes.

She rolled onto her right side and snuggled down into the bed as Andrew covered her bruises and scratches with the cool sheet. He sat on the edge of the bed and gently scratched her back. The sedative given at the hospital was kicking in and she softly moaned her appreciation before falling asleep. He kissed her cheek, noticing the nasty bruise forming on her shoulder too, she was going to be sore in the morning. She might think she was getting up for work, but he had other plans and he took her cell phone and quietly slipped out of the bedroom. Down the hall in his office, he called Shannon's work number and left a voice mail in the general mail box stating that Shannon would not be to work in the morning. Then he turned the phone off so that the alarm would not sound at six am.

Tuesday 4:20am

He reached his right arm around her, cradling her throat in his elbow and resting his hand over her left shoulder. His left hand covered her mouth with the chloroform-soaked cloth. She struggled to scream for a moment and then went limp in his arms. He almost fell forward with the sudden shift of her weight as she lost consciousness. He leaned back, bent at the knees, and took one step backward to steady his balance. He continued backwards, dragging her toward his van parked in the alley. The door was unlatched and he used his left hand to slide it open and then turned slightly to lay her upper body across the bare metal floor. Her long, blond hair spilled around her and he was careful not to step on it as he jumped into the van. Reaching under each of her arms, he pulled the remainder of her body into the van. Her hair caught on something but then broke free as he laid her on the blanket, fixed her arms at her sides and straightened her skirt.

He paused for a second to look at her creamy skin highlighted by the moonlight shining through the open door. Then he bent down and took in her soft floral scent and pressed his lips against her neck just under her delicate chin line. He traced the flow of her warm flesh down to the soft curve of her breast peeking out of her blouse. He sat back and watched the swell moving up and down with each shallow breath, imagining how it would feel to slice his sharp blade into that perfect flesh and see the beautiful, contrasting crimson of her blood softly escaping from her body.

* * * * *

Steve jumped and sat straight up in bed! His heart was beating against his chest and he was drenched in sweat! He looked around and saw only the dark outline of his bedroom. He took a deep breath and tried to release it slowly in order to calm his racing heart. Looking around the room again, searching for any motion and finding none, he reached over and turned on the bedside lamp.

“What a shitty dream!” He said aloud. “More like a nightmare.” He grabbed the water bottle on the night stand and realized it was empty. Pulling back the covers, he swung his legs off of the bed and felt for his slippers. Not there. The bare wooden floor was cold under his feet as he walked out into the hall and saw his slippers in the bathroom. It was only September, but he had heard the warnings that it would be getting colder in a few weeks, so he needed to make a habit of keeping his slippers in the bedroom. He stopped and put them on and then continued down the hall into the kitchen area.

Steve took the pitcher of filtered water out of the fridge and refilled his water bottle. He looked at the clock on the microwave and saw that it was 4:37am. No point in trying to go back to bed for a little over an hour of sleep. He flipped the kitchen light on, poured some of the filtered water into the coffee maker and placed the pitcher back in the fridge. Opening the coffee can released that great coffee aroma and he began to relax a little. As he scooped the grounds into the filter, he noticed he was still shaking. He pushed the start button on the coffee maker and sat down at the tiny kitchen table in his apartment.

Another deep breath in and slowly out. "I haven't had a nightmare in years." He stated emphatically, and out loud. His voice sounded strange in the quiet little apartment next to the gurgling of the coffee pot. He got up and walked around the breakfast bar into his small living room and then over to the wall unit and turned on the TV for noise.

Steve went back to the bedroom to make his bed while the coffee brewed. Picking up the pillow he noticed it was wet with his sweat. The sheets were damp too. He would need to wash everything. He ripped the blankets and sheets from the bed and threw them into a pile on the floor. "Damn" out loud again. That meant going to the laundry mat and he had just been there over the weekend. He cursed himself again for renting a unit with no washer and dryer. He was new to the valley and had wanted to make sure he liked it here before buying a house, so that meant renting.

Steve selected a clean, white button-down shirt and a pair of dark blue Dockers pants from the closet and then pulled an undershirt, Jockey shorts and socks from the drawer. He laid everything on the dresser and hung the pants and shirt from the hook on back of the door. He returned to the kitchen to fix a cup of coffee and then sat on the couch to watch the early-morning edition of the news. It was Tuesday, September 6th. Clear sunny weather was expected with a high of 80 degrees. A piece on Patriots Day, the anniversary of 9/11 coming up on Sunday. Everyone asking the question..." how will you remember loved ones lost that fateful day?"

Steve, being the Director of Human Resources for a large legal firm was quite relieved that it was falling on a Sunday. He didn't have to wrestle with the various employee issues involved in dealing with such a political and emotional anniversary on a workday. Better for people to spend the remembrance of such a controversial day with the individuals who shared similar values; their families and friends.

As he sipped his coffee, an anchorwoman informed everyone that up next, would be the breaking news regarding a young woman found in the canyon by hikers late last night. Her identity was unknown but it was clear she had been brutally tortured and murdered. The sick feeling of Steve's dream came back and he swiftly picked up the remote and turned off the TV. He got up, placed the now lukewarm coffee on the breakfast bar and headed off to shower.

Tuesday 8:55am

Shannon was at the gate. Only a sliver of the full moon was peeking out from behind the clouds. She was frantically trying to open the gate but couldn't see well enough to release the chain. She looked back down the street. She couldn't see him, but knew he was there. Her hands were shaking as she fumbled at the carabiner. She felt his breath on her neck and tried to scream but nothing came out! She jolted awake!

The sun was shining in through the window and the clock showed 9:07am. Andrew was gone. She reached for her cell phone but it wasn't there. Andrew must have taken it. She felt the stiffness beginning to set into her joints. She noticed her robe lying across the bed and her slippers on the floor, Andrew had thought of everything. She dawned her robe and slippers and shuffled out of the bedroom.

She discovered Andrew and the dogs out on the front porch, Andrew was poised to toss the tennis ball and the dogs were whining and begging with delight. He threw the ball and reached his hand out to her. She smiled as she walked over to him and avoided his slobbery outstretched hand. Instead she put hers on his shoulders and leaned in to kiss him. Murphy and Molly came back, the ball proudly secured in Molly's mouth.

"I took the dogs for a walk this morning and picked up some of your fake coffee." He grinned, "It's in the fridge waiting for you. And you should take an ibuprofen too."

"Oh, you're a life saver!" Shannon turned and scuffed her slipper-covered feet back into the house, concentrating only on the ice coffee that would make all the world right.

* * * * * * *

After enjoying her ice coffee on the porch with Andrew, Shannon showered and got dressed. She called into the office and let Thomas know she was OK. Thomas let her know that the entire office was up-in-arms trying to guess why Shannon's husband would call in for her. They had considered everything from a horrible car accident to winning the lottery. Thomas respected her privacy and knew she would explain when she was ready. He figured it had to be something serious because Shannon never missed work. That was part of what made her such a great advertising agent. She was warm and friendly and incredibly outgoing. She wasn't at all competitive and everyone in the office loved her.

Thomas ended the conversation with Shannon by reassuring her that staying home for the day was the right thing to do.

She hung up the phone and placed it on the dresser. She made the bed and looked around the room. She gathered up the jeans and shirt she had worn the night before. The jeans were torn and she figured it would be best to throw them both into the trash. She couldn't imagine ever wanting to wear them again. Walking outside to the large trash bin, she remembered her driver's license and debit card were in the back pocket.

"That was close." she thanked herself for remembering, but when she reached into the pocket it was empty. She checked all of the other pockets but again came up empty handed. She threw the clothing into the trash can and went back inside.

"Andrew, honey? Did you find my ID and debit card in my pants pocket?" He was in the office on the phone and signaled her to wait one minute. Shannon stood in the doorway and watched him working at his desk. His dark hair was lightly dusted with the highlights of gray and his big brown eyes reminded her of the Sunshine Family dolls from her childhood. He had striking, rugged features, a strong jaw line and distinct cheek bones. He was incredibly handsome and she felt the same fluttering in her heart as she had the first time he spoke to her in their college English class all those years ago.

Andrew was speaking to a client about the book he was editing. Andrew worked from home and was just beginning to build his business as an independent editor after working for a publishing firm for several years. They were finally able to make it on Shannon's salary and she was supportive of him striking out on his own.

Andrew hung up the phone and looked up at his beautiful wife standing in the doorway. "What are you looking for my gorgeous angel?" He asked.

"My driver's license and debit card." She stated with frustration. "Did you take them out of my pocket or did I lose them?" She was still so emotional from the night before.

"I don't have them, sweetie. Where do you think you might have lost them?" He hated to even bring up the details of the night before.

"Maybe the hospital." She thought out loud. "I had to put all of my clothes in that locker for the X-rays. I bet they fell out. I'm gonna drive over there and see."

"Why don't we just call?" Andrew asked.

"No. I need to do something anyway. I can't just sit around the house all day wondering how the hell he got away last night!" She headed back toward the bedroom to grab her purse.

"I'll drive you." Andrew followed her.

Shannon turned to face Andrew, purse slung over her shoulder, "I'll be fine, Honey." She said softly as she looked up into his concerned eyes. He was a full head taller than she was. She reached her hands up to cradle his face and he leaned over and kissed her gently on the lips.

"You stay home and get some work done and I won't be gone long. How about if I bring home some fresh sushi for lunch?" Andrew agreed that sounded tempting and made her promise to call after she retrieved her cards from the hospital, he wanted to be ready to call and cancel her card if she didn't find it.

Tuesday 10:05am

Steve sat in his office inside the very old and very classic building that housed one of the largest legal firms in the valley. It was ornately decorated with dark wood and a grand, curving stair cases. The ceilings were high and everything seemed larger than life. He sometimes thought that the over-stuffed leather chairs and deep mahogany desk in his office gave the opposite impression to employees than the one he wanted them to have. He needed people to feel that he was on their level, an advocate, not some stuffy member of management. Mostly the lavishness of the building was for clients, but it did create both a positive and negative feeling for the employees. It was positive because employees enjoyed working in such a prestigious space, and negative because it created a sense of separation; an "us versus them" kind of feeling.

Steve tried to focus on work. He had an employee getting ready to go out on Family Medical Leave for a pregnancy, and another claiming a worker's comp injury of carpel tunnel syndrome. He was also recruiting for a paralegal and the candidates were not that interesting. Tomorrow he was conducting a lunch-and-learn for the supervisors on Coaching, Counseling and Discipline.

His mind kept drifting back to the dream – the nightmare. It felt so real. In fact, that was what made it so disturbing, he wasn't that kind of person. He'd heard of men dreaming about other men, in a sexual nature, and being deeply disturbed because they weren't gay. And psychiatrists claim it has nothing to do with being gay or heterosexual. They say you can tie the strange events of your dreams to some other aspect of your life, like the need to control someone or some other bullshit like that. Only he couldn't figure out why he would be dreaming of hurting someone. The sexual attraction made sense, but the logic of it all stopped right there.

"You find me any good candidates yet?" Brad interrupted Steve's thought process as he stepped through the doorway.

"Oh, yeah," Steve looked up, "I was just going through some of the resumes I've received. Nothing really jumps out yet. Have you considered offering more money? At this pay rate, you won't get much; mostly newly graduated students and experienced people who couldn't cut it in their last job. If you want someone with great experience, you will probably have to pay for it."

"I know." Brad breathed a sigh. "I guess you can repost the position and raise the pay grade one level, but I also want you to clearly require two or more years of experience."

"Good choice." Steve responded. "I'll repost the job today."

Brad thanked Steve and left. Steve watched the door for a minute wondering if he should get up and close it. He needed to focus. Instead, he decided to take an early lunch.

Tuesday 10:12am

Shannon parked outside the emergency room in the visitor parking area. She wanted to retrace her steps just to be safe. She entered through emergency room doors and walked up to the admitting desk where a thin, young girl sat wearing jeans and a plain blouse. Not really professional, but not really sloppy. It occurred to her that the definition of business casual was deteriorating over the generations. Her mother had always taught her to 'dress for the job you want, not the one you have.'

"Excuse me," Shannon peered at the girl's name badge, "Trisha? I was here last night for some X-rays and I was wondering if anyone might have found my ID and debit card."

Trisha looked at her with a blank stare, paused, and then responded that she would need to get her supervisor. She disappeared behind the reception area into an office and then re-appeared with a distinguished looking grey-haired woman in a plain skirt and jacket.

"Hello, I'm Louise. Can I help you with something today?" She seemed genuinely interested in helping her.

"I was here last night for an X-ray" Shannon began, "and I think I may have lost my ID and debit card out of my pants pocket, possibly when I put my clothes in one of the lockers you have?"

Louise responded, "Sure, it happens more often than you realize. Let me call up to administration where they keep the lost items. Why don't you have a seat in the waiting area?" Louise disappeared back into where ever she came from and Shannon walked across the waiting area to an empty seat. She looked around the room. There was a heavy-set woman sitting with a chubby young man; her son most likely. He was holding his right arm in his lap with a bag of ice balanced on top. She wondered why they hadn't gone to an urgent care center; the emergency room was so expensive. She figured they probably didn't have insurance, and hospitals can't turn people away. There was also an older gentleman who looked like he was waiting for someone. Before she could size him up, Louise came back.

"OK Miss, can you tell me your name and date of birth? I'd ask you for your ID, but it appears I have it here in my hand." Louise smiled kindly.

"Shannon Medford, ten, thirty-one, eighty-four." Shannon rattled off dutifully.

"Yes, a Halloween baby!" Louise confirmed and handed both the ID and debit card over to Shannon.

As Shannon stood up, she reached for the cards and thanked Louise for all of her help. She headed toward the emergency room exit and then stopped, turned, and called after Louise just before she disappeared behind again the reception area.

"Louise?" she paused, "You seem like a very kind person. Can I ask you a personal favor?" Louise looked at Shannon and raised her eyebrows. Shannon took that as a 'yes' and walked over toward Louise.

"I know you can't release personal, patient information to strangers, but I was wondering if they brought the girl here from the accident a few nights ago. Do you know who I mean? The girl that ran out into the road and got hit by the SUV?" She paused for a second, looking for signs of recognition in Louise's eyes. She began again slowly and sadly, "I was one of the people who gave her CPR until the ambulance arrived."

Louise took a breath and let out a sigh while placing her arm around Shannon's shoulders and leading her down the hall, behind the reception area and into her office. They both sat down; Louise behind her desk and Shannon in the chair opposite.

"You are correct," Louise began, "I cannot give you private patient information. But I can confirm that the young woman was brought here." Louise took a breath and chose her next words carefully. "We still don't know what happened. She still has not been able to tell us anything. In fact, we still don't know who she is." Another pause, "if it weren't for you, she might not still be alive. And that is really all I can tell you, other than thank you, for being there, and helping."

Shannon looked at Louise and could feel a tear trying to well up in her eye. "No, thank you. It makes me feel good knowing that I could do something to help, and that she is still fighting for her life." Shannon was about to get up and show herself out when Louise asked,

"Do you mind if I ask why you were here having X-rays so late last night? I really don't mean to pry, and you certainly don't have to answer."

She was a little shocked at the question, but then figured it made sense, given the level the conversation had turned to. She began carefully,

"I kind of had a nasty fall in front of my house last night. I guess I blacked out for a minute or two, well, long enough for my husband to call an ambulance. They wanted to make sure I didn't have any kind of neck or back injury." She looked at Louise to see if that was going to satisfy her. And then she had an overwhelming need to tell the entire story.

"Actually, it is much more disturbing than that. Someone started following me home from the grocery store, and the faster I walked, the faster he walked. I ended up running home and he was running after me. But after I fell, he was gone! My husband didn't see him. I guess he realized my husband was coming out of the house, or maybe he heard my dogs barking and ducked away somewhere. The police took my statement here at the hospital last night, but I couldn't remember much about him. He wore dark clothing and was pretty much average height and average weight."

Shannon and Louise both sat there for a few seconds. Then Louise broke the silence,

"Wow! What a rough couple of days you've had! I certainly hope you are taking some time at home for yourself, to regroup, and let your heart settle. Do you have someone at home to help you?

"Yes, my wonderful husband saw to it that I slept in today and that my boss didn't expect me at work. In fact, I was supposed to call him to let him know if I got my cards back!" She reached across the desk to shake Louise's hand and thanked her profusely.

"You've helped me more than you know!" Shannon smiled and walked out of the office. As she left the hospital, she pulled her cell phone from the exterior pocket of her purse and hit the speed dial picture of Andrew. She knew she was late checking in and prepared her carefree, happy voice so that when Andrew answered he wouldn't be worried.

Tuesday 11:45am

Alex arrived fifteen minutes early for his shift which ran twenty-four hours, from noon to noon. He worked for the fire department, but he was trained as a paramedic and typically worked the ambulance. He went to the locker room, stashed his stuff, changed his clothes, and then slumped on the couch in the small TV room to chill for a minute. He was exhausted as a result of too many recent, sleepless nights.

Alex had never had problems sleeping in the past, which was why this job was so perfect for him. He could fall asleep easily and do it anywhere. During a twenty-four-hour shift, you were either practicing drills to stay certified, or you were eating, watching TV or sleeping. You might even catch a basketball game out back now and then. Calls came in at all times of the day or night, so you slept when you could.

He was also one of the lucky people who didn't have a squeamish stomach. He was able to look past the blood, protruding bones, or gaping wounds, and focus on performing the necessary life-sustaining techniques needed between the accident site and the hospital. However, Alex had been somewhat bothered by a call he he'd recently been on; a vehicle versus female pedestrian. For some reason, he couldn't get it out of his mind and decided it was the culprit nibbling away at his restful sleep.

Alex had also recently moved in with his girlfriend, Victoria, and this was his first, serious relationship. He figured it was some kind of subconscious awareness now that he had someone important in his life. Maybe it was the realization that if something bad happened to Victoria, he wouldn't be able to handle it free of emotion. He'd grew up without brothers or sisters, but now he officially had someone in his life to worry about.

While he sat there thinking, the rest of the team had shown up, changed into uniform, and filed into the TV room or kitchen area in preparation for their shift change meeting. The two shift captains came into the room, Bradford was going off shift and Murray was coming on. The retiring shift captain always gave a quick review of the prior shift activity and covered any unfinished business. Bradford did exactly that and then Murray took over. He reminded everyone to adhere to uniform guidelines since there had been a few complaints recently. He also told everyone to watch the bulletin board because benefits open enrollment was coming up, along with vacation bid schedules for the next quarter. There were certifications expiring and the year-end pay increase percentages would be posted if they got approved.

The meeting ended and everyone either left or settled in. Bradford walked past Alex and slapped him on the back, “Whatcha been up to, Mr. Jones? I don’t get to see you much anymore.”

“I’m good,” Alex replied with a warm smile. Alex looked like a California boy with sandy blond hair, lightly tan skin and kind, blue eyes. He wasn’t too tall, but had a nice build. If you saw him out of uniform you would think he was a beach-bum, surfer boy.

“How is that nice young lady you’re dating?” Bradford asked. He caught a glimmer in Alex’s eye.

“She is doing quite well.” Alex stated and then he added, “We moved in together.”

“Well congratulations!” Bradford slapped Alex on the back even harder than the first time.

Tuesday 5:30pm

Shannon was walking her dogs back from the park. It was great having a park that took up an entire city block located so close to their home, in fact, her street ran right into it. Walking to the park and making the loop on the walking trail had become a daily routine. Spring and autumn were the best times because it wasn't too hot in the evenings. This summer, she and the dogs had cut their walk a little short several times due to the heat, but this evening was perfect and a gentle breeze made all the difference. She knew that when the snow came in late October, it would be tough to get the dogs to go out even for a potty break. Murphy and Molly had such short hair and their stomachs were actually bare. They were completely spoiled and lived in the house year-round.

As they approached the intersection, Shannon looked up and down the wide street. This was the only busy street on their walk back to the house. There were two lanes of traffic in each direction, divided by a median lane. The street was made even wider by a parking lane on each side. The last Mayor had started a program downtown which provided orange, safety flags for crossing at every busy intersection. Some people used them and some didn't. The kids liked to drag them off and occasionally the narrow flag buckets attached to the light poles were empty.

Shannon stepped up to the curb where the crosswalk began and gave a quick tug on the dual leash. The dogs stopped and sat dutifully. It was still light outside and she didn't see the need to use one of the flags. She waited for the intersection to be clear of cars from both directions and then instructed the dogs, "OK". The three of them began to cross. The evening was beautiful and fairly quiet, and the street was empty except for a bicyclist coming the other way, most likely heading to the park.

Suddenly, she heard the screech of tires skidding toward her! She looked to her right and bright headlights blinded her eyes! *'Oh my hell!'* She thought inside her head, *'the dogs*!' She looked toward Molly and Murphy and the world once again, began to move in slow motion. They hadn't noticed! Couldn't they hear? She looked back to her right as the car closed in. She tried to lurch forward into more of a run, yelling "go!" loudly to the dogs.

She became suddenly aware of how cold and dark it was. Her entire body clenched and braced for the impact. She ran into Murphy and stumbled around him, nearly falling and her joints twisted with pain.

The quiet hit her like a brick wall. The intersection was empty. Murphy looked up at her like he was being admonished for doing something wrong and his big brown eyes were full of sadness. She continued to run and called for the dogs to hurry. The dogs, on either side of her, caught up as they all reached the sidewalk and Shannon stopped and looked around. Her heart was pounding and she was breathing in heavy, jagged breaths. Resting her hands on her legs and bending slightly, she tried to catch her breath and stop her head from spinning. She was shaking.

"What the hell!" She said out loud. The dogs looked up at her and cocked their heads to one side. Molly came up and sniffed her face and gave a little lick. Molly was always trying to give kisses and constantly getting in trouble for doing so. She wagged her tail and gave a small bark. Murphy stood up and sniffed at Shannon too. Shannon straightened back up and responded to the dogs, "I'm fine. Losing my mind, maybe, but fine." She gave them both a quick scratch on the head.

They continued on toward home and Murphy and Molly tried to stop and check out the house with all the cats lounging on the front porch. This was also a part of their routine, but she was feeling uneasy and wanted to get home. She gave the leash a jerk and called the dogs. They arrived at the last cross street, this one very small with minimal traffic. Shannon didn't even make the dogs stop and sit. She looked in every direction, felt a little scared, and then just took off running while she could see that the streets were empty. All three jumped up onto the sidewalk at the other side of the street and kept running. Murphy and Molly were enjoying the run and tried to break into a full doggie gallop. She did her best to keep up, but then had to tug on the leash and get them to slow down. They settled into a trot as they came up to the fence line signaling their house. She recalled the anxious feeling from the night before and was afraid she wouldn't be able to get the chain off of the gate. For the second time, in less than twenty-four hours, she was scared and shaking and just wanted to be in the safety of her own home.

As she lifted the latch, Andrew came out of the front door to greet her, only this time he didn't know he was coming to her rescue. She closed the gate behind her and handed the leash to Andrew. She fiddled with the chain and Andrew commented,

"Man! You must have had a good work out. You're shaking, your cheeks are red, and you're a little sweaty around the edges! Go in and get a drink and I'll take care of the mutts."

Tuesday 6:20pm

Steve pulled into his designated parking space under the carport. He turned the key off and the SUV engine went quiet. The radio continued to play until he opened the door. Then all was silent. He could hear the crickets grinding their legs in unison, signaling the night was beginning to set in. He clicked the lock button on his key fob and heard the horn beep, confirming the vehicle was secure. He followed the sidewalk to his first-floor apartment. Only two more months on the lease and he could buy a house. He had recently found a local realtor and begun looking at properties. Steve knew he wanted to live on the East side and stay within close range of the down town area. He disliked long commutes.

Moving into a house and getting everything settled would give him a good excuse not to work so late every night. And who knows, maybe he would meet someone worth dating. Steve Waters had spent the first four months in this new town getting the firm's HR department in order, learning the area, and deciding whether this was a place where he could truly settle down.

He turned the key in the door lock and then repeated the process to unlock the deadbolt. He entered his dark apartment and switched on the living room light. His coffee cup was still sitting on the breakfast bar and memories of his early morning came flooding back, bringing the nightmare with them. He had managed to put it out of his mind all afternoon by staying busy with work, but now he was home, alone, and famished. The TV would have to keep him company while he threw a steak on the grill and could hopefully find one last beer in the refrigerator.

* * * * *

Steve sat on the couch with his feet propped on the coffee table. The only evidence of his steak was the fat he had trimmed from the side. A nearly empty beer bottle stood next to his Styrofoam plate on the coffee table and the last sip was sure to be warm and flat. The patio door was open and the screen filtered in a nice, cool breeze. Steve knew he would probably eat better, because he would shop better, once he had a real home. He was going to have to find a house keeper to come in and do the serious cleaning at least once a week.

Hell, he could even have her do the grocery shopping, why not? Women loved to shop! He snickered out loud at his little joke.

The credits rolled as some silly sitcom theme song played on the TV. The news would be next. Steve got up and collected his plate and beer bottle, then threw everything in the garbage and placed the fork and steak knife into the dishwasher. Returning to the living room, he closed and locked the patio door. He laid the stick back into the track behind the door for good measure and then headed down the hall for a nice hot shower.

Tuesday 9:45pm

Shannon was completely relaxed in the claw-foot, cast iron tub she had refinished for the master bathroom. The previous summer, she had donated several boxes of leftover wood flooring to Habitat for Humanity. They returned the favor by selling her the antique tub for only Ninety dollars. Another good citizen had previously donated it and she was happy to be the new owner.

She had never been more appreciative of this deep, long tub brimming with hot water and laced with bubbles. The hot water soothed the stiffness in her knee, hip and shoulder, created by the fall. The bathroom mirrors were completely fogged up and the only light came from the dancing flames of several strategically placed candles. It had been a long day and she was actually a little afraid to go to sleep tonight.

She soaked until the water began to cool, and then pulled the plug. She stood up and took the large, fluffy purple towel from the faux antique towel stand and folded it around herself. She was glad they had made the investment in the more expensive, soft towels. She stepped out onto the mat and began to dry off. She had washed her hair that morning, so it was tied up in a knot and held in place by a stick. A few wisps of her auburn hair hung down and curled against the nape of her neck.

A knock on the door made Shannon look up from drying her long legs. Andrew cracked the door and peeked in, "You doing OK?"

"Yes" she replied, "I was about to start shriveling like an old grape, so I decided to get out."

Andrew smiled and walked into the bathroom. He took the towel from her and began to dry her back. He gently toweled down to the two dimples created by the skin attaching to the back her pelvis. He knew from his editing career that they were known as the dimples of Venus.

He brought the towel back up and wrapped it around her shoulders, bringing the ends together in front of her. He kissed the back of her neck. She put her hands over his, taking the towel and turning to face him. She dropped the towel and put her arms around his neck and pulled his face down to her lips. They kissed for a minute and then he picked her up in his arms and carried her out of the bathroom, through the unfinished master bedroom and down the stairs where he laid her on the bed. He stood in front of her and unbuttoned his shirt, which he laid on the bench at the foot of their bed. He unbuckled his belt and unbuttoned his 501 jeans. He pushed them down, stepped out of the legs, and then laid them with his shirt.

She watched his muscular physique as he moved to the light switch and turned off the light. He came back over to her and pushed his boxer shorts down to the floor, and climbed in next to her. His body was so warm and his skin was amazingly soft. He smelled of a Drakkar Noir, the cologne she bought him every Christmas. She breathed him in and wrapped her arms around his strong back as she nuzzled into his neck.

He was kissing her, his warm tongue flirting over hers. And then his soft lips and hot breath moved to her neck and down her breast to find her erect nipple. She felt his hands exploring her freshly clean body and then finding their way up to her neck. She could feel how large and strong his hands were as they closed around her delicate neck.

His hands began to tighten and she called out his name, “Andrew.” He moaned and pressed his thumbs harder against the front of her neck while his fingers squeezed at the back. She could feel the pressure and started to cough. She clawed at his hands and began to cry and tried to scream! She couldn’t get him to release his hands and they were painfully tight around her throat now! She ripped at his fingers in panic and then slapped Andrew’s face!

“What the hell!” Andrew yelled!

Shannon quickly realized that she was clawing at her own neck and his hands were nowhere near hers. He was leaning on his left elbow and cupping her breast with his right hand.

“Why did you do that?” Andrew asked with surprise.

“I thought,” she paused, “It felt like...,”

“Felt like what?” Andrew demanded.

Shannon took a deep breath, “I thought... It felt like you were choking me!” She blurted out.

Andrew looked at her and saw her eyes were dark with embarrassment and even a little fear. He looked at her neck and saw the redness forming there where she had been clawing at her own flesh.

“Honey,” Andrew asked softly, “are you OK? You just don’t seem like yourself.”

Shannon felt her eyes well up with tears. Andrew saw this and grabbed a tissue from the night stand. Then he pulled the sheet over and around her, while slipping his left arm underneath her. He pulled her toward him and she snuggled her face into his neck and broke down and cried.

Tuesday 11:10pm

After his shower, Steve made his bed with the extra set of fresh sheets from his linen closet and then climbed in, wearing only a clean pair of boxer shorts. He was tall, so his feet nearly reached the end of the king mattress. He had thick, dark hair and tanned easily. His features were handsomely rugged, and only enhanced by the thick, five-o'clock shadow he sported at the end of each day. His body showed the evidence of hitting the gym three times a week, but surprisingly, his chest only sported a sprinkling of dark, curly hair.

Plenty of women had been interested in him since he first moved to the valley. He just hadn't had the time to date, nor had he met anyone with that intelligent sense of humor he loved so much.

Steve read for a while and then folded down the corner of the page in his book before placing it on the night table. He got out of bed and lowered the window to just a couple of inches from the frame so the cool air would continue to seep in and then he switched off the overhead light. The large green letters of his alarm clock glowed through the darkness and showed the way back to the bed. Steve threw the blanket back and pulled only the sheet up to his waist line. He fluffed and punched the pillow until it fit strategically under his head and settled in to sleep. "No dreams tonight, OK?" He muttered out loud. Then he focused on the distant sound of the crickets chirping outside and drifted off to sleep.

Wednesday 2:40am

Steve descended the large, winding stair case from the second floor where his office was located. It was barely after closing time, but everyone seemed to have gone home for the night. When he reached the bottom of the stairs, he walked across the large reception area and into a small, back foyer. He opened the door leading to the employee parking lot only he found himself at the top of another small stairway. It was dark and he could make out a single, bare bulb hanging from the ceiling at the bottom of the stairway. Steve took the steps slowly and heard a soft moan, like someone having a bad dream. He reached the bottom and stepped down onto the hard concrete. He could smell something musty like old, wet dirt.

The basement room opened up to the left and another single bulb was mounted to one of the wood beams crossing the ceiling. The dim light shined down over a metal table and a young woman with long blond hair was lying, unconscious on top of it. Her wrists and ankles were held prisoner by wide leather straps that were somehow attached to the corners of the table. Another strap ran across her rib-cage. She was dressed only in her bra and panties. Her skirt and blouse had obviously been cut off and lay in a shredded pile next to the wall.

The young blond woman moaned again and moved her head slightly. Steve walked over to a dirty stone ledge that ran the length of the basement room, parallel to the metal table. The ledge served as a countertop, lined with candles and one silver tray displayed several vials and syringes. He selected one of each and then watched his own hands carefully stab the needle into the rubber stopper on the vial, pull the plunger back and fill the syringe. He walked over to the woman and carefully pierced the skin inside her right elbow. The needle was almost horizontal to her arm and slid smoothly into the vein. He slowly pushed the plunger until the syringe was empty. She made a stronger, short moaning sound, as if she was somewhat aware of the sharp, stinging pain.

He pulled the needle out of her arm and a small trickle of blood escaped from the tiny hole. He felt a stirring in his groin. The blood was so beautiful against her creamy skin!

He placed the spent syringe back on the tray where he saw a scalpel. He picked it up and watched the sharp metal blade catch the light as he turned it side to side. He was excited to use the tool, but knew he would have to wait until later when she began to come around again. For now, he needed to prepare. He moved to the dark corner of the basement to an old, wooden Victrola phonograph and placed the needle on the outside edge of a record. As he turned the crank, an eerie sound came from the box. It was music, playing way too slowly to discern, but as he cranked faster, he could make out a violin and then some kind of horn. It was beautiful and eerie all at the same time.

Next, he found a large box of matches and lit the various candles standing ready on the long stone countertop. He pulled the chain to kill the dirty overhead light above and the soft light from the candles danced in the dark perimeter of the room making it feel even more macabre. Again, something stirred in Steve and he felt that sensation of butterflies in his stomach.

He walked over to the young woman and stroked her golden hair. He slowly gathered the long strands along one side of her face and neck and gently laid it over her collar bone and down into the swell between her small but firm breasts. He allowed the knuckles of his right hand to brush against her skin. Another bolt of electric excitement shot through him.

He leaned over her and gently buried his face in her hair. He breathed long and deep and then stood upright. He placed one hand gently on each shoulder and slowly traced his fingers down her arms. He moved to her stomach and felt her flat belly under both of his hands. He continued downward and allowed his fingers to slip between her thighs and gently stroke the inside of her legs all the way to her ankles. He stood at the end of the table and cupped each foot against either side of his hips. He looked at her. Where would he begin? Not her neck, she would bleed out too quickly, perhaps her inner thigh. There was plenty of soft flesh there and if he was careful to avoid her arteries, she would only bleed enough for him to begin his crimson masterpiece.

She moved her left foot and he felt the pressure against his hip. She was coming back to him and he was ready. Steve returned to her side and again picked up the scalpel. He placed his hand on her left cheek and softly kissed her lips. They were cold. The basement was cold, and she was hardly dressed for the damp air surrounding her. Her eyelids fluttered and then opened. Her bright blue eyes searched for something recognizable. The pupils were tiny pinholes in the bright light but then they widened in horror as she realized her situation!

"There, there, my dear." Steve cooed in a gentle voice. "You mustn't struggle. It will only make things worse." But he was giddy with the idea of her frantic reaction! He brought the scalpel into her view and watched as she froze in horror. He slowly moved his hand down toward her leg and she began to pull against the straps that kept her prisoner. Steve leaned on her abdomen with his left forearm and all the weight of his upper body. He placed the scalpel between his teeth and with his right hand he checked the tautness of each leather strap while she began screaming. He stood there watching her, the scalpel back in his hand now.

She finally stopped screaming and pleaded softly, "Please, no" over and over again.

He placed his hand on her left thigh, the skin warm now from all of her movement. The blood was flowing through her body and would only make what he was about to do even more beautiful. He pressed the scalpel against the inner thigh of her left leg, high up toward her panties and began to press inward and downward.

Steve sucked in a deep breath of air and nearly choked! It was dark! How was it suddenly dark? It took a moment for him to realize he was sitting upright in bed, in his room. Another damn nightmare! And he was soaking wet again with his heart about to pound right out of his chest.

The green digital light from the alarm clock glowed 2:59am. He flopped back down onto the pillow and stared up at the dark ceiling. There was no way he was going back to sleep now. He wondered if any laundry mats were open twenty-four hours. He decided to shower, make some coffee, and then pursue that avenue since he was out of clean sheets.

Wednesday 3:15am

The bells beat out their warning sound and Alex sat up and grabbed his uniform pants from the end of the military-style bed. He pulled them on. As he stood up to zip and buckle, he slipped his feet into the boots he had left perfectly in position. Next, he grabbed his uniform shirt off of the wall hook near the head of the bed. He buttoned as he walked. Everyone was moving out to the bays, preparing to gear up and get into their vehicles.

The radio dispatcher came over the loud speaker, "House fire at 756 Elm Street, smoke inhalation and possible injuries."

Alex went straight to the ambulance and climbed into the passenger seat as Jay jumped in on the driver's side. The garage doors went up and a fire truck led the way with sirens wailing and the ambulance on its tail.

The streets were pretty much empty, but the few cars that were on the road pulled over for the passing emergency crew. The smoke was visible from the end of the block as they approached the house. The emergency vehicles lined up along the street, in front of the house, and the fire crew jumped out and began their routine. Alex jumped out with a medical kit and went directly to the neighbor's yard where a very pregnant woman lay on the lawn.

Her husband was kneeling next to her and supporting her head and shoulders while the two of them coughed. Another young woman was sitting with a toddler nearby. The neighbors had brought out blankets for the pregnant woman. In between coughing fits, the pregnant woman shook with the chill of the night.

Alex called after Jay, who was approaching with an oxygen pack. Before Jay even settled the equipment on the ground, Alex secured the oxygen mask and placed it over the woman's face. He gently picked up her wrist and looked down to take her pulse. He was shocked to see several long lacerations on her inner forearm and wrist area. Alex asked the woman, "What is your name, ma'am?"

"Cheryl" the pregnant woman half coughed.

"Cheryl, did you get these cuts on your arm as you were trying to evacuate your home?"

Cheryl raised her arm and both she and her husband looked in surprise.

"What?" Cheryl muffled through the oxygen mask as her husband grabbed her wrist.

"Did you hurt yourself!?"

"No!" Cheryl returned.

Alex apologized and asked Cheryl if he could finish taking her pulse. As he returned her arm to the blanket at her side, he saw that her skin was smooth and free of any wounds. "It must have been a trick of the light" he finished. Then Alex asked the husband if he was feeling OK. His coughing seemed less severe compared to his wife's.

Jay attended to the toddler boy who was trying desperately to get away from the neighbor and back to his mother. He was doing just fine and showed no signs of smoke inhalation.

Alex retrieved the ambulance gurney and a special blanket that was designed to warm a victim in shock or, like tonight, in cold weather. He and her husband helped Cheryl scoot over onto the special bed which had been lowered to the ground for her. Alex placed the blanket over Cheryl and then took her pulse again. It was beginning to steady. She was coughing less but the oxygen was still important to her and her baby.

Jay handed the toddler off to his father and then helped Alex to raise the gurney fully upright and wheel it over to the ambulance. The gurney was designed so that the legs would collapse back up under the bed frame enabling them to push it into the ambulance. Alex jumped in with Cheryl while Jay coordinated with the neighbor to bring husband and child along to St. Francis Hospital. Then he climbed into the ambulance and started up the motor and switched on the siren.

Alex sat beside Cheryl and prepared all of the materials he would need to start an IV.

"You're doing just fine." He encouraged her.

Alex selected her left arm and began to look for a full, healthy vein on the back of her hand or inner wrist. As he examined her arm, he saw more lacerations. They were long and looked fresh. Blood should have been coming from the wounds but none was present. He lifted her arm and turned it in the light for a better examination. Cheryl shot him a worried glance and he met her eyes for a brief moment. When he looked back, the skin on her arm was again, smooth and perfect. The vein on the back of her hand showed in the light so he laid her arm down, swabbed with alcohol and picked up the IV catheter needle.

"I'm sorry if this pinches a little." He said as he slid the needle parallel to her hand and into her vein. He connected the IV bag and gently squeezed it a few times and then hung it from the collapsible IV stand attached to the gurney.

"How's she doing?" Jay called from the front

"Settling in and breathing steadily." Alex answered back.

"We're almost there." Jay stated more for Cheryl's benefit than Alex's.

"When are you due?" Alex asked.

"November 11th, and I better not be early! I don't want any tricks for Halloween." Cheryl actually gave a small smile. Alex knew this was a good sign.

They both felt the ambulance pull around into the emergency entrance and come to a stop. Jay jumped out and went around to the back and opened the doors. Alex moved to the head of the gurney, preparing to push it out of the ambulance. He looked down into Cheryl's face to give her a reassuring smile, but then he jerked back and hit his head against the ceiling. Her eyes were sunken in and completely dull! Her pupils were fixed and the skin around her eyes was a dark grey. Her face was completely white, as if she had lost *all* of her blood!

"Are you OK?" Cheryl asked.

Alex was shocked to hear her speak, but then he saw the color had returned to her face and her eyes were lively and full of suspicion. She probably thought he was crazy at this point.

"I'm so sorry! I just haven't been sleeping well." It was all Alex could think of to say.

"Let's go, klutz!" Jay called him back to the task at hand and they both moved into action expelling the gurney from the ambulance.

The ER crew met them outside the doors and Alex rattled off the stats regarding the smoke inhalation, oxygen therapy, IV, and how the patient was thirty-two weeks with a healthy fetal heart rate. The ER crew disappeared into the hospital with Cheryl, while Jay and Alex waited for a replacement gurney.

"What is with you tonight? You look a little shaken." Jay interrogated Alex.

"I don't EVEN know!" Alex threw back in a self-deprecating tone.

Wednesday 4:04am

Katrina Dempsey was returning from her break and walked past the ER. The patient of focus was a woman who looked pretty far along in her pregnancy. Close by her side was a man with a cute little boy. "Happy family", Katrina thought, hoping nothing serious was wrong with the mother.

She took the back stairs up to the third floor, she never used the elevator unless she was with a patient. In her hectic life, there was little time for exercise and so the stairs were the next best thing. The third floor was quiet this time of night. Most patients were either sleeping or heavily sedated.

One of her patients, in particular, was in a coma. Jane Doe Seventeen was the official name on the medical record because she was the seventeenth Jane Doe patient admitted to the hospital since it was first opened in 1905. She came in via ambulance three nights ago, apparently having run out into the street and been hit by a car. The strangest part was that she was dressed in only her bra and panties.

Her body was covered with lacerations, not from the accident, but from someone actually cutting her - torturing her was more like it. She had lost a lot of blood too; they had given her two units so far. Luckily, she hadn't broken anything more than her right wrist in the accident, but her head had taken a serious hit to the pavement, which most likely caused the coma.

Katrina sat down at the nurse's station and told Brenda to go ahead and take her break. Brenda double checked the monitors and then took her coffee mug and went off down the hall. Katrina picked up her water bottle and took a long drink. She had a personal rule not to drink coffee all night. Firstly, because it would make it difficult for her to sleep when she got home, and secondly because it wasn't healthy. She had one cup when the shift started and then it was either water or green tea after that.

Having just turned fifty-eight, Katrina was focused on many more healthy years as a nurse. She was always surprised at the nurses who did not take care of their own health when they had firsthand knowledge of the difference it made, and the risks of not doing so. Katrina had also maintained a healthy weight over the years. She had a kind face and had allowed her hair to gray naturally.

Katrina settled in while Brenda took her break because upon Brenda's return, they would each take a turn to complete their rounds.

Katrina's patients included Mrs. Watson, who had just undergone a hysterectomy in room 310, and Ms. Kirby in 308 was to be released in the morning. There was Georgette in 306 with a small tumor attached to one ovary, and 304 housed Mrs. Thompson who just had her gallbladder removed. Finally, in 302 was Jane Doe Seventeen.

Brenda arrived back from her break with a steaming mug of coffee. It smelled sweet, like the Irish creamer Brenda always added for flavor. Katrina didn't want to be tempted by the aroma so she took one last drink from her water bottle and set out to make her final rounds.

Each patient was sleeping peacefully, largely because of the meds they had been given earlier that night. Katrina checked the vitals of each woman, which was a completely different process than it had been many years ago when she had first become a nurse. These days the machine monitor by the bed kept track of everything. A blood pressure cuff on the patient automatically checked pressure at set intervals, and each patient wore a plastic finger clip on the end of one finger to track their pulse. The clip made Katrina think of a cross between of one of those metal finger splints and a clothes pin, only plastic. You squeezed one end to open it and slipped the monitor over the patient's finger. It simply clamped on to the end of the finger and detected the pulse present in the fingertip.

If the large monitor detected anything out of normal range, it played a beeping alarm, which also registered at the nurse's station. The monitor in Jane's room was set to measure more than just the regular heart rate and pulse/oxygen levels, it also recorded brain activity. The nurses wanted to know immediately if she had any change in her current status.

Everyone else was tucked in, safe and sound, so Katrina pulled the chair over to the bed and sat next to Jane Doe. The bed was against the left wall from the doorway and the large picture window opposite the door was covered by the drawn shades. Katrina sat between the head of the bed and the window. The overhead light in the room was off, but the reading lamp was on. This was common practice for patients who might wake up and not know where they were. Waking up in the dark with various attachments coming off of your body could be quite upsetting, and possibly even dangerous.

Jane Doe had an IV providing more than the standard saline solution, it was enhanced by the nutrients necessary to feed her body since she obviously couldn't eat. If she didn't wake up soon, they would install a feeding tube through her nose and down into her stomach.

Jane Doe's arms lay on top of the bed covers and her left wrist was set in a removable brace. Katrina took Jane's left hand in her own. It was cold so Katrina placed her other hand on top of it to sandwich in some warmth. As she sat there holding the girl's hand, Katrina caught a glimpse of a dark figure in the doorway of the room. She jumped! She dropped Jane's hand and stared in the direction of the figure, but there was no one there. All she could see was the open doorway and the dimly lit hall beyond. She wondered if someone was up and walking around?

Katrina focused on Jane again. The girl was shaking slightly so Katrina placed both of her arms under the bed covers. She left the room and came right back with one of the heated blankets. She laid it across the girl's feet and then unfolded it several times until she could tuck it in around Jane's shoulders. The blankets were purposely folded in a manner that allowed them to be unrolled, so to speak, over the patient.

Katrina left the room again and made a mental note to come back and check on Jane. She didn't want the girl to get overheated. These things were especially important for a person who could not react or adjust to their environment.

Back at the nurse's station Katrina asked, "Hey Brenda, who's walking around on the floor?"

Brenda looked at Katrina, leaned her head to the left a little and responded, "No one?" with a questioning tone.

"Oh. I just thought I caught a glance of someone passing in the hall. Must have been my imagination. Well, you might as well get your rounds over with." Katrina sat down and made an entry in the patient log regarding the warming blanket with a reminder set to go off in one hour.

Wednesday 6:11am

The sun was beginning to rise in the morning sky, so Katrina and Brenda again took turns to conduct their final morning rounds. Part of the routine was opening the blinds in patient rooms as requested, and Katrina did so for each of her patients because the cheery sunshine aided in recovery for most. For others it was a celebration of the arrival of their release date. In the last room, Jane Doe Seventeen was surely in need of some sunshine.

After adjusting the blinds, Katrina moved to check on Jane. She had warmed up nicely with the extra blanket and luckily never became overheated.

In the light, Katrina could tell that Jane was a pretty girl in spite of her injuries. She had long blond hair which was half covered by the head dressing. It was placed there to cover the wound which resulted from drilling at the back of her head in order to relieve the fluid creating pressure on her brain. Her eyes were closed and the lids were slightly blue-gray from the loss of blood. She had a bruise on her left cheek as well. Other than that, the skin on her face was creamy and flawless.

You couldn't say the same for the rest of her. She had long deliberate lacerations in various places on her arms and legs. Whoever cut her knew what he was doing because he managed to miss all of the major arteries and was careful not to go too deep. Then again, maybe he hadn't finished, maybe she had just gotten away before he could.

Standing between the window and the bed, Katrina moved closer and took Jane's hand in hers one more time to check her temperature. This was not body temperature measured in Fahrenheit, but body temperature measured by the warmth of the hand and indicative of how comfortable the patient was under her current blankets. She decided to leave the extra blanket and post comments for the next nurse to check on her as the day warmed up.

Katrina stood there for a minute, holding Jane Doe's hand, and wondering. She wondered when the girl might wake up. She wondered how she had gotten to the place where a car struck her and landed her in a hospital. She wondered what horrible place she had been in, and how she was brave enough to escape.

As she began to wonder what kind of horrible person could do such a thing to a sweet, young woman, a man in a white lab coat entered the room. He walked slowly and held a scalpel out in front of him at waist level. Katrina didn't recognize the man and wasn't sure why he would be carrying the scalpel. He kept moving forward toward the bed where Jane slept.

"Can I help you? This is a private room." Katrina stated in her best I'm the nurse and I'm in charge voice. Katrina stepped away from Jane's bed, releasing her hand in the process. She took one warning step toward the man, hoping he would realize his place and stop or leave. Instead he kept coming toward the bed and answered Katrina.

"I'm Baxter Maynard from the lab, I'm here to collect more blood Samples." He held out the item he carried in his hand. It was a lab kit consisting of one catheter needle, several vials and some rubber tubing.

Katrina let out a sigh of relief. She had imagined the scalpel. She turned back to Jane and saw that she was shivering again. She would change out the blanket from last night for a new warm one while Mr. Maynard did his phlebotomy work.

Wednesday 6:30am

Steve left the laundry mat with ticket in hand. It was the only location close to him that opened at 6am. He had dropped off both sets of sheets along with a few dress shirts and pants. They promised to have them all laundered and ready to go after work today.

The sun was shining and the air was slightly crisp, it was a perfect, early autumn morning. Steve climbed into his SUV and headed out to find a McDonald's. An Egg McMuffin and a very large hot coffee sounded pretty good. He started the engine and pulled out of the parking lot into the nearly empty street. Heading toward work, he didn't have to go more than two blocks before he saw the golden arches on the left. Steve took advantage of the drive-through, secured his much-awaited breakfast, and continued on down the road to work.

He was the first one to arrive, specifically because it was nearly two and a half hours before the regular opening time of 9am and most of the staff rolled in between 8:30 and 9. Luckily, they had entrusted him with a key to the employee entrance off of the back-parking lot.

As Steve opened the door he was reminded of the horrible dream from the night before. He was going in the opposite direction, in instead of out, but he still braced himself for something other than the back corner of the main floor lobby. He breathed a sigh of relief when everything looked normal.

The sun was beginning to shine in the through the front windows and casting strange shadows around the very expansive first floor lobby. He hit the bank of light switches on the right-hand wall and everything came back to normal perspective. Egg McMuffin bag and coffee balanced in his left hand, portfolio in his right, he headed up the stairs to his office.

Steve had been working diligently for a couple of hours when he realized that his coffee was all but gone and extremely cold. He took the cup to the end of the hall where the employee lounge was located and poured the remains down the sink and placed the paper cup into the recycling bin.

There were ceramic mugs in a cupboard above the sink and a dishwasher as well. The firm saved a great deal of money not buying Styrofoam cups and it made the green team happy not to add to the landfill. Steve selected a cup and filled it from the fresh pot of coffee someone had recently brewed. He was impressed with how responsible everyone was, making sure all the dishes made it into the dishwasher and starting new pots of coffee when old ones were empty. The cleaning woman came in at 4:30 each afternoon to turn off the pot, load it into the dishwasher and run it.

Brad joined Steve in the employee lounge. “Wow! You beat me to the first cup of coffee.”

“It’s actually my second, and the first one was a big one.” Steve pointed to evidence in the recycle bin.

“Hey, you better be careful you’ll be jittery all day.” Brad warned as he filled his own cup. “Bad night of sleep?”

“You have no idea!” Steve led the way back to his office and Brad followed.

They both sat down with Steve at his desk and Brad in one of the deep leather chairs.

“Lay it on me,” Brad began, “But you should be the one in the leather chair with me behind the desk. Just think, I could have been a shrink instead of a lawyer. We both listen to people’s problems.” He chuckled.

“I don’t know.” Steve seemed to miss Brad’s attempt at humor. “I’ll never catch up on my sleep if I keep having these awful nightmares.”

“You know”, Brad’s tone became serious, “you should really talk this out with someone. Ever since the accident you haven’t really been yourself. In fact, aren’t you always preaching about the amazing benefits our Employee Assistance Program provides? Make an appointment with one of those counselors.”

And with that, Brad stood up and moved to the doorway. The look on his face was sheer satisfaction. This would be the easiest problem he solved all year.

“You are probably right. Thanks.” Steve thought for a moment and realized that Brad *was* probably right. He smiled and said, “I’ll make a call this morning and then I’ll get back to the business of finding you an outstanding paralegal.”

Brad gave Steve the thumbs up, “See you at the lunch and learn,” and headed off down the hallway with his coffee.

Wednesday 9:30am

Shannon walked out of the staff meeting and headed back to her office. They were promoting the March of Dimes haunted house this year. Every year Brewer and Brown budgeted to promote one charitable event and she was excited they were able to do something for Halloween. It was like an early birthday present.

Shannon and her team were in charge of getting donations, which included decorations, cash, and small advertising space. Small advertising space could be anything from the marquees that restaurants used, to flyers, place mats, and local print publications. She would have to set up a meeting with her team and divide up the areas of responsibility, divide and conquer, so to speak.

Everyone had been happy to see her return to work. Her co-workers were all very kind and didn't really pry. She had basically conveyed to everyone that she had spooked herself walking home from the store which resulted in a trip and fall, which her husband made out to be worse than it actually was. This, of course, was met by all of the concerns for her walking alone at night. They meant well, but she was slightly offended by the whole helpless woman idea. Still, she *had* been chased by some weird homeless man.

A knock came on her door frame and she looked up to see Lisa standing in the doorway.

"There is a police officer here asking to see you." Lisa said with a puzzled look on her face.

"You can bring him back to my office. I'm sure it's nothing." But in the back of her mind, Shannon wondered if they had actually found something to substantiate her claim that a man had been chasing her. She didn't want to have that conversation in full view of her co-workers.

Lisa disappeared and returned in less than a minute with a man in a suit, not a police uniform. Shannon got up from behind her desk and greeted him. She thanked Lisa and closed the door as Lisa left.

"Please, have a seat." She indicated one of the chairs across from her desk. She walked back around to her desk and asked, "Is this about the other night?"

"Actually, yes. But let me start by introducing myself, I'm Detective Howard." He reached across the desk and shook her hand. "I wanted to ask you some questions about the accident Sunday night."

Shannon cocked her head to one side and responded, "You mean Monday night?"

"No. The accident was definitely Sunday night. You were one of the first people to help at the scene of the accident? You administered CPR?" He was trying to jog her memory, although he thought it strange that she couldn't remember clearly.

"You're here to talk about the car accident?"

"Yes. Has there been another accident?"

"Oh. No, not really. It's just that, well, I had a small accident on Monday night. I fell walking home and apparently was knocked out for a minute. Nothing really important."

"But you thought it was important enough to believe I was here to discuss it with you. Is there more to the story?"

"Well, it's just that I was sure someone was following me, chasing me, really. And no one else saw anyone, so no one really believes me."

"It's interesting that you should say that," Officer Howard began, "because I wanted to ask you about the girl who was hit by the car. She appears to have been abused by someone, possibly even abducted and some of her injuries were definitely not caused by the accident. We have been trying to find out what happened to her and I thought you might be able to help."

"She hasn't been able to tell you what happened? The nurse said she was unconscious yesterday, but is she still unconscious? She didn't die, did she?!" The words flew from Shannon's mouth.

"I am afraid she is in a coma and we only have the evidence of her wounds and witness testimony to go on, which is why I'm here. So, can I ask you some questions?"

"Absolutely! Anything I can do to help."

"According to the initial police report, you were out jogging that evening?"

"I was walking my dogs in the park and I try to take a different route every time I go so it was a weird coincidence that I was even there when it happened. I like to vary my route partly because my dogs enjoy sniffing out new areas, and partly because I don't want to be predictable, you know, for stalkers or predators." her voice trailed off.

"That is very wise of you." Detective Howard reassured her. "Can you explain to me how the accident happened, in your own words?"

"I was walking the dogs on the east side of the park, you know, on Seventh East. We were heading back home because it was starting to get dark. I told the responding officer that the accident must have happened around 8:40pm."

"I heard a car screech like it was slamming on the breaks, and I heard a scream too. It came from behind me and the dogs figured it out before I did, they definitely wanted to see what was happening, and they were barking in that scary, protective mode. I turned around and saw a yellow SUV stopped in the lane closet to me and I could see the girl lying in the street. I knew I had to help so I tied my dog leash to the door handle of the SUV and ran over to the girl.

She looked really bad, pasty white, and all bruised and cut up. And it was so strange, she was only wearing her underwear and bra!" Shannon looked at Officer Howard and he just waited patiently, so she continued.

"I felt her neck for a pulse. I couldn't really feel it. I held my hand over her mouth and nose but didn't feel any breath. I was afraid to move her head, but I was afraid she wasn't breathing. The man who apparently hit her called 911 and when he was off the phone, I asked him if he had a blanket or coat or anything to put under her neck to hold it steady so I could give her mouth to mouth.

I remember wondering if I might end up with some kind of disease. For all I knew she was a drugged-up prostitute. But she didn't *look* like a drugged-up prostitute. She looked like a nice girl that had something horrible happen to her. The man brought his suit jacket and rolled it up. We carefully slid it under her neck and I started breathing for her, but then I remembered our recent CPR training at work. You don't actually have to breathe for them that often. You want to concentrate on getting their heart beating. And they say the chest compressions will actually force air in and out of the lungs." Shannon realized how silly she was for explaining this to the officer.

She went on, "I just started compressing her chest when another man came by with a blanket and he put it over the bottom half of her. The SUV driver took a turn doing the doing chest compressions and I just held the girl's hand. Even though it seemed like forever, the ambulance eventually arrived and the paramedics took over. Then each of us, as witnesses, had to fill out a statement regarding what we saw."

"Murphy and Molly were going crazy by then, howling and crying. They didn't understand at all. One of the police officers was nice enough to give me and the dogs a ride home, even though it was only about three blocks." She paused, "And that's the story." She looked at Detective Howard with a pleading expression that said please make it all better.

"Thank you. I am sure that must have been hard for you. Do you have any idea where the girl might have been coming from?" Officer Howard looked hopeful.

"No, but it seems that by the way she fell, she could have been running across the street toward the park. Does that help any?"

Wednesday 1:50pm

Steve turned onto Park Street and looked for the number 620 on the right. The street was narrow and lined with old homes, but no office buildings. There was a long, two-story brick building on the right that was all but hidden by a line of trees, shrubs and giant rose bushes growing along the sidewalk. He parked next to the long stretch of trees and bushes. He got out and walked around to find what appeared to be a historic looking set of town homes. Number 620 was the second unit from the far end of the building.

Steve realized how much he felt like he had gone back in time. Once on the sidewalk in front of the building, you couldn't see any of the street or other houses because of all the greenery blocking the way. The bricks of the building had been painted a creamy, banana yellow that was peeling so you caught a hint of the original brick color underneath. He couldn't put his finger on it, but thought maybe it had a French feel.

He approached the door of the unit he was looking for. Sydny Samuels, interesting name, was the EAP counselor who happened to have an opening in her schedule today. He opened the door and had a view of the stairs leading to a second floor. To the right was a closed door with a small sign mounted at eye level. He followed the instructions and sat down on the bench in the tiny foyer to wait.

It wasn't long until two women came out of the room. Steve identified Sydny by the way she hung back in the doorway for all the 'good-bye' and 'see ya next time' salutations. Once the other woman was out the door, Sydny turned her attention on Steve.

"You must be Steve." She smiled and extended her hand. She was about average height and had straight, dark hair that was shoulder length and framed her face. Her eyes were blue, a rarity for people with such dark hair. Her smile was broad and showed beautiful straight teeth. Overall, she appeared to be a genuinely nice person.

"I am." Steve stood up and took her hand. He was impressed with her strong hand shake. He hated it when women gave him the limp-fish hand, like they wanted to have their hand kissed or something. Or maybe they perceived their hand to be a delicate flower. A strong handshake was a sign of a confident person.

Sydny led Steve into her office on the downstairs level of her townhouse. She made a mental note that Steve would be one of those you would describe as tall, dark and handsome. She wondered what could be bothering him so deeply. Men did not choose to go to counseling as easily as women. No ring on his finger, so possibly single and probably not a wife pushing him into counseling. They usually wanted to come with their husbands and Sydny had to politely un-invite them from any future visits. More evidence he was probably single.

"Have a seat." Sydny indicated the three, large over-stuffed chairs centered around the coffee table. She didn't have a couch because she felt it created too much of a stigma around the traditional "shrink" profession. Steve selected the chair that looked out the front window and Sydny sat in the chair to his right.

"Let me start with some basic information. I am a counselor, not a psychiatrist. However, everything you tell me is confidential, unless I believe that you are a danger to yourself or others. Your EAP benefits plan covers eight visits and if you wish to continue beyond those eight visits, we can transfer over to your mental health plan. They pay fifty percent of each visit, and you are required to pay your portion after each of those appointments."

"Now that we have the business aspect out of the way, I want you to know that this time is for you. Share whatever you are comfortable sharing. If, at any time, you feel like we are not a comfortable fit, I won't be offended, and the EAP will assign you a new counselor."

"So, tell me what brings you here today." Sydny turned the air space over to Steve.

Steve took a deep breath and let it out slowly. He squeezed the arms of the large over-stuffed chair and repositioned himself as if uncomfortable, all while Sydny waited patiently.

"I'm not sleeping." Steve paused, "Actually, I am having bad dreams so I am not sleeping." He clarified.

"Would you like to tell me about your dreams?" Sydny probed.

Steve raised his hands to his face like he was planning to pray, but then rubbed his fingers outward across his forehead and stopped at his temples. His thumbs were resting under his chin. He looked at her. He appeared as someone who had a bad headache. Then he folded his arms across his chest. It was a common defensive-protective posture that people took when they were uncomfortable.

"In my dreams" he began pensively, "there is a pretty girl with long blond hair. Each time I dream of her, I feel like I'm someone else; the thoughts and feelings are mine, but the actions are not me. Does that make sense?"

After a long pause, Sydny encouraged, "When you are comfortable, continue on."

"The thing is, in my dream, I keep thinking I am going to cut the girl." Steve made a face of pure disgust. Now that it was out there, he was ashamed. After the dreams, he was always scared, but now he had to take ownership of the awful dreams.

"Do you know this girl?" Sydny asked.

"No."

"Where do you meet her, in your dream?" Sydny prodded him.

"I don't exactly meet her. She is always just there. In my first dream, she was in a van. I guess I must have kidnapped her and somehow knocked her out. In my second dream," Steve stumbled over his words, "This is why the dreams are so awful!"

"It's OK." Sydny assured him, "They are exactly that; just dreams, and if we can understand them, we can figure out why you are having them. Then we can make the changes or take the steps needed in order to stop them."

Steve continued, "In my second dream, the girl is strapped to a metal table in a basement, I think. A metal table like you see in movies, for autopsies." The look of disgust returning to his face, Steve let his head fall back against the chair and he looked up at the ceiling.

Sydny sat patiently. She knew that you couldn't push people in these situations.

"In my dream last night, I actually did cut her with a scalpel. It was awful, but I enjoyed it! Then I woke up and was horribly sick at the thought!"

"The important thing for you to remember, Steve, is that you have the appropriate feelings of remorse while you are awake. I would be concerned if you didn't feel bad about the dreams. Let's change the subject for a minute. Tell me what is going on in your life, specifically any major happenings or changes over the past six months."

Steve was relieved. He didn't want to discuss the dreams anymore.

"Well, I just moved here four months ago for a new job. I am looking for a house to buy so I can move when my lease is up in the two months. Life is pretty normal, work is normal. I go to the gym three times a week and eat fairly healthy."

"That is quite a lot of change all at once, anything that happened recently? Something that is closer in time to the start of your nightmares?"

"Yes!" Steve sat up straight in his chair as if he had found the answer. "The accident!"

"Tell me about the accident." Sydny urged him to continue.

"I was driving home from the gym Sunday evening, it was starting to get dark outside. Oh, yeah, and I had stopped at the grocery store for some steaks. I was at the intersection of Seventh East and Ninth South waiting for the light to turn green. When it did, I took off. I was traveling south next to the park. Just as I was picking up speed, a woman came running out into the street! I slammed on the breaks but I still hit her! I don't think I hit her that hard, but her head really smacked the pavement when she fell! I jumped out and ran to check on her.

As I called 911 another woman came running over. She must have been walking her dogs in the park or something and I remember that she had a double leash for two dogs, and I had never seen one before. She tied her dogs to my passenger side door handle and it all seems like it happened in slow motion. She came over to the girl and started to check on her. She asked if I had something to put under the girl's neck while she felt for her pulse.

I grabbed my jacket from my SUV and rolled it up. The woman helped me to carefully put it under the girl's neck and then she began to give her mouth to mouth resuscitation.

I remember thinking that I hoped neither of them had AIDS. The woman puffed a few breaths and then started pumping on her chest. It made me think of my CPR training. She was doing everything right; focusing mostly on the heart and only pausing to give a breath every few minutes.

Another driver came with a blanket from his car and covered the girl as much as possible to still allow us to give her CPR. I could tell the woman was getting tired so I took a turn doing the chest compressions while we waited for the ambulance.

The woman just sat there and held the girl's hand. The crazy part that just keeps sticking in my mind was that the girl was only dressed in her underwear. I mean, she had on a bra too."

Steve sat silently for a few seconds and then Sydny saw the light come on in his eyes.

Steve spoke slowly, “I thought they were from the accident; the cuts on her arms and legs! She had long cuts on the insides of her arms and legs and even on her stomach!” He slumped back into the chair as if suddenly all of the anxiety had drained out of him. “Now it all makes sense.”

“I think you’re right.” Sydny agreed.

They both sat and enjoyed the little bit of sunlight coming in through the window for a few moments. It was getting darker, earlier as autumn was setting in. In less than two weeks the neighborhoods would begin decorating for Halloween.

“Well,” Sydny began, “I think you have discovered the root of your problems. And it only took one visit. It seems that your mind is trying to deal with the trauma of the accident and also solve the puzzle of how she came to be in the road in that condition.” She smiled genuinely and it showed in her bright blue eyes. “Why don’t you plan to come and see me in a week? We can see if your sleep gets any better now, and just make sure you aren’t being overwhelmed by all of the big changes in your life right now.”

“That sounds good.” Steve agreed. “And hopefully I will be back to normal and I can ask you about the neighborhoods my realtor is steering me toward, get a second opinion, so to speak.” Steve chuckled at the little “doctor” joke he had made.

“Absolutely!” Sydny smiled at his joke. “I am sure the EAP can understand the importance of the therapy process for buying a new home in a new state. I have Wednesday at 4pm open again next week. Can you make it?”

Steve pulled out his smart phone and went to the calendar application. He selected next Wednesday and made a notation on the 4pm time slot. “It’s a date. I mean, an appointment.” Steve awkwardly corrected.

They both stood and walked to the door.

Wednesday 5:38pm

Alex had enjoyed his afternoon off puttering around the small, two-bedroom he now shared with Victoria up on the east bench. He mowed the lawn and finished cleaning out the garage so they could each park inside for the winter. He also fired up the grill on their small back patio and was boiling the brats in beer as Victoria pulled into the driveway. He adjusted the burner on the gas stove to low and went out to the front porch to meet her.

"Hey beautiful!" Alex greeted her as she was getting out of the car. "You hungry?"

"I'm starving! All I had was a salad for lunch."

"Well, what do you want with your brats?" Alex opened his arms as she came up the porch stairs. They hugged in the early evening sunshine and then Alex opened the door for her to go in.

He returned to the brats in the kitchen and she went down the hall to the bedroom to change out of her skirt and heels and into her favorite sweat pants and T-shirt. She yelled back toward the kitchen,

"Do we have any of that German potato salad left?"

In the bedroom, Victoria stepped out of her skirt and walked to the closet to hang it with the others. Alex walked into the room apologizing,

"I'm sorry, babe, I ate the last of the potato salad for lunch."

He saw her standing there facing the closet. She was thin and athletic with long dark hair. She unbuttoned her blouse and pushed it off her shoulders, letting it slide down her arms as she turned to face him.

Alex's words stopped in his throat as he saw the deep gash across her left breast. He ran toward her and grabbed her by the arms. Her blouse dropped to the floor. Victoria's face showed surprise as Alex drug her over and sat her forcibly on the bed. He ran across the hall into the bathroom and came rushing back with a hand towel. He stopped dead in his tracks.

Victoria was sitting on the bed in her bra and panties. She was completely shocked and speechless. The two stared at each other for a moment and then Victoria broke the silence.

"What on earth? I almost thought you were going to hit me?"

"You know I would never hit you!" Alex fell to his knees on the floor in front of Victoria. "I thought you were injured! Oh, honey, I am so sorry!" He put his hands on her knees and leaned forward to rest his head in her lap. Victoria put her hands on his head and stroked his hair.

"What on earth did you think was wrong with me? You scared the heck out of me!"

Looking up into her big brown eyes, he apologized more, "I'm so, so sorry. I thought you were bleeding. I thought you had managed to somehow cut yourself, or scratch yourself. I don't know."

She placed her hands on either side of his face and softly kissed him. "I'm fine, I'm OK. Man, the paramedic in you really over reacted for something like a scratch! Let me get dressed and we can go find something to eat with our brats." She kissed him again and then stood up to retrieve her sweat pants hanging on the wall hook.

Twenty minutes later they were sitting at their small card table out on the patio, eating bratwurst and potato pancakes. The sun was beginning to set and the air was starting to cool. Victoria wore her university sweatshirt while Alex was still comfortable in his short-sleeved T-shirt. He looked across the table at her and noticed the sunlight reflecting off of her hair.

"I just don't know what I would do if something happened to you. I've never really worried about the bad things that I've seen happen to other people, but I didn't know those people and it was always my job to help them. I more than know you, I love you! And I can't be there to protect you, every minute of every day. I guess it kind of freaks me out."

Victoria reached her hand across the small table and grasped his. "I know, honey. But I'm going to be fine. And I love you too."

<u>Wednesday 7:40pm</u>

The sun was getting low in the sky and the air was cool and perfect for an evening walk. Shannon was clad in her yoga pants, one of Andrew's over-sized sweatshirts and accessorized by Molly and Murphy tugging and tail-wagging on the end of a leash. The leaves were beginning to turn and falling from the trees, which meant the dogs were compelled to sniff and nibble as many as possible along the way.

They were going north, away from the park, for a shorter walk around the block for this evening. Returning in the direction she had come the other night, she recalled her frightful experience and shivered. 'Someone dancing on my grave.' She thought morbidly.

Their journey took them passed the small alley way the separated the last house from the fenced-in corner house. It didn't look scary during the day, and she wondered where it led. And then she wondered if the man following her had run back and hidden in the alley way Monday night.

Her thoughts were interrupted by a glimpse of an old car through the fence slats. The missing slat that always gave her a peek at what she thought was a pool had been replaced, and the water pump was quiet for the first time since early spring.

Rounding the corner to the left, the tall fence turned in toward the house and was intersected by a short, decorative fence guarding the front yard and all of its trees, bushes and various, odd yard decorations. It was way too busy for her taste.

The dogs continued to pull her along passed a few other cute, historical homes and then a very small apartment building before turning left again at a side street. This was one of her favorite routes to take. On the left side of the small street was an apartment complex followed by more of the smaller historic homes. Occasionally she saw the couple who lived in the olive-green house, with the tiny front porch trimmed in by white decorative railing and two ornate pillars. A cloth-covered, card table and two folding chairs barely fit on the porch where she had seen them eating dinner and drinking beer in the early evening. This was a couple who knew how to enjoy the simple things in life.

She smiled and led the dogs across the street to walk by the townhomes that reminded her of Europe. Tall trees intermingled with extra-large rose bushes and vines, and completely blocked the view from the street, but inside the tree line was a view of the long, two-story, cream-colored building. The peeling paint created both a rustic and romantic feel. Three rectangular and neatly trimmed strips of lawn stretched out in front of the building, separated by three short sidewalks, which lead to double entryways framed in under matching latticework archways.

The whole set up made her think of Italy or France and she was jealous of her friend, Sydny, who lived in the second unit from the end. To be honest, she and Sydny were more acquaintances than friends. They had met one day while Shannon was walking her dogs last spring. Catching Sydny outside, she had asked about the amazing townhomes, and after several more walk-by chats, they had agreed to go for coffee. Soon coffee become a semi-regular Saturday morning event for them.

The dogs tried to wander off across the lawn, and calling them back, she saw Sydny through her downstairs window. They waived at each other and Shannon made a mental note to invite Sydny over for dinner soon.

Once, on a previous walk, she and the dogs had ventured behind the long building, sneaking down the driveway on the north. They found a large, black-top parking area with a thick run of trees along the fence the back and side of the property. The result was a dark cool space that would be great for the summer but terrible in the winter; the snow would never melt back there. A sunken patio area at the south-western corner had a quartz stone floor and an old rusty patio table and chairs blanketed with fall leaves and looking abandoned.

They had returned to the front by way of a narrow passage way between the fence and the other side of building. Shannon remembered an open, screen-covered window that she couldn't see through, but had still felt like she was invading someone's privacy, so she quietly hurried the dogs back the front sidewalk.

She was brought back to the present moment by Molly doing her business on the lawn in front of the last unit. She grabbed a plastic bag from her pocket and laid it on the ground behind the dog just in time. She had gotten pretty good at this trick, all she had to do was fold the bag over and pick it up. It sure beat trying to scrape the mess off of someone's lawn.

"Now to find a garbage can," she said aloud.

She looked down the narrow walk way she had once snuck through, hopeful someone had chosen to store their garbage there. Instead, she saw someone leaning against the building in the shadows at the far end. She couldn't really make him out and figured he was watching her to ensure her dogs didn't leave a present on his lawn.

They continued on their walk; the dogs sniffing and snorting, while Shannon searched for a trash can. She tried to focus on getting rid of the stinky package and not on the man watching, which brought back the creepy feeling from the other night.

The tree line ended and she crossed back over to the east side of the street. She continued on to the corner and found a garbage can and dropped her baggie into it. As she did so, she looked back in the direction they had come. The man was standing on the sidewalk now. Her heart gave a little jump, but then she felt silly. She again encouraged the dogs to continue the walk, trying to sound cheery, "Let's go!"

They reached the corner and continued on to the left where she decided to jog the rest of the way around the block. This excited the dogs because they loved running.

Every so often, she looked back and saw nothing, until she turned last corner of her block and saw him round the corner from Park Street. Now her heart pounded and she picked up the pace, allowing the dogs to bolt into a full run.

She was getting short of breath and her legs couldn't match the pace of the dogs. She feared she would take another tumble and so she pulled the dogs back as she approached her own yard. Shannon looked again and there was no sight of him as she and reached over her fence to unhook the chain on the gate. Once the gate was opened, she nearly fell over the dogs trying to get them in. Dropping the leash, she latched the gate, refastened the chain, and leaned way out to look up the sidewalk, past the neighbor's bushes growing out through their fence. She waited and watched, and then saw him rounding the corner. She ran to porch, calling the dogs, flung open the screen door, shoved through the front door and yelled at Murphy and Molly to come in.

"Andrew!" She shouted. "Andrew, come here!" She closed the front door and moved into the living room. Shannon stood in the center of the living room looking out the large picture window with the dogs going ballistic at her side.

Andrew came into the living room. "What's all the fuss? Why are the dogs still tethered together?"

She reached her hand out to him, "come here, and hurry!" Andrew took her hand and walked up beside her. She had that look of fear in her eyes again. He put his arm around her.

"Honey, what's wrong?"

"Just wait. He's gonna come walking past the house any minute."

"Who?"

"The man who followed me the other night! He was following me again!"

"Honey, are you sure it isn't just someone out taking a walk?" Andrew tried to calm her.

"No! He was hiding behind a building on Park Street and he came out and started following me. I saw him!" Shannon's voice was shaking.

Molly and Murphy continued to bark in reaction to her emotion and Andrew ordered them to be quiet. There was a moment of silence as they all waited, but no one walked past the house.

Andrew gave Shannon a squeeze, "I'm gonna go take a look outside."

He left her standing there looking out the window, went out the front door and up to the fence. The dogs tried to run after him, but he was too quick, and they were tripping over each other and the leash.

She watched him lean over the gate and look up and down the sidewalk. The sun was setting and the sky was turning to dusk.

He turned back to look at her and shook his head, "no".

She watched him release the chain and open the gate, go through the gate and latch it behind him, leaving the chain dangling. He stood on the sidewalk and looked south and then turned to look north. Again, he looked back shaking his head.

She was kneeling on the couch as she looked out the window now. She didn't like Andrew standing out there like a giant target. She waived for him to come back into the house.

He came back to the gate and began to open it and then paused to look down the street one more time. Shannon felt like she was watching a horror movie, where you yell at the screen to tell the stupid sorority girl to hurry up and get back inside the building before the psycho comes up and plunges a knife into her neck!

"Hurry up!" She yelled at the window. Murphy and Molly were up on the couch next to her, barking furiously with a similar message.

Andrew finally came through the gate and latched it behind him. He shook his head at her again, moving in painfully slow motion as he reconnected the chain. The entire way back toward the house, he continued to shake his head "no" and held his hands up in a gesture of futility. She watched him until he disappeared on to the porch.

She untangled and unhooked the dogs and then slumped onto the couch as he came through the front door. The dogs jumped off the couch and ran to meet him, going crazy sniffing his legs to find out if he had encountered any strange beings while out on his short jaunt.

"Babe, there was no one anywhere up or down the street. Whoever it was, he was probably just walking and went on in another direction."

Shannon put her head in her hands and mumbled, "Why won't anyone believe me?"

Wednesday 8:28pm

Katrina sat next to the bed holding Jane Doe Seventeen's hand. The room was dark other than the glow of the monitor's green light. Jane's hand twitched in Katrina's so she leaned over to look at Jane's face. Her eyes were moving under her eyelids. Katrina placed her left hand on Jane's cheek and whispered softly, "Honey?" Jane began to moan in a low, soft tone. Her hand twitched again much more distinctly. Katrina gently squeezed it and tried again, "Sweetie? Can you hear me?" Jane began to move her head and her moaning became louder. Katrina tried to calm her, "It's ok Sweetie, you're in the hospital." But Jane only responded by shaking her head and moaning the words "no, please, no."

Katrina checked Jane's pulse on the monitor and saw it was rising. She looked back at Jane to see her face contorting into the frightened look of a person experiencing a nightmare. Jane's eyes came open and she screamed!

The beeping continued but the room was completely dark and Katrina realized she was dreaming and her alarm clock had gone off. She reached over and hit the snooze button. She needed ten more minutes to decompress from that dream.

Wednesday 8:53pm

Steve whistled as he poured the spaghetti noodles into the strainer over the sink. The steam rose up toward his face and he set the strainer in the sink and turned off the stove. He grabbed a plate and scooped a pile noodles onto it, followed by two big ladles of sauce. He continued to whistle as he went into the living room and settled in to watch the ten o'clock news.

He was feeling much better about life after meeting with Sydny, mostly because he was able to talk through his dreams and make the connection relating his dreams to the stress of the accident, but also because Sydny seemed like an amazing woman.

Steve ate his spaghetti, only half paying attention to the news. He was tired from a long workout at the gym and a long day. The saying, "confession is good for the soul" came to mind. Only *his* was a different kind of confession — a confession that something was bothering him.

He turned off the TV, rinsed his plate in the kitchen, and put the leftovers into a Tupperware container; lunch for tomorrow.

He completed his usual bedtime routine and settled in to read for a while. He was having a hard time concentrating and the fatigue of the day was wearing on him. It was much later than his usual turn in time.

He opened the window slightly to let in some fresh air and then climbed into his bed, freshly made with clean linens that smelled of fabric softener from the laundry mat. Turning off the bedside lamp, he settled in for what he hoped would be a simple night of dreamless sleep.

Wednesday 9:45pm

Shannon lay on her side, in bed next to Andrew. The moonlight streamed in through the slit in the curtains highlighting the outline of his face. He breathed heavily in his sleep. He was so strong and handsome. She snuggled in closer and gently kissed him on the temple. She wrapped her arms around his right arm at his side and draped her leg over his. He was warm and he stirred gently in response to her body.

She wished she could fall asleep as easily as Andrew did, but she was never able to shut off the worries of the day at bedtime; they played over and over again in her mind.

Tonight was especially eventful with thoughts of the girl in the hospital and the strange fact that someone kept following her, even if no one else believed it. She hated the idea of sleeping pills, but wished she could have one tonight. She wondered if Sydny was actually able to prescribe sleeping pills to her clients and then felt guilty for thinking of using her friendship in that way. The doctor from the ER might do it for her. She would have to call in the morning.

Lying in bed wasn't working so she decided to get up and make some hot tea, or perhaps she should try hot milk. She unwrapped herself from Andrew, who moaned and turned toward her, trying to wrap his arm around her. She caught his hand and held it as she slid out of bed, then kissed it and tucked it back under the blanket.

Scooting into her slippers, she could hear Molly stirring outside the bedroom door. The dogs knew her walk. If Andrew was getting out of bed, they didn't stir from the cozy warmth of their own, he usually didn't feed them. But if Shannon was getting up, something was going on.

She wrapped up in her robe and quietly opened the bedroom door. Both dogs were standing in wait, their tails wagging and thumping against the wall of the small foyer. She opened the front door to let them both out for a quick potty break, peering through the screen door to check the gate first.

Every once in a while, some rotten passer-by would open their gate. She knew that at least once in the past, someone had come in nosing around their yard and when the motion light and the dogs scared them off, they certainly didn't stop to latch the gate.

Shannon had her thumb on the latch of the screen door when she paused, the porch light was off, pending the motion of the dogs running out onto the sidewalk. The lights in the house were all off and the street lamp across the street glowed in the cold, dark air. There was someone on the sidewalk just at the corner of the neighbor's fence line and just left of her driveway. She would wait for him or her to pass by the house, otherwise Murphy and Molly would pitch a fit of barking and growling if she let them out now.

She watched and waited, but the person had stopped just in front of the big mess of rose bushes at the corner of the neighbor's yard. The hair on her skin stood up and she shivered.

The whining of the dogs caught her attention and she reached down to pet them both, whispering in a hushed voice that it was ok. She looked back toward the sidewalk and the bushes. Now no one was there. She pressed her face against the glass of the screen door and tried to see if he or she had changed their mind and gone back the way they had come. Nothing.

Now the idea of letting the dogs out to bark at the stranger seemed like a good one. If the person was still close by, the dogs would scare them off, so she opened the screen door and the dogs bolted. They were excited with anticipation at this point. She expected them to go charging off toward the neighbor's fence, but instead they ran straight out to the gate and then both began circling and sniffing for the perfect spot to relieve themselves.

Shannon stood in the doorway and waited patiently for the dogs. Everything was lit up brightly by the porch light. Molly came back first, as always, and Shannon let her in. She waited while Murphy wandered around looking for something else on which he could mark his territory. He settled for the trash can, which by now had been marked so many times that if it were a tree it would be dead. Finally, he sauntered up to the door to be let in. Shannon closed both doors, locked the deadbolt and turned the porch light off and slowly on again to reset the motion sensor.

The dogs followed her into the kitchen and sat patiently while she filled the tea pot and lit the gas stove to heat her water. She looked at them and knew they were hoping for some kind of scrap from whatever she might be cooking. "I'm sorry, Babies, only tea this time." She scratched each of them under the chin and said, "Go get on your bed."

They obeyed immediately because this was the normal routine and always resulted in a dog biscuit.

She checked the flame under the tea pot and then went back into the living room to tuck the dogs into their bed, which was made up of a long foam mattress covered in a flannel sheet and a feather bed. Shannon had found the feather bed at a thrift store for eight dollars. She figured the old house got so cold in the winter that it would help to keep the dogs warm. She covered each dog with blankets that also came from the thrift store. They had a collection of warm, fluffy baby blankets that she rotated out each time she washed their bedding. The dogs truly were her babies.

She walked over to the baker's rack and opened the dog treat jar to retrieve two bone shaped biscuits. Both dogs perked up and expertly caught the treats she tossed in their direction.

She went to sit on the couch and noticed the living room curtains were still open. Even though the living room light was off, she still didn't like the idea of anyone trying to look in the window, so she released the tie cords at each side and she pulled the curtains together. She peered out toward the driveway again and he dark shadow of a person was back, lurking behind the bushes just beyond the driveway entrance. Her heart raced and she looked toward the dogs, then toward the hallway to the kitchen. She could wake Andrew, but then it would be just like all of the other times. She looked again, and the person was gone.

"OK" Shannon said out loud. "That's it. I'm not gonna play this game anymore." She got up and walked to the kitchen, turned off the burner under the tea, turned out the light and left the room. She made her way down the hall, pausing only long enough to ensure the dogs were still quietly tucked in before going back into the bedroom. She laid her robe at the end of the bed and climbed back in next to Andrew. He rolled over and spooned in behind her. "Honey, you're so cold, you're shivering." He whispered.

Wednesday 9:55pm

Katrina stowed her purse and lunch bag in the bottom drawer of the cabinet at the nurse's station and settled in to read over the notes from the previous shift. She would be working with Brenda tonight, but Tammy was finishing up her final rounds before leaving. Katrina scanned the computer notes for each patient and stopped when she came to the Jane Doe Seventeen record. Her dream was still fresh in her mind and she wondered if the poor girl would wake up anytime soon. Something terrible must have happened to her.

Nothing too interesting in the notes; they had kept her warm with the heated blanket and checked on her repeatedly. The IV had been changed regularly too. Well, after Brenda was settled in, she would go check on the girl.

Tammy came back and Katrina let her have the computer to finish her notes.

"How was your evening, Tammy?" Katrina went to the cupboard to get her coffee mug.

"Not bad." Tammy responded. "Pretty quiet actually, I even had a minute to catch up on the late-night news. Did you see that girl who's been missing for the past couple of days? It makes me wonder, what with our mystery guest 'n all."

Katrina paused and looked at Tammy, "Oh my goodness. Do you think they could be related? I mean, it seems like once every two or three years some poor woman goes missing and it ends up being the husband who did her in. I would hate to think we have some kind of maniac lurking around."

Tammy shivered and went on with her typing and finished the notes from her rounds.

Katrina shuddered and left to get coffee but returned in time to find Tammy putting on her coat.

"You need to take advantage of hospital security and have them walk you to your car. We all should, every night." Katrina ended in a matter-of-fact and motherly tone.

Tammy made a face that said *what a pain!* and then said goodnight to Katrina and headed off toward the elevator.

Katrina settled in with her hot coffee and cocoa mix and waited for Brenda to show up and the other night nurse to finish her rounds. She was a new nurse on staff and Katrina hadn't learned her name yet. She decided she should introduce herself when the woman came back, or she could look at the computer notes with Brenda after the woman left. Katrina leaned back in her chair. She didn't feel like she normally did at the beginning of a shift, she felt more like it was the end, when her energy was waning after a long night. It was probably the dream, not the most restful situation.

"Oh well, thank goodness for mocha." She raised her cup to the empty nurse's station and took a long careful drink.

Thursday 12:47am

The ringing jolted Alex out of a dream that was immediately gone when he reached to answer the phone. He looked at the digital clock glowing green from the dresser across the room. He expected it to be morning, but it was only 12:47am. No wonder he felt like he had been hit by a bus, he must have been in some deep REM sleep. "Hello" his voice came out cracked and groggy. It was one of the guys from the station asking Alex to come in and cover for a sick colleague that had been sent home.

He wasn't due to go back on shift until noon that day, but the overtime pay would be nice. Plus, he would most likely be able to go back to sleep once he got settled in at the station. He agreed to go in and hung up the phone. Alex continued to hold the cell phone in his hand and rolled over quietly to kiss Victoria.

"You're going to work?" she pouted in a sleepy voice.

"Yes, sorry. Go back to sleep. I'll kiss you again before I leave the house."

He slid out of bed and felt his way toward the hall and stubbed his toe on the door-jam leaving the bedroom. He bit his tongue in order not to shout his favorite profanity.

"Are you OK, sweetie?" Victoria was more awake now.

"I'm fine, just not used to the new house yet." He closed the bedroom door behind himself and turned on the hall light. He had meant for the shower to wake him up, but his throbbing big toe was doing the trick. Alex entered the bathroom and flipped on the light and closed the door. He pulled the shower curtain back and turned the hot water on to let it warm up. He lifted the seat and relieved himself.

"Remember to put the seat down" he repeated over and over in his head.

The shower was steaming so he turned the cold handle while testing the water with his other hand. Once the temperature was just right, he kicked off of his boxer shorts and stepped over the ledge of the tub, closing the shower curtain behind him. The hot water felt great on his face and he stood there for a few minutes and then remembered he needed to wash up in a hurry and get in to the station.

He finished the shower and grabbed a towel. As he dried himself, it occurred to him that he would have to use the light to find his uniform but wanted to be considerate of Victoria, she had to work in the morning. He remembered the flash light application on his cell phone. Genius! He wrapped the towel around his waist and grabbed his cell phone from the shelf above the sink. He found the application, activated the light, and flipped the switch for the bathroom.

The flashlight worked really well and he snuck into the bedroom, steering it toward the closet and finding a freshly laundered uniform hanging at his end. He grabbed his boots and turned toward the dresser. His hands were getting full, with a uniform over one arm and boots in his left hand. He pulled the drawer open with his cell-phone hand and tucked a t-shirt and boxers under his arm. From the second drawer he pulled a rolled-up pair of socks and stuck them between his teeth.

Alex turned back toward the door, and as the light crept across the bed, he saw the dark crimson red of blood soaking through the sheets. He fixed the light on Victoria's face, which was completely white with her empty eyes stared up at the ceiling! Alex dropped everything creating a loud thudding noise and the cell phone went dark.

"Oh my gosh, Alex! What happened?!" Victoria sat up and turned on the bedside lamp.

Alex stood there staring at his beautiful, healthy girlfriend, who was looking back at him with frightened eyes. There was no blood. Alex stood frozen for a few more seconds, processing the facts. The room had been dark. The minimal light from his cell phone cast strange shadows. He had already over reacted once in the last twenty-four hours.

"I'm so sorry!" Alex pleaded, "I guess I can't find my way around the room in the dark. Please forgive me for waking you up again!" Alex felt completely stupid as he stooped to pick up all of his clothing and the phone. With his arms full, he walked over to the bed and leaned in to give Victoria a kiss. Victoria looked at him with her brows furrowed.

"Are you sure you're OK sweetie? You look really tired." She kissed him again and reached her hands up to his cheeks. His face was drained of its natural glow. "Sweetie, please sit down for a minute." Victoria coaxed.

Alex slumped onto the bed and let the clothes in his arms fall around him. "Just for a minute", he breathed, "and then I have to take off."

Victoria pulled him onto his side so that his head was in her lap. She stroked his hair and he heaved a long sigh.

Thursday 4:16am

"Everything is quiet on my end." Brenda stated as she came behind the counter of the nurse's station and sat down in front of her computer screen. "Your turn to do rounds and then it won't be long until we can head home for a nice long nap." She began typing the notes from her recent check of all of her assigned patients.

Katrina took a swig from the water bottle that always replaced the coffee half way through her shift and then set out to check on her half of the patient floor. As she entered each room, she quietly picked up the clipboard hanging at the end of the bed and annotated the time and any pertinent actions taken, followed by her initials. Most commonly, she was waking patients up in the wee hours of the morning to give them prescribed meds. Some were administered intravenously. Most of the patients went back to sleep for a couple more hours before breakfast was served.

As she moved down the hall, she thought about the paperless system that the hospital was about to install. No more clipboards. Each nurse would have a portable device that would record all of their notes directly into the main data base system. This would kill two birds with one stone. She also worried about everyone's records being electronic and all the movies she had seen where vicious criminals hacked the system.

Jane's room was dark and quiet as usual, except for the side lamp and the monitoring machines. Jane was lying on her side facing the window as they had been rotating her to prevent bedsores. It was time to return her to her back and tomorrow she would be rotated to her other side. Katrina slid the recently placed feeding tube out of the way. She carefully straightened out Jane's right leg, placed her hand behind Jane's back and gently pulled on her right shoulder to roll her onto her back. She adjusted Jane's arms at her sides and fixed the blankets and the feeding tube. She walked to the end of the bed to make her notes on the clipboard.

She felt him standing there in the doorway before she even looked. The hair on the back of her neck stood on end and she turned slowly, half expecting the man to vanish just as she looked his direction. He was still there and dressed in dark clothing. The dim light from the hallway shined around him and made it more difficult to make out exactly who he was. The nurse call button was at the head of Jane's bed and Katrina began to walk casually around the bed toward the window side of the room when he spoke to her.

"Excuse me, I'm sorry if I startled you. I'm Detective Howard. I have my ID." He paused and reached into his jacket pocket.

She breathed a sigh of relief, but remained a little cautious. "Can you please move to the hallway where we have more light?" she responded. She wanted to get him out of the room so she wasn't trapped inside. He probably *was* a cop or he wouldn't have made it past security. At least she hoped that was true. She moved slowly toward him, giving him plenty of time to move out into the hall. As he did, she could see that he was wearing the kind of clothing you would expect a plain-clothes detective to wear, and the light shined on his badge as she approached. It too looked real.

"How can I help you?" Katrina asked as she stepped into the hallway and passed him so that she had easy access to the nurse's station.

"Again, I'm terribly sorry and I hope I didn't scare you." Detective Howard repeated. "I've been working the case involving the victim," he corrected, "the young lady in the room. I was really hoping that she might have awakened by now, or maybe even said something in her sleep that would be helpful?" He looked at Katrina and she saw the genuine concern in his eyes.

"But why not come during the day, Detective?" You would have better odds of catching her if she was conscious, and there are more people on staff to answer your questions?"

"You're right to think so, um, Mrs.," he paused

"Ms. Dempsey. Katrina Dempsey." She finished.

"Thank you, Ms. Dempsey. Normally I would come during the day. In fact, I did come during the day a couple of times after she first arrived, but I just had a feeling I might get lucky and I couldn't sleep tonight, so I was up early anyway. Do you mind if I ask you a few questions?"

"Sure, but call me Katrina, and why don't we go sit at the nurse's station. Would you like a cup of coffee?"

"I'd love one," Detective Howard followed after her. "and you can call me Derrick."

Katrina led Derrick around the counter to the nurse's station and then over to the drink station. As she did, she introduced him to Brenda.

"Here you go. We have soda, water, coffee, tea and hot chocolate. This is here for the patients and the families. The cups are over here."

As Derrick poured himself a cup of coffee and added a cream packet, he asked both nurses,

"Are either of you aware of whether your coma patient has come to at all?"

Both Katrina and Brenda agreed that they were not and Katrina remembered her dream.

"And she hasn't said anything in her sleep, like someone dreaming?" He continued.

Again, Katrina considered her dream but nodded "no" along with Brenda.

"Why do you ask?" Brenda came closer. "We know we're supposed to notify the police if she wakes."

"I know." Detective Derrick Howard breathed a heavy sigh. "And honestly, I really shouldn't discuss the details of this investigation with anyone, but another young woman is missing. And I have a feeling, based on other facts I cannot discuss, that the two are related. So, I am looking for any new leads I can find."

Thursday 5:23am

"Ahhhh!" Steve heard himself shout. He was sitting up in bed again, breathing heavily and drenched in sweat. The clocked glowed 5:23am from the dresser and his alarm was set for 6am. This was a far worse way to wake up! This nightmare thing was getting really old. He threw the covers back and swung his feet out onto the floor. He put his elbows on his knees and his face in his hands. As he rubbed his eyes, he became increasingly chilly as the early morning air cooled his sweat-soaked body.

Steve stood up and went into the bathroom for a hot shower. Standing under the hot spray with his eyes closed, he realized that if this continued, he was going to need to stop at a store and buy a few more spare sets of sheets, and he certainly didn't want to deal with the laundry mat today. He wondered if Sydny would be available again today and made a mental note to call her first thing after he arrived at work.

Thursday 5:45am

Derrick left the hospital feeling both a little guilty and frustrated. He knew he shouldn't have barged in on the nurses at that hour, but he also felt like the nurse, Katrina, had been holding something back. He chalked it up to doing the job protecting patient confidentiality.

Unfortunately, he had three other bodies that showed up in the crime scene data base that were too similar to be coincidental. They'd all been runaways or drifters that no one reported missing, and they had all three been cut in a similar fashion to the unknown victim in the hospital. *And,* they had all died from having their throats cut, currently the only difference between them and the Jane Doe. Somehow, she had gotten away before suffering that fate.

But now a girl was missing, that people in the community actually knew. Maybe the perpetrator was getting sloppy after having lost one of his victims.

There was one other difference between all the victims; they had different hair types and colors which meant the perp wasn't sticking with a very specific kind of girl; he was more of an opportunist. Derrick wondered if he had picked the girls up while hitch-hiking, or found them on the street near a homeless shelter.

Detective Howard believed the now-missing Laura Roundsley to be his latest victim. She was a student up at the university who was on a full scholarship. She had no family and was raised in the foster care system. She did have friends who knew her well enough to know she liked to run in the park in the early evenings, but not well enough to miss her when she didn't show up for class for a couple of days.

Running in the park was not such a bad idea, except that the sun was setting earlier each day with winter approaching. She lived a few blocks from the park and had last been seen shopping at the grocery store just north of the park on Tuesday night.

All of that added up to a lot of coincidence for Derrick, too much to swallow without thinking about it at least twice.

Thursday 8:01am

Steve arrived at the office early again. He settled at his desk, ate his Burger King breakfast and sipped on his coffee. Between bites he searched through his Rolodex for Sydny's business card. He laid it out squarely on the corner of his desk pad in preparation for his phone call once he finished his breakfast.

Steve heard someone come in down the hall. According to his cell phone, it was 8:16am and he wondered if he should wait until 9 to call Sydny. If she didn't work out of her home, he might not be so concerned, but the rule of thumb for calling people at home was never before 9am or after 10pm.

Janice, the office administrative assistant, came to his doorway and said hello. She had a few forms he needed to sign, and an invoice for the latest job posting. She was pleasant and very efficient. She had two elementary-aged children; a boy and a girl, as evidenced by the pictures on her desk.

As he handed the forms back to Janice, he looked at her and wondered what the worst night was for her. A sick kid who kept her awake coughing? A fight with her husband? Maybe even the stomach flu. He would trade her any day of the week right now. He immediately took the thought back, he wouldn't wish his dreams on anyone.

Steve looked at Sydny's card, reminding himself it was there and ready to go once the clock hit 9. He tried to focus on his email in-box and managed to pass the last twenty-five minutes. He responded to his last unread email and then looked at the clock on the computer monitor: 9:08am.

He slid the business card closer to read the phone number, dialed nine for the outside line and followed by entering Sydny's number. He listened as it rang once, then twice, and on the third ring he realized he might get an answering machine. The fourth ring began and was cut off by someone answering on the other end. "This is Sydny." Came the polite response.

"Good morning, Sydny, this is Steve Waters. I'm sorry to bother you first thing in the morning, but I was wondering if you might be able to fit me in for a second appointment sometime today."

"I actually have quite a bit of time later this afternoon." Sydny asked, "Things haven't gotten any better?"

"No, I actually think they are worse." he responded in a tired but relieved voice. "What is the latest you can see me? Later in the day works out best for my work schedule."

"How about 4pm?"

"That's perfect. I'll see you then. And thank you, really, I mean it." He hung up and felt like he might be able to focus on the day ahead of him.

Thursday 9am

Shannon walked through the building saying hello or good morning to everyone as she passed. She appreciated working with such an optimistic, dedicated group. She opened her office door, balancing her ice coffee and purse in her left hand, and then unloaded everything onto her desk. She hung her jacket on the coat stand her team had given her last year for her birthday. Again, she counted herself lucky.

She picked up her coffee and took a long draw from the straw. Today was what she often identified to her team as a "two-coffee" day. She'd hardly slept last night, actually, she had hardly slept for the last *several* nights. This reminded her that she was going to call Sydny and as much as she hated the idea, ask her to recommend a physician that could prescribe her something to help her sleep. They already had a Saturday coffee date, but maybe she could bump up the date and get together this evening.

She grabbed her cell phone and scrolled down through her contacts until she found Sydny's name. She tapped the screen to initiate the call.

Thursday 3:45pm

Steve pulled over parking parallel to the bushes and trees that protected the historical townhouse where Sydny lived and practiced. He locked his SUV and walked along the street until he found a break in the tree line and snuck through to the sidewalk inside. He followed the pathway up to Sydny's door, opened it, and was just getting ready to have a seat in the tiny foyer when the inner door opened and Sydny greeted him with a smile.

They both entered what should have been the living room and Sydny motioned to the three large, comfy chairs as she had done on his first visit. He selected the same chair, facing the window as before. Sydny sat in the chair to his right and waited patiently.

He took a deep breath and tried to begin. "I don't know..." he trailed off. He sat for a moment with Sydny patiently looking across the small space at him. "I'm not sure how to even start. I haven't even really been able to focus on work today and the more I think about it, the more it seems to bother me."

"Take your time." Sydny directed him.

"Well, obviously I'm still having the bad dreams. I really believed it would stop after our last discussion. Everything made sense to me because the girl I dreamed about was similar to the girl I hit. I can't really remember what she looks like now, but I know she had long, blond hair. Anyway, my guilty feelings about hitting her resulted in bad dreams and even though I realize it really wasn't my fault, I still feel horrible." Steve paused again for a minute before continuing on.

"Well that doesn't even make sense anymore, not now."

"Why do you say that?" Sydny asked.

"Well, it's because the girl in my dream is different now," he took a breath, "new." Steve stopped, as if he had just presented the most mysterious situation he had ever come across in his life. He looked at Sydny, who was patiently waiting for him to continue.

Finally, she prompted him, "So are you having the same dream with a different girl or a new dream altogether?"

"It *feels* like the same dream," Steve began, "but it's *not* the same dream. What I'm trying to explain to you is that *I'm* the same in the dream – the person I am, who isn't me. But the girl is different now."

"You say that the person you are in the dream, isn't you?" Sydny tried to clarify.

Steve breathed in and out slowly. "It's me, I feel myself. But it isn't me because the thoughts aren't mine. It's like I am inside someone else's body, feeling their thoughts and looking through their eyes but I can't control what they do!" Steve was frustrated.

"OK, how about if I just let you tell me the dream, and I promise, no more interruptions." As Sydny said this, Steve looked at her and felt like he could really trust her, so he began again.

"The beginning of my dream was fairly normal. I am at the grocery store. In fact, it seemed like the large market store just a few blocks from here. I'm shopping, only I don't know what I'm shopping for. I see the girl with the short dark hair. She has one of those baskets, not a big cart. She puts a box of toothpaste into the basket and I know it was Crest, the kind with baking soda. How funny that I would remember that!

Next, she walks back toward the dairy and I realize that I am following her. I keep my distance because I don't want her to realize that I am following her. She adds some cottage cheese to her basket and I follow her all the way across the back of the store to the produce area. She stops and looks at a few things here and there along the way and each time, I stop and look at something as well. After adding bananas to her basket, she heads back to the escalators at the middle of the store and goes up to the self-checkout area. I wait for her to get almost to the top of the escalator and then I quickly walk up the stairs between the escalators.

I see her in line for the self-checkout stations and I walk around all the checkout aisles and go out the automatic doors. It's dark. I walk to the side of the building where the parking lot lights don't have such a strong effect and I wait.

Can you believe it? I'm actually waiting for her to come out of the store! Only I'm hiding at the side of the building!" Steve looked across the small room at Sydny. She lowered her chin slightly and raised her eyebrows as a non-verbal clue to continue.

"Well, she eventually comes out of the store with a grocery bag in one hand and her purse over the opposite shoulder. I watch her, expecting to see her get into a car, but *somehow,* I know she won't. She just walks passed all the cars to the street, and that's when I start following her again.

She headed south and walks a few blocks in that direction. In fact," Steve sat up straight in his chair, "She crossed the street at the intersection just before the spot where I hit the girl who's in the hospital! Maybe that's why I'm having the dream! What do you think?"

"I think it could be. Maybe you should finish the dream so we know for sure." Sydny encouraged again.

Steve settled back into his seat, speaking a little easier now. "Well, like I said, she crossed the street and went east for a few more blocks. The street was all residential; no gas stations like you see as you go further toward the center of town.

This is where the dream starts to get really creepy. I start walking faster, but I'm trying to be quiet. I get pretty close and she turns and looks back at me. I can tell she isn't really scared yet, but she walks a little faster.

We are almost to her house now. And I actually *know* which house is hers. The neighborhood is quiet. She looks back at me again and then I can see her looking around for a house with lights on. Now I know she is thinking through her options in case I turn out to be really following her and she picks up the pace again.

I don't want her to scream, so I call out to her, 'Excuse me, Miss, I am so sorry to bother you, but do you know which house the Thompson family lives in?' This gets her to stop and look at me. I slow down so she won't feel so threatened. She looks at me and I can see her searching her mental hard drive for a family in the neighborhood with the last name of Thompson. I slowly walk toward her and say, 'I feel like such a fool. I parked down the street because I thought I was close, but now I've walked around for nearly ten minutes and I thought I might be able to catch you and ask before I walked all the way back to my car.' She looks at me again, and I noticed that her shoulders relaxed a little so I move closer to her and tell her I'm sorry again for bothering her and I hope I haven't frightened her. I stop just within arm's reach of her with my hands in my pockets and I look at the ground and shake my head from side to side. This really sets her at ease and she tells me that she is sorry she doesn't really know the neighborhood that well.

She looks down the street behind me, and I follow her searching gaze. Then when she looks up the street, I pull both of my hands out of my pockets and grab her. I have a cloth soaked in chloroform, which I hold tightly over her mouth. She drops her grocery bag and purse and begins clawing at my hands. I pull her back against me and put her in some kind of neck lock while she struggles. Eventually she passes out and I drag her down her own driveway.

I have the same van as before, parked behind her house. I drag her into the van and I remember being disappointed that it wasn't a full moon. And this is the worst part! I thought about how her blood would flow warm and sticky in the darkness! I thought about how it would smell sweet and taste of copper!

That's when I woke up. I can't handle any more of these dreams!" Steve was on the edge of his seat leaning toward Sydny as if he was waiting for her to throw him a life line and save him from the treacherous waters of his dreams.

Sydny's face had gone slightly pale and the encouraging look was gone from her eyes.

Steve asked her, "Are you alright?" He felt awful, having described every sordid detail of his dream

because it had obviously made her sick.

"I'm fine." Sydny suddenly became aware of what must be showing on her face and forced herself to relax and give Steve a soft smile.

"Please forgive me, I should never get emotionally involved. It's just that you tell your dream with such tortured emotion and I was feeling bad for you."

She hoped this would explain the look on her face. The truth was that she realized the girl in Steve's dream could very well be the same girl who had gone missing two nights ago. The idea that she had a serial killer sitting in her home office had more than danced across her mind. She felt her heart speed up and realized she needed to keep calm, she needed a distraction.

"Would you like a cup of tea?" Sydny stood up and began toward the kitchen area of her town home. She paused and looked at him.

"No. Thank you for asking." Steve stood up as well.

As they both stood for an awkward moment, Sydny realized that she could never make it out the front door with Steve standing where he was. She thought about the back door off of the kitchen. She looked at him, trying to decide how to get him to leave without alarming him.

"Sydny, I feel like I've dropped a bomb on you. Maybe it would be better if we continued this session at my next visit. Maybe that would give you time to research some kind of ancient American Indian dream catcher solution." Steve was trying to put her at ease by making a joke.

Sydny realized this was her opportunity and jumped in. "You're right. I do need to order some dream catchers on line" she managed a smile, "I should always keep a few spare ones around the house."

"Can I call you next week when they come in and put you on the schedule for another visit?" Steve chuckled. "That sounds great." He began to walk toward the door.

Sydny summoned her courage and followed him, she needed to be supportive and not give away the nagging fear that was growing in the back of her mind.

"I'm so sorry to end your visit like this, but I do have another appointment." She felt both guilty and scared at the same time, "and I think it you did a great job today of working through this new dream. You probably need some more time and I promise to call you for next week." Sydny really did mean it. She might need to lure him back here after she called the police. She opened the door and Steve paused, turning to thank her.

"I really do understand" he said, "It's a lot to take in, trust me, I know." Steve seemed so sincere. As he turned to leave, Shannon opened the outer door.

Thursday 4:55pm

Thank goodness Steve had respected the privacy of her next "patient". Sydny was not inclined to introduce Shannon to him, especially given her new fear that he might be a very, mentally ill man. She had quietly gestured for Shannon to go inside her office area while she reassured Steve that she would have more time for him next week.

Shannon was waiting in the front room, which could now function as a normal living room. She had only been in Sydny's house once before so she looked around the room while waiting for the last patient to leave. Whoever he was, he was definitely handsome. She wondered if Sydny could ever meet a nice guy in her line of work. Even if she was interested in someone like the gentleman that just left, who knew what kind of issues he might be dealing with? Shannon immediately felt bad for thinking something so awful about the man.

As she continued to look around the room, she noticed there was nothing personal in the room. "Smart" she thought to herself. You don't want patients to know anything about you, just to be on the safe side.

"Hey, thanks for waiting!" Sydny was standing in the foyer locking the outer door. She came into the office area and shut that door behind her and locked it too. "Sorry, I just had a strange day. How are you?"

Sydny could hear Shannon talking about how she was basically fine, life happens, etcetera, etcetera... but all she could think about was how she needed to make a report to the police. She hated to do it, but they could keep an eye on Steve just in case. She wondered if it was possible that he had actually abducted the latest missing girl and really couldn't tell the difference between a dream and reality. It would even make sense that he had abducted the girl he said he hit with his vehicle. She would have to check on his story and see if the accident even happened. She could feel the nervousness coming over her as she stood there listening to Shannon. Only Shannon had stopped talking.

"Sydny, are you OK?" Shannon was asking.

"Oh, I'm sorry. Please forgive me! My mind was wandering." Sydny answered. "Can you do me a favor, Shannon?"

"Sure."

"Can we just stay here and have coffee? I can brew some, and I have some of that Ghirardelli chocolate and whipped cream. We can make mochas." Sydny pleaded with her eyes as well.

"Of course! You look like you could use a break. Where is the coffee? I'll brew some and you just sit down." Shannon went into the kitchen in search of the coffee maker. There was a white ceramic cookie jar next to the coffee maker and she opened it on a hunch. The pleasant aroma of coffee wafted into the room.

"Thank you." Sydny said softly as she slumped into one of her big chairs. She could hear Shannon putting water and coffee into the coffee machine. As the pot began to brew Shannon returned from the kitchen and came to sit in one of the big chairs by Sydny.

"I know you can't talk about it, but please let me know if there is anything else I can do for you."

"I'm fine." Sydny replied. "Tell me how you are doing, you sounded like you've been under a lot of stress lately."

Shannon suddenly sat up straight in her chair. "Oh, my, gosh!" she said in deliberately slow pace. "I know your client! He is the guy who hit that girl! The one that ran across the street in just her underwear! She was all cut up and I don't know if it was from the accident or something else! He was terribly upset. He jumped out of his car and we both worked together; he called the police and he even managed to find someone with a blanket to cover her so she wouldn't go into shock! He even helped me to give her CPR!" Shannon's words erupted from her like water breaking free from a damn, and Sydny just took it all in.

Sydny began slowly,

"Shannon, you know I cannot discuss anything that Mr. Waters has shared with me, but you are right. He said he was there, at the accident. And it must be you he talked about coming to help and having two dogs. What else can you tell me about the situation? It might be really important, important to how I proceed with his counseling. Can you help me?"

"Well, it was last Sunday night..." Shannon began and relayed the entire story to Sydny, just as she had to Detective Howard earlier this week.

Sydny took notes now and then on a note pad she had sitting on the coffee table. She specifically wrote down the detective's name. When Shannon was done, Sydny stood up and went to the kitchen for coffee.

"Oh my goodness! You have had a tough week!

"No," Shannon followed her to the kitchen, "that is only the beginning of my story." The two women looked at each other in the kitchen and Sydny broke the silence,

"Let's make our mochas and sit back down, then you can tell me the rest."

The two women sat in the living room while Shannon recounted the incident of being followed home from the grocery store, going to the emergency room, losing her ID and going back the next day. She told Sydny how she confirmed that the girl Steve had hit was in a coma at the hospital. She explained the strange feeling of waking dreams as she experienced the car that almost hit her, only to vanish again, while walking the dogs, as well as the mysterious man who kept following her. She told Sydny how frustrated she was that no one believed her, not even own husband.

The two women sat and sipped their coffee. Sydny felt like she had been emotionally dumped on for the second time in one day, while Shannon felt a little relieved to tell her story to someone that was willing to listen.

Dusk crept in, outside the town home window and Sydny didn't want Shannon walking home, so she suggested she call Andrew to pick her up. There were too many strange things going on in the neighborhood and Sydny didn't want to have to worry about her new neighborhood friend. Of course, Shannon agreed.

Thursday 9pm

Steve sat in his living room eating take-out, teriyaki chicken from the Japanese Steak house downtown. He'd stopped after his appointment with Sydny as well as deciding to skip the gym this evening. He was mentally worn out from recanting his dream and he has a bad feeling that he may have really freaked her out.

"Just my luck." He thought. "I meet a smart, attractive woman, and it is under the kind of circumstances that will make her think I'm nuts."

Steve took another bite of chicken and then picked up the remote. He started flipping through the channels and found nothing but the news. Nothing good would be on for a while. He clicked to the next channel and froze in position. The face on the screen of his TV was the girl from his dream last night! It was a photo that was quickly reduced to the upper right-hand corner of the screen. A reporter was saying something and then the image was lost and replaced by the scene of a car crash on the freeway.

Steve frantically flipped up and down through the news channels looking for the story of the girl. Finding nothing, he cut the power to the TV. He set his plate on the coffee table and went over to the small desk against the wall, opened his laptop and logged on. Steve used Google to search for the local news. He tried to remember which channel he had flipped to when the photo of the girl had appeared and then decided to pick the local Fox network and search for the words 'missing girl'.

The story immediately filled his screen and Steve read through the details. Her name was Laura Roundsley and she had gone missing two nights ago. She'd been walking home from the grocery store and was believed to have been abducted in her own back yard. One of her neighbors found the grocery bags thrown behind the house. She told the news reporters that stray cats had been eating the bread from one of the bags and so she had knocked on the front and back doors and then called the police because Laura never answered.

Steve sat back in his chair. It hit him hard at that moment. Sydny had been so upset because she knew about the missing girl! She probably thought he had something to do with it. Two nights ago, he had been at the gym. But why would he dream about this girl? He had no connection to her. His mind spun with questions. Should he call

Sydny? Should he call the police? Should he drive by the house where the girl was reported to live? Should he even try to go to sleep tonight?

Thursday 9:40pm

Alex had been at work since 2am this morning and it had been a pretty uneventful day so he was able to take a nap to catch up from his sleep interruption last night. His regular team came in at noon and they had their shift meeting, followed by some drills.

Victoria brought him Mexican, fast food at 5:30, after she got off work, and they'd eaten together in the day room and watched TV. The news recapped the story of the missing girl, Laura Roundsley and encouraged volunteers to join the search team. It had all been very concerning for Alex so he made Victoria promise to call him the minute she got home. He made a mental note to go and purchase some better deadbolts and security chains for their new home. He wondered how much an alarm system would cost per month. My, how his life had changed since he and Victoria became serious.

Victoria called to say goodnight around 9pm. She had an early day at work tomorrow and wanted to let him know she was safely tucked in and the house was locked up tight. He suggested they should get a dog now that they had a big back yard and Victoria giggled at the idea of a puppy. He was thinking more of a guard dog, besides, who had time to train a puppy? He told Victoria he loved her and they both said goodnight.

Alex walked out the back door of the station house where some of the guys were playing basketball even though it was pretty dark outside. The lights on the back of the station house were not sufficient to light up the entire basketball court and the game would have to come to an end soon.

He walked out into the cool dusk of the evening to get some fresh air before turning in for the night. He'd heard somewhere that catching up for one bad night of sleep took a week of good nights, and he knew the likelihood of that as a paramedic working for the fire department. A few minutes later, the guys ended their game and began walking back into the station house. Alex turned around and followed them.

Some of the guys settled in to watch TV in the day-room while others hit the kitchen for a snack. Alex flopped onto his cot, fully dressed and lay there thinking about all of the strange events of the past few days, he wondered how much of it was caused by fatigue and worry, and as he pondered, he fell fast asleep.

Thursday 10pm

Shannon had gone safely home with Andrew, and Sydny had locked up her townhouse nice and tight. She even went around checking that all of the windows were locked, shades down and curtains drawn. She'd made a call to the local police station and left a message for Detective Howard to call her back regarding possible information on the disappearance of Laura Roundsley. Then she had settled in upstairs with a hot cup of tea and her laptop.

She sat in bed with the TV on low volume and the computer on her lap, making her session notes from Steve's visit today. She stopped typing to pick up her tea from the night stand and as she took a sip, she glanced at the television screen. The late news was on, showing the search for Laura Roundsley had ended for the day but would resume tomorrow. They showed the picture of Laura again. She looked so young and happy that day in the park. Sydny wondered if anyone ever thought about their picture being used in such a somber manner when they were actually having it taken.

She was analyzing the details of Steve's session in comparison to the disappearance of Laura. She needed to be clear tomorrow when Detective Howard called her back and she made the final decision to violate patient confidentiality and report the information to the police. She was required by law to report two conditions; when a client is believed to be a danger to him or herself, or to someone else.

Laura had been abducted two nights ago, and Steve had dreamed of the action one night ago. Steve seemed unaware that the girl he dreamed about was real. The girl Steve hit with his SUV had been found in her underwear. Steve believed she had been hurt prior to the accident. Steve dreamed about torturing the girl. Shannon had confirmed that the girl was injured in more ways than the accident had caused. Could Steve have hurt her prior to that day and not remember it? What were the odds that he could have abducted her, tortured her and then hit her running across the street? Or had she escaped from him and he had gone after her to stop her? She would need to know so much more about the accident.

Then the next stream of questions flew into her head. Why did Shannon think someone was following her? And if someone had followed her home from the grocery store, was it the same man who abducted Laura? Did he go after Laura because he was unable to catch

Shannon? Was it Steve who went after Shannon because he knew she lived in the area after the accident? His dream of abducting a girl on the way home from the grocery store was so close to what Shannon had described. Had Steve been lurking around the neighborhood following her? Or was it someone else? But if this person had abducted another woman, why follow Shannon?

Sydny was making herself more upset. She took another sip of the hot tea and tried to relax. She definitely was not feeling clear about anything. Tomorrow she would cancel all of her afternoon appointments and do some research of her own. She wanted to visit the hospital where the mystery blond girl was being treated, and she wanted to talk to the detective who had visited Shannon.

The next unanswered question was how she was going to get information without betraying Steve? Funny, she thought to herself. Why was she so worried about betraying Steve? Why did she have a gut feeling that he was not the guilty person circumstances pointed to? Why was she allowing her personal feelings to get in the way?

Friday 3:12am

Alex was awakened by three audible beeps and the loud speaker. Jocelyn was the working dispatcher on shift and was reporting an unconscious victim found at Johnson Park, northeast side adjacent to the duck pond and horseshoe range. "Ambulance crew to report immediately". Jocelyn repeated the call as per protocol while Alex and his teammate moved quickly to the ambulance bay.

Alex climbed into the driver seat, taking his turn at the wheel, and Jay jumped in beside him. As they backed out of the bay, Jay picked up the radio microphone and held down the transmit button while speaking into the microphone, "Unit 24 in route to Johnson Park. Please repeat the details of 911 call." The voice of Jocelyn came over the speaker,

"Report of woman found unconscious in Johnson Park, northeast corner with proximity to small duck pond and horseshoe range. Called in via cell phone by Trent Wilson, who should still be on site."

Alex turned on the siren and headed directly to the park. It was 3:17am and there was no traffic. He turned onto Ninth South, very near where the girl had been hit not even a week ago, and then turned right into the park from the north entrance. Unfortunately, the park only had vehicle access around the perimeter, so Alex had to drive the ambulance over the curb and down the wide concrete sidewalk where people walked their babies in strollers and ran with their dogs during the day. As they got closer to the center of the park Jay spotted a man waiving his cell phone back and forth in the air. Who knew that the cell phone application for a flashlight would become so valuable? Technology had really changed the world. Instead of lighters, people used cell phones at concerts now.

Jay pointed toward the man with the cell phone light and Alex drove off of the sidewalk and onto the grass pulling in close once he saw the girl lying on the grass. The man had obviously covered her with his sweatshirt jacket, but her white legs shined bare in the ambulance headlights. The full moon of last weekend was waning now and caught behind nighttime clouds.

Jay and Alex both jumped out and grabbed their gear. Jay quickly unfolded a silver heat blanket while Alex kneeled beside the girl to check her pulse. Her body was ice-cold and her face was grey and colorless. As he felt her neck for a pulse, he recognized her immediately as Laura Roundsley. He found no pulse in her neck and could see that her throat had been cut. Alex carefully pulled the sweat jacket aside and saw the long, shallow cuts on her breasts, upper and lower arms. He could also see the same type of cut along her abdomen and down her inner thighs and calves.

Alex took a breath and decided not to over react. This had happened before. He closed his eyes for the count of three and then opened them. The cuts were still there.

Jay gently lowered the sliver heat blanket over her body and stopped to look at Alex. They were both kneeling on either side of Laura.

Jay paused, "Alex. What are you doing?"

Alex answered very calmly, "Jay, take a look. Tell me what you think." He sat back and gave Jay room to examine the girl. He expected Jay to find a pulse as he picked up her wrist and then make some kind of wisecrack about how Alex was losing his touch.

Instead, Jay lifted the sweat shirt,

"What the hell happened to this girl?" They both looked at each other and then back at Laura.

"Can you find a pulse?" Alex asked Jay who responded by shaking his head back and forth and stating, "Wouldn't expect one after her throat being cut like that."

Alex took another deep breath as he watched Jay examine Laura. This just didn't make sense to him.

Jay asked the man who found her, "You found her unconscious? Did you try to administer CPR?"

The man answered, "I, I just assumed she was unconscious so I covered her and called 911. I don't know CPR or anything. I'm so sorry."

Jay looked across at Alex and saw the strange look on his face. "Alex! We've got to call it in and get a unit out here to secure the area. It's a crime scene."

Alex snapped out of his trance and ran to the ambulance. He called in the victim information and stated possible ID for Laura Roundsley. Dispatch would notify the police.

He went back to the body. Jay had left the warming blanket over the girl, and had pulled it up to cover her face. He was talking to the man who found her, explaining that he would have to stay and give his statement to the police. Then he encouraged the man to sit on a nearby bench and got a second warming blanket to wrap around him.

He couldn't have his sweat jacket back now because it had become part of the crime scene.

Alex looked down at the figure hidden under the thin silver of the heat blanket. Images flashed through his mind. First was the Jane Doe victim, hit by the SUV, with lacerations on her arms and legs, which was followed by the image the pregnant woman with the imagined lacerations on her arm. Then Victoria popped into his head, standing there in her bra and panties with a fresh gash across her breast. Alex shivered and Jay called his name.

"Alex, why don't you come over here and sit with Mr. Wilson for a minute. I'm going to get some juice out of the bus for him to drink."

Alex walked over and sat down next to Mr. Wilson, thankful for a distraction.

"Are you doing OK?" He asked.

"I don't know. Did I screw up? Is she dead because I didn't give her CPR?"

"No." Alex answered and his voice cracked. He cleared his throat and continued. "She's been gone for a while, there was nothing you could have done other than call us, which you did."

"I've never seen a dead person before! How was I supposed to know?"

"It's OK, really." Alex tried to calm him. "It is such a dark night and I am sure you were shocked to even find her here. You did the best you could under the strange circumstances. It's not your fault."

Alex could see the squad car lights coming into the park as Jay returned with a juice box for Mr. Wilson. He stood up and felt a rush of dizziness. He braced himself against the arm of the bench, and as the dizziness subsided, he saw the first squad car pull off the center walk and onto the grass. The eerie red and blue lights bounced off of the silver shrouded body.

<u>Friday 3:32am</u>

Derrick's cell phone and pager went off at the same time. He opened his eyes in the dark and reached over to the night stand where both his phone and pager were charging. The pager simply showed 911, which meant to call in to the station, and the caller ID of his phone registered the station dispatch. He answered the phone and received instructions that a body had been found in Johnson Park, possible identification, Laura Roundsley. Officers had been dispatched to secure the crime scene. He acknowledged the dispatcher and hung up the phone.

"Great!" He said out loud. He hated it when missing person's cases ended this way. He switched on the lamp standing near the head of his bed and swung his feet to the floor. Sitting on the bed, Derrick leaned his head right and then left creating cracking sounds that filled the quiet room. Then he dragged himself off to the shower.

* * * * * * * *

Ten minutes later he was in his car heading to the park. Emergency calls always warranted the two-minute, wake-up shower. Two more minutes to get dressed, followed by securing his gun, badge and a bottle of water.

He didn't live very far from the park, and chose to enter at the southern entrance. He could see the lights bouncing off the trees to the east, so he drove through the center and then parked. There were already four vehicles parked on the grass; two squad cars, the coroner's vehicle and an ambulance.

The officers were already cordoning off the area with yellow crime scene tape secured between a mix of trees, the bench, and tall, thin stakes driven into the ground. He walked over and lifted the yellow tape to duck under.

A bright flash sliced through the cold, dark night. Someone from the coroner's office was taking pictures. Detective Howard watched as another officer removed the thin, silver blanket that was covering the body. He took another picture and the flash illuminated a dark, hooded sweatshirt draped over the body. After three more shots at different angles, the officer removed the sweatshirt.

Derrick was standing close enough now to see that it was, in fact, Laura Roundsley. Each flash of the camera enabled Derrick to see the long lacerations on her arms and legs, and finally the deep gash across her throat. The body was alabaster white. She had definitely been killed somewhere else and probably exsanguinated before being brought here.

The body was lying perfectly straight with her arms at her side. She had been posed, still clothed in her bra and panties and the perpetrator had taken his time. No rushed, dump-job with the body rolled up in a sheet or shower curtain and then quickly dropped in random position. She had been carried over and carefully laid onto the ground. Her arms and legs had been straightened and her hair had been smoothed flat under her head. But she had also been left out in the open for the whole world to see, in only her underwear.

"Did you find any tire tracks coming into this area?" Detective Howard asked.

Officer Banks responded, "No, the only evidence of vehicles in here are ours and the ambulance. Would have been nice, though. Would you like to talk to the gentleman who found her?"

"Ya, that would be good."

"I'll let you know as soon as Officer Jordan is finished getting his statement."

Derrick looked around. The two paramedics were sitting in the back of their bus filling out statement forms. The coroner's team had finished with pictures and was now carefully placing the victim's body into a long, black body bag. An officer would have to stay here to secure the scene until morning, when the lab would come out and gather any other physical evidence and take additional pictures.

Officer Banks waved at Detective Howard and pointed at the ambulance. Officer Jordan was helping their witness over to the ambulance where he sat down and one of the paramedics began checking his vitals. As Derrick approached, he could see the man better in the light from the bus. He looked to be in his mid-forties, with scraggly hair and the beginnings of a beard. His shirt was dark and worn, and his jeans looked dirty as well. He was wearing one of the silver medical blankets around his shoulders like a shawl. It was *his* sweat jacket that had been placed on the victim.

'Homeless' Derrick thought to himself. "Hi, I'm Detective Howard, can I get your name?"

"My name is Trent Wilson. I'm sorry. I don't know CPR." His voice was gruff. He was obviously upset and possibly even in shock.

"It's OK." Derrick responded. "You did everything right. You called 911, didn't you?" Trent nodded. Derrick continued, "Do you mind telling me how you happened to be in the park so late tonight?"

Trent frowned. "I couldn't sleep, and the shelter was full. I thought maybe I'd walk around for a while and maybe find a nice bench for a nap. Then I saw her, lying in the grass. I thought it might be someone I knew. But then I got close and I could tell something was wrong. And she didn't have no clothes on, so I covered her up. She was so cold that I figured she might be sick, or hurt, so I called 911." His looked down at his feet.

"You live at the shelter, no home address?" Trent nodded. Derrick continued, "Can I ask how you got a cell phone?"

"Ya, I got that free phone from the government, I get 250 minutes a month and I can call 911 for free. The shelter helped me do the application last month. Only problem is when I can't charge it cause the shelter is full. My battery was almost gone tonight. I wish I could've found her sooner so I could've saved her." His voice cracked with the emotion.

"Don't beat yourself up, I think the girl was already deceased before she was brought here. There was nothing you could have done, and everything you did do was just right." He gave Trent a minute to collect himself and then asked, "Did you happen to see anyone else in the park tonight while you were walking around?"

"No. The weather is gettin' colder now. Everyone wants to go to the shelter."

"OK, thanks." Derrick patted him on the shoulder and turned to Officer Jordan. Will you make sure to get me copies of everyone's statements, by the morning?"

"Absolutely."

Derrick visited with the two paramedics for a minute. Jay Blackwell reinforced what Trent had said. Once they had realized the girl was deceased, they left everything as they found it with the exception of the warming blanket. Alex Jones didn't have much to say. He looked like he was in shock himself. Derrick wondered why the young man had ever become a paramedic if the sight of the victim's body made him queasy. Surely, he saw all kinds of gory injuries in his line of work. Anyway, nothing else stood out so he decided to let the teams finish up. He would head home, take a real shower and grab some breakfast before heading into the office to review all of the new information.

Friday 4:01am

Shannon opened her eyes but couldn't see anything. She reached to rub her eyes, but her arms were pinned at her sides. She felt cold, achy and stiff. She shivered and realized that her chest and ankles were also restrained. She rotated her right arm so her palm was up and then bent her fingers toward her wrist, trying to feel what was holding her down. She could feel the cold metal of a big, bulky buckle.

She held still for a moment and thought to herself, "This is a horrible dream, I need to wake up." She took a deep breath and could smell the familiar dank smell of her basement. Was she in her own basement? Had she been sleepwalking? None of this made sense to her.

The feeling of panic began to burn in her chest. She tried again to move her arms and then to pull her knees up. She was stuck, held to some cold, metal surface by wide straps on her ankles and wrists, and across her upper abdomen. Her arms and legs burned in pain and she felt like she was all scratched up. The panic took hold of her and she began violently writhing, trying to kick and flail her arms. Her right arm came free and she felt the sting of a gash along the meaty part of her palm where it joined her thumb.

Shannon froze for a second and listened. Dead silence. She pressed her right hand to her mouth and bit the flesh to ease the pain. She tasted the blood running from her hand.

"Where the hell am I?" she asked out loud. The sound of her crackled voice scared her. It was weak and didn't really even sound like her. The fear gripped her again and she quickly reached to free her left wrist. She could feel the big buckle with two metal posts instead of one like most belts had. The heavy strap felt like leather.

She pictured the kind of straps used to hold down a prisoner or mental patient. She fumbled at the strap and it slipped in her hand as the blood ran over it, making it difficult to grip. She managed to get her index finger under the strap and work it lose and then free of the metal posts. As she pulled her left arm free, she heard a thump coming from above her.

She froze again. She opened her eyes wider in the dark trying to see anything, but there was nothing but quiet and darkness. She became more aware of the stinging pain along her arms and legs. She reached her left hand to her right bicep and felt a horrible gash running the most of the length of her upper arm.

'I have to get the hell out of her!' She screamed in her head. She tried rolling to the right but the strap across her ribs held her back. She fumbled with the buckle using both hands and finally worked it open.

She leaned over on her right elbow and then braced her left hand next to it on what felt like the edge of a metal table. She pushed with all of her strength and then repositioned from her elbow to her hand, continuing to push to sit up.

Every move was racked with pain and Shannon wasn't sure she had the strength to continue. She took in another deep breath of musty air and moved her left hand back over to her side and pushed up more. She felt her stomach muscles strain and then she finally sat up. She reached to her right ankle to undo the strap but only found the bed covers over her legs.

Shannon looked up and read the digital clock across the room on the dresser. The time read 4:17 and she could see the outline of her bedroom from the glow of moonlight filtering through the sheer curtains.

She looked at her right hand, no cut, no blood.

Friday 4:49am

Jay drove back into the station with Alex in the passenger seat of the ambulance. Alex was ashen and quiet the entire way back from the park. Jay was glad he had offered to drive. The girl in the park had really taken a toll on Alex, which was strange, because Alex and seen much worse over the years. Jay wondered if being in love had changed the way Alex looked at the tragedies they encountered. He was certainly in bad shape this morning.

Jay turned off the ignition and they both quietly exited the ambulance and walked silently back into the firehouse. Jay made his way over to the captain and Alex collapsed onto the couch.

Four minutes later Captain Murray walked over to Alex and sat down next to him.

"Hey Alex," began Captain Murray, "You've been on longer than a standard shift and you've had a rough night. I just called Zachary and he'll be in to cover the rest of your shift. I just need to know if you feel ok to drive home, or I can call Victoria to come and get you? What do you think?"

Alex looked at Captain Murray and frowned. "Sir, I can finish my shift. I just think I'm feeling a little under the weather 'cause I haven't been sleeping well."

"I know. So maybe it isn't such a bad idea for you to go home now and catch up on your sleep."

Alex gave the Captain a look of consternation as he was trying to come up with his rebuttal, but then he just breathed a heavy sigh and nodded his agreement. He thought for a moment, Victoria would be getting up soon but he didn't want them to call and alarm her by asking her to pick him up. He was exhausted, physically and emotionally. Still, he didn't want to worry Victoria so he agreed and went to collect his keys to drive home. He stopped to say good night and the Captain handed him a card.

"Do me a favor and call this number after you have had a nice long rest." Alex gave him a puzzled look. "It's our Employee Assistance Program, they have counselors available for our guys to talk to, especially after a traumatic event. They help us through the tough times, and you have certainly had couple of those this past week. Promise me you'll call."

Alex nodded and took the card. He just wanted to get home.

Friday 5:28 am

Alex pulled into the driveway and turned off the engine of his Subaru. He looked at himself in the rear-view mirror. Dark circles were forming under his eyes. He had never felt this awful in his life. He got out of the car and went to the front door of the new home he was making with Victoria. He inserted the key into the lock and turned it as quietly as he possibly could and tried to push the door open. Then he remembered the deadbolt. He was happy that Victoria had locked it.

Once in the house, he locked the door behind him and tip-toed down the hallway to the bedroom. Victoria was still asleep in the bed. She looked like an angel to him. Her dark hair flowed aimlessly around her on the pillow and over the sheets. One strand lay gently across her cheek. Alex sat on the edge of the bed and softly slid the wisp of hair away from her cheek and behind her ear.

She opened her eyes and smiled up at him. She lifted the bed covers for him to lay down beside her. He wanted to tell her how strange things had been and hope that she would make sense of it all; telling him it was all just a manifestation of the level of stress in his life. Instead, he climbed in next to her and allowed her to drape her arm and leg over him. She was spooning him with her tiny body, the opposite of their normal cuddling, but it felt like the safest place in the world so he closed his eyes and was out almost instantly.

* * * * *

When the alarm went off at 6:10 am, Victoria kissed Alex on the side of his neck and carefully climbed out of bed. She gathered her work clothes and cell phone and quietly left the bedroom. After getting ready, she filled her travel mug with coffee and slipped out the front door.

Friday 6:15 am

Steve awoke to his alarm, breathed a heavy sigh and stretched in the bed. No dreams last night, at least not that he could remember. The Ambien had definitely worked. He was glad he'd saved the old prescription. The challenge now would be getting a refill since he only had three pills left. He wondered if Sydny could write him a refill. He would have to give her a call when he had a free minute at work. He pulled himself out of bed and headed for the shower.

Friday 7:30 am

Sydny was sitting at her desk with a coffee and notebook. Her first patient was scheduled at 9am. She would begin making cancellation calls at 8:15 to clear her afternoon schedule. In the meantime, she was making a list of everything she hoped to accomplish this afternoon. She wanted to research the accident, stop by the hospital, and hopefully speak to Detective Howard since she was expecting him to call back. That would be the biggest hurdle for her since she wanted to ask him questions that he would likely not answer. She wanted to tell him what she knew, but still felt uncertain about what she actually did know.

'What a mess!' she thought as she opened her laptop. She had more than an hour before her first morning appointment. She opened the Internet and Googled the Fox news page to search for the accident last Sunday and any published details. Before she could search, the main story popped up showing Laura Roundsley had been found dead in the park! The story mentioned several lacerations on the body, but not the cause of death. This knowledge changed everything, Sydny had to cancel all of her appointments for the day and get in touch with Detective Howard.

Friday 8:49am

Detective Howard made it in early after his second shower and a quick breakfast at the diner. He had reviewed the latest reports, checked his email and listened to his voice mail messages. Most people could get ahold of him on his cell, but the non-emergency calls came to his desk phone. He was planning to run by the Medical Examiner's office to see what they could tell him, but first he was perplexed by a voice mail left late last night by a Sydny Samuels. She didn't say much but let him know she was a counselor and concerned about some information she had received from a patient. He knew it could be just some crazy nut-job and she was obligated to pass on the perceived threat, but it could also be important, which his gut was more inclined to believe.

He was just about to dial the return number when his phone rang. He answered, "Detective Howard."

There was a pause and he was about to hang up when he heard, "Um, hello, my name is Sydny Samuels and I left you a message last night."

"Yes, I was just about to return your call. How can I help?"

Sydny stammered, "I think I may have some information that will help regarding the girl who was just found, Laura Roundsley, but I don't feel comfortable talking over the phone."

Detective Howard got that feeling in his stomach that he always got when he found a clue to a case. He offered, "You can come to my office, or I can come to yours. What do you prefer?"

"I think I will come to you if you don't mind. I don't think I can sit around here anymore and I have other errands to run later. Is that OK?"

"Absolutely, how soon can you be here?"

"How about 10am? Sydny had not gotten a hold of her 9am appointment and wanted to wait for her arrival, reschedule her, and then head out.

"That's perfect." Responded Detective Howard. That would give him time to visit with the ME and check on their progress while he waited.

"OK. Thanks," said Sydny, "I'll see you then." and hung up the phone.

He hit the red phone disconnect button, grabbed his jacket and left his office. The medical examiner's office was up the hill at the

University complex; a short 10-minute drive. He walked out the back door of the city police offices and jumped into his car.

Traffic wasn't bad now that rush hour was over. He pulled into one of the parking spots reserved for the police and launched from his car, he had the high energy feeling he got when he started getting somewhere on a case. The first thing he wanted to do was compare the lacerations on the body to the Jane Doe in the hospital, and the other three unsolved cases he had linked together.

Dr. Rutherford had been on since the body was brought in early this morning. He was just wrapping up his autopsy notes when Detective Howard walked in. Some medical student was attending to Laura's body; finishing the sutures and making sure she would be as presentable as possible for whomever had to identify the body. It was clear who she was, but standard procedure required an ID from the next of kin, or in her case, a friend.

"Hey Joe," Derrick put his hand on Dr. Rutherford's shoulder.

Joe looked up, "I hate the young ones." He clicked the save button on his computer program and stood up and shook Derrick's hand. They had worked together before, mostly on less gruesome cases.

"What can you tell me?" Derrick asked.

"Well," Joe began, "cause of death was the throat incision which opened up the carotid arteries causing the victim to bleed out. All of the other incisions on the arms, legs and body were more superficial. I can only imagine those were inflicted for some form of torture. The victim was obviously killed somewhere else and then dumped in the park. The body had very little blood left upon arriving here."

Dr. Rutherford never used terms such as 'she' or 'the girl', it was all very scientific and impersonal. Derrick knew it was part of the job.

"Can I take a look at the superficial incisions?" Derrick asked. "I want to compare these to the Jane Doe victim we have up at the hospital. In fact, perhaps you could send me a copy of your diagram and notes to share with her doctor. I really think these two cases are connected and I have to stop this guy!"

"Anything I can do to help, Derrick." Joe led Derrick over to Laura's body and pulled back the sheet.

The room had that strong smell of rubbing alcohol and medicinal fluids mixed with a growing scent of rotting Parmesan cheese, it was the only way Derrick could describe it. He looked down at the body. He remembered the flashes of the camera that illuminated each incision in the dark. But now he could see the harsh reality under the bright lights. The throat incision was gaping but clean of any blood. The other incisions were also clean but not deep. They were almost perfectly symmetrical; one at an angle across each breast, and one on each upper arm. Each leg had a slash along the inner thigh and then on the calves. There was an incision across her abdomen. Occasionally there was a slight jagged edge which he could only imagine was a result of her trying to pull away.

What kind of human being could inflict this kind of torture? Derrick felt slightly sick, but very strongly pissed off. He nodded at Joe who then replaced the sheet. Derrick looked at his watch. The time was 9:33 and he needed to get back on time to meet Ms. Samuels.

As Joe walked back to his computer Derrick asked, “You’ll be sure to send me those diagrams and notes? And let me know if you find any other trace evidence?” Joe nodded and Derrick turned to go.

Friday 9:55am

Sydny pulled her Land Rover into the police station parking lot. She felt anxious, was she about to betray a patient? Or catch a killer and save a life? She walked into the building and up to the front desk. She introduced herself and stated her appointment with Detective Howard. Just then, a tall man with dark hair graying at the sides came up to her. He was dressed in a casual suit and introduced himself.

"I'm Detective Derrick Howard, I overheard you asking for me. You must be Ms. Samuels." He held out his hand.

"Yes, I am. And please call me Sydny." She replied as she shook his hand.

"Please, let's go to my office." Detective Howard gestured down the hall. "Would you like a water or coffee?" he asked pointing to the break room on the right.

"I would actually love a bottle of water, do you have any that isn't cold, just room temperature?" Sydny inquired.

Detective Howard walked into the break room and retrieved a bottle of water out of the storage cupboard. He came back to Sydny waiting in the hallway and handed it to her.

"My office is just down here." She followed him into an end office and he pointed to seat across from his desk. "Make yourself comfortable."

Sydny took a seat and put her purse on the chair next to her, opened the bottle of water and took a long drink. Detective Howard settled behind his desk and grabbed a note pad and pen from the slightly cluttered desk.

"May I ask how you got my name and number?" asked Detective Howard?

"Oh, ya, sorry!" responded Sydny. "A friend of mine; I got it from a friend of mine who helped out with an accident last week. Shannon, her name is Shannon Medford." Sydny trailed off.

"Oh," Detective Howard answered with an intrigued tone as the feeling came back to him; more pieces of the puzzle. "go on, what can you tell me?"

"Well, let me start with just the relevant information before I disclose any names. I want to make sure it is absolutely necessary to violate the confidentiality of one of my patients."

"OK, that works."

"I started seeing a patient through the Employee Assistance Program earlier this week. He was having trouble sleeping due to some graphically violent dreams. On his first visit, he told me he dreamed of abducting a girl with long blond hair. He had also dreamed of having her in some kind of old basement on a metal table where he began cutting her leg with a scalpel." She looked over at Detective Howard feeling embarrassed.

Detective Howard was on the edge of his seat. "Is there more?" he asked?

"Yes. At first it made sense because the man had witnessed (she wanted to be careful how much she disclosed) a terrible car accident and the victim was blond, with cuts on her body." Sydny paused to gage Detective Howard's reaction. He just kept watching and waiting for her to continue so she did.

"But then things got really strange because the next time he came to see me his dreams had changed. He dreamed of abducting a girl with dark hair on the way home from the grocery store downtown." Sydny stopped. She knew this was too much and she would be forced to disclose Steve's name.

Detective Howard proceeded cautiously. "Ms. Samuels, Sydny, you said your patient witnessed the accident of last Sunday night that resulted in our blond, Jane Doe victim who is currently in a comatose condition at the hospital." He took a breath. "There were three individuals who helped the victim, one woman, being your friend Shannon Medford, the other two men were Steve Waters, who struck the victim with his SUV, and Joseph Norton, who helped with blankets from his trunk. There were, of course, other men and women in cars and at the park, who witnessed the event. I am afraid I am going to have to ask you who your patient is."

Sydny took a deep breath and then let it out slowly. "I know, I understand, it's Steve Waters." They both just sat silently for a moment, and then Sydny began again.

"I think there are a few more important things you should know, the first is that Steve may very well be having these dreams solely based on the horrific circumstances of hitting the girl and witnessing her body all cut up. And before you say it, he might even have seen a picture of Laura on the news and not even realized it, but transferred it to his dreams."

"However," Sydny began again, "My friend Shannon has reported that someone has been following her and that concerns me because it could be Steve, or it could be someone else who is committing these horrible crimes!" Sydny's emotional state was starting to get the better of her.

Detective Howard softly commented, "Yes, and I just spoke with Shannon the other day and she told me about the man who followed her home from the grocery store. Apparently, no one actually saw the man following her but this is too much to just be coincidence. I'm definitely going to have to interview her again.

More silence as the two of them sat there until it was broken by Sydny, "What will you do with this information?"

"Well, your timing is perfect. I have been interviewing key witnesses to the accident and just so happen to have an appointment with Mr. Waters this afternoon."

Sydny looked concerned. "Don't worry, Sydny, I won't disclose the information you have given me, but I will be sure to ask a lot of extra questions that might give me some insight into Mr. Waters. In the meantime, do you have another appointment set for him?"

"Yes, he is scheduled for 4pm next Wednesday, but I had promised to find an earlier time slot for him. What should I do?"

"Call him and let him know that you are booked solid so you can't change the time, but you look forward to his next regular visit. That way he won't be suspicious and you won't have to deal with him. If we decide he is a person of interest, we can arrest him on Wednesday before he comes by. Are you OK with that?"

"Yes, Detective Howard, I think I live with that. I just feel so," She trailed off.

"Please, you can call me Derrick. And thank you so much for coming in, you really did do the right thing." Derrick reached for a business card and walked around the desk to hand it to Sydny as she stood up. "If you think of anything else, don't hesitate to call me on my cell number here on the card. Day or night, doesn't matter." And he escorted Sydny back to the front of the station.

Friday 11:30am

Shannon sat in her office and looked at the clock on the computer which showed it was only 11:30am, still at least half an hour 'til she could leave for lunch. She'd been reviewing some marketing strategies for the March of Dimes Haunted House, but wasn't really concentrating that well.

Last night at Sydny's had been pretty overwhelming, with all the talk of the accident and being followed home. She had forgotten to ask if Sydny could recommend anyone to prescribe something to help her sleep.

After Andrew brought her home, she had taken couple of Benadryl tablets in the hopes they would make her drowsy enough to sleep without dreams, then she had climbed into bed with a book next to Andrew, who had been reading a client's book. He liked to read ahead at night and then review the chapters on the computer the next day to do the editing. She didn't know how he could stand to read it twice, but he was good at his job.

It hadn't taken her long before she put the book away and snuggled in next to his chest, pushing her head under his arm just like the dogs always did to her on the couch. But in the end, it hadn't worked that well so she then made an attempt of hot tea, and when she did finally sleep, it was restlessly.

Now Shannon was feeling tired before it was even lunch time. She grabbed her cell phone and found Sydny's name in her contacts. She tapped the green phone symbol to dial the number.

Sydny answered on the Bluetooth connection in her Land Rover. The background was a little noisy. "Hey Shannon, can I call you back when I am done running errands?"

Shannon agreed and said she just wanted to ask a quick question whenever it was convenient. They agreed to speak later and both hung up.

She wondered why Sydny was out running errands during the day. She had expected to get her voice mail and then a return call between appointments. But then again, Sydny had to take a day off here and there to just get *life-stuff* done.

Her train of thought was interrupted by Lisa as she popped through the office door all excited and proud, "I got the first batch of place mats designed for the March of Dimes Haunted House! And we have 38 local restaurants ready to use them this year!"

Lisa placed one of the paper place mats on Shannon's desk. The artist had done a good job of capturing the haunted house in cartoon form. It was an old Victorian about five times the size of her house. The lettering was in the *Chiller* font but wasn't really scary. The address, hours of operation and dates were listed across the bottom, and if you looked closely, you could see a dark figure in one of the high windows of the house. This gave Shannon the chills.

"Great!" Shannon said. "Great work you and the team have done. Will you be distributing these today?"

Lisa nodded with excitement as she rattled off some elaborate plan they had for some of the restaurants to pick up their boxes, while others were being delivered by volunteers, and so on.

Shannon wasn't really listening, she was thinking of haunted houses and dark, dank basements. Suddenly her nightmare from last night came back to her and she remembered the pain of slicing her hand as she pulled it free from the leather strap and buckle. She instinctively grabbed the back of her right wrist, cradling it in front of her and examining the fleshy part where her thumb joined her hand.

"Are you OK?" Lisa asked.

She looked up. Lisa's face showed genuine concern. "Ya, I'm OK." She looked back at her hand and wrist. "I think it's just sore from typing." She paused. "You better get going! You have a lot of exciting stuff going on."

Lisa smiled, grabbed the place mat and left to go show it off to the next person on her list.

Friday 11:58am

Victoria saved the spreadsheet she was working on and looked up at the clock on the wall, it was almost noon. She'd been running financial reports all morning for her boss and really needed a break. She pressed the control-alt-delete buttons and then enter, to lock her computer. Jenny had invited her earlier to grab a burger for lunch, but she'd declined because she intended to run home and check on Alex. He hadn't been himself lately and working extra hours was making it worse.

As she grabbed her purse from the desk drawer and headed out of the office, she realized she had never worried about Alex like this before. He had always been so confident and go-lucky in his attitude toward life. Now suddenly he was worrying about every little thing that could possibly happen to her.

Perhaps the job was finally taking its toll on him. Certainly, being one of the responders to that awful accident where the girl was hit by a car and left in a coma was bad enough, but now he had to be the one to find Laura Roundsley's body in the park. And he said they both had cuts all over their bodies. She thought his was the type of job that would require some mandatory counseling from time to time.

Victoria reached her car and started the ten-minute drive to their new home. She liked the commute so much better now. Before, it took her 35 minutes to get to work. Being a couple meant affording a better home and she was so excited for all the fun decorating and gardening projects she had in mind.

The next thing she knew, Victoria was in the driveway parking next to Alex's Subaru. She drove a gun-metal black, Audi TT that was about 11 years old, that she had purchased used and managed to pay off a within a few years. She loved it so much and couldn't imagine getting a new one, the body style of hers was the best. She was glad it was paid off, because the maintenance on the thing could be a bit pricey as well, but the gas mileage was great and it handled really well. Driving up the canyons was a favorite Sunday activity.

Victoria killed the engine, got out and went to the front door. She hadn't locked the deadbolt when she left this morning so her entry was fairly quiet. She plopped her purse and keys on the kitchen counter and went down the hall to check on Alex. He was still passed out in the bed pretty much where she had left him *and* he was still in his uniform, minus his shoes. She slowly unbuttoned his shirt and unbuckled his belt. As she unbuttoned his pants he stirred and reached to take her hand.

"Shhhhh," She soothed him. "I'm just gonna help you get out of your uniform.

He opened his eyes and smiled faintly, then cooperated by scooting out of his pants before allowing her to pull them off of his legs. She laid them across the bed and then helped him work one arm and then the other out of his shirt. He rolled onto his side, scooted across the bed and patted the mattress.

Victoria sat down next to him and pulled the sheet and comforter up to his shoulders. She kissed him on the temple and instructed him to stay in bed at least until she got home after work. He was incredibly tired and appeared to go right back to sleep.

Victoria walked around the bed and adjusted the window blinds to block out most of the sun. The room darkened a little and was more conducive to a long nap.

She went back around the bed, grabbed Alex's uniform to lay them across the chair by the closet, and noticed white business card about to fall out of his front, pants pocket. She grabbed it and read the words Employee Assistance Program. Leaving the clothes on the chair, she snuck out of the room and closed the door behind her.

Victoria went to the kitchen and placed the rumpled card on the counter and set about making a cheese quesadilla for lunch. As she threw the tortilla on the plate and sprinkled it with grated cheese, she wondered what an employee assistance program was. Popping her food into the microwave, her mind returned to the thought she had earlier about mandatory counseling.

She went to the desktop computer at the small desk built into the back, dining room wall and Googled Employee Assistance Program and read the results. Apparently, larger companies offered this as one of their benefits; employees could get counseling help for any number of problems ranging from financial and legal troubles to drugs and divorce.

The microwave dinged to signal her lunch was ready so she grabbed her plate and sat back down at the computer. While she ate, she did a little more research. She wondered who had given the card to Alex and hoped he would take advantage of the opportunity to chat with someone about all of the ugliness in his job this past week. Noticing the time, she placed her empty plate in the sink, grabbed her purse and locked the front door behind her.

Friday 2:25pm

Steve was in his office finalizing comments on a written warning prepared by one of the attorneys for his paralegal. Apparently, the young lady continued to have issues making it to work on Monday mornings despite being coached twice and given a verbal warning all during the period of the last three weeks. It was time for more serious disciplinary action. He hoped the paralegal would change her act because employment at this firm was highly competitive and she could be replaced in a heartbeat. It was also critical that any for-cause terminations, even in an At-Will employment state, be done by the book, especially when carried out by a law firm. Hence, the need for an HR Director and a great job for Steve.

The reception line rang through to Steve's phone and he hit the speaker button. "Steve, there is a Detective Howard here to see you. He says he has an appointment with you at 2:30."

"You are correct, Elizabeth. Please let him know I'm on my way." Steve pressed the disconnect button on his phone, stood up, stretched, and headed out the door.

He descended the elegant staircase leading to the main floor and saw the detective still at the reception desk chatting with Elizabeth. As he approached the desk, Detective Howard looked up and extended a hand. They shook hands, made the formal introductions and then Steve led the detective back upstairs to his office where they both sat at the small conference table.

"I have to say," began Steve, "I really hope you get this mystery solved with these girls! Being just partially involved has really messed me up. I am not sleeping well at all, and I am not even a victim." He felt a little selfish as the words left his mouth. "I don't know how you do it, you must deal with a lot of unpleasant situations in your line of work as a detective."

"To be honest," Detective Howard replied, "I can't imagine being in Human Resources, I wouldn't want to deal with everyone's work problems."

"Ya, I've heard that before. I guess we're all cut out for different things and that is what makes our great, diverse world." Steve took a breath. "So how can I help you with your investigation? I know when I gave my statement the night of the accident, they told me someone else would likely follow up. I guess that's you, Detective Howard?"

That's true, Mr. Waters, I would like to go over the accident with you again and find out if you've remembered anything more, or might even be able to answer some extra questions for me."

"You can call me Steve, and you bet, I really want to help that girl. I can't believe I hit her, on top of whatever other horrible things had happened to her." Steve looked down and shook his head.

Detective Howard could see that Steve felt genuine remorse. Could he possibly be having some kind of psychotic break and abducting girls but not remembering it? Well, that was part of the reason he was here, to find out.

"Steve, will you start from the beginning and tell me in your own words how the accident happened?"

Steve went through the details just as he had relayed them to Sydny. Detective Howard referred to his notebook and added a few things as Steve recounted the events to him.

Then Detective Howard began with his 'clarifying' questions. "I see that you told the officers on scene that the accident happened around 8:45pm, does that sound right?"

"Yep. It was getting close to dark and you know that is about 9pm these days."

"And you stated that you were traveling south on Seven Hundred East. Can you tell me where you were coming from?"

"Sure. There is a 24-Hour Fitness gym across from the shopping center on Seventh, and that's where I do my regular workouts."

"So, you really hadn't traveled that far before the young woman ran out into the road in front of you." Steve made a note in his notebook to confirm Steve had been at the gym that night.

"No. And I am sure glad I was only just taking off from the stop light. I can't even imagine if I was going the full thirty-five miles per hour. She might not have even made it! I am not sure how I could have lived with that."

Detective Howard reassured him, "Well, that didn't happen, so don't waste time stressing about what might have happened. Sounds like you're already stressed enough. The next thing I wanted to clarify is what time you finished up with the paramedics and police."

"The paramedics arrived pretty quickly, I would say even before 9pm. After they took care of the girl, one ambulance crew stayed for a few extra minutes to make sure none of us were in shock, and that I hadn't been hurt either. We were all fine, although the young lady with the two dogs seemed to be really shaken up."

Steve paused and in his own head he shouted, 'that's where I saw that woman before!' He was realizing that the woman coming into Sydny's place the other night was the same woman who helped with the accident. He wondered how she ended up going to see Sydny. It was a really strange coincidence!

Detective Howard watched the gears turning in Steve's head and wondered what he was thinking. "Did you remember an important detail?" He prodded.

"Oh, sorry, I was just thinking about the girl with the two dogs. After the second ambulance left, she un-tethered her dogs from the door of my SUV and that's when the police had each of us write down a statement. I thought she should've just left the dogs where they were, but turns out they calmed down immediately when she untied them and kept them by her side. I think it was after 9:30pm when we finally finished up. One of the officers gave her and the dogs a ride home. I guess she didn't live that far away, but like I said, she was pretty shaken up."

"And where did you go after the accident?" Detective Howard hoped Steve wouldn't get suspicious of his questions.

"I went home too. I was physically AND emotionally exhausted. Don't even think I ate dinner that night."

"It says here that you live at 1925 West Hope Avenue in apartment 21A."

"Yes, for now, I'm hoping to buy a house soon."

"Well, I wish you luck with that, you really have to know the valley well and pick the right neighborhood for yourself. How long have you lived here?"

"I've been here for four months. I relocated to work for Smith, Brown and Kittredge, so I am just learning the area. I do like the neighborhoods around the park, though. I just hope this all gets resolved because I don't have good memories of the area so far."

"Steve", Detective Howard asked carefully, "Is there anything else you can remember or think of that might help us?" He leaned closer and focused his eyes on Steve's.

Steve took a breath. "I don't know that I remember anything else, or that I saw any special clue, but I just have a bad feeling about the girl and all of the cuts on her body." Steve paused. "I just wish I did know something that I could tell you to catch the son-of-a-bitch who did that to her." Anger gleamed in Steve's eyes. It was quickly followed by sadness.

Detective Howard felt for the man, but that didn't take away the concerns regarding the suspicious behavior reported by Ms. Samuels. He would just have to do his homework and find out what else was going on.

Detective Howard rose to his feet and extended his hand as he thanked Steve for his time. Steve responded in kind. "I'll walk you back downstairs."

Friday 3:15pm

Alex bolted upright in bed, sweaty and disoriented. He wasn't at the station and he wasn't in his apartment. Then he recognized the bedroom in the new house he shared with Victoria. The clock on the dresser showed 3:16 in the semi-dark room. He remembered that Victoria had come home and checked on him at lunch, so she must have closed the blinds.

He still felt tired, but he was wide awake. He'd been having a nightmare where he found Victoria lying lifeless, with an ashen face, dead eyes and cuts all over her body so there was no way he was going back to sleep.

He threw on a pair of sweat pants hanging on the wall hook by the closet and wandered out into the kitchen for a snack. As he rifled through the cupboards, he saw the half-crumpled business card on the counter. Obviously, Victoria had found it and tried to flatten it back into normal condition. Then he saw the desktop computer screen across the dining room boldly displaying the words, Why Employee Assistance Plans Are Right for Your Business.

Alex grabbed an apple out of the fruit bowl and took it, along with the card over to the computer. He fell into the chair still feeling quite tired. He bit into the juicy apple, read a few lines of the article, and then looked at the business card in his hands.

Victoria was obviously worried about him. Hell, he was worried about him. What could it hurt to make a call?

They didn't have a house phone because it didn't seem like there was any point these days. Everyone had cell phones, wireless internet, and satellite TV. He wandered back to the bedroom in search of his cell and found it on the night stand. He pushed the home button to bring up the unlock screen, dragged his finger over the pattern, and the picture of Victoria he'd set for the background came into view. He slid the screen to the right with his thumb as he walked back to the dining room, retrieved the card and dialed the number.

"Employee Assistance Program services. How may I help you?" Came a woman's voice.

"Um, I was wondering about the counseling services. I'm not really sure how this works." Alex stated in a less confident voice than usual.

"Sure. Can you tell me what topic you are seeking counseling for? For example, financial? Legal? Substance Abuse? Family and Divorce?

Stress Management?" The girl rattled them off like they were everyday occurrences.

"I think stress management, I work as a paramedic and I've had a couple of bad calls lately."

"OK, let me get some information from you and then I will forward this to one of our counselors to make you an appointment." She asked for his full name, employer, address, date of birth, etc. and let him know that it was standard practice for someone to call with an appointment time within twenty-four hours, but warned that since it was Friday, he may not hear back until Monday. Alex asked how it would work with his work schedule and she answered that the counselor assigned would coordinate that with him.

She asked if there anything else she could do for him and he told her no, and then said in his head, 'Can you make these day-mares go away!' He thanked her and said goodbye.

Friday 3:42pm

Sydny sat in her 'patient' meeting room slash living room thinking about her conversation with Detective Howard. She was feeling really bad about disclosing Steve's private suffering to the detective, but she was also a little scared.

She'd stopped by the hospital to inquire about the coma patient but they were not allowed to release any information, and since she didn't know a name and was not next of kin, they had sent her packing.

She had grabbed a salad to go, and then come home to research anything she could find on the internet regarding the accident, the victim, and the missing, but now found, Laura Roundsley. She figured Shannon might be able to give her more detail as well but would wait until evening to give her a call.

Now what to do? It was quarter to four and she had canceled all of her appointments for the day. Usually Sydny worked hard all day and then felt great about taking a walk or relaxing with a good book. Today she just felt defeated.

Her cell phone rang from across the room where she had left it her purse and the ringer indicated it was the EAP coordination office. She always programmed specific ring tones for important callers.

"Something to focus on!" She jumped up and grabbed the phone in anticipation. "Sydny Samuels." She answered.

Becky, one of the benefits coordinators, rattled off Alex's information and Sydny took notes in a notebook she pulled from her purse.

"Thank you." She hung up.

Ok, she thought to herself. Young man, works as paramedic, work stressing him out, specifically some of the calls he has responded to lately. "Well if he has been dealing with anything like the Steve or Shannon, he probably is having a tough time." She said aloud.

Sydny stopped. She stared into the open space of her living room. Again, she spoke out loud, pronouncing each word like a separate sentence, "Oh – My - Lord." What would be the odds that this young man was called out when Laura Roundsley's body was found?

She grabbed her phone again and dialed the number on her notepad. The chance of actually getting him was slim, but she was burning with the need to know if she was right!

The phone rang three times and as the fourth ring began, she mentally prepped to leave a professional message.

"Hello?" at the last minute, a young man answered.

"Hello, my name is Sydny Samuels with EAP Support Services and I am trying to reach Mr. Alex Jones."

"Wow! That was fast, I only called half an hour ago. I'm Alex."

"I am glad I was able to catch you, Alex. I understand you are interested a few counseling sessions to work through some stressful events in your work life."

"Yes, I guess that's what I am interested in. The only problem is that I work for the fire department and my schedule is pretty hectic."

Sydny was overwhelmed with curiosity and was trying very hard to sound calm and patient. "Are you working today?"

"No, I am actually off until tomorrow at noon. I don't suppose you work on Saturdays."

"Not usually, but I have been known to make exceptions. I am also open for the remainder of the day today and my office is open until 6pm. She felt like she was pushing him. She felt a little selfish, to be honest.

"Um, I could probably do 4:30 today. Is that too short of notice?"

Sydny's heart jumped. "No, that would be perfectly fine. Let me give you the address." She recited her address and then closed with, "OK, I'll see you in half an hour, be sure to drive safely."

Friday 4:11pm

Alex locked the front door and climbed into his Subaru. He'd washed his face, reapplied deodorant, and dressed in jeans and a T-shirt. He started the car and backed out of the driveway. The address Ms. Samuels had given him was only about ten minutes away.

He hit the green call button and then dutifully said, "Call Victoria on mobile." The mechanical voice of the Bluetooth system came back "Calling Victoria, The Girlfriend, on mobile. Press the hang up button to end the call". The ringing sounded over the speaker. It always made him laugh that the car said her name exactly the way he listed her in his phone contacts list. Someday he would change it to be Victoria, The Wife.

"Hey, Sweetie! Why are you awake?" Victoria answered the phone.

"Well," he replied, "I called that EAP number from the card you took out of my pants, *and* googled on the computer, and they were able to get me in this afternoon, so I am on my way. I wanted to call and let you know that you'll probably beat me home."

"Oh, good. I'm proud of you! You've been under a lot of stress lately! And I didn't take the card from your pants, it was falling out." She said matter-of-factly.

"OK. Well, I love you and I'll see you in a bit."

"I love you too. What do you want for dinner? Want me to pick something up?"

"You know what? Just go home and order a pizza. Get anything you want. We'll sit on the back porch and enjoy the evening sun."

"Sounds good. Gotta go, someone's at my door. Love you." Victoria hung up.

Alex followed the directions on his navigation system and it led him right past the park. He shivered. The navigation told him to turn right onto Park Street, which he did. The directions took him almost to the end of the street where a checkered flag on his screen indicated he would reach his destination.

The thing he hated about navigation was that it didn't always indicated which side of the street the house or business was on. Luckily, Ms. Samuels had told him she was on the west side of the road behind a thick wall of trees and rose bushes. He parked on the street and walked around to the sidewalk.

Wow, he thought to himself. If I wasn't going to live in a house, I'd certainly pick a cool old townhouse like one of these. He saw the door labeled by the number 620 and went up and rang the bell.

Sydny came to the door and smiled at Alex. He liked her at first sight. She led him through a second doorway and into an open living room with three large, comfy chairs.

"Have a seat, doesn't matter which one." Sydny pointed. "And we can get the administrative business out of the way first thing."

A pitcher of water and two glasses were on a small, round coffee table centered between the three big chairs. Alex choose the one closest in from the doorway. Sydny sat straight across from him, and the chair facing the window sat empty creating a point of balance to their little triangular meeting.

"As I said, my name is Sydny Samuels, but please call me Sydny. I am not a psychiatrist, I am a counselor and if you are not comfortable after today's session, you may request a new counselor to meet with, and know that it won't hurt my feelings. Everyone has a different personality and some people just fit better with others."

Alex knew he was going to be just fine with Sydny and his anxiety about the process was already wearing off.

"Secondly, the next time you come for a visit, feel free to open the outer door and have a seat on the bench in the foyer. If I have another appointment, you don't need to stand outside waiting, that's what the foyer is for. Make sense?"

Alex nodded, "So how does this work?"

"Well, your employer pays for up to eight counseling sessions per year, and that is for each kind of services, some of which you are probably already aware, like legal or financial counseling. If you decide you want to add extra sessions, we work through your health insurance to bill the rest. People usually come to me to work through a specific challenge in their lives, and not for any on-going condition, so eight sessions is usually more than enough. Does that answer your questions?"

"Yep. I guess the only other question I have is, how does this work here today?"

"Pretty informally, why don't you start by telling me a little about your job?"

Alex explained to Sydny that he worked for the fire department as a paramedic, and had been doing it for about 5 years now. He sometimes wondered about going into nursing or even becoming a doctor, but he really liked things the way they were. He explained that he'd never had a squeamish stomach and was a quick thinker and fast on his feet in an emergency.

When he was a teenager, his little brother fell off the trampoline and while all of the other kids panicked at the sight of the bone protruding from his brother's arm, he was quick to action, taking his brother inside and hollering for his parents to take them to the hospital. That was when he first knew he wanted to be a paramedic when he grew up.

"And what about your personal life?" Sydny asked.

"That is definitely a big deal," Alex responded. "I just moved into a house with my girlfriend, Victoria. I would classify this as my first serious relationship. In fact, I think I will ask her to marry me someday soon."

"Well, that is a big deal." Stated Sydny.

"It is! In fact, it's just since we moved in together that I think I have started looking at my job differently. I worry about her and I seem to imagine bad things happening to her because I am worrying so much."

"What do you mean by imagining bad things are happening? Sydny prodded.

"Well, the other day, I thought she had somehow cut herself. I actually saw the cut on her chest and I ran to grab a towel, but when I got back nothing was wrong with her."

"That's interesting." Sydny both thought and said aloud. "What do you think would trigger that kind of imagined injury? Do you deal with a lot of strange injuries in your line of work?"

Alex sat forward and looked at her, pausing for a moment. "Just because I imagine a few weird things, that doesn't make me crazy, does it?"

"Not at all!" Sydny responded with genuine understanding. "The things we imagine and dream are often our mind's way of dealing with the stressful events in our lives." She looked him straight in the blue eyes and searched for his trust.

"OK." He said, "Then let me tell you about some of the strange things I've been imagining, but first, let me tell you about the stressful event that I think started it all. Last week I went out on a call to find a young girl who had been hit by an SUV after she ran out into the road."

Sydny's heart paused for at least two beats. She folded her hands in her lap and bit down on her lip. She couldn't believe what she was about to hear.

"So, without disclosing things I really shouldn't, and because it was on the news, I can tell you that the girl was only dressed in her underwear and that she had several lacerations on her body. They were not lacerations from being hit by a car; someone had done something bad to her." Alex looked at Sydny and she was listening very intently, so he went on.

"Well, the next time I went out on a call, I imagined cuts that weren't really there, on the arms of a pregnant woman. I even imagined her looking dead and exsanguinated, you know, drained of all her blood. Then another time, I imagined my girlfriend having cuts, and even saw her lying in our bed with blood all around her! That was in the middle of the night when I got a call to go in to work, so I guess the shadows in the dark room played tricks on me.

For the first time in my life, a patient has really freaked me out. But that's not the worst of it, last night, I went out on the call where we found the body of the missing girl from the news. I'm sure you have seen it."

Sydny nodded that she had and quietly stated, "Laura Roundsley."

Alex asked, "If I tell you some specific details, I need to know how confidential this process is, because I can get into a lot of trouble. Police often withhold certain details during a murder investigation and we aren't supposed to talk about murder victims."

"Everything you say to me is protected just like when you speak to your attorney or clergy person. The only way I can share what you say, is if you become deceased, or if I believe you are about to hurt yourself or someone else. I am bound by the same laws of confidentiality as any therapist, does that make you feel more comfortable?"

"Yes." Alex breathed a sigh of relief. "Well, I want to tell you, in confidence, that when we found Laura's body in the park, I saw lacerations on her arms, chest, abdomen, legs and neck. She was also in her bra and panties. The man who called 911 had found her and covered her with his sweatshirt. Sadly, he thought she was unconscious and called for an ambulance. But what I want you to understand is that when I first looked at her, I thought I was imagining the cuts like before."

Sydny's head was swimming! Two men, both at the scene of an accident where the victim had cuts all over her body and was clothed only her bra and panties. Both men imagining, or dreaming about similar victims. It was a very strange coincidence that they would both be so drastically traumatized by the girl who ran across the street! And it didn't seem that they could be working together or having a shared delusion. At least it would be the rarest thing she had ever come across, even in all of her studies.

Alex broke her train of thought, "What do you think?"

"I think you are under a great deal of stress! Can I ask you a question or two?"

"Sure."

The night of the accident, did you interact with any of the witnesses? I know it sounds weird, but I just want to understand everything that happened to you that night."

"Yes, I usually do get a little information from other people on scene. When I arrived, two people were taking turns giving CPR; a man and a woman. The woman had started mouth-to-mouth and had also done chest compressions.

The other man was doing chest compressions when I arrived, and he was the poor sap that hit her with his SUV. He was overwhelmed with guilt, but had managed to stay focused on helping the girl until we got there.

My partner, Jay, took over the CPR and I intubated the girl and then used the paddles to get her heart started again, then Jay, and I put her in the ambulance and got her to the hospital.

There were other people there but I didn't talk to any of them. And the second ambulance stayed behind to check everyone else out, which is standard procedure.

I really feel for the guy that hit the her, it definitely wasn't his fault. Everyone kept saying she just ran out into the road. It's a wonder that she didn't get hit by traffic from the other direction, but if the light was still red when she ran into the street it makes more sense.

She made it almost all the way to the park but got hit in the far lane. I just wonder where she was coming from. And of course, I have to think that it could have been her body we found in the park if she hadn't gotten away from whomever did that to her."

Alex paused and his gaze went somewhere beyond the room. "That must be why I am having these crazy thoughts about my girlfriend,

Victoria. It scares the hell out of me to think that there is some psycho out there doing horrific things to girls."

Sydny had just been taking it all in like a suspenseful movie playing out on an imaginary silver screen in her head.

Alex came back to the moment and noticed the look on her face. "Did I freak you out?"

"No. Honestly. I guess I just feel the same way you do, seeing the news about Laura and worrying about a potential serial killer in our town."

Alex looked at his watch. He wanted to get back to Victoria and she would be home soon. He wanted to hold her all night and keep her safe. "Do you have any advice for me?"

"I don't so much give advice as I do listen. Talking about stressors usually helps people identify what is causing them trouble. It creates an awareness and an understanding, which typically reduces the stress. I am hoping that by getting this all off of your chest by talking to me, you can relax a little more at home with your girlfriend. I don't imagine you share these kinds of events with her."

"No, I don't, and not just because of confidentiality reasons; I don't want to bring that ugliness into our lives."

"Well then, you have done the right thing by coming to me. I'll be your support system for getting all of that ugliness sorted out and swept away so you can go back to your regular life, sprinkled with happy moments instead of scary ones." Sydny smiled. "Do you want to schedule another time to come back and let me know if things are settling down?"

"Yeah, that would be great! I actually feel better already."

Friday 5:08pm

The little clock in the right-hand, bottom corner of the computer showed 5:08. Shannon had not had a productive day. Thank goodness she had a great team, they worked well together and each took full responsibility for the success of team projects. She hoped they hadn't noticed how disconnected she was today. The phrase TGIF came to mind and she couldn't agree more.

She shut down her computer and put on her long, burnt-orange sweater coat. It was the perfect coat for the fall weather. She had seen it in a catalog when she visited her mother, and that Halloween, her mother had sent it as a birthday present. Her mom was great that way. She grabbed her purse from the bottom desk drawer and walked out of her office.

She said goodnight to a few people as she walked through the building. Not many were left on a Friday night after 5pm. She left through the front door and walked to her Jeep in the parking lot. She loved the fact that putting her hand inside the handle triggered the door to unlock. Of course, the key fob in her purse had to be in proximity, but she loved the function. She climbed in, threw her purse on the passenger seat, closed the door and pushed the start button causing the seat to move forward into her preset position.

The jeep was the best investment she and Andrew had made. They'd been able to pay half of the purchase price in cash up front to reduce the amount financed. It was an investment and they planned to keep it for at least 10 years. It was great for taking the dogs up the canyon for a hike, and pulled the small cargo trailer they had purchased for home renovation projects. She backed out of her spot, hit the comedy channel on her XM radio and headed home.

Friday 5:32pm

Detective Howard sat in the store director's office on the second floor in the back of the large building. They'd entered through the 'employee only' doors and walked down a narrow hallway to get there. Eight monitors sat side-by-side on a long credenza, each with a different view of the 2-story store. Each monitor was connected by an HDMI cable to an intricate CPU that obviously recorded the store footage. A large, flat-screen TV was mounted to the wall next to the CPU.

The store director was queuing the playback for what he had identified as zone eight; the east side, upper entrance of the store. This is where Detective Howard had explained that a witness had last seen Laura Roundsley before she disappeared. Only he didn't add that the so-called witness was Dr. Samuels' patient, who supposedly dreamed he followed Laura out of the store. If they were able to find Laura on the footage, that would help the case, and if he could place Steve Waters at the store at the same, time then he would have a viable suspect. He had pulled Mr. Waters' driver license photo, and that along with the thirty minutes he spent interviewing the man, would make it easier to spot him on the video.

The Jane Doe, vehicle-versus-pedestrian victim had been found last Sunday night, so that was the day Detective Howard had requested they begin viewing the footage. They were about to start watching from 9pm on since Steve would not have been able to get to the store before then, being tied up with the police just finishing up at the accident site.

"I'm sorry to keep you here so late on a Friday night, and I do really appreciate it, this could be the break in our case that we need."

"Anything I can do to help, and I never go home before 7pm anyway." Replied Jason Borg, the tall, slightly balding store manager. "Besides, I have a daughter attending the university and I don't know what I would do if something awful like this happened to her! I hope I can help you catch the person that did this." His dark eyes blazed with genuine concern and a little fear.

Detective Howard handed a photo of Laura Roundsley to Jason. "You have probably already seen her picture, but if you can help me scan for her, I would appreciate it. We believe she came up the escalator and paid through the self-checkout stands." He didn't mention Steve Waters because it wouldn't be right to put pre-conceived notions of guilt about him into Jason's mind.

"Ok, sounds good." Jason replied. He sat in the chair next to Detective Howard, and pointed the remote at the large screen TV. "The program will run at a fast-forward pace that still allows us to track images and movements. That seems to work best for going through three hours of footage in a short time."

The store closed at midnight, so it made their jobs a little easier creating a hard stop on the footage timeline. If they didn't find anything, he would ask to go through the next couple of nights using the same timeframe. According to the dream Mr. Waters had, it was dark when the girl was abducted.

Detective Howard shook his head slightly and thought to himself how absurd it was that he was basing his search on a dream. Well, if they didn't find anything, he could have the surveillance tapes sent to the station for a comprehensive review.

They scanned the footage for Sunday night, staring at the screen for 20 minutes only to find nothing. The same was true for the Monday night footage. About 10 minutes into the Tuesday night footage, Jason spotted Laura Roundsley coming up the escalator.

"There!" he nearly jumped out of his seat. "Can you rewind it back by 5 minutes and can we watch it at regular speed?" Asked Detective Howard.

"You bet," stated Jason and fiddled with the remote. The TV screen showed the scene moving in reverse and then played forward again in real time. They both watched intently as various people sporadically rode up the escalator. A woman with a sleepy toddler in one arm and a basket filled with groceries hanging from the crook of her other arm stepped off the escalator. Shortly afterward Laura could be seen walking the last few steps of the escalator and then standing in line for the self-checkout stations.

As the two men observed, Detective Howard watched all of the others coming up the escalator or from any other direction in the store to the check-out line. He observed a few individuals by-passing the checkout line and just walking out of the store with no purchases.

Laura checked out at the far station next to the store associate stand. She scanned and bagged each of her items and then paid with a card. They continued to watch as she picked up her two bags and walked out of the store. The view cut off just before she went through the doors due to the angle of the camera. The feed continued to roll for another fifteen minutes and Detective Howard saw no sign Steve Waters.

"OK. I think that is all I need to see tonight." Detective Howard began. Is it possible for me to get a copy of the footage for that camera for the past week? I can have an officer stop by and pick it up tomorrow if that's OK?"

"Absolutely! I will make the copy tonight and have it ready for pickup tomorrow morning. Just tell your officer to ask at the customer service counter."

Both men stood and shook hands. Detective Howard expressed his gratitude and then Jason walked him back down the hall and out into the store.

As Derrick walked toward the exit, he thought about Steve Waters. He had confirmed that Steve had been at the gym the night before the accident. But Laura Roundsley had been at the store on Tuesday evening, so Sunday night alibis didn't really matter anymore. On the other hand, if Laura was abducted Tuesday night on the way home from the store, there was no sign of Steve being in the store with her. But there was more footage to review before writing Mr. Waters off as a suspect.

Derrick walked out through the automatic doors that Laura Roundsley had walked through on the last Tuesday night of her life. He went to his car and headed back to the station to update his case file. The case was officially going somewhere based on this strange new lead, *from a dream*.

Friday 6:21pm

Alex and Victoria were sitting together on the couch enjoying their pizza and watching their favorite movie, *So I Married an Axe Murderer*. What better way to decompress and forget the stresses of life for a while?

Victoria picked up another slice, placed it carefully on her paper plate and then sat back and folded her legs up on the couch causing her to lean right against Alex's shoulder. He responded by placing his left arm around her. She rested her head on his shoulder for a minute. He pushed the last bite of pizza into his mouth and then rested his head on hers. He chewed against her head and she giggled and pulled away.

"So how did your visit go with the EAP people today?" Victoria took a bite of her pizza and stretched the cheese further and further away. It was like the silence that stretched out between them.

Leaning forward to get another slice Alex answered, "It was good. The lady was nice. She just listened." He paused. "It was just nice to talk about all of the crazy stuff that has been happening."

"You know you can always talk to me too." Victoria stated quietly. She looked into his eyes and waited for an answer.

"I know, babe, I just don't want to share some of the horrible things I see with you. Once you have that image in your mind, it never goes away. You should never have to have that stuff in your head." They looked at each other for a minute and then he kissed her on the forehead. "I feel so relieved now after meeting with her. That's a good thing, so you can stop worrying so much about me."

"Ok." She said and settled back in next to him to finish her pizza.

Friday 6:58pm

Sydny sat in one of two over-stuffed reclining chairs in her upstairs sitting room. Since her living room was a patient meeting room, she had turned one of the three upstairs bedrooms into her own living room. It wasn't a large room, but was a perfect fit for her two recliners, small coffee table and big screen TV on the wall. A small, half-circle end table rested against the wall, centered between the recliners. It held one lamp that softly lit the room and her glass of wine.

Sydny had selected a recorded episode of one of her favorite TV Sitcoms but wasn't really paying attention to the characters on the screen, she was reliving the narrative from Alex that afternoon. She should have re-heated a slice of the lasagna she'd made earlier in the week but didn't really have an appetite. She picked up the glass of wine and took another sip. The warmth traveled down and settled in her stomach.

Her mind raced. Alex had found the body of Laura Roundsley. He 'd seen the evidence of the torture described by Steve; the long cuts on her arms, legs and body. Did that confirm Steve's dreams were correct? Or did it confirm that Steve was actually some kind of delusional serial killer?

And what about the similarities between Steve and Alex? Alex imagined the cuts, while Steve dreamed of making the cuts. Both were involved with the Jane Doe accident, so both could easily be displaying signs of post-traumatic stress from the event. Or perhaps just one of them was displaying these symptoms and the other was blocking out the horrible reality of his actions.

Sydny wondered what Detective Howard had found, and she dreaded the idea of seeing Steve again next week. What if he had another "dream" and called for an emergency session like the last one? What would she do? What would she say? Would she agree and then call Detective Howard to come and arrest him? But what if she was wrong?

Sydny finished her glass of wine and got up to refill it. The upstairs hallway was dark but the front foyer light leaked up the stairway. As she descended the stairs, Sydny wondered if she had locked all of the doors and windows. She checked the deadbolt on the front door as she went by, and then checked the front room windows and the sliding door in the dining room, which was locked and braced by a metal bar to keep it from sliding. The window above the sink was also closed and locked.

She pulled the bottle of wine from the wine drawer in her refrigerator and filled her glass. When she was done, she hit the night light on the front of her refrigerator and turned out the kitchen and dining room lights. She left the small lamp on in the corner of the front room and shut the door to the Foyer.

The top of the stairs opened on the opposite side of, mirroring the downstairs foyer. A small wall desk held the wireless modem and the alarm system panel. She double checked the system was armed for the night and then headed back down the hall to her sitting room with her glass of wine.

Friday 7:32pm

Shannon had arrived home from work to find Andrew was manning the barbecue on their large front porch and Murphy and Molly were milling about in the front yard. Her favorite bottle of wine was chilling on the table between the patio chairs and there were two wine glasses waiting to be filled. Andrew instructed her to go in and change and then come join him.

They ate outside in the comfortable evening air, protected from the begging dogs by one of the baby gates across the entrance, which forced them to lounge in the yard. Shannon and Andrew had found that baby gates were quite convenient and could be moved around the house depending on what was going on in their home. When they hosted dinner parties, it was better to put up the gate and contain the dogs in the back half of the house than to lock them in the bedroom because the dogs cried incessantly when they were locked up. They were much better sitting behind a gate where they had a view the people in the house who might even stop and pet them on the way to the bathroom or kitchen.

The sun was low behind the house and Shannon and Andrew sat on the dimly lit porch feeling full and sipping their wine. The air was cooling off and she zipped up her hoodie. Andrew loved the cool air.

Friday 8:20pm

Steve sat on the couch eating the Chinese take-out he had grabbed on the way home. He had stayed late at the office, well past everyone else, to catch up on his less than productive week. He took another bite of his cashew chicken but had barely made a dent in the white carton of food. The TV was off but his tablet on the credenza played soft jazz music that came through the Bluetooth speakers.

The day had been too long, and the visit from the detective was stressful. He felt like he'd told the story about the damn girl he hit way too many times. He just wanted to know that she was ok and then maybe the awful dreams would stop. But he also wondered about the girl found in the park. He had dreamed about her too! Surely, he had seen her on the news and placed her into his dreams. Sydny, she had to know about her too.

His heart began to beat faster as he wondered what Sydny thought. Had she made the connection that he was placing the girl from the news into his dreams? He could tell that she was a little freaked out at the end of their last session.

Well, maybe he wouldn't need to bother her for a while. He hadn't dreamed last night, which was due to the left-over sleeping pill he had taken. Unfortunately, he had forgotten to find out if Sydny could write him a refill. Well, at least he still had three left and he would take one tonight.

Friday 9:30pm

Katrina's alarm went off on schedule, but she was already awake and hit the button on the alarm to silence it. She lay there in the darkness of her room. She knew it was dark outside even though her thick black-out blinds always kept out the light of day. It was Friday night and the last night of her work-week. Friday's were always the hardest. She had so many things she wanted to do over the weekend and one more shift stood in her way.

Katrina turned on the bed-side lamp and got up. She really wanted a cup of coffee but that would have to wait until she got to the hospital. She found a bottle of water in the fridge and took a long drink as she meandered back down the hall to the bathroom. A nice hot shower would wake her up. She felt more like she had been drugged than like she had just completed a good night of sleep.

* * * * *

10:57pm

Katrina finished putting her personal items away in the cupboard behind the nurse's desk area and prepared to grab the much-needed cup of coffee before officially beginning her shift. She was working with Brenda again tonight. She liked Brenda. When they worked together, there was no drama, no gossiping, just good company and hard work.

She headed out to the cafeteria for her coffee. There was a small coffee maker at the nurse station, along with a fountain soda machine, which were primarily for visitors of patients on the floor. The cafeteria had a large, commercial Keurig coffee maker with a variety of coffee flavors, teas, ciders and hot chocolate.

She returned with her sweet-smelling coffee and settled in to review the electronic notes on each patient. A couple of new patients had come in during the day and were only expected to stay one night. Jane Doe was still in a coma and her feeding tube was clean and functioning well. She had been sent for a CT scan which showed continued, healthy brain activity, and that her head wound was healing well. It was just a waiting game with this patient and with no identity, there was no family to make any decisions for her.

Katrina reviewed her notes from the day she was brought in; almost a week ago, Sunday evening. She'd come in without identification, obviously, since she had come in without any clothing. Her only personal effects were the bra and panties she was found in. Those had been taken by the police as evidence, along with a rape-kit, her DNA swab, and scrapings from under her finger nails. Katrina made the educated guess that none of that had panned out since they still didn't know who she was or what had happened to her.

A female police officer had come and taken pictures of her wounds last Monday after Jane Doe had been stabilized. They'd drilled into her cranium to alleviate the pressure of her head wound, which was caused by hitting the hard surface of the street, which, in turn, was caused by being hit by a vehicle.

Not much else had changed over the course of the past five days. Heated blankets had been used repeatedly to keep her body temperature up. The Physical Therapy department came in once daily and exercised her arms and legs to ensure good blood flow and muscle activity, and the nurses changed her position frequently to prevent bed sores.

Brenda was sitting beside her, reviewing her own patient notes in the computer. "Can you believe it?" she asked. "They found that poor girl who was missing, Laura Roundy, in the park!"

"Roundsley." Katrina corrected. "And no, It's awful."

"Do you think they're connected? That Laura and our Jane Doe? I heard they found the same kind of cuts on her arms and legs and that her throat was cut too. My cousin's girlfriend works for the county."

"To be honest," Katrina began, "I remember that detective who visited saying he thought they might be connected back when Laura Roundsley was still missing. That would make our Jane Doe the victim of a serial killer! And since she isn't dead, and might wake up, wouldn't that mean her life is in danger? What happened to her has been all over the news. Whoever did it to her must know that she is in the hospital!"

"OK, now you're making me nervous." Brenda declared. "But you know we have security, and the women's ward is always under careful watch just because of the female patients we treat."

"You know, I still have that Detective's business card. I'm going to call him in the morning and find out what they are doing to keep her safe, and for tonight, I'm going to make sure security is paying close attention." Katrina picked up the phone and dialed the security extension.

Saturday 2:37am

Katrina made the last stop on her rounds walking into Jane Doe's room and saw the moonlight shining in through the blinds. The small figure of Jane Doe lay under the covers in the bed. The tiny, bed-side lamp joined forces with the moonlight to illuminate Jane's face. The bruise on her left cheek had turned to a darker green-blue with yellow tint and was getting splotchy. This was the body's way of healing; breaking down the blood under the skin's surface into small pieces and carting it off to be disposed of as waste. The dressing on her head was new as it had to be changed regularly to prevent infection and allow observation of the healing process.

It had become routine now for Katrina to pull the chair by the window over to Jane's bedside and hold her hand for a while. As she sat there, she felt the warmth of Jane's hand and knew it meant she was healing. She reached over with her free hand and gently laid the back of her fingers against Jane's cheek. Jane's head flinched! Katrina pulled her away and clasped Jane's hand with both of hers as she stood up and pushed the chair back with her legs. She bent over Jane, staring intently at her face, expecting to see her eyes open, but they didn't. She continued to watch patiently in the soft light and Jane's eyes began to move under her eyelids. This was a good sign!

Katrina encouraged her softly, "Sweetheart, you're OK, you're in the hospital."

Jane's eyes continued to jerked back and forth under her eyelids. Katrina watched and waited. Then she felt a quick squeeze from Jane's hand. Or did she? Did she imagine it? Katrina looked up at the monitor to see what kind of activity it registered. The heart rate had picked up and her pulse-oxygen rate increased. Katrina looked back at Jane and could see she was breathing more distinctly. She continued to look back and forth between Jane and the monitor, and then she felt someone to her right. She looked toward the window and the dark shadow of a man leaned toward her. Katrina jumped back, dropping Jane's hand and shouted, "Hey!"

She was alone in the room with the exception of Jane. Jane's hand had fallen onto the bed beside her still body. Her eyes showed no movement and her breathing was barely audible. The monitor displayed a resting heat rate and all of the other stats were reflective of a sleeping patient.

Katrina tucked Jane's arms under the blankets and headed back to the nurse's station. She would review the monitor readings from there. Surely, she hadn't imagined the whole thing. As she approached the station, she called out excitedly to Brenda, "Jane Doe showed some voluntary movement!" She was excited. She sat down in her chair and used the mouse to open Jane Doe's monitor tracking system on the computer. She set the replay feature back ten minutes. Brenda rolled her chair over closer to Katrina and they both sat and watched the computer screen mimic the monitor.

Five minutes passed and nothing changed. Brenda turned to Katrina, "Are you sure something happened?"

"Yes, she moved her head and squeezed my hand, she was definitely dreaming. I even thought she might open her eyes!"

They focused on the computer screen again, which played out the steady stream of squiggly lines representing each of Jane's vitals. It was hypnotizing. Then a couple of the lines jumped! The squiggly lines became more extreme for about fifteen seconds and then returned to their steady slow pace.

Brenda and Katrina looked at each other.

"You should call the neurosurgeon on call." Brenda prodded.

"You are so right!" Katrina replied and picked up the phone.

Saturday 2:48am

Shannon awoke shivering in the cold, the kind that made your bones ache. It was pitch dark and the smell of musty dirt hung in the air. She felt for the comforter but couldn't find it. She tried to sit up but pain ripped through her chest and stomach muscles. She rolled to her right but her ankles were caught in position and her elbow hit hard on the cold surface underneath her. Pain shot through her upper arm.

She anchored her hands at her sides and pushed against the cold, hard surface to sit upright. Where was she? She sucked in another breath of the musty air. Her eyes searched the darkness and she listened intently. Her heart was pounding in her ears and each breath was horribly loud. Was someone else in the room with her? She began to shiver and her heart raced faster.

She sat, frozen, listening to the beat of her own heart, accompanied the rasping sound of each uncontrolled breath. She listened for what felt like at least two minutes. There was no other sound but hers. Her eyes adjusted to the darkness but still she only saw, darkness. Ahead to the right, was it her imagination or could she see what looked like the outline of stairs? She could make out the first couple of steps from her vantage point. Could it be light creeping in under a door at the top? She stared longer, trying to open her eyes wider, trying to focus.

As she sat there in the darkness, the pain came throbbing back. Her wrists were sore and her right hand stung from a gash across the meaty flesh where thumb met palm. She felt the same sting of pain along her arms, stomach and thighs. She had to get up! She had to get out of here!

Shannon remembered the restraints at her ankles and reached down to feel for the buckles that would free her. Every move triggered fresh pain. She worked at the long, double-pronged buckles, yanking the big straps loose; first her right ankle and then her left. Her stomach burned and she felt the warm, sticky sensation of blood caking in the creases.

Each buckle made a loud clanking noise as it fell loose onto the metal table. She froze again, listening for any sound. Nothing. Her eyes searched for the floor underneath the table she was perched upon. She carefully swung her right and then left leg over the edge. It took all of her strength. She pointed her toes downward but felt nothing.

Bracing both hands on the edge of the table, she lowered herself down. Again, the pain tore sharply across every surface of her body. She felt more blood trickling down her inner thigh.

Her toes finally touched what felt like smooth, cold concrete and she exhaled as she lowered her weight onto her violently shaking legs. Her feet were now flat on the cold floor and the icy edge of the table supported her lower back. She brought her arms forward and they felt heavy as she reached out in front of her like a person blind-folded.

Shannon turned toward the shadowy shape of the stairs. Her legs were weak and her steps were tentative and short. She didn't know what she would step on or run into. Finally, she felt a wall with her right hand. It had the paper feel of sheet rock and was cool to the touch. She moved along the wall, sliding her hand against it until she reached a corner and looked up to see the faint outline of a door at the top of the stairs.

She listened again. Once more there was nothing. She put her left foot onto the first step and felt the gritty bare wood of an unfinished flight of stairs. She shifted her weight onto the first step and expected it to creak, it didn't. Lifting herself was like walking after a long workout on the elliptical machine. Her legs felt like Jell-O. Her left hand found a hand rail and she clung tightly to it with her right hand still trailing the wall. She took another step followed by another, and another.

She was about half way up the stairs when the hard wood finally responded with a creaky groan. She froze again, shaking and listening. Again, there was only the sound of her own breathing, and the more she tried to control it, the louder it became.

Shannon heard a thump from above her and she strained to hear more. Still frozen in position she screamed in her head, "What are you doing? You have to get out! You have to hurry!" It felt like watching a horror show and yelling at the victim on the screen. She willed her legs to move but nothing happened. She made a fist and dug the fingernails of her right hand into the gash on her palm. She gritted her teeth and growled to herself, "move!"

Her heart was pounding so loudly she figured anyone near her would hear it. She lifted her right foot and the stairs creaked again. She kept going as quietly as possible. A couple more steps creaked under her weight and then she was at the top. She put her hand on the door handle and tried to turn it gently, quietly. It didn't move. She twisted harder. The handle barely moved and then stuck. Was it locked?

Shannon's heart began to beat faster than she even thought possible. She felt light-headed from sucking in too much oxygen. She forced her-self to slow her breathing; in through her nose and out through her mouth. She wasn't sure how long she stood at the top of the steps trying to calm her heart and breathing. The blood leaking from her stomach was drying on her skin. She hadn't heard a single sound. Maybe no-one was upstairs.

It had to be an old house based on the unfinished, musty basement smell. She wondered what she would find behind the door. Should she go back down and try to find a light? Should she find a hiding place and try to ambush her captor if he came down? Or should she hit the door and try to break it open and then run? Where would she run to? What if he heard her? What if there were more locked doors?

Shannon's fear was consuming her. She didn't understand how she had gotten here. She was freezing and her entire body ached and shivered. And then she felt someone grab her from behind! She jerked around and shrieked!

"Shannon!" Andrew yelled. "Honey! You're dreaming!" He wrapped his arms around her and pulled her close.

Shannon opened her eyes. She was in her bed and Andrew was behind her. She suddenly felt overheated and began to shake. Her heart pounded in her ears.

"It was just a nightmare." Andrew soothed in a sleepy voice.

She pushed the comforter off of her body and rolled over to face Andrew. "Oh my gosh! That's the worst dream I've ever had. She began to cry and Andrew pulled her close and stroked her hair.

"It's over now, Baby."

Saturday 6:02am

Derrick had gotten up with the sun, dressed in jeans and a long-sleeved, cotton shirt and arrived at the station with his protein drink in hand. He had so many pieces of the puzzle and he needed time to lay them all out. The station would be busy with the regular weekend crew, but the detective's department would be quiet on a Saturday morning, giving him a reflective space in which to work.

He sat down at his desk and put the half-drank protein shake on the corner of the desk. The report from the medical examiner had arrived and been left on his desk. Derrick opened the envelope and removed the annotated drawing. The standard female form was printed on the paper twice, representing the front and back, and the lines and notes had been added by Dr. Rutherford. This was a color photo copy, so the doctor's notes were all in blue and the lines were drawn in red. There were nine long lines drawn very thinly with red ink on the front-facing body diagram. One ran down the inside of each upper thigh, one along each of the inner calves, two more working out from the armpits and across to the inner elbows, one diagonally across each breast, and finally one across the abdomen just below the navel. Next to each was 'SPFL' – the abbreviation Dr. Rutherford used for superficial.

One thick red line was drawn across the throat with the words 'cause of death' written next to it.

There were several X's indicating bruising on each wrist, ankle and across the rib cage just under the breasts. The girl had been bound and tortured.

Derrick wondered if Ms. Samuels recorded her sessions with her patients. He would love to hear Mr. Waters tell his dream and see how many details matched. He pulled his notebook out of the drawer and made a note to call Ms. Samuels on Monday.

Next, he pulled his case binder out of the drawer. Each time he investigated a complex crime, he kept a binder with all of his investigative notes, pictures, etc. for reference. He thumbed through the plastic page protectors. There were pictures of Jane Doe, a medical report from the hospital, her DNA report and an analysis of what was found under her nails. The rape kit had turned up with nothing. There was also a picture of Laura Roundsley, provide by a college friend, followed by a picture of her body found in the park.

All of the report information for the vehicle accident with Jane Doe was included in his binder.

He still needed to type up his notes from the meeting with Mr. Waters and put that into the binder behind the notes from his meeting with Mrs. Medford earlier in the week.

He placed Dr. Rutherford's diagram and notes into a protective plastic sheet and added them to his binder. Then he reviewed that last few pages, which included the four other unsolved murders he had found when he ran a national database search for similar crime criteria.

One girl had been found five years ago, in a field south of the valley. Another had been discovered by joggers on a morning hike along the river parkway three years ago. The third had been found out on the desert, near the state line, by a group riding four-wheel ATVs. Most recently a young girl had been found in the canyon. Time of death was estimated to be at least one month prior. And now Laura's body had been found in plain sight at the park downtown.

Derrick wondered what that meant. It seemed like the killer was careful about where he dumped his victim's bodies. He had chosen a variety of remote dumping grounds which were all far away from the area where Jane Doe was hit, and where the latest victim had been found. It also seemed that he also had never taken a victim that was known by members in the community, like Laura. All of the victims that Derrick had tied together so far, were run-away or transient young women. Of course, the other disconcerting thought that entered Derrick's head was wondering how many other bodies had never been found.

Jane Doe made sense, but Laura did not. If Jane Doe has escaped, the perpetrator may have been forced to abduct someone local because he didn't have the patience to seek out a new victim that wouldn't be missed. He wondered if the killer had left Laura's body in the park to send a message to Jane Doe. For all he knew, Jane Doe could identify him to the police and he was trying to scare her. That triggered the question as to whether Jane Doe was safe with the standard hospital security.

His train of thought was interrupted by the ringing of his cell phone. He answered it to find Katrina Dempsey on the other end of the line.

"Mr. Howard, this is Katrina Dempsey from the hospital and I wondered if I might ask you a couple of questions?"

"Absolutely, and remember, you can call me Derrick."

"Yes, thank you, I was just wondering, when you were here earlier in the week, you said you thought our Jane Doe and the missing, but now found, Laura Roundsley might be connected."

"You are correct, I did say that."

"Well, now that the missing girl has been found, do you still think they are connected?"

"You know I can't answer any questions about this investigation, but yes, I still believe they may be connected. Why do you ask? Did Jane Doe wake up?"

"No," Katrina paused, "She didn't wake up, but she did display some momentary movement last night, but that isn't why I am calling. I was thinking that if the two girls are connected, if the same person hurt them both, then wouldn't that mean our Jane Doe's life might be in danger?"

"Ms. Dempsey, Katrina, you seem like a very intelligent and caring person, I can understand why you are a nurse. I want to assure you that we won't let anything happen to Jane. In fact, I was just preparing the paperwork to arrange for a couple of officers to take shifts at the hospital specifically *for* her safety. As you have stated, now that Laura Roundsley has been found and we have collected all of the reports on both victims, it has been determined that there could be a risk for the victim in the hospital, uh, your Jane Doe."

"Thank goodness." Katrina responded.

"Absolutely. And I am so glad you called. Can you tell me a little more about what happened last night? You said Jane Doe moved last night?"

Katrina relayed the events of the prior evening back to Detective Howard and explained that the neurosurgeon on call had come in to examine her. "I'm sure if she wakes up, they will notify you first thing." She concluded. Then she thanked him for his time and hung up.

Derrick was hopeful that the girl in the hospital would wake up soon and be able to provide valuable information that would lead to the arrest of the sick individual committing these crimes. Then he remembered that he was supposed to send an officer to pick up the additional footage from the store. He decided he would go himself. He wanted to get someone reviewing all of the store footage right away to confirm whether or not Steve Waters was in the store, at all on the day Laura disappeared.

Saturday 7:03am

Alex awoke to the glow of the clock. The blinds were still closed as Victoria had adjusted them yesterday afternoon and tiny slits of sunlight tried to peek in between the slats. This allowed Alex to make out shapes in the room like the dresser standing guard in the corner, and the chair awaiting someone's company by the door.

He slept on the side of the bed closest to the door and Victoria was next to him somewhere under the blankets. He rolled over to look at her. He could hear her breathing softly as she lay on her left side, facing him. The comforter was pulled up over her shoulders and her ear, casting a shadow over her face.

Alex gently reached to pull the comforter down and then froze. What would he see? He hadn't had any hallucinations recently, but he was spooked enough to stop and mentally prepare himself. "It's not real." He whispered as he eased the comforter down.

Victoria's shoulder was soft and bare in the shadowy glow. Her dark hair spilled over her neck and cheek. He ran his fingers along her forehead and behind her ears to sweep the soft strands away from her face. Her skin was flawless. He traced his fingers over her shoulder and hooked the lace strap of her camisole, pulling it down along her arm.

Alex softly kissed her shoulder and then moved to the delicate line of her jaw. He kissed her again and Victoria took in a deep breath. She stretched a little; arching her back. He kissed her neck and breathed in the beautiful scent of her. He reached around and placed his hand against the small of her back and pulled her closer to him. She wrapped her right arm and leg over him and moaned as she pulled him up against her. Alex rolled over on top of her and continued kissing her neck. He moved slowly down to the swell of her breasts, kissing and exploring with his lips. He pushed the camisole down with his chin and continued to explore.

He got up on his knees and pulled the remaining lace strap down over her right shoulder and returned to the task of kissing. Victoria ran her hands through his thick, soft hair and then down over his broad shoulders. He pushed her camisole up from the sweet curve of her hips and began kissing her stomach. He worked his way up to the perfectly, rounded curvature of her breasts, covered only slightly by the camisole which he then pushed up and over her head. Victoria pulled it away and threw it toward the chair by the door.

Alex sat there on his knees looking at the angel who lay in his bed. She stared back up at him with her dark eyes. He felt an overwhelming sensation of love, mixed with a strong primal need to protect what was his, and the two were meshed together by a dark desire.

He leaned in and kissed her hard and long. She pulled at his back, trying to bring him in closer but he pulled away and went back to the business of kissing every square inch of her amazingly soft, warm skin.

Saturday 7:59am

Steve looked at the clock and couldn't believe he had slept so long. The morning light was coming through his bedroom window. He stretched and sat up, swinging his feet down to the floor and finding his slippers. "Thank you, Ambien." He said aloud. His feet found their way into the slippers and he stood up and walked over to his robe hanging on the back of the door.

Today he planned to hit the gym, do his grocery shopping, and then pay bills. He made his way to the kitchen and started the coffee pot. He stood there for a second and thought how nice a double espresso shake would taste after his long and restful night of sleeping. He clicked the coffee maker back to the off position and headed back to the bedroom.

He threw on his workout clothes; shorts and T-shirt, and then sweat pants and zip-up hoodie. He'd shower at the gym after he worked out. He grabbed a duffel bag and threw in some jeans, a sweatshirt and clean underwear, then sat on the bed and put on his running shoes. After a quick pit stop in the bathroom to brush his teeth, he grabbed his duffel, keys and phone and headed out the front door.

He drove over to the coffee shop on 21st Street. He went through the drive-up lane and got his double espresso shake. The first sip was heaven! He pulled back out onto the street and headed east, then made a left onto Seventh, which was a straight shot to his gym.

As he drove by the park, he was flooded with memories. It was almost exactly a week ago that he had taken off from the stop light headed in the opposite direction, when the girl had run out in front of him. He remembered the fading light turning to dusk. He remembered thinking she was wearing a bathing suit as he slammed hard on his breaks. He still hit her. It was the most sickening feeling that he'd ever had in his entire life. He could remember the look in her eyes right before the front of his SUV struck her. It had all seemed like slow motion to him. His vehicle had slowed, but not fast enough to come to a complete stop before striking her across the right shoulder and chest causing her to abruptly reverse direction like she had been hit by gale force winds. She went down like a limp rag doll and he couldn't remember if he actually saw it or imagined it, but when her head hit the street, it bounced.

Steve felt sick and pulled over to the side of the road. He threw his vehicle into park, opened the door and threw up what little coffee he had already consumed.

Saturday 8:27am

Andrew was sitting at his computer editing an article when he saw Shannon walk down the hallway to the kitchen. "I can't believe you let me sleep so long." She mumbled as she walked by.

"You were exhausted!" he shouted toward the kitchen. "You had a really awful nightmare last night and you needed the rest."

She pulled a bottle of mocha from the refrigerator door and closed it. Then she placed her insulated coffee cup under the ice dispenser and filled it. At the counter, she unwrapped the plastic and popped the cap off the coffee. As she poured the liquid over the ice, she breathed in the aroma. This daily ritual gave her a sense of calm. She stirred the ice around to make sure the liquid was cold and then took a long draw of the icy, bitter-sweet coffee. It was just perfect. She preferred it to any coffee shop concoction and it was only a fraction of the price.

Shannon came back down the hall and turned into Andrew's office. She placed her coffee on his desk, sat sideways across his lap and put her heavy arms around his shoulders and snuggled her face into his neck. He stopped trying to type and put his arms around her. He breathed her in. The back of her neck always smelled sweet and her unruly auburn curls smelled like something soft that he couldn't quite define.

She sat back and looked into his eyes. He looked back at her and stated, "Happy Saturday Morning." With a smile.

"You spoil me." She leaned her head slightly to the right and gave him a smile.

Saturday 9:20am

Katrina sat at her kitchen table looking out through the sliding glass door into her back yard. The leaves on the trees had turned mostly yellow, orange and red. Many of them had fallen and were scattered around her small back yard.

She always sat at the table and enjoyed some kind of breakfast after a long night of working. Today she was enjoying warm oatmeal with brown sugar and a splash of milk. On a normal work day, she would stay up doing chores and personal stuff until her bedtime of 1pm, but since it was her weekend, she would only take a nap today. Her Bunco group usually got together on Saturday nights and she liked to catch a matinee movie with her sister on Sunday afternoons.

The morning air had been cool when she left the hospital but the day would warm up. Fall was a beautiful time of year, and since she was off for the weekend, she planned to rake up the first of the leaves creating a light blanket over her grass.

Before she had left the hospital that morning, Detective Howard, true to his word, had sent an officer over to sit outside the room of Jane Doe. 'The Victim' she thought to herself. What a horrible way to refer to the poor girl.

Katrina thought back to the moment when Jane almost woke up last night. She was so excited and then so disappointed all within just a single moment. Jane was young and beautiful and probably had her whole life ahead of her, if only she would wake up. The longer she stayed in a coma, the worse her chances were. These kinds of cases were the worst for Katrina.

She finished her oatmeal and went to the kitchen sink where she washed the bowl and spoon. She placed them neatly in the drying rack and then decided to brew some hot tea. Coffee was a bad idea since she planned to get her nap in before her afternoon activities. She checked the large., white kettle on the stove and then added some water before placing it back on the burner. With a click of the knob on the front of the stove, gas flames jumped to life under the kettle. She turned the dial to the medium setting and then set out one large, blue tea cup and selected a packet of Chamomile and Lavender from the wooden tea box at the back of the counter. She opened the tea packet and lay the bag gently in the cup with the string and paper draped over the edge. Then she turned and headed down the hall to her room where she would change into jeans and a sweatshirt for the chore of raking the leaves. It was going to be a glorious day.

Saturday 10:00am

The bathroom was full of steam and the hot shower was ready for Alex. He could still smell the sweetness of Victoria on his own skin and hated the idea of washing it away, but he climbed in and immersed himself in the hot, pounding spray.

They had made love more passionately than ever before and then just stayed in bed holding each other. He had dozed off and Victoria had sneaked away to prepare a breakfast of toast, coffee and fresh fruit. Victoria brought him back from dreamland with a soft kiss and the warm aroma of the coffee she brought him.

They'd eaten breakfast and then Victoria had instructed him to go shower while she tidied up the house. Their plan was to take advantage of his weekend off and do some grocery shopping.

Alex stood in the shower with the water reverberating off of his upper back. It felt so good, he didn't want to move. He wanted to stand under the water until every muscle in his body relaxed, and then he wanted to get out and climb back into the bed with Victoria in his arms and stay there forever.

He heard the bathroom door open and Victoria announced, "You should be done by now! Step aside, I'm coming in." He pulled her under the stream of soothing water and held her tightly. Then she turned him around, scrubbed and rinsed his back and kicked him out of the shower.

he stood there in the small steamy space trying to see his own reflection in the mirror. There was nothing but a shape. He wiped the mirror with his hand, which enabled him to see a blurry slice of his face. He stared and wondered, 'what will I see today?'' He wondered if this was how victims felt after a traumatic event and the fear of encountering it again; Post-traumatic stress or PTSD it was called. Alex thought it could become disabling if it really got a hold of you.

Saturday 11:00am

Derrick retrieved the store security footage from the customer service clerk where it had been waiting as promised by Mr. Borg, and returned immediately back to the station and assigned one of the rookies to sit and review the tape. He printed a full-page picture of Steve Waters' driver's license photo and mounted it on the wall next to the TV so that the young officer knew what he was looking for. Derrick knew it was going to take all day to review the footage, even at an accelerated speed. He instructed the young man to take a break now and then so that he could stay fresh and focused, and emphasized that this was a critical task. He wrote down his cell number and ordered the young man to call him immediately if he saw the suspect in the footage.

Saturday 11:30am

Steve had not enjoyed his time at the gym as anticipated. He'd thrown away his completely-full Espresso Shake and tried to work out on empty stomach *and* without any morning caffeine. Every push and pull of the weights had been accompanied by images of the girl bouncing off of his SUV, followed by her head bouncing off of the dark asphalt of the street. He'd tried running on the treadmill and focusing on the TV mounted on the wall. It hadn't helped, especially when a news segment teaser came on to announce, *"Police still baffled by the unsolved murder of Laura Roundsley. Are our parks safe? Watch the noon addition of Channel 9 news."*

That had been all he could take and Steve had showered, dressed and left the gym feeling exactly the opposite of what he had expected when he started out that morning.

He was now in his SUV and didn't know where he wanted to go. He definitely didn't want to go back past the park so he made a detour by going north. He would loop around and head back home. He turned left onto 600 South and then made a left onto Park Street. Had he done this on purpose? He pulled over next to the trees and bushes that lined the sidewalk in front of Sydny Samuels' townhouse. Most of the leaves had turned to dark, earthy colors and many had fallen to the ground. He could see the large window on the first floor where she conducted her sessions. The blinds were down, but adjusted horizontally which allowed a view both in and out. Was that Sydny standing in the front room? He wanted to knock on her door and ask permission to sit in the safety of her front room where bad dreams were only bad dreams and happy endings were possible. He wanted to hear the comforting sound of her voice telling him that it all made sense, and that the nightmares would go away as soon as his mind had worked through the trauma of the accident. And mostly he wanted all of this nastiness to be behind him so that he could ask Sydny out for coffee and get to know her better. She seemed like the kind of person he would enjoy spending time with.

But then he remembered the nervous look in her eyes at the end of their last meeting. The fact that his dream had sounded like an admission to the murder of Laura Roundsley scared him more than it could have scared her. He felt like an idiot, an idiot lost in a world with no one to turn to. He put the SUV into gear and drove away.

Saturday 11:38am

Sydny had stayed in bed longer than usual this morning due to the extra dose of wine last night. She'd gotten up at 6am, taken an Ibuprofen with a big glass of water and then climbed back into the warm, king-sized bed.

The sun had been peeking through the dark curtains of her eastern facing bedroom windows just before 9am, which finally enticed her to emerge from under the fluffy comforter and pile of pillows. She hadn't yet turned on the heat for the season, so the room had been crisp and cool. She had added the task to her mental to-do list while she drew a bath in her large garden tub.

The remainder of the morning had consisted of laundry, vacuuming, and running the dishwasher. She was dusting the front room when she looked up and saw the bright yellow SUV pull over and park behind the half-naked tree line. She froze for a minute and searched the memory bank of her mind. Had she scheduled Steve to come over for an appointment? She rarely saw clients on Saturdays. No, she had not, he was scheduled for next Wednesday. What was he doing? Maybe it wasn't him, just someone with a similar vehicle. She watched, frozen in place like a statue, for what seemed like minutes, and then the vehicle drove away.

Saturday 1:08pm

Alex and Victoria were at the grocery store with a half-loaded shopping cart. Victoria had a list on her phone and they were strategically going up and down each aisle collecting the necessary items. "We need cheese." She directed Alex.

He grabbed a large bag of grated cheese and showed it to Victoria. "No, Sweetie, that costs twice as much and we can grate the cheese ourselves, get the 2lb block there." She pointed.

This was the dance they had been doing since the beginning of their shopping trip. Alex was used to purchasing for convenience and Victoria was a budgeter and a planner. Even though Alex grumbled each time she made him select the cost-effective item, he secretly enjoyed it. He knew that she was going to make the best wife and mother. And since they had purchased a home, it made sense to follow a budget.

"What about beer, Babe? Do I have to buy the discount stuff?" Alex teased with a smile.

"No, Sweetie, you buy whichever beer tickles your fancy because I plan on stopping by the wine store. In this area, we must not be chintzy!" She giggled.

They continued on through the store and every once in a while, she let Alex throw in something silly and unnecessary. He was a patient man and she loved him enough to let him have whatever he wanted. But she also knew the importance of managing money. Even though they were doing OK financially, she remembered her father and how he bankrupted her mother because he had some kind of addiction to spending money. The family bank account had been frozen more than once based on her father's tax debt and her mother had decided it was pointless to work and pay daycare when her paycheck kept getting garnished for dad's bad debts.

Saturday 3:47pm

Rookie cop, Glen Hayden was not happy about sitting in the office reviewing footage of a stupid grocery store. This was not what he had signed on for. He figured it was some kind of hazing and this footage was a test they used on new cops all the time. If he missed the man in the picture, they would give him hell, so he had not taken a break all day.

It amazed him how many people rode up the escalator, used the self-checkout and then left the store. There were so many college students! It made sense with the university located a few blocks up the hill. Many of the students wore red, university T-shirts and sweatshirts so they stuck out. He wondered if that made them easy targets for criminals.

Glen looked up and the clock on the wall read 3:51pm. He looked back at the TV screen and caught a glimpse of a man leaving the store, was it him? He quickly grabbed the remote and rewound the footage just slightly and played it again. He watched the figure coming off of the escalator and walk to one of the checkout stations. It certainly looked like the guy. Glen continued to watch and as the man picked up his grocery bag and turned toward the camera, Glen hit the pause button. He used the remote to send a print screen to the computer and then compared the image from the store to the driver license picture. It looked like a match. He had done it! He was nobody's fool! He had passed the test. Now to call Detective Howard.

Saturday 4:32pm

Derrick was on his way back to the station after receiving the excited call from officer Hayden. The rookie officer's attitude had instantly soured after Derrick instructed him to write down the time stamp from the footage capturing Steve Waters and then continue his review. The kid acted like this was a *'Where's Waldo'* activity and once he had been found, the project was complete. He had a lot to learn about good detective work.

Derrick pulled into the station and parked by the back door. He entered with his electronic badge and went straight to the tech room where officer Hayden was sitting, slouched over, with his eyes glued to the TV monitor. Glen straightened up when Detective Howard came through the door.

"Detective Howard! I haven't seen anything else since we talked. Do you want to see the footage? I have the time stamp written here." Officer Hayden grabbed the remote and paused the screen with one hand and picked up the notepad with the other.

"Was it Tuesday night?" asked Derrick.

"No, it was last Saturday." Replied Glen, noticing the strange look on Detective Howard's face.

"Last Saturday? You haven't gotten to Tuesday's footage yet?"

"No, I started at the beginning, which was Thursday, over a week ago, but I found him, do you want to see?"

Derrick slumped down in a chair next to Glen and nodded. Well, this would at least place Mr. Waters in the store, proving that he shopped there.

Glen reversed the footage with the remote, stopping a couple of times to check the time stamp. He hit the play button about two minutes prior to the annotated time. Both men sat and watched the TV screen as the camera feed played out in real time. Glen considered asking Detective Howard about all of the college students and whether or not they were easy targets, but then decided not to. He was beginning to get the feeling that this was not any kind of test or hazing activity. Detective Howard was way too serious and focused for this not to be real. And then a moment of complete awareness slapped Glen metaphorically across his brain! The girl that was found in the park! Was she abducted Tuesday night? Glen felt so stupid. No wonder Detective Howard was upset, he was looking at the wrong day.

Now he knew he was going to catch hell from all of the detectives. He had been given a chance to help in a real investigation and had blown it.

"There." Glen pointed feebly at the television screen as Steve Waters came into view riding up the escalator.

"Huh." Derrick said out loud and then leaned forward resting his elbows on his knees.

Maybe he hadn't messed up completely, Glen thought to himself. Both men leaned forward and watched the screen. The time stamp showed Saturday evening at 8:38pm. They observed Steve scan one small item and place it in a bag at the front, self-check-out station to the left. He didn't pay with a card, instead he fed a single bill into the cash collector and then scooped out a coin or two from the change cup. Derrick wondered what he might have purchased that would be small and cost less than a dollar.

They watched Steve pick the small item up out of the bag and stick it into his pocket. He then grabbed the receipt, wadded it up and dropped it into the trash can under the register station.

"Gum." Glen said out loud.

"Yes, gum. But why go all the way to the grocery store and not a convenience store to buy gum? And why go all the way down stairs to buy gum when it was at every check-out station on the upper floor?" Derrick asked out loud. "Can you rewind it again? I want to watch it one more time."

Glen did as instructed and both men sat quietly taking it all in.

"Go back again." Derrick directed. "Go back about 30 minutes and let's play it in fast motion. I want to look for a female that might have come out ahead of him."

"That Roundsley girl?" Glen asked with excitement. He was now feeling a little better about this assignment and his ability to contribute.

"Yes. Do you know what she looks like? I have a picture in my office. Rewind the footage and I'll be right back."

Derrick left the office and returned in less than 60 seconds. Glen had the footage cued up and hit the play button as Derrick leaned back from taping the photo of Laura next to the photo of Steve Waters. They watched the entire 30 minutes of footage in fast motion and Glen pressed the pause button when Steve came into view again. No sign of Laura.

"One more time." Derrick directed.

While Glen reversed the footage, they both sat in silence until he pressed play and hit the fast-forward button once to kick it into accelerated motion. Just as it was anticipated that Steve would come riding up the escalator, Derrick took the remote from Glen and hit the play button. They watched again in real time as Steve made his single purchase and left the store.

The footage continued to play. "What are you thinking?" Asked Glen.

"I don't know." Responded Derrick. He continued to watch the images on the television.

Glen didn't want to make a fool of himself so he sat quietly and watched too. More college students and a mother with two wiggly kids came around from the side and got into line at the self-check-out. A strange man who looked to be in his forties and mentally handicapped, got in line with a baby in his arms. No, not a baby but a life-sized baby doll. When he got up to the station, he struggled to put his dollars into the cash feeder. A scrawny young blond girl was in line behind him. Her clothes looked dirty and worn. She stepped forward and appeared to be asking the handicapped man if she could help him. He gave her his dollars and she fed them one and a time into the slot designed for bills. She smiled at him and made a gesture toward the doll. He smiled back and then awkwardly scooped his coin change out of the dish with his free hand and shoved it into his pocket. The girl waived goodbye to him and then scanned her bottle of Pepsi and placed it in a bag.

"Stop!" Derrick demanded and then remembered he still had the remote in his hand. He pointed it at the Television and hit the pause button and they both stared at the face of the blond girl on the television screen for a good minute.

"Who is it?" Glen finally asked. "Do you know her?"

"Hold on." Derrick hushed Glen harshly and then he hit the play button, setting the frozen blond girl back into motion. They watched her slide some coins into the receptor, pick up her bottle of Pepsi and walk toward the door. She disappeared under the camera and out the door. Derrick reversed the footage slightly and watched her leave again. Just as he was about to rewind one more time, the dark figure of a man slipped under the camera and out the door.

"Did you see that?" He asked Glen. Someone following her? He was standing off to the side and then walked out behind her. Derrick reversed and replayed the girl exiting. The blond girl walked straight toward the door, moved under the camera and was gone, but just two seconds later, a tall man wearing what looked to be a dark heavy coat and hat came from the side of the door and turned under the camera to go out. The camera only caught the side and back of him. Could this be Steve? Had he been waiting for her? But he would have had to put on a coat and hat, re-enter the store and wait off to the side where he knew the camera would not capture his presence.

"I don't understand," said Glen, "That's not Laura Roundsley, do you know her?" Glen watched Derrick as he reversed and replayed the footage several more times.

Finally, Derrick responded, "I believe that young woman is the victim currently laying in a coma at the hospital. Her identity is unknown at this time and she is listed as a Jane Doe." Derrick turned and stared hard into Glen's eyes. "None of this has been connected or reported to the media. You will not speak of this to anyone. It would not only compromise my investigation, but it would put her life in danger."

Saturday 8:41pm

Steve spent the remainder of his day at home, with his TV on; some football game didn't pay close attention to. He vacuumed and emptied the dishwasher. He liked having a clean place to start the new week. Work created enough stress and he liked to come home, barbecue or eat take-out and kick back in the evenings.

His day had not gone as anticipated and he hadn't eaten all day either. He opened the door to both the fridge and freezer and stood there taking inventory. In the freezer was a frozen dinner and two cans of concentrated orange juice kept company by a cannibalized bag of ice. The fridge hosted a carton of eggs, a jug of milk holding slightly more than a sip, and a mystery box of Chinese takeout that escaped Steve's memory. There were condiments; one bottle of Sam Adams in the door of the fridge, and a wilted half head of lettuce in the drawer. He really needed to hit the grocery store. It had been on his agenda for the day, but that agenda had all gone to hell.

He closed both doors and went to the pantry where he found a package of Ramen noodles and a can of peas. That would work. He could fry up an egg to throw in with the cooked noodles and then sprinkle on some peas. Thank goodness he had one beer left to wash it all down.

As he was cooking, he considered taking in the 10 O'clock news, but then thought better of it. He'd had enough real-life news to tie him over for a lifetime. Dinner would be the last activity of his day and then his Ambien would be his dessert.

Saturday 9:30pm

The day had been fairly uneventful and Shannon had puttered around the house in her sweatpants while Andrew worked in his office. The dogs followed her from room to room, waiting to see what excitement the day would bring. They were used to at least one walk and usually going in the Jeep with her to the home improvement store on the weekends. Shannon always had some project she was working on in the old house and everyone at the home improvement store knew the dogs by name, and gave them treats.

Instead of a walk, Shannon had taken them out front and thrown the ball for them until they were panting like crazy with their tongues lolling from their mouths. She let them lay in the grass for a while and then made them come in for a drink. She had taken a nap, followed by a hot bath late that afternoon. Her bruises were turning yellowy-green and beginning to dissipate.

Later that day, Andrew had dragged her out of the house for dinner. She had been too tired to cook and almost too tired to go out, but it turned out to be a nice evening at one of their favorite restaurants. It was a small, hole-in the-wall Italian place with an adjoining bar that had become popular with the college crowd. The restaurant served a salad soaked in homemade dressing that left everyone reeking of garlic but was utterly amazing!

Shannon had enjoyed her glass of wine, her garlic-drenched salad, and being waited on, but it was nice to be back home again. She went into the bedroom and changed into her sleeping attire; tank top and boxer shorts, while Andrew let the dogs out one last time for the evening.

As he was tucking Murphy and Molly into their doggie bed and tossing them each a treat, Shannon came up behind him and put her arms around him. She rested her head on his back and he covered her hands with his. "Let's go to bed. I'm full, and tired, and could use a good night of sleep. . . with no dreams."

Andrew hit the light switch and followed her into the bedroom closing the door behind him. It was early for a Saturday night but the week had been long and the weather was changing, resulting in darker, cooler nights. They each had a book on their night stand and decided to read quietly rather than turn on the TV.

Once Andrew was settled on his side of the bed, she snuggled up next to him with her book. She made him lift up his left arm and put it around her shoulders so that she could lean in against him. They read for a while, but Shannon kept fighting to stay focused. After reading the same paragraph three times, she placed the book on the night stand and burrowed under the covers against Andrew's warm body.

Sunday 1:58am

The smell of must, accompanied by shivering cold made Shannon open her eyes. She looked around in the darkness. Her back was stiff and her muscles ached. She tried to move and felt the restraints on her wrists, ribs and ankles. It was a familiar feeling, followed by fear. How could she be here? She had been here before, but she had gotten away, right? She pulled her arms against the restraints. Her right hand slipped through just a little so she tugged again as hard as she could. Her hand came lose and a sharp pain ripped through the meaty flesh of her thumb and palm. She reached over to her left wrist and worked at the buckle. It all felt like a dream as she freed her left hand and then began working on the strap across her ribs.

She could barely get herself into a sitting position. Every surface of her body stung like she had been thrown into a thorn bush. She bent over to reach her ankles and felt a warm, stickiness across her stomach. She could smell the coppery scent of blood as she freed her ankles.

The feeling of Déjà vu came over her as she carefully lowered herself to the floor and felt for the wall and then found the stairs. Working her way up, each creek of the stairs made her freeze in fear, and her breathing was loud in her ears. She panicked for a moment when she thought she heard a sound, but then convinced herself to keep going by digging her nails into the cut on her palm. At the top of the stairs, she carefully tried the door handle, knowing in her gut that it was locked. And then the memory of someone behind her made the hair stand up on the back of her neck. She whipped her head around bracing for the dark stranger, but no one was there. She froze, trying to see anything in the darkness of the stairwell yawning deep behind her. She saw nothing. She heard nothing.

She turned back toward the door and studied the small sliver of light slipping in underneath. She listened again and contemplated how hard she would have to hit the door to break it open. She moved her hand from the door handle to feel surface of the door. It was flat, and made of wood. There were no raised and sunken panels like the doors in most new homes. This door felt like the cheapest kind of door that could be purchased at any home-improvement store. It was a basement door and didn't need to be anything but simple. This gave Shannon confidence. She listened again for a long time while she told herself over and over it was the only way out. All she had to do was hit the door as hard as she could with the entire weight of her body and then run in whichever direction looked like a way out.

"Just do it. Just do it. Just do it." She whispered softly into the darkness. She held the handrail for support and leaned back. Then she took the biggest breath her bruised and gashed chest would allow and hurled her right shoulder and hips toward the door.

Shannon felt the jolt of pain run through every limb of her body as she went hurling through the doorway. She braced herself to hit the dingy green linoleum but then she pivoted around to the left and slammed into the door frame. She hadn't let go of the banister. She dropped to her knees and released the banister, her left hand came down to the floor next to her right. She sat there on all fours, looking around a dimly lit kitchen. Everything was dingy and worn. The fixtures were antique along with the appliances. The refrigerator was in a corner to the right and an old gas stove and countertop was to the left. The sink was a large porcelain basin about three feet in front of her. The light was coming from another area of the house, the living room? The hallway? But what caught her eye was the back porch off to right just past the refrigerator. She began to crawl slowly toward it. Each advance pulled at the slices on her arms and legs.

The back porch was dark, but she could see a porch light shining through a curtained window in the outer door. The linoleum on the floor gave way to a concrete pad at the doorway. She felt dirt and grit under her hands and the tiny pieces of debris stabbed at her knees. She brought her right foot under her and braced herself against the wall to stand up. She felt the skin on her stomach slowly unfold as the dried, sticky blood peeled away by the motion of straitening into a standing position. Her hand went to her stomach in an effort to stop the pain.

Shannon walked the last two feet to the back door and steadied herself against the door jamb with her left hand. She grabbed the door handle and tried to turn it with her right. Her hand just slipped and she noticed the blood smearing on the brass knob. She wiped her hand on the back of her panties and tried again. This time the handle turned but the door would not open. She pulled and jerked and heard herself cry out "No! No! No!" Then she saw the deadbolt and turned the lever with her left hand. She jerked again, this time with both hands, and the door came open. It hit the big toe on her right foot and she muffled a yelp the best she could.

There were three old, wooden steps leading down to an overgrown sidewalk and a wooden fence that butted up against a rickety old garage. The gate in the fence was secured by a sliding bolt lock. she looked back over her left shoulder and heard the sound of a key in a door off in the distance. She jolted and took off down the wooden steps. She tripped on the last step and her knees skidded on the sidewalk. Her hands grazed the concrete with a stinging sensation. She heard a strange noise coming from her mouth and jumped up as quickly as she could. The adrenaline coursing through her body erased all of the pain and she lunged at the gate. She tugged at the bolt, trying to slide it back, and then looked over her shoulder and saw him standing in the kitchen peering down into the basement. He turned in her direction and yelled, "Stop!"

The bolt slid jaggedly and the gate gave way into an alley. Shannon ran out into the dusk of the night without looking back again. The alleyway butted up to a small side street and she ran to the right toward streetlights and then recognized the park across the wide street. She continued on, running into the street and jumping up over the narrow median. She had to reach the sidewalk and the safety of other people. There was a woman with two dogs on a leash and she yelled out to her. Suddenly, the bright lights blinded her and then the darkness swallowed her up.

Sunday 9:47am

Shannon stood in the foyer with Murphy and Molly sitting dutifully in front of her. They could barely contain their excitement or their sitting position. They knew they were going for a walk and it took every bit of strength they each had to sit still long enough for Shannon to retrieve the collars and leash that hung on the doggie-butt hooks on the wall. One was pink and one was blue and the tails curved up serving as hooks.

Once both dogs were secured, she opened the front door and they jumped over the threshold. They stopped, barely, dancing in place while she followed them out and locked the door.

Andrew was having coffee with a client this morning to talk about an editing job and wouldn't be back for at least another hour, so she, in turn, had made plans to meet Sydny for coffee.

Shannon followed the dogs to the gate where they once again sat and waited. She looked up and down the sidewalk before opening the gate. There was a lot of foot traffic, as well as skateboarders and bicyclists who traversed up and down their sidewalk. This wasn't the kind of surprise she wanted to encounter. She and Andrew had once seen a bicyclist go by with his dog tethered to his handlebars. His dog stopped to bark at Murphy and Molly through the fence and the bicyclist had gone headfirst over the front of his bike. It hadn't been a pretty sight and she wondered why people didn't think those kinds of things through.

The sidewalk was clear, so they proceeded out through the gate. The dogs waited one last time with their tails going berserk as she latched the gate and hooked the chain. She was taking them with her to meet Sydny for coffee at The Blended Bean on the corner of Ninth and Fifth.

They headed south toward the park. The dogs were itching to run so she worked up to a jog and let them trot a little. If she let them do any serious running at the beginning of their walk, they would run out of steam and then it would be a fight to get them back home.

All three sprinted for a block and then slowed back to a walking pace. Reaching the corner at Nine-Hundred South, she stopped, selected a flag and waited for traffic to clear. Being Sunday, the traffic consisted of only two cars. Murphy let out a tiny whine and Molly looked up at her as if to ask 'can we go now?' They crossed street, but instead of entering the park as they usually did, they veered right toward the coffee shop located across from the western corner of the park.

It was a crisp morning but the sun was bright in the clear blue sky and Shannon was dressed in matching sweat pants and zip-up hoodie over a bright white T-shirt. Layers were important because a person could quickly warm up from a brisk, autumn walk under a sunny sky.

As she neared the corner, she saw Sydny sitting at one of the outside tables in front of the shop. They waived to each other and the dogs picked up on the excitement, pulling hard against their harnesses. Once again, Shannon had to give the 'sit' order and wait for the traffic light to change. There was no crossing signal at this small intersection so they waited for the light to turn green and crossed with the parallel street traffic.

The dogs pulled harder and harder as they made their way through the parking lot and toward the building and people. An average observer would never believe Murphy and Molly were capable of being scary, protective, watchdogs by the way they greeted every stranger out on the street. If Shannon liked a person, they liked the person, they really only became territorial and protective at home.

The dogs went nuts as Sydny greeted them with head scratches and baby talk, telling them how big and beautiful they were. Their entire bodies wiggled with the crazy back and forth motion of their tails. It always made Shannon think about the saying 'the tail wags the dog' and she had some vague notion of a movie that had been made with a similar title.

After an exciting moment of puppy greetings, Shannon and Sydny exchanged the traditional *'how-are-you'* and shared a brief hug.

"What are you interested in this fine, fall morning?" asked Sydny, "I'll go in and order and you can snag that table in the sun over there." She pointed to the farthest table at the corner of the building.

"Sounds good." Shannon took a ten-dollar bill from her sweat pants pocket and handed it to Sydny. "I'll have a twenty-ounce, decaf mocha made with drip coffee and whipped cream. Oh, and cinnamon and nutmeg on top, please."

As Sydny turned to enter The Blended Bean, Shannon went to the table and settled in with the dogs. She sat with her back to the building facing East. The Blended Bean looked like it used to be a corner convenience store, the kind without gas pumps, and not many of those had survived the last couple of decades.

The front of the building faced the park and was mostly floor to ceiling tinted glass framed in by a reddish-brown brick frame. A single, glass door stood in the center and upon entering customers had a view of the U-shaped coffee counter straight ahead, tables and booths to the left and a more comfortable seating area with over-stuffed chairs and couches to the right.

Outside, metal picnic-style tables with attached benches lined the front of the building and people sat, soaking up the morning sun as they read a paper, or a book or visited with a friend and sipped a hot, steamy concoction. One man sat at the far table enjoying a cigarette with his coffee. Shannon watched the smoke gently coiling up through the crisp air and thanked him mentally for sitting at the opposite end, away from her and the coffee shop entrance.

Murphy and Molly had settled next to Shannon with the assistance of some dog treats from her pocket. They raised their heads as Sydny approached with a steaming paper cup in each hand. She handed one to Shannon and placed her own on the table before swinging a leg over the bench and sitting down with her back against the glass wall.

Shannon cupped her mocha with both hands and took a gentle sip. "This beats any other hot mocha out there." She said with a smile.

"They definitely make their coffee differently. It seems like at most places, the chocolate syrup separates and collects in the bottom. I wonder how they keep their chocolate from doing that?" asked Sydny.

"They use powered chocolate and constantly blend it with milk in a bubbler and then when they steam it, it is already well mixed. I only know that because one of my co-workers has a son who works here." Replied Shannon.

The two women sat silently for few minutes, enjoying their hot drinks and basking in the sun as it tried to warm the autumn morning.

Shannon broke the silence, "So how's that poor guy, Steve, doing? No, strike that, I know you can't tell me, but if he is having as difficult of a time as I am, I feel bad for the guy and I'm sure he appreciates your help working through it all."

"You're having a difficult time?" asked Sydny.

"Yes, the dreams are getting worse. But hey, we didn't meet for you to give me free counseling." Shannon smiled at Sydny, "We came to drink coffee and chat, so what have you done for fun lately?"

"Shannon, I haven't don't anything fun lately. You know I can't betray confidences, but you and Mr. Waters aren't the only ones having a difficult time processing that awful accident. I met with another client this week who was also involved and that person is having a rough time as well. So as a friend, I am happy to help. I can only imagine how traumatizing it must have been to see that girl not only get hit, but be in that condition, and the post-traumatic stress you're all experiencing is quite justified."

"Wow!" Shannon took another long sip of her mocha. "I won't try to guess who the other person is, but I probably know in my head." Shannon paused for a moment and then asked, "Is it dreams? I mean is that a common side effect when people have scary experiences?"

"Nightmares are a common way for a person's mind to work through trauma. You're not crazy." Sydny smiled. "Have you been dreaming about the accident and the girl?"

"No," Shannon sat across the table and stared at the white lid of her coffee cup. "I've been having dreams that I *am* the girl." She looked up at Sydny to see what her face might register.

"Really?" Sydny looked intrigued instead of concerned. "How so?" She prodded Shannon.

"Well, first I dreamed of being followed home. But I actually thought that was just from the night I was followed home. Then I started dreaming of being locked in a basement. Only, I didn't know it was a basement at first."

Sydny sat up and swung her other leg under the table to face Shannon squarely. Her eyes were glued to Shannon's and she waited for her to continue.

"I had the dream a couple of times before I figured out the basement part. In the dream, I was strapped to some kind of cold, metal table and I had cuts all over my body. I already figured out that part came from seeing the cuts all over the girl in the street. I guess my mind is trying to create some kind of story about how they got there." She waited for Sydny to confirm this theory.

"What made you think you were in a basement?" Sydny encouraged.

"Well, it smelled the same as our basement, with an old musty smell mixed with the scent of dirt. And in the dream, I get one of my hands free and unstrap myself. I get off the table and feel along the wall until I find the stairs. I can see a bit of light coming in from under a door at the top. I had the dream three times before I finally got out of the basement and ran out the back door. I actually made it out to the road which was Seventh East where the girl was hit. But again, that has to be my mind trying to make sense of everything."

"Do you want to know the strangest part of all?" Shannon looked at Sydny and saw her nod 'yes'.

"Have you ever been hurt in a dream, but you never actually felt any pain?"

Again, Sydny just nodded.

"In these dreams, I can feel the pain of every single cut on my arms and legs and stomach. I feel the aches in my muscles from the cold, and I feel fatigue like that of an intense workout. The only time I have ever felt that worn out was after wind surfing in Hawaii when I was just a beginner."

Sydny just sat and stared at Shannon. Shannon broke the silence, "I'm going to walk around the park today and see if there is even a side street that looks like the one from my dream. I need to prove to my mind that it is making things up and hopefully get the dreams to stop."

Sydny reached her hand across the table and covered Shannon's. "I'm so sorry that you are having a tough time. I think it's good that you're trying to reason through the dreams. Just be careful, please."

"Well I've certainly ruined the mood this fine Sunday morning!" Shannon smiled, "Let's talk about something uplifting. My group is marketing the March of Dimes Haunted House again this year and the ad campaign is pretty cute."

"I'm not sure Halloween is much of a deviation from nightmares!" Sydny chuckled. "I am looking forward to the kids trick-or-treating in our neighborhood. But we still have over a month to go. Do you and Andrew go all-out decorating in October?"

"Yes, I love it!" Shannon's eyes sparkled. "Halloween kicks off the holiday season and I enjoy every minute of it until Christmas is over and then I pack it all up and it's out of my system until the next year."

They continued on, chatting about the upcoming holidays until they finished their coffee. Murphy and Molly could tell it was time to continue on their walk and became restless as the two women said goodbye and agreed to do this again in the near future.

<u>Sunday 11:13am</u>

Sydny walked back to her town house on auto-pilot, deep in thought, comparing the similarities of Shannon's dreams with those of Steve's. They had both mentioned the basement and the smell of it. They both spoke of the metal table and the straps. The cuts were explainable; the victim who ran into the street had those same cuts on her body, so that was the one part that made sense. Shannon dreamed of being followed home, but like she said, she was followed home. Or was she? Did she imagine it? But then why dream about it? But set that all aside, what about Steve's dream of following and abducting two different girls?

Theory one, Sydny explained to herself, was that Steve had actually abducted two girls, tortured them both, and even killed one and dumped her body in the park. So, what are the holes in this theory?

First, if he had abducted the girl in the hospital, it would be one hell of a coincidence that he hit her while she ran across the road. Or had he recognized her running in the street and hit her on purpose? Or, had he gone after her when she escaped? Then why not find a way to kill her in the hospital? That might not be so easy, there would be surveillance cameras all over the hospital. Or even at the accident site, could he have faked CPR so she would have died?

But then she considered Shannon's dreams. How would she know so much about what Steve had actually done to the girl in order to dream about it? If she did know, it would make sense that he followed her, *if*, he was actually the person following her, and *if* she somehow knew what he had done. Shannon's head was swimming.

An even crazier theory would be that Shannon was in on it with him? That was ridiculous because why would either of them come to her and tell her about it? Unless they were toying with her and she was going to be their next victim. No, and while it might make sense that Steve was delusional or schizophrenic and didn't know what he was actually doing, they couldn't both be experiencing the same shared delusion.

She felt stupid for even entertaining that one. She knew Shannon had lived here for years and that Steve had only moved here several months ago, another hole in the crazy theory.

Well, the next obvious theory was that one of them was involved in what happened to those girls, outside of the pedestrian-versus-vehicle incident. The dreams made sense with the post-traumatic stress that would be expected. The part that didn't make sense was the basement detail.

She stopped for a second, she physically stopped on the sidewalk and stood there for a moment. She went back to her college days and thought about her education in logic. It was all explainable, and the most common explanation was usually the correct one. She began walking again as she listed out the logical reasons for their common dreams.

First, all of the homes in the area had basements. Most of the homes downtown were historic homes with old, musty, unfinished basements. Shannon owned one and Steve was in the market to buy a home soon.

Second, how many movies had been made of victims on metal tables being tortured and cut with scalpels? How about movies about morgues and mortuaries? The cuts on the victim Steve hit were placed in a manner that would make it obvious she must have been laying down when they were inflicted. And you know she had to be restrained in order to be cut like that.

Third, it only made sense that she had been abducted at night, and fourth, she was hit running across the street toward the park, which was surrounded by historic homes.

Laura Roundsley had been found in the park and her picture had been on the news for several days. Both Steve and Shannon had to be familiar with the neighborhoods around the park; Shannon lived close by and Steve worked and went to the gym downtown.

She had made the logical connection explaining both of their dreams. She felt much better now. The sun even seemed to shine a little warmer as she continued on her way back to her home.

The thought of Detective Howard crept into her head, what had she done? She had betrayed a confidence of a client and made him a suspect in a crime. But she hadn't heard back from Detective Howard, so maybe that was a good sign.

Sunday 11:25am

Shannon allowed Molly and Murphy to drag her along the northern side of the park veering off the sidewalk here and there, as they caught an interesting scent. She could hear the Sunday drum circle in the distance and visualized the group of modern-day hippies assembled with their dreadlocks and tie-dye shirts playing bongo-style drums.

Another collection of interesting characters frequenting the park on Sundays were dressed in Karate style clothing with Star Wars robes, practicing sword fighting and other strange maneuvers. Honestly one of the things she loved about the park was the eclectic range of people who frequented it. She loved the diversity of the downtown area overall.

Her thoughts quickly turned to the body that was recently found somewhere in the center of the park. She imagined the missing girl from the news laying half-naked in the center of the drum circle with cuts all over her body and the drummers wildly pounding on their bongos like it was some kind of bizarre sacrificial ritual. Had she been found in only her underwear and bra? Did the news say anything about how the girl was found or killed? Perhaps she just super-imposed the details of her dream onto this other girl.

Shannon shivered from her own thoughts and realized she was almost to the corner. She reined the dogs in by wrapping their leash around her hand several times and then instructed them to sit as she pushed the cross-walk button. The light changed and she encouraged the dogs with an "OK" command.

As they crossed, she remembered the night of the accident, the cars backed up into the intersection, and how many people had just gotten out of their cars to stand and stare. The memory triggered rays of heat spreading from her heart and radiating through her body. She felt overheated and slightly nauseated. Once they were safely across the street, she took off her hoodie and tied it around her waist.

She was one of many people out walking with dogs this morning. Across the street at the park, people were running, roller blading, and strolling on both the private drive and the outer trail that circled the park.

Suddenly Shannon became aware that she had seen *herself* walking with the dogs in her dream. How strange, it had to be another piece of the puzzle her mind had created in an effort to make sense of everything.

She and the dogs made their way south and the dream began to replay in her mind. She was suddenly chilled by the cool night air of her dream, in spite of the bright morning sun. She shivered and stopped to put her hoodie back on.

Murphy and Molly trotted along with Shannon in tow looking like she was in a trance. They came to a small side street to the left and she stopped and looked up to read the street sign. "Beckford Avenue." She said aloud. Murphy and Molly looked back at her for direction and then followed her as she slowly turned left onto the narrow street.

It was so narrow that it looked like it should be one-way, but it wasn't. Two homes stood like sentinels on either side, facing Seventh. The house on the left was a turn-of-the-century, red brick, that had been updated with some stucco for contrast and had a new shingle roof. On the right, was a two-story brick painted a yellowy-cream color and protected by a line of trees paralleling the narrow street. The back section of the house was a wooden porch converted into an add-on room; typical of many of the historic homes surrounding the park.

Both houses had back yards enclosed by chain link fences. The house on the left had a modern cinder block garage that had been added at the back corner of the property, with a garage door that opened onto the small street.

Shannon recalled the dream, had she run past these houses? She only remembered running toward the lights of the wide street and the park.

Just after the cinder block garage a true alley way opened up to her left. Murphy and Molly were going crazy trying to sniff everything they could get to along both sides of the street. This was unchartered territory and they were thrilled, but Shannon was not so thrilled; she was nervous. She tugged at the leash and the dogs followed her as she continued on.

A wood-framed garage in desperate need of fresh paint was leaning behind its cinder-block neighbor at the corner. The single wooden garage door opened into the alley that intersected with Beckford Avenue.

She stopped and looked up the alley and noticed the garage was met by a tall, wooden gate mounted between it and a matching fence running the length of a back yard. She turned the corner and walked to the fence but then stopped and stood frozen while the dogs whined and sniffed wildly along the fence line.

She pictured herself in the dark, on the other side of that fence, desperately working at the slide bolt and looking back to see the dark figure standing in the kitchen. Could this really be the same house from her dream? She wanted to see the back yard but the fence was too high. She walked a little further, looking for a knot hole or loose board with the dogs at her heels still sniffing and snorting.

One of the fence slats was warped and created a narrow opening for her to peer through. She could see the back of the house. It had an old porch addition just like a hundred others in the neighborhood. There were three rickety wooden steps leading up to a back door with a square, curtain-covered window.

Molly released a low, guttural growl and Shannon froze again. She slowly turned to look at the dogs. They were both standing stiffly, staring at the fence and Molly's scruff was standing on end from the nape of her neck to her tail. Shannon slowly looked around expecting to see someone watching her in the alley but saw no one. She looked back through the fence to find the yard was also empty.

"It's ok." She said to the dogs. "We're leaving. This place gives me the creeps too." She turned to retrace her steps toward Beckford Avenue and had to tug forcefully at the leash because the dogs were still focused on the fence and yard beyond.

Once she had their full attention, she and the dogs picked up the pace and made their way back to Seventh. Shannon was jogging by the time she turned north and only slowed back to a walk after she passed the brick and stucco house. The next house had to be the one she was just standing behind in the alley way. Murphy stopped and hiked his leg to urinate on a light pole directly in front of the house.

This house was also a turn-of-the-century brick and stucco bungalow. The major difference was the front porch spanning the full width of the house. The front door was centered between two large picture windows, both of which were covered by heavy curtains.

Shannon stood and stared. She wondered if her mind had concocted the entire dream in response to the unsolved mystery about where the girl had come from last Sunday night. She must have driven by Beckford Avenue and this house a hundred times on her way home from various places. And how many houses all around the park had pretty much the same back porch and fence? She'd been in so many similar homes when she and Andrew were house hunting. They, like so many others, were looking for a historic home ready for renovation. People bought them cheap, fixed them up and then some sold for a profit while others settled in and made a permanent home. She and Andrew were the latter, it would take them years to get their house into the condition they wanted, but it was an investment in their future.

Shannon realized that she had been standing there for quite some time when Molly began sniffing at her sweatpants pocket in hopes of a treat. She reached down and scratched Molly's head and then reached into her pocket for two treats. Murphy came up next to Molly and they both sat back on their haunches with paws up in front of them. This was the 'sit cute' pose. They didn't even wait for a command these days, just began going through the poses in hopes of receiving the treat more quickly. She tossed them each a treat which they caught with precision. She looked back at the house and said "Let's go home, babies." As they continued on their way, she thought she saw someone peeking out of the far, left window, but then again, maybe she imagined it.

She and the dogs made the journey back to the house, crossing the main street with the light and then using the flags at the park entrance to cross Ninth South. The remainder of the trek was quiet with only two cars passing them by. Because of the park strip in the middle, Sixth East was not a common through-street. Cars could only make left hand turns where the other small streets intersected, causing a break in the park strip. Shannon loved it because it made for a quiet neighborhood. She and the dogs often traveled down the center, enjoying the grass instead of the sidewalk.

Today the grass was brown and covered with the turning leaves from the strategically planted trees. The city had not yet sent out a crew to rake up the leaves that cracked and crunched softly under foot. Every once in a while, Murphy or Molly would try to catch a sniff at the ground under the leaves, resulting in snorts, sneezes and scattered leaves.

They were almost parallel with their own house now, so she gently tugged at the leash and crossed over to the sidewalk with the dogs. One more lonely vehicle passed by heading north toward the grocery store and small shopping center up the road. It was a dingy, old white van. It took her back to early memories as a young girl in California, when it was common knowledge that all vans belonged to child molesters. She chuckled as she watched it continue on up the street.

At the gate, the dogs waited for two seconds while she unhooked the chain and lifted the latch, before pushing through. She heard another vehicle coming toward her, slowing its approach, and looked up expecting on of her neighbors. It was the van again. She thought they might be lost, or perhaps they had turned around to come back to one of the houses on this side of the street. The van continued to slow and she guessed driver needed directions. She turned to and waited to offer assistance. As the van pulled in alongside of her, she noticed the windows were tinted, and behind her and the fence, Molly, once again, let out her long, low, guttural growl.

Sunday 12:33pm

Andrew turned his Audi sedan into the driveway. He knew he was going to catch hell for being gone so long, but his meeting with the new client had gone well, and he was going to get several projects out of this business deal. He was actually surprised that Shannon hadn't texted him with her usual "are you lost?" message. She was considerate not to call when he was meeting a client, but liked to remind him when he forgot to check in and made her worry. Well, hopefully she had an equally long and enjoyable coffee date with her friend from up the block.

Andrew noticed that the dogs were in the front yard and they came at the fence by the driveway like crazed animals. Molly was barking her head off and Murphy was acting strange. Then he noticed they were still tethered together on the dual leash. Shannon must have just gone inside. It wasn't normal for her to leave them out front alone. Maybe she'd gone in and they had come running back out when they heard him drive up. He stopped and rolled down his window.

"Hello, silly puppies!" Andrew engaged the dogs, "Where is your silly mama?" He was met by more of Molly's incessant barking and Murphy made a growl that turned into a bark. It was like a command, 'listen up, you!"

"Shannon!" Andrew shouted and waited for her to come out of the house. He couldn't see the door from this angle. No response. "OK, OK, just a minute." He tried to console the dogs. He hit the button causing the window the roll back up and continued on down the driveway to the back of the house.

He parked then let himself in the back door with his key. He weaved his way up the long hallway to the front of the house and found the front door both closed and locked. He opened the front and screen doors and the dogs barreled through the entrance with Molly tripping over the leash. Murphy jumped over her and then came to a stop because he couldn't go any further.

"Slow down!" Commanded Andrew. He had to jerk at the leash a bit to loosen it and unhook first Murphy and then Molly. The dogs ran to the living room and jumped up on the couch to face the large picture window. They both barked at the window and then at him. Molly jumped down and ran into their bedroom and then back out and down the hallway to the kitchen. Andrew followed her and called Shannon's name a couple of times.

Had she come home and then left again? Maybe she went to the neighbors for a minute and left the dogs in the yard. He checked the remainder of the house with both dogs at his heels and then went out the front door to go check the neighbor's houses. Both dogs howled and barked in the foyer where he left them. He guessed they were doubly upset now that he was leaving them behind just like Shannon had done.

He walked out the gate and latched it behind him. He could see both dogs were back on the couch and barking at him through the window. He walked right to the home owned by Nathan and Matthew. They were not often there since they were still renovating the home and lived farther south in the valley, but the weekends were the best times to catch them. Andrew knocked on the door even though there were no cars in the driveway. He waited a minute and knocked once more. No one answered. He walked to the side of the wide porch and jumped down into the driveway which ran on the opposite side of their own and walked the length of the gravel drive to the rickety chain link gate that was held closed by a twisted wire. He didn't see anyone in the back yard or on the dilapidated back porch. He figured the porch would be the last part of the house the couple renovated.

Andrew headed back up the driveway and out to the sidewalk to look up and down the street. Then he went back past their own house and waived at Murphy and Molly, still barking at the window, and walked up to the door of the northern neighbor's house. He thought her name might be Ann, but wasn't sure. He expected at least one of the nine children to be playing out front, but then remembered they would still be at their church services. That then led to the frustrating thought that no one would be home here either. He tried the doorbell anyway and waited only momentarily before he rang it again. With one more loud knock, Andrew gave up.

He wondered about the other neighbors? Both the family to the north and the tree-lady, as Shannon called her, to the south would also be at church. It didn't make much sense. Andrew walked back to the front gate of his own home and paused with his hand on the carabiner that latched the chain to the gate. He looked up and down the street again. The dogs barked madly at the front window. He shifted his weight as he leaned in to unlatch the gate and felt something crunch under his left foot. He looked down to find a smashed dog treat, the little kind Shannon called 'pocket treats'. He wondered how the dogs had missed that tasty morsel. And then he noticed several more scattered on the edge of the sidewalk and in the gutter just in front of Nathan and Matthew's house. There was no way she dropped all of those and the dogs didn't gobble them up.

For the first time, Andrew felt an emerging pang of concern. He opened the gate and closed it swiftly behind, quickly latching the chain. Then he considered, had the chain be connected when he had walked out just a few minutes ago? Shannon would never have left the dogs in the yard without securing the chain.

He made it to the front door in half the strides it normally took and had to shove past the dogs and down the hall to the kitchen. He already had his cell phone in hand and was listening to the ringing of Shannon's phone. She didn't answer but her voice mail kicked on. He hung up and dialed again. This time he left a message, "Hey honey, where you? The dogs were in the yard so you can't be far. Call me back right away!" He hung up and hit redial one more time as he searched the list on the side of the refrigerator.

She kept a list of phone numbers in case either one of them had to locate the other in an emergency. He searched the list for a name that began with 'S'. What was her name? He could only remember the mental note he had made the other night when he drove over to pick Shannon up; both of their names started with the letter 'S'.

He got voice mail again and hung up. He entered the text message, 'are you lost?' and pressed the send button. Murphy and Molly were sitting on the kitchen floor watching him in silence. Molly's back legs had slid apart on the slick tile surface. She looked like she was half frog and half dog. She had always had this problem with slick surfaces and had apparently become accustomed to holding her legs steady even though she was half way into the Chinese splits. Andrew looked at her and thought about all of the times Shannon had made her move to sit on the floor mat in the kitchen so she wouldn't hurt her hips. Where was Shannon now when Molly needed her!

He turned back to the phone list again and read each name aloud, "Megan, George, Nathan, Mathew, Ann, so that was her name, Tiffany, Kory, Owen, Sydny, Brady, Sydny!" He shouted as he finally discovered the name he was looking for. He opened the phone and then dialed the number.

The phone rang four times and then was answered by a professional voice mail message. Andrew remembered that she was a counselor or something. He waited for the beep and then responded, "Hey, Sydny, this is Andrew, Shannon's husband. I think she went to coffee with you today. I was just trying to get a hold of her. Can you call me back? Thanks."

Sunday 12:59pm

Sydny heard the phone ringing out on the coffee table, but it was the general ring tone so she let it go to voice mail. It wasn't anyone she knew, so it was probably a solicitor. And even if it was business, it was the weekend and she had a pretty strict rule about her private time, especially Sundays.

She continued on with the enchilada dish she was preparing. Every other Sunday she made several casserole dishes and then froze them for the week. It was easier to make them all at the same time, and then pull one out in the evening and pop it into the oven. After it was cooked, she would eat some and put the rest into single serving containers and freeze them again. This gave her a variety of leftover dinners to choose from throughout the next week or two. And if she decided to go out to dinner or order pizza, the leftovers didn't go bad in the refrigerator.

As Sydny scooped the meat and beans into individual tortillas, added cheese and rolled them up, she wondered who was calling her on a Sunday afternoon. It couldn't have been Shannon because she had recently been assigned her own ring tone. Could it have been Steve? Or Alex? Had she given both of them her number? Yes, she had.

She placed the last enchilada roll into the casserole dish, scooped the hot enchilada sauce over all of the rolls, and then sprinkled grated cheddar cheese over the top. She covered the dish in tin foil and then placed the plastic lid on the glass dish. It had a piece of masking tape that labeled the dish with the word 'enchiladas'. She slid it onto a lower shelf in her freezer and then washed her hands.

Sydny walked into the living room-office area, picked up her phone and sat in one of the large chairs. The phone screen said she had one missed call from a local number. It almost looked familiar. She hit the voice mail icon and listened to the message. It was Andrew. No wonder the number looked familiar, it was just one digit different than Shannon's. He was looking for Shannon, but they had parted ways this morning after coffee. Perhaps she was still out walking her dogs in the park. Andrew had sounded slightly concerned in the message so she tapped the little green phone icon at the top of the voice mail screen and waited. The phone rang only once before Andrew's voice came on the line.

"Hello? Sydny?"

"Yes, is this Andrew?"

"Yes. Thank you for calling back. I was just wondering, I mean, you're not still with Shannon, are you?"

"No, we had coffee and finished up about a quarter after eleven. I think she was going to take the dogs for a walk. Do you think she's still at the park?" Sydny hoped this would put him at ease.

"No, the dogs are here." Andrew responded sounding worried."

"Well maybe she ran a quick errand?"

"No!" Andrew's voice was sharp this time. "Her Jeep is here and the dogs were in the yard! They were in the yard still attached to the leash!" Now Andrew was truly panicked. And the feeling came through the phone and seized Sydny's heart like a vice.

"Um," Sydny began but was cut off by Andrew.

"Did she say anything to you at coffee this morning? I have no idea where she could be!"

Sydny's heart was racing. What had Shannon said? They had talked about her dreams and they had talked about Halloween. And then it came to her, along with a feeling of nausea growing in her stomach,

"She said she was going to walk around the park and look for a street she had seen in her dream, but she obviously came home, right?"

"I'm assuming, I mean, the dogs were in the yard. But it doesn't make sense! If she was going to walk some where she would have put the dogs in the house. Hell, she would have put the dogs in the house even if she was going to drive somewhere."

"Maybe she popped over to the neighbor's house for a minute?" Sydny sounded hopeful.

"No!" again with frustration, "I already checked and no one is home."

"What if your neighbor had an emergency and she was helping? What if she went to the hospital with someone?"

"Then why wouldn't she call me back or answer her phone or text me?" Andrew asked desperately.

"I'll tell you what," said Sydny, "you get off the phone and wait for her call. I'll check with the local hospitals and see what I can find out. I know a detective that I can call too."

"Oh, my lord!" said Andrew, "What if she was hurt or hit by a car and whoever responded put the dogs in the yard and took her to the hospital?" His panic was mounting.

"Don't think like that." Sydny soothed. "Just hang up the phone and sit down for a minute. I'll call you back within ten minutes, I promise."

"OK." Andrew sounded defeated as the connection terminated.

Shannon was a little more panicked, but she forced herself to remain calm as she walked up the stairs to her office area. She needed to look up the number to the local hospitals. There were three in just the downtown area alone. And if she could get in touch with Detective Howard, he would surly know an easier way to check everything that had been reported today so far.

Sydny sat down at her computer and typed in the password to unlock the screen. She would start with the university hospital first. She looked around for a notepad or something to write the numbers down once she had them. What about Detective Howard? How would she get in touch with him? But then she remembered he had given her his business card on Friday. What had she done with it? It was probably in her purse. Where was her purse? She jumped up and went back downstairs and searched all of the usual places she left her purse but had no luck. It was probably in the bedroom and then remembered she had taken some cash and a house key to coffee this morning and left the purse hanging on a hook in the closet.

She took the stairs back up, two at a time and found the purse hanging right where she had left it. She grabbed it off the hook and dumped the contents onto her bed. Almost everything in her purse was organized into a wallet, a small cosmetic bag, a sun glass case, a pill box, and the coins were in a zipper pocket. The only lose items were two pens and a receipt. No business card. She looked in the zipper compartment with the coins but it wasn't there. Then she opened the wallet and looked in the pocket where she normally put receipts. Not there. She opened the side with the credit cards and there was the business card tucked sideways into one of the credit card pockets. She pulled it out feeling relieved because this was somehow going to make everything all right. Detective Howard would have the answers. It would be something simple and silly. They would laugh about it later.

Sydny went back to her computer and picked up her cell phone. After she punched in the direct number for Detective Howard's cell, she sat down on the edge of her office chair. She couldn't quite relax yet. She listened as the phone rang once, twice, three times. 'Please, please, please, no voice mail' she thought to herself. A fourth ring started and then was interrupted by the deep voice,

"Detective Howard."

She let out a deep breath, "Detective Howard, this is Sydny Samuels. Do you remember me?"

"Of course, I do. Do you have more information for me? Has Mr. Waters been bothering you to come back for an early appointment?"

"No, no, he hasn't bothered me, but I do think I might have made a mistake about him."

"Really? Because I am beginning to think you were actually on to something. Is that why you called?"

"Um, no." Sydny was confused but she had more important things to worry about, "I'm calling because I need to ask you a favor and I hope that you won't be upset. It will seem silly to you but it would mean a great deal to me and to my friend's husband."

"OK, what is it?"

"Well, my friend, Shannon Medford, might be missing and I was hoping you could check your police computer to see if any accidents have happened in her neighborhood, like maybe she helped with a car accident or something and had to leave suddenly."

"You're *friends* with Shannon Medford, the woman who helped with the car accident a week ago?"

"Yes."

"The accident where Steve Waters hit the girl who is now in the hospital?"

"Yes." Sydny was getting frustrated.

"OK. Just tell me what happened, why do you think she might be missing or helping with another car accident?"

Sydny began with their coffee date, leaving out the topic of conversation, and mentioned that when they parted, Shannon was planning to walk around the park. She continued on to explain how Andrew, Shannon's husband had arrived home to find the dogs in the yard, still on their leash, but that Shannon was missing and he had already tried to call her and checked to see if she might be at one of the neighbor's houses but had no success.

"I'll tell you what, Sydny, why don't you drive over to Andrew's house and let him know I'm going to check with the station to see if there is any record of a call, police or ambulance, and have them run her name. Then I'll meet you there. I am assuming you know where she lives?"

"Yes, I've driven by there once before. Do you know where it is?" Sydny asked feeling stupid.

"Yes, I have her address listed in my investigative notes and I know she lives just north of the park."

"OK, I'll see you there. Thank you so much for your help!"

Sunday 1:42pm

Andrew was sitting in the overstuffed chair kitty-corner to the couch. He sat staring at his cell phone, willing it to ring. Murphy and Molly lay on the floor at his feet. Occasionally Molly released a high-pitched, soft cry. Both dogs knew something was wrong. Andrew searched his mind for a valid reason why Shannon was not at home with the dogs. Did she mention something to him earlier in the week and he just hadn't paid attention? No, that wasn't the case. The week had been crazy and mostly she was just trying to catch up on her rest. She'd missed work Tuesday and had been having nightmares all week. Did he know what her nightmares were about? Had he even asked her? No, he knew, she dreamed someone was following her, trying to hurt her.

The blood in Andrew's veins turned to ice. Shannon had claimed someone chased her home Monday night, and then again Tuesday she said someone was following her on her walk. But no one had believed her. Why had he not believed her? Had she been followed again today? Had she been taken right in front of their house? All someone had to do was approach her as she opened the gate for the dogs and then ask her directions. She would have closed the gate to keep the dogs in and then been completely vulnerable!

Andrew felt the nausea swell up from his stomach and ran down the hall to the bathroom. He barely made it to the toilet before he violently vomited up the coffee and bagel from that morning. His stomach heaved several more times as he braced himself over the seat. Cold sweat broke out across the back of his neck. He shuddered.

He needed to calm himself down. He was no good to Shannon this way. He moved to the sink and rinsed his mouth several times and then gargled with mouthwash. He went back to the living room to retrieve his phone. It was time to call the police. As he made his way into the living room, he saw a dark Land Rover pull up and park parallel to the sidewalk. Was it Shannon getting a ride home? No, it was a woman about Shannon's age. She was about the same height but had straight, dark hair that framed her face and stopped abruptly at her shoulders. From Shannon's past description he guessed it must be Sydny. She approached the gate and looked at the chain trying to determine the best way to unhook it.

Andrew opened the front door and called out, "You must be Sydny."

"Yes, I am. Can I come in? I relayed your concerns about Shannon with a detective I know. He is going to check around and let us know what he finds."

"Here, let me get the gate." Andrew walked out followed by the dogs who immediately recognized Sydny and ran excitedly to the fence. He let her in and they all went back to the house. "Do you think your detective will call you right back, because I think I've made a big mistake and we need to call the police right now."

"Yes, actually Detective Howard is his name and he is on his way over here. Why do you think you've made a mistake?"

"Shannon told me twice this week that someone was following her but I didn't believe her. I thought she was just spooked from last Monday night and the nightmares she's been having. But if you think about it, someone could have grabbed her just after she let the dogs into the yard. It would explain why they were out here." Andrew opened the screen door and turned to look at Sydny. She looked just as worried as he did.

They both went inside, accompanied by the dogs and then took a seat in the living room to wait for Detective Howard.

Sunday 2:02pm

Derrick had been watching football with his feet propped up on the coffee table and an unopened bottle of Bud in his hand when he received the call from Sydny. Thank goodness he had not begun to drink yet. He had been witness to too many drunk driving accidents and fatalities over his career and had made it a cardinal rule never to drink and drive.

Sunday's were the only days he ever had a beer or two, unless he was on vacation. He went once every summer to visit his sister and her boys in Idaho. They would go camping and fishing and roast marsh mellows by the fire at night. After the boys were asleep in their tent, he would enjoy a couple of beers with his sister. She had become a widow at a very young age and raising two boys alone was tough. Derrick always made it a point to demonstrate how a responsible man behaves in front of the boys. They really didn't have any other male role models.

He was now on his way over to the home owned and occupied by Andrew and Shannon Medford. The address was still in his pocket notebook even though he had typed his notes from her interview earlier this week, into the computer at his office. He was hoping to hear back from the station before arriving at the house. Life would be so much easier if they could locate Mrs. Medford at the hospital being a good Samaritan again. He hated working the cases where women were abducted. Case in point, things had not gone well for Laura Roundsley at all.

Derrick took the Sixth South exit and continued on toward Sixth East. Still no call from the station. He drove across Main street and then State Street. With each intersection, he hoped that Mrs. Medford would return home or call her husband to tell him where she was. He came to the light and turned right on to Sixth East. Only a block and a half to go. Their house was numbered so that it would be on the right side, about half way between the six hundred and seven hundred blocks. He hit the Bluetooth call button on his steering wheel and directed the car to call the station. The dispatcher answered as he pulled over behind a Land Rover, which was likely to be Sydny Samuel's vehicle.

He stayed in the car for a minute and gave the dispatcher his name and asked for the desk sergeant on duty.

After a short wait, the desk sergeant answered, "Detective Howard, we haven't been able to locate calls or incidents in the vicinity of Liberty Park or anything within a five-block radius. Nothing under Shannon Medford either, other than a vehicle versus pedestrian accident that occurred one week ago, but we are still checking."

"OK, if you find anything, hit me on my cell phone, and thanks." Derrick hit the phone disconnect button on the steering wheel and turned off the car engine. He got out and approached the gate. Mr. Medford had come out, followed by Ms. Samuels and two dogs who seemed to be unhappy about something. They must be the dogs Shannon spoke of when she recounted the story of the accident to him in her office earlier this week. He wondered how such a tiny thing could control what looked to be almost 200 lbs. of dog. But then he also wondered who would even consider abducting a woman accompanied by these same dogs.

Sydny stepped around Mr. Medford to greet Detective Howard, but the dogs made it to the fence first and were barking with uncertainty at this new visitor. They were waiting for an indication from their master as to whether or not he was to be considered friend or foe. Derrick had experienced this enough times to know that he should wait to be invited into the yard, but Mr. Medford didn't seem to be making the connection.

"Andrew, do you think it would be better to put the dogs inside somewhere first?" Sydny asked.

"Ya, that would be better." Andrew responded and began to call Murphy and Molly back to the house. They didn't listen at first but then he took a stern tone and called them, "Here!"

Both dogs reluctantly went back to the house with Andrew. He opened the screen door and then ushered them into the bedroom. He knew they would end up on the bed, but didn't care. He closed the door and turned around. Sydny and the detective were coming up the sidewalk so he opened the screen door and ushered them through the foyer and into the living room where they each took a seat.

Detective Howard began,

"Mr. Medford, I met your wife earlier this week when I interviewed her about the accident that happened last Sunday evening. Ms. Samuels tells me that you think she may be missing."

Before Derrick could add anything else, Andrew took over,

"Yes. Someone has to have taken her! She wouldn't leave the dogs in the yard unless she was right next door and none of the neighbors are home, I checked. And her Jeep is here and I found dog treats on the sidewalk!"

Derrick didn't understand, "Dog treats?"

"She must have dropped them or they fell out of her pocket when someone grabbed her. She told me someone was following her! Why didn't I believe her?"

"When did she tell you someone was following her?"

"Last Monday night, the other day when she walked the dogs. Who knows when else? She probably stopped telling me because I didn't believe her!"

"I do recall that when I interviewed her last Wednesday, she thought I was there to investigate someone following her home on Monday night."

"And you didn't believe her either? Now what do we do?" Andrew begged for the answer with his eyes.

"Well, let's start by dissecting her day, step by step."

Andrew was frustrated but took the time to explain how their morning began and how they each had coffee plans. He hadn't heard from her all morning. His meeting with a new client went long and he just figured Shannon and Sydny had also enjoyed a long morning together.

Sydny then recounted their time together at the coffee shop. She explained that Shannon was having bad dreams brought on by the events of the accident a week ago. She was careful not to violate any confidence by sharing information about Alex or Steve. She did relay the fact that Shannon wanted to walk around the block looking for a street from her dream but Sydny concluded that Shannon had never found it as evidenced by the fact that she had come home with the dogs. She closed with the phone call from Andrew, at which time Andrew retold how he had arrived home to find the dogs still leashed in the front yard.

Detective Howard leaned forward in his chair, elbows on his knees and folded his hands together. "OK, we know Shannon was with the dogs around 11:15am and the dogs were found here in the yard at about 12:30pm. So, what are the possibilities? She may have come home and then checked on one of the neighbors, leaving the dogs in the yard. If the neighbor had an emergency she may have helped out. I have checked with the desk sergeant and there is no record of her from any call this morning. He is also checking the hospitals and will get back to me. Now keep in mind that if she was at the hospital helping someone, they may not have her name on record.

"But why wouldn't she call?" Blurted Andrew.

"There are some areas in the hospital where you cannot have a cell phone turned on. There are many rational explanations. She may have dropped her phone and broken it or the battery ran out."

"But she would use a land line and call me." Andrew was desperate for Detective Howard to understand the seriousness of the situation.

"Yes, you could be right. Often times these things work out to have a simple explanation. And what if we are making a hasty assumption that she even came home with the dogs? What if she was helping out in some capacity and sent the dogs home with a friend? Or if she tripped and broke an ankle and went to the hospital by ambulance and an officer brought the dogs home?"

"Yes, but wouldn't that have shown up to your desk sergeant?" asked Sydny?

"Derrick didn't want to alarm them any further, but he had to say it, "What if she was unconscious and had no ID on her person?"

"Then who would know to bring the dogs home!" Andrew said not as a question, but a frustrated statement. He stood up and placed his hands on his hips, "I think she has been taken and we need to get everyone out looking for her!"

"Do the dogs have a home address on their tags?"

"No, just a phone number!" Andrew was losing patience.

"OK," Derrick responded very calmly, "I believe we should treat this like a missing person report. Will you sit with me and help me get all of the information I need to put out a bulletin and get the search started?" Detective Howard knew the forty-eight-hour rule but in his gut, he also knew there were too many strange elements to this situation.

"Let me go and get my laptop and we can enter the report electronically and expedite the process."

He got up and left the house, closing only the screen door behind him, pulled his phone from his pocket and dialed as he walked to the gate. He announced himself again to the dispatcher and she transferred him to the desk sergeant. The conversation ensued while he opened the gate, unlocked his car, retrieved the laptop from its anchored spot on the center console, closed and locked the car, and went back through the gate where he paused to finish the conversation. There were no reports of Shannon Medford at any of the hospitals, nor anyone fitting her description. It was going to be a shitty afternoon and evening. Hell, the entire past week had been shitty and it was only getting worse.

Sunday 4:38pm

Detective Howard had taken all of the information necessary to put out what he had described as an all-points-bulletin on Shannon Medford as well as asking for a recent photo of Shannon to take with him. He had made the request for officers to canvas the park where Sydny had last known Shannon to be. He'd done his best to reassure Andrew and told him it would be important for him to stay home and stay by the phone in case Shannon tried to contact him or came home. And with that he had left.

Sydny had stayed with Andrew for about another half an hour but had run out of things to say. Everything she *could* say seemed false and contrived. She certainly didn't want to come off like a counselor, and that was the only role she knew how to play. What really made matters worse was that she, herself, was impacted by this event as well. She felt horribly scared for Shannon and felt guilty for letting her go off in search of some strange detail from her dream.

She reminded herself that Shannon was an adult and could go anywhere she wanted, and that bad things happened to people every day. There just wasn't much you could do about it. Only it had never happened to someone close to her before. The not knowing was the worst. It was like Schrödinger's Cat, with the possibility of being alive or dead all at the same time. Shannon could be just fine or in the worst imaginable situation ever.

She had finally excused herself, wished Andrew luck, and told him that everything would be OK. She had taken and squeezed his hand with both of hers at the gate, reminded him he could call any time, and then gone to her vehicle. As she drove away, Andrew had still been standing at the gate staring off across the street while the dogs milled about in the yard.

Sunday 5:09pm

Steve arrived home with his groceries and backed his SUV into his designated parking spot. He made three runs to unload his grocery bags into the kitchen and then hit the remote button on the key fob to lock his vehicle. As he placed the various food packages into the refrigerator, freezer and small pantry, he hoped he had not forgotten anything. He was mentally and emotionally exhausted and didn't want to leave the house again until tomorrow morning when he had to go to work.

He had never been in a negative funk like this before. He was normally energetic and very optimistic about life. He thought that perhaps it was due to the lack of physical activity and poor diet. How long had it been since he truly had a good workout? Last Sunday, he thought and shivered. No wonder. Well, he had one Ambien left and planned to get a good night of rest and start the week fresh tomorrow, and then he would get back to healthy eating and regular exercise. The fact that he hadn't had a nightmare for the past two nights was also a positive sign.

He finished putting his groceries away and then opened the fridge to evaluate his options for dinner. One of the new bottles of Sam Adams in the door called his name, so he grabbed it and popped the top. He took a long, refreshing swig and then decided that a cold beer needed to be accompanied by a freshly grilled steak.

He retrieved the one T-bone he had left in the fridge, the rest had gone into the freezer, and placed it on the counter. He went to work seasoning the piece of meat and then went out to light the grill. He left the patio door open and closed the screen behind him. Now what to do while he allowed the meat to sit and the grill to heat? He decided that some football would do the trick.

The half-consumed beer had never left his hand, and it accompanied him now to the couch, where he picked up the remote and planted himself on the couch across from the TV. The screen jumped into action as players clad in white and red uniforms scrambled after a ball sailing through the air. He wondered if he was catching college or pro ball and let his mind drift, only half watching the game. It will be nice to be out of this apartment, he thought. He knew the area well enough to start looking at homes. He definitely liked the downtown area where he did his shopping and attended the gym. He even liked the park, and the impact of the accident seemed to be lessoning with time. He could see himself getting a dog and running the track with a companion as so many others did.

The woman at the accident, who had stopped to help with the dogs, must run in the park all the time. He remembered that he had seen her earlier today, when he had gone out for some breakfast, well it was more like lunch based on the time of day. She must live east of the park, since she was crossing the street in that direction. Probably heading home after a nice run with her two big dogs.

He wondered if there were any nice homes for sale over in that neighborhood. All of the streets and neighborhoods surrounding the park were dotted with interesting, historic homes. Some were in great shape and some were in very sad condition. He didn't think he wanted a fixer-upper, and he knew that the further east you went, the nicer and costlier the homes became. There, he had just given himself something positive to focus on for next week. It was time to find a good Realtor and start looking.

Sunday 7:15pm

Katrina's weekend had been wonderful. The time spent in the yard raking up leaves on Saturday made her feel rejuvenated. The air had been crisp but the sun warmed her bones and the exercise warmed her muscles. She had taken a short nap to restore her energy and then enjoyed a great evening with friends playing Bunco.

Today had started out right, with a good night of sleep that was only broken by the soft sunlight coming in through her bedroom window. This was definitely the thing she missed most working the night shift.

She had puttered around her house in her house-coat and slippers, sipping her coffee and doing all of her regular preparations for the coming work week. Finally, she had showered, dressed and then started a load of scrubs in the washer before heading over to her sister's house.

She and her sister, Martha, had eaten lunch at Chili's in the mall and then watched a matinee at the adjoining theater, as was their weekly ritual. The ride back to her sister's house had consisted of the same conversation it always did, with Martha expressing her disapproval of the 'filthy language' Hollywood infused into all of their movies these days.

Katrina and Martha always picked PG or PG-13 movies, but Martha was correct, the ratings seemed to be slipping over the years. Katrina wasn't as bothered by the language, probably because in her line of work she encountered all kinds of people and language, which included some of the doctors and other medical staff.

Martha was 14 years older than Katrina and really did come from a different generation. She had never worked because her late husband was a successful salesman and when he passed, tragically young, of a heart attack, he had left Martha with a good life insurance policy and had been smart enough to buy insurance on their mortgage. Between Social Security and the life insurance, Martha led a modest, but comfortable life.

Katrina was happy for her older sister, knowing that she had no work skills and had never even learned to drive. Her little house was slightly east between the down town area and the university up the hill. Though small, it was probably worth quite a bit, and Martha was able to walk to a small neighborhood market or use the passenger train and bus system to get to the larger store or downtown mall.

Before dropping her sister back at home on Sundays, Katrina always took her to the grocery store to stock up for the week. Martha was always prepared with a list in her big, bulky black purse and they spent about an hour perusing the aisles. The checkout process was never expedient as Martha also brought along all of the coupons she had collected that week, and by the time Katrina helped her sister unload and unpack all of the groceries and say their 'goodbyes' the sun was getting low in the skies.

As Katrina drove away with a few of her own groceries tucked safely in the trunk, she remembered that she had left her travel mug and snack bag at the hospital. She was such a creature of habit and organization, that she hated being unprepared for her shift, so she headed toward the hospital to grab both.

Katrina parked in the visitor parking lot since she would only be a few minutes. She used her employee badge to go up the back stairs and was thankful that she always kept it in her purse. Monica greeted Katrina with a surprised 'hey, how are you?' because the two of them rarely crossed paths at work.

"Hey, Monica. I just stopped by to get a few things I left here over the weekend. How are you?"

"I'm good." Monica responded, "And my shift ends in less than three hours, so that makes things even better!"

Katrina went behind the counter and saw that her mug and snack bag were still stored neatly on the lower shelf where she had left them. She remembered how exciting things had gotten with Jane Doe last week and figured that was why she left her stuff behind. And with that thought she asked,

"Has Jane Doe awakened? Is she showing more signs of activity?"

Monica responded with a bit of confusion, "Jane Doe is just the same as always, so sad, I'm beginning to wonder if she will ever wake up."

"Oh." Katrina replied with in a soft, sad tone. I thought for sure that she was beginning to come back to us last week. Do you mind if I walk down and check on her?"

"Go for it." Monica stated, "It can't hurt."

Katrina set her mug and snack bag on the counter and walked out of the nurse's station and down the end of the hall. She saw the officer sitting on one of their rolling desk chairs right outside Jane's door and remembered her conversation with Detective Howard regarding the safety of Jane, especially if she awakened and could remember what had happened to her.

As Katrina approached the officer, she fished her employee badge out of her purse. The officer looked up at her with deep brown eyes and she noted that he looked very young, even though a swatch of gray was beginning to show through his thick, dark hair at each temple.

"Can I help you?" He asked.

"Yes, I'm Katrina Dempsey, I work the night shift and have been caring for Jane Doe for the past week. I'd like to peek in on her and see how she is doing."

"I'm sorry, ma'am," Replied the officer, "but you're not on my roster of employees for today's shift so I can't allow you into the room." The officer picked up a clipboard from beside his chair and double checked it as he made this statement to Katrina.

"Oh." Katrina responded feeling deflated. She put her badge back into her purse and stood there looking at the officer. The doorway was just past him and she looked into the room to see that the blinds were still open but the last of the early evening light was losing the battle to illuminate the room.

As she stood there contemplating whether or not to ask Monica to escort her into the room, she saw Jane lift her arm slowly off the bed and reach out a shaky hand toward the door, and then Katrina heard her, barely audible, say, "Hurry," and her hand dropped back to the bed.

"Oh, my goodness! She is awake!" Katrina tried to push past the officer but he was out of his chair and spun her against the wall so quickly she stopped breathing for a moment. Then she shouted, "Monica! She's awake! Monica! Come check on her!"

Monica came rushing down the hallway and asked the officer, "What are you doing? Let her go!"

"She tried to enter the room and I had to restrain her." The officer stated.

"Jane is awake!" Katrina pleaded.

"You can let her go." Said Monica as she pushed past them both and entered the room.

The officer stepped back and released Katrina, and then both of them watched from the doorway as Monica stood over Jane, blocking their view. After only a minute, Monica turned to them both and stated, "No change in her condition. Her pupils are still unresponsive and I don't know what happened, but she isn't awake."

Sunday 8:36pm

Andrew had spent the past couple of hours pacing and then sitting and staring out through the large picture window. Every so often he had walked out to the gate and looked up and down the street. Murphy and Molly had followed his every move, and when he sat and stared, they laid at his feet, softly whimpering.

It had finally dawned on him at about 7pm that he should feed the dogs and they had eaten slowly, which was strange for them. He knew that they could sense something was wrong.

He'd just come in from checking the street again. The dogs had done their business and would normally be ready to settle in for the night, but tonight there was a tension in the air that animals were acutely sensitive to. As Andrew stood in the center of the living room, watching the quiet street in front of their house, Murphy and Molly posted themselves on either side of him, like sentinels. Dusk was creeping in on the day and Andrew pictured Shannon lost somewhere as the cold and darkness descended upon her.

What was he doing? How could he just stand around waiting? He had to go and find her!

"Let's go for a ride." He said to the dogs. They both jumped up and darted to the front foyer. Andrew followed them and suited them up with collars only. He grabbed the dual leash, double checked that the front door was locked and then said, "Let's go."

They ran ahead of him down the hallway to the back door. Andrew grabbed the spare Jeep key off the hook and hit the remote button twice, activating the hatchback door. The dogs waited dutifully at the back door and when he opened it, they trotted out and jumped into the back of the Jeep in perfect unison. Andrew locked the house door, went out into the cool evening air and realized he had forgotten a coat. He made sure all tails were positioned safely inside the Jeep and then pushed the button activating the door to close.

He went back into the house and grabbed not only a coat for himself, but a warm coat for Shannon and a large blanket out of the hallway cupboard. If, no, *when* he found her, she would be cold. He went back out of the house, locked up and climbed into the Jeep, throwing coats and blankets on the passenger seat. Molly came up and licked his ear as he started the engine. Normally he would chastise her for this, but not tonight.

He backed the Jeep up and negotiated the terrain until he was down the narrow driveway. Reaching the sidewalk, he hit the brakes and looked up and down the street for a good ten seconds, scanning for signs of Shannon, but the street was empty. He headed right toward the park. At each intersection, Andrew slowed and looked up and down the side roads. Murphy and Molly went back and forth to the windows as if they too were looking for their human mother.

Reaching Ninth South, Andrew stopped and waited as one single car passed by before he crossed and entered park. He drove slowly on the one-way road that circled the park with his window down and the heat going on low, he didn't want the noise of the heater to obstruct his hearing. He had even lowered the rear passenger window so that he dogs could put their heads out. Somehow this made sense to him. They recognized people more by smells, walking patterns and sounds, than by looks. The dogs might be better equipped to recognize Shannon from far off than he would be.

The lamp posts lining the circular drive and various paths in the park were lit up for the evening and few cars remained in the angled parking spots that bordered the road. The dogs sniffed at the air as Andrew allowed the Jeep to creep along. He alternated his search from left to right, knowing that the running track ran along the outside of the circular drive and had wide strips of grass and trees in spots that insulated it from the inner and outer streets that framed the park.

Andrew came to the half-way mark on the south side of the park and had to exit and then get into the center lane so he could re-enter the park and complete the circle. He made the return trip around the park in excruciating silence, broken only twice by the footsteps of a lone runner on the path and chatter of a couple walking hand and hand in the park. Molly barked at both, as was her M.O. and Murphy only sniffed.

At the north end of the park, Andrew pulled up to the exit. A car pulled out of the parking lot of the coffee shop and then onto Ninth Street toward him. He waited for it to cross his path and then pulled out into the center lane heading west. Why hadn't he thought of the coffee shop? He would go there and ask about Shannon.

The coffee shop parking lot harbored only two other cars in a lot that was normally so full, people parked on the grass and street to get their morning fix. The dogs became excited as he parked the car. He wondered if it was because they knew this was a place to get treats or because they remembered being there with Shannon.

Andrew exited the Jeep and locked the doors with the key fob. He could hear the dogs whining and barking in protest at being left behind. He walked into the coffee shop and went to the left side of the U-shaped counter where a pimply-faced boy that Andrew figured to be about sixteen greeted him and asked for his order. Hell, Andrew figured, I might as well get a coffee. I'm going to be up all night anyway.

"I'll have a Grande, double espresso with Cinnamon and extra milk." The kid repeated back his order and then hit some buttons on the cash register,

"Four, seventy-eight." He said before turning around and busying himself with making the coffee.

Andrew pulled five dollars from his wallet and then grabbed one more for a tip. He laid the bills on the counter and then pulled out his phone and flipped through the pictures until he found a good one of Shannon. When the boy came back with his coffee, he asked, "Have you seen her today?"

The young man picked up the five-dollar bill and left the one on the counter. He hit another button on the register and the drawer opened. He looked at the picture and then exchanged the five-dollar bill for some coins which he placed on top of the one still laying on the counter.

"Nope, but I've seen her before. She comes in on the weekends, in the mornings. She always has those cool dogs. But I traded shifts today, so I wasn't here this morning."

"Do you think someone might still be here that would have seen her this morning, or even this afternoon?" Andrew asked with a hopeful tone.

"I can ask Tammy. She was training someone this morning, and she is helping me close tonight." He stepped back and looked to his right, "Tammy! Can you come here a minute?"

"Hang on a sec." The answer came.

Andrew took a sip of his coffee and nearly burned his tongue. He set it on the counter and took the lid off, never letting go of the phone and the picture of his smiling wife.

A young woman, only slightly older than the boy and sporting a dark pony-tail, came walking out from the back of the shop. "Can I help you?" She asked.

The young man jumped in, obviously feeling important, "Hey Tammy, do you know this lady? She comes in all the time on the weekends. She has those big dogs, the sweet ones. Did you see her today?"

Tammy put her hand on the phone and angled it toward her for a better look. "Ya, I've seen her before, but I didn't see her in the shop today. Wait, I think I did see her walking up with the dogs this morning, but she didn't come inside."

"Do you remember what time?" Asked Andrew.

"A little before lunch, I think." Tammy looked at him and waited. "Are you a cop?" She asked suspiciously.

"No, I'm her husband and I'm trying to find her."

"Ben said there were cops in here this afternoon looking for some lady." Tammy said this to the boy and then turned back to Andrew, "Weird, I hope you find her." The tone was genuine and Andrew felt defeated.

"Thanks." He mumbled and picked up his coffee. He put the phone back in his pocket and walked away leaving the dollar bill and change on the counter.

"Dude, you forget your change." The boy called after him. He didn't care. He walked out of the shop and back toward the Jeep.

The dogs were barking and Molly had jumped into the front passenger seat where she'd already made several doggie-nose prints on the window. Andrew wondered if the dogs could actually find a scent for Shannon and follow it. It was worth a try, what else was he gonna do? He went to the back of the Jeep and opened the hatch by squeezing the handle. The dogs waited as the gate slowly lifted. They knew the routine and sat patiently waiting for Andrew to attach the leash to each collar. He gave them the official "OK" and they jumped from the vehicle and began sniffing and pulling at the leash. Andrew hit the close button inside the back door of the Jeep and then the lock button on the key fob. He heard the Jeep horn beep behind him as the door closed and latched into place.

The dogs took off, pulling him toward the front door of the coffee shop and then suddenly veered off to the left. They went to the far table against the front of the store and sniffed around under it.

Andrew wondered what this meant. Did they smell something that spilled? Had Shannon been sitting there today with Sydny? Had she given them treats that left crumbs under the table? Murphy gobbled up something and Molly bull-dozed her way under him searching for whatever he had beaten her to. He let them sniff around until they got it out of their system.

Once they settled a bit, he posed the question, "Where's mom? Where is she?" Both dogs perked up and looked at him cocking their heads to one side and then the other. "Where's mom?" he asked again. "Go find her."

Both dogs went back to the business of sniffing, only they moved quickly from the table back into the parking lot. They sniffed and circled and nearly tripped each other but then tried to pull in opposite directions. Andrew realized he had only sent them into a frenzy looking for more treats or a toy. But then they both took off in the direction of the street and the park, causing Andrew to lurch forward and pick up the pace. He had no idea what they were really after but decided it couldn't hurt to follow them.

When they got to the street, Molly tried to go right on the sidewalk and then came back and looked at him. "Where's mom?" He asked again and the dogs stepped out into the street. Andrew held them for a second as he double checked for cars. The streets were quiet so he let up on the leash and followed them across into the park. They walked along the outer sidewalk that ran parallel to Ninth South. They sniffed like bloodhounds but seemed to get sidetracked by every tree, bush, and stick on the ground.

When they arrived at the front entrance of the park, the dogs headed toward the center along the concrete path that cut straight through the park. Andrew continued to follow and then Molly veered off to the right even more. It was clear that Murphy was going to follow her where ever she went, but Andrew was not sure what scent she was actually following. She continued to sniff along the ground and then stopped and dug her snout into the grass. Murphy joined her and they fixated on the grass and dirt. Andrew realized they had found the spot where another dog had urinated. He jerked the leash and said, "Let's go. Let's find mom."

The dogs reluctantly broke away from their find. Now they just trotted along like they were on a normal walk in the park. Andrew coaxed them back to the main path and asked the question again.

"Where's mom?" Both of them bounded off in the direction of the park entrance, back the way they had come. He trotted along with them, trying to keep their run to a minimum. He followed them back out of the park and then to the cross walk where they stopped and turned to him. They were waiting for permission to cross the street, they wanted to go home. Was it because this was the direction Shannon had come or was it because they knew the way home? Andrew felt tired. He decided to take the dogs back to the Jeep and head home. Maybe they would be better at searching around out in front of the house.

"Let's go." He said and turned back toward the coffee shop. They came along reluctantly, sniffing a little here and there. They crossed the street and went back to the Jeep in the lonely parking lot. Andrew used the key fob to trigger the back to open and then let go of the leash. The dogs ran and jumped in. When he got to Jeep, he removed the leash, threw it into the back and hit the button. He watched to make sure neither dog turned around, placing a tail in harm's way as the door slowly came down. Then he climbed back into the driver seat and placed his coffee in the cup holder. He hadn't even consumed any beyond that first sip in the coffee shop.

He watched the display screen as he backed the Jeep up and avoided the two cars that likely belonged to Tammy and the boy. Then he headed back home. He kept careful watch along each sidewalk and side street as he drove. The dogs went back to the windows, looking here and there, and leaving smudges on the glass. Shannon was always washing the windows in her Jeep. How could she stand it?

He suddenly became very angry at the dogs. They were a complete pain and what good were they if they couldn't protect her? He yelled at the dogs to lay down! They both stopped and lowered themselves into the prone position as he made the U-turn around the park strip and then came back up and entered his own driveway. He pulled to the back and parked the Jeep in Shannon's designated spot. He pushed the button to stop the engine and then turned over his shoulder to look at the dogs. The tip of Murphy's tail flickered up and down and then came to a stop. His big eyes implored Andrew not to be mad at him. And then Molly jumped up and licked him again.

Andrew knew it wasn't their fault, and he knew that Murphy would always take the guilt for both of them and Molly would always be in the I-love-you mode. "I know." Andrew said as he stroked the out-of-control Molly and then Murphy as he slinked forward for some of the attention and forgiveness.

Andrew went through the process of getting the dogs back on their leash and out of the Jeep. Instead of going in the back door, he walked the dogs back up the driveway and whispered, "Where's Mom? Go get her." This command always worked in the house, why wouldn't it work now? He wondered with a sickening, sadness growing in his stomach.

The dogs pulled him out to the sidewalk and then toward the front gate. They sniffed around the sidewalk at the gate area, and then over to where he had found the pocket treats earlier today. They dug their noses through the leaves building up in the gutter and then Molly stopped and let out a growl. Her head was hanging low but she looked forward. Her scruff was raised all the way along her back to her tail. Murphy came over to her, sniffed the ground and joined her in the low-pitched growl.

"It's OK," Andrew soothed, "Good dogs. What did you find?" he pulled them back gently but they didn't want to come. He pulled a little harder and ordered, "Come." Andrew led the dogs back to the gate, opened it and ushered them inside. He dropped the leash and closed the gate.

Had Shannon done the exact same thing today? Shivers ran down his spine. He walked back over to the spot the dogs had fixated on, squatted down and looked at the leaves. It had gotten quite dark. He heard the dogs making low growly barks over his shoulder as he sifted through the leaves. The only thing he found was a large, blue button. It reminded him of an old Pea Coat he had once had. Were the dogs really upset over this?

Andrew straightened up and went over to the fence. He reached over the gate and let the dogs smell the button which resulted in more growling and then Molly bared her teeth and snapped at him. Andrew jumped and pulled his hand back. They both barked in unison for a moment and then settled down. Andrew spoke calmly, reassuring them it was OK. Molly wagged her tail and Murphy headed toward the house. It was cold and it was time to go in. He put the button in his pocket and went through the gate. The dogs followed at his heals and they all went inside.

Sunday 11:35pm

Shannon awoke feeling chilled to the bone. She shivered and sucked in a deep breath. The air was musty, dark and cold. Her joints ached and she struggled to see through the darkness. Her back was stiff and sore from a coldness that permeated her bones. She knew she was uncovered and her bare skin tightened with goose bumps. Then she recognized the cold, hard surface of the metal table she lay upon.

"I'm dreaming again." She groaned aloud, and was startled at the raspy sound of her own voice in the darkness. She tried to bring her hands to her face and rub the sleepiness from her eyes but they were jerked back, secured at her sides; not by straps, but by metal with chains that clanked against the surface of the medical table. She was handcuffed. That didn't make sense, or did it? Previously in her dreams she had escaped the leather straps. Was her mind playing tricks on her? How would she escape now?

She lay there shivering and listening in the dark silence. She felt different, she didn't feel like

she was dreaming, this felt very real. Her body was racked by a painful shiver and her head began to throb, but the stinging sensation along her arms, legs and stomach was missing. She lifted her head and let it drop back against the table. "Wake up!" She demanded.

A creak sounded from somewhere above her and she froze. She heard footsteps and remembered the stairs with a door at the top. Her heart beat quickened and her breath hitched in her throat. Was she dreaming? How could this feel so real? It couldn't be real, but she knew she was not dreaming! How did she get here? The questions raced through her mind and then she remembered having coffee with Sydny. Was that yesterday?

She heard the door at the top of the stairs open, and then nothing. She waited and listened, trying to hold her breath silent. The slow decent of footsteps sounded softly in the darkness. She was suddenly warm as fear swept over her body like a heavy blanket. She heard the groan of one wooden stair and remembered her dreams again. How could this possibly be? Tears welled up in her eyes and her breathing became choppy as she struggled not to make any noise.

Her mind raced, searching backward in time and trying to understand how she had gotten here. She remembered coffee with

Sydny and walking the dogs along the park. She remembered walking home. She remembered being in front of the house.

The footsteps stopped and she endured another few seconds frozen in time, straining, but hearing only the sound of her own heartbeat pounding in her ears. Then she felt the presence of someone by her side. She held her breath again. Fingertips grazed her cheekbone and she jerked away as a tiny shriek escaped from inside her. This caused the strap across her chest to bite into her skin and her wrist bones stung against the pinch of the handcuffs.

Shannon half felt, half heard, the person move behind and around to her left. A match scraped across a flinty surface and then bloomed into flame, followed by the popping of a newly lighted candle wick. She smelled the sulfur and her eyes registered strange shadows and shapes dancing around her. The surroundings became clearer as the dark figure lit two more candles, moving along what appeared to be a tall wooden bench running the length of the room to her left.

Overhead she saw the dirty wood framing of the floor above. Old, grimy pipes were suspended beneath the floor, stretching across the room and occasionally running through a floor joist. Larger aluminum piping tracked here and there, carrying air from a furnace that was somewhere in a shadowy corner. To her right was the unfinished, sheet rock wall she remembered trailing with her hand. "Please be a dream. Please just wake up." Shannon whispered.

Music began to drift out of a corner behind her head. It sounded like an old record player spinning dreary opera music with a lint-covered needle riding a warped vinyl surface. She became aware that the man was somewhere behind her again.

"Not a dream," Came a low, raspy voice, "but I do hope you are feeling comfortable."

Monday 1:14am

Yellow flames flickered and danced in time to the eerie music pulsing in and out of a dark, musty corner. The darkness swelled, cool and deep.

The blanket was heavy, comfortable and he sank into his pillow, and the darkness.

Damp, musty air cooled his skin. Auburn softness, scented with lavender looped around his fingers. Relaxing, comforting, quiet.

The air was thick, dark and the scent of copper filled his nostrils. A warm glow of soft yellow flame waivered in the darkness.

.....And so, Steve slept, and dreamed, and slept.

* * * * * * * * * *

5:45am

The alarm clock droned loudly and Steve slowly came to the realization that it was time to get up. The room was dark and the glow of his phone cut through that darkness displaying two words; *snooze* and *dismiss*. He reached over and tapped the screen which then showed 5:45am. He lay back on his pillow in the quiet of the room. He felt groggy and drugged, unlike the past two mornings when Ambien had been his miracle drug. He couldn't remember dreaming so he must have slept, but the feeling in his head and body didn't align with that truth.

Steve half rolled and half pushed himself into a sitting position with his legs draped over the edge of the bed. He turned on the bed-side lamp and rubbed his eyes. It was Monday and he needed strong coffee and a hot shower.

Monday 6:51am

Andrew sat in the over-stuffed arm chair in the living room staring out through the big picture window. He observed the warm glow hinting at the eastern mountain range and knew that the sun was due to rise just after 7am.

He had tried to sleep at one point during the night, shoving in between Molly and Murphy who had taken over the king-size bed, but who was he kidding? Murphy had experienced some kind of nightmare in the wee hours of the morning, growling and barking, and he was joined by Molly's waking reaction of going berserk, as if someone had broken into the house. This, of course, awakened Murphy, and it took a while to calm both dogs down again. Andrew wondered if the dream was a remnant of what had happened to Shannon that day. He would give anything to know what Molly and Murphy had seen. Shannon always joked about knowing what the dogs actually thought, and now he found himself praying for the same thing.

He'd given up on sleep shortly after the doggie, nightmare fiasco, and finally fed them at 6am, keeping to their regular schedule. They had been out for their morning business and were now coiled up together on the couch, half dozing and half keeping an eye on Andrew. They were keenly aware that something was wrong. For the first time ever, Andrew really observed the dogs. Murphy was on his right side with his head curled around toward his chest and front paws drawn up under him. His back was to the back of the couch and his right leg was drawn up but his left was stretched out almost straight. Molly had climbed onto the couch from the opposite direction and essentially plopped down on top of him with her head resting on his outstretched upper thigh. Her hind quarters had squished down between Murphy's curled head and the couch. She also had her left leg tucked under her and the right stretched out behind her.

In his chair, Andrew recalled Shannon making comments about Molly pushing in on top of Murphy. She always said that Murphy loved Molly so much, that he would let her do or have anything she wanted. Then he considered how much he loved Shannon and berated himself for not listening to her. Why wasn't he devoted like Murphy? Tears stung in his eyes, his shoulders began to shudder and he dropped his head into his hands and cried violently.

Monday 7:20am

Alex sat beside Jay in the front seat of the ambulance. Jay was driving like a crazy person and taking corners at dangerous speeds.

"I think you should slow down!" Alex stated in a concerned tone.

"What?" Jay shot Alex a serious look and then returned his eyes to the road. "I can't hear you over the siren." He shouted.

"You're gonna flip the ambulance if you don't slow down!" Alex shouted back to Jay.

"But it's gonna be too late!" Jay responded.

Alex looked around. It was dark and the streets were empty. They were careening east on

Thirteenth South, parallel to the southern end of the park. Suddenly Jay slammed on the brakes and jerked the ambulance left into the park entrance. Alex's body floated forward and then to the right but there was no impact and no pain. The interior road in the park curved around to the right, but Jay jumped the curb and drove onto the grass. The ambulance shot up the side of the small grassy hill and then leaned scarily in Alex's direction. He thought for sure they would roll, but the ambulance just kept going.

A banging sound came from the back bay of the ambulance and Alex realized he had heard it several times now. As he rested his weight and his right elbow against the door, he craned his head to the left and looked around his seat back to see their gurney with a patient strapped down for safety.

"You're gonna hurt the patient if you don't slow down!" Alex shot at Jay.

The ambulance made it down the grassy hill and continued on at an angle across the park toward Seventh East. They bounced and tilted from side to side as Jay swerved around the big trees that had been planted decades ago. Alex looked wildly from Jay to the path ahead and then back to the patient.

In that moment, everything slowed down and he noticed that the patient was clothed in only her bra and underwear. Her blond hair, slightly dirty and limp, fell around her shoulders as she slowly sat up.

Lacerations on her stomach oozed with sticky, crimson blood and her legs were ghostly white except for the dark slices along the fleshy parts. Her arms came up and she reached her hands out toward him. More dark gashes along her delicate skin caught his eyes. She looked at Alex and locked her dark blue eyes with his. She curled the fingers of her right hand, leaving only the index finger pointing forward and gasped out a single word,

"Hurry!"

Alex followed the direction of her pointing finger and looked out the window to see the ambulance had left the park and was bouncing and jerking over the median of Seventh South, barely squeezing between two trees.

Jay didn't slow down at all as the big vehicle jumped the sidewalk and plowed across the grass toward the porch of an old, brick house at full speed. Alex raised his arms over his face and yelled,

"Jay!"

Alex felt someone shaking him and he opened his eyes. Victoria had one knee on the bed as she leaned over him calling his name and shaking him.

"You're having a nightmare again." She softly stated.

Alex looked up into Victoria's eyes. She released him and gently sat back onto the bed. He sat up and wrapped his arms around her tightly.

"I'm sorry, babe. I thought this shit was passing and I was getting back to normal." He held her for a few minutes and she held him tightly in return.

"I'll call and make another appointment with the counselor before I go into work today."

"Sounds good, sweetie. I think that's why you made such good progress in the first place. You need to talk this stuff out."

Alex released her and cupped her face in his hands. "I love you so much!"

Monday 7:28am

Steve hit the seek button on his radio as he drove to work, and the speakers came to life with the chatter of two morning talk show hosts prattling on about a secret sound contest. They were cut off by a short buffer of silence while the radio scanned for the next channel and then a high-pitched, female voice was screeching rhythmically to a tech-no beat.

The next pause was a short relief which gave way to soft musical tones that reminded him of his grandmother. Again, the music disappeared, and in the silence, his mind was instantly filled by a distant memory of Victrola music. Before he could make sense of it, the memory was shoved aside by AC/DC singing “Back in Black”.

He hit the power button on his center dash, leaving a vacuum of silence in the interior of the SUV. He tried to drag the musical memory back to the surface of his mind, but it was nowhere to be found. Where had it come from? It felt important, and a little bit unsettling. He continued the drive in silence until he arrived at work feeling very uneasy.

Monday 8:11am

Sydny was lying in bed when her cell phone vibrated on the night stand. Her first appointment wasn't until 10am and she hadn't slept well all night. The idea of climbing out from under the comforter was not a pleasant one.

The sun was shining in through the windows and the heat had kicked on for a minute so it wouldn't be that bad, but facing the morning chill was the least of her worries. Sydny had spent her waking moments trying to come up with a logical explanation of where Shannon could be, infused with a few restless, dreaming moments that incorporated Steve's nightmares with Alex's day-mares and Shannon's, well, both day and nightmares.

Sydny took a deep breath and exhaled slowly before sitting up straight in her bed. She pondered the similarities and the connections between the three people. It was obvious, they had all experienced the same horrific tragedy together. But was there more? Every aspect of her professional education, training and experience told her that no, there was a logical, reason for each of their post-traumatic stress symptoms.

Something in the back of her mind nagged at her. Steve had seemed truly unaware of how he had dreamed of a real victim. On the other hand, he probably just hadn't realized he'd seen a photo of Laura Roundsley on the news while she was missing. There were a lot of similarities between Shannon's and Steve's dreams, but they were only generalized similarities. And Alex didn't have any dreams, only hallucinations of the same types of cuts he had seen on the girl from the accident. So that was completely understandable. No, there was no real connection between them all other than the accident.

Sydny peeled back the comforter and put on a pair of thick sweatpants, slipped her feet into her slippers and grabbed a sweat jacket off the back of the door. After she stuffed both arms into the jacket, she picked up her cell phone and took a look at the missed call. It was Alex. She had programmed his contact data into her phone after their first appointment and giving him her direct number, but her phone was on silent. She tapped the voice mail icon and then hit the speaker button. Alex's voice spoke to her as she descended the stairs.

"Good morning, Ms. Samuels, this is Alex Jones. I hope I'm not bothering you during an appointment, and I know we have an appointment on Thursday morning, but I was just hoping you might have some time sooner. I think talking to you really helped and things have been going well, but I just had the worst nightmare, so I don't know. Anyway, sorry, I'm rambling. But if you could call me back when you have a chance, that would be great. Thank you."

That nagging feeling came back to Sydny as she walked into the kitchen and started the coffee pot. She went back into the living-office area and looked at her schedule for the day. She kept the schedule on her lap top upstairs, but each night printed the schedule for the next day before going to bed. She knew the 10am slot was filled but was happy to discover that she was open until 1pm after that. She'd penciled in a note to call Detective Howard during the break. She could do that too.

Sydny went back to the kitchen and made herself a cup of coffee with a little hot chocolate and whipped cream and then settled into one of the big arm chairs and called Alex back. His phone was answered by a woman with a very kind voice.

"Alex's phone, this is Victoria."

"Hello, Victoria. This is Sydny Samuels calling for Alex."

"Oh yes! Hold on just a moment, he is expecting your call." The phone was muffled for a moment and then the male voice of Alex, "Ms. Samuels?"

"Please, Sydny is fine." Responded Sydny. "I received your voice mail this morning and I know it is short notice, but I have an 11am appointment available if you can make it. If not, we can look for another time possibly later today."

"No! I mean yes, 11am is perfect. I can just ask my captain to have one of the guys stay for 30 minutes to cover me because I'll be a little late for my shift at noon."

"Are you sure? I can look at my calendar and find another time."

"No, that couldn't be more perfect. I'll see you then. And thank you!"

Monday 8:30 am

Andrew had waited as patiently and as long as he possibly could and it was now 8:30, so he picked up the phone that had not left his person for almost 21 hours now and called Sydny. The phone rang several times and then went to voice mail. His heart sank as he prepared to leave a message.

"Sydny, hello. I hope I am not bothering you. I just haven't slept all night and I, well, I don't know really why I'm calling you. But, well, if you have a chance, maybe you can call me back."

He ended the call and leaned back in the big chair still holding the phone in his lap. Molly and Murphy had snuggled into one of their combined positions on the couch again and they both looked over at him with equal sadness.

Andrew jumped as the phone rang in his hand. He looked at the display with hope and then saw that it was Sydny. He felt both sadness and relief at the same time.

"Hello Sydny." He answered.

"Sorry I missed your call. How are you doing?" Sydny thought about adding that she was about to get in the shower when he called, but then it didn't really matter.

"Well, not sure if you heard my voice mail, but I haven't slept all night."

"That's completely understandable. Do you think you might be able to get some rest today?" and then she added, "Have you heard anything?" It was a loaded question and she wasn't sure she wanted to know the answer.

"No, nothing. But there was something strange last night."

"Really? What happened?" Sydny coaxed him to continue.

"Well, I took the dogs out walking and driving through the park hoping they might actually be able to figure out where Shannon had gone. Kind of silly, I guess."

"No, it's not silly at all." Sydny comforted him.

"Well, anyway, when we got home, I parked and then walked the dogs up to the front gate, again hoping they might smell something and they did. They found a big button in the leaves in the gutter."

"A button?" Sydny questioned.

"Yes, it looks like it came from an old pea coat. And the dogs did not like it. They growled and when I picked it up and held it out for Molly, she almost bit me, she was so upset!"

"Andrew, that could be evidence! You need to call Detective Howard right away. You didn't call him last night?"

"I don't know, I just ..." His voice trailed off.

"It's fine, you're fine. It was late and it will be fine. You can call him right now and let him know."

"Oh my lord, what have I done? I should have called the police last night! What if It's too late?"

"Andrew. Andrew!" Sydny stated his name as gently and firmly as she could. "Everything is going to be fine. You are going to hang up the phone and call Detective Howard right now, and I am going to come over and bring you lunch just after noon. Then you can tell me what Detective Howard says. Can you do that for me?"

Andrew nodded.

"Andrew?" Sydny asked again and he responded, "Yes, I'll call right now. Thank you."

Andrew ended the call and walked to the kitchen to retrieve the business card from its hanging place on the refrigerator. Detective Howard had his work number on the front but had written his cell on the back. Andrew tapped the numbers and put the phone to his ears. He looked down and saw that Molly and Murphy were sitting in the doorway to the kitchen watching him.

"Treat?" he asked and they both turned excitedly back to the living room. Just as he was reaching into the treat jar Detective Howard answered his phone,

"Detective Howard."

Andrew tossed a treat to each dog and responded,

"Hello, this is Andrew Medford, I was wondering if you had any new information for me?" The words sounded ridiculous and Andrew felt like an idiot.

"Mr. Medford. I am sorry to say that I don't have anything helpful to tell you at this point. We are sending officers over to the coffee shop again this morning to find out if anyone remembers seeing her there, or leaving for that matter. We're also sending a few officers to canvas the park and find out if any witnesses saw her walking with the dogs. I'm just getting ready to brief the group here in a few minutes. How are you holding up?"

"I'm not, really. And I feel like the worst husband in the world! Last night I was walking out front with the dogs and they sniffed something in the gutter right where I found all of the dog treats. It was a button from a coat or something and the dogs were growling at it. Do you think that could mean anything? Should I have called you last night? I'm such an idiot for not calling you last night!"

"Mr. Medford, you are not an idiot. You are calling me now and that is a good thing. Can I send an officer over to collect the full details *and* the button and see where you found it?"

"Ya, OK, um I guess that makes sense, I'll just be here."

"Perfect. As soon as I finish briefing the officers, we will get the search started and one of them will come by. His name is Hayden, Officer Glen Hayden. He should be there within the hour, will you be OK until then?"

"Ya, I'll be OK, I'll be here." Andrew ended the call and went back to the chair. Molly and Murphy had gone back to the couch. The sadness in the room was palpable.

Monday 9:15am

Katrina had stayed up until nearly 1am finishing her laundry, preparing some snacks and meals for the week and finally reading a book before turning in for the night. Sundays were always a transition night for her. She couldn't stay up all night but if she stayed up late, and in turn slept late the following day, she was able to last through her first evening shift of the week and then would be plenty tired when arriving home Tuesday morning.

Last night had been different; tossing and turning for about 5 hours and then finally getting up for a hot shower. She'd made the decision to stay up for the day, but planned a late afternoon nap before getting ready for work. Her lunch was packed, the laundry was done and the house was clean. She did spend a couple of hours reading by her small fire place.

Katrina thought it was late enough to call Detective Howard. She didn't know if he ever worked late at night, so she wanted to be considerate just in case. She believed that most people with day jobs were at work by 9am, so this would have given him some time to settle in for the morning. She was using his business card as a book mark, so she went to the wall phone at the entrance of her kitchen area and dialed the numbers for his cell phone. She hoped it was still OK to call him on his cell, after all, he had told her several times in their past conversations to use that number.

His voice came on the line, "Detective Howard."

"Good morning, Detective Howard, this is Katrina Dempsey. Do you have a minute to chat?"

"Is Jane Doe awake now?" Detective Howard asked.

"I don't think so, I'm not at the hospital, I'm calling from home."

"Well to be honest with you, now is not the best time. There's another missing woman and I'm just releasing a task force focused on finding her."

"Oh, I'm so terribly sorry. I didn't mean to bother you, of course you have more important things to worry about."

"Ms. Dempsey, you obviously called for a reason, is it something you can tell me quickly and then perhaps we can chat more later?"

"Well, I," Katrina paused, "I just wanted to tell you that I was at the hospital early yesterday evening and I checked in on our Jane Doe, and she reached out to me and tried to speak."

"She spoke, but she isn't awake? What did she say, exactly?" Probed Detective Howard.

"She only said one word, she said 'hurry'. Does that mean anything to you?"

"I'm not sure, but I do appreciate you calling me. We'll talk more later. You'll be at the hospital tonight?"

"Yes, at 10pm."

"OK. Please call back immediately if she wakes up, or says or does anything else. And thank you again!"

The phone went dead and Katrina hung it back in the wall cradle. She looked at the phone and wondered why she didn't get rid of it. The only calls she ever got were sales people and sometimes her sister, but mostly she called the cell phone number as did all of her bunco friends. It was just an added expense.

Katrina wasn't sure if she felt better or not after speaking with Detective Howard. Oh well, she had done her duty. She decided to sit back down and read. Maybe if she got tired, she could take that nap.

Monday 9:42am

Steve re-read the first paragraph of the Department of Labor bulletin for the third time and let out a heavy sigh. He hadn't processed one word. He closed the email and flagged it so that he would be prompted to open it at a later time. The memory that had evaded him all morning was tugging at his brain and diverting it from processing any other information.

He leaned back in his chair and clasped his hand behind his head. He closed his eyes and took another deep breath. The office was quiet and his door was closed. He had to find a way to clear his mind and focus on work. He wondered what the actual process was for meditation. Weren't you supposed to focus on your breathing or something? He took another breath and slowly exhaled. He repeated this a few times.

He did start to feel a little better and began to relax. He breathed in again and caught the faint scent of lavender. He recalled the lavender bush that grew in the front yard of his grandmother's house. The image transformed to that of candle light illuminating thick auburn curls intertwined around his fingers, accompanied by eerie music floating out of the darkness.

He jerked straight up in his chair. That was it! He *had* dreamed last night. Somehow, even through the Ambien, he had dreamed something horrible that he could only remember in glimpses. He picked up his cell phone, found Sydny Samuels contact number and hit the dial icon. The phone rang several times and then went to voice mail. He waited for the instructions to leave a message and then began to speak. Just as he was identifying himself, he heard the call waiting tone. Upon inspection of his phone screen he saw that it was Sydny. Feeling relieved, he answered.

"Hello."

"Hello, Mr. Waters, I'm sorry I just missed your call, how are you doing?" Sydny asked.

"Thank you so much for calling me back. I know you have a busy schedule and I already have an appointment for later in the week, but I wondered if you might have some time today? I'm dreaming again and I can't even focus at work."

"I think I can find some time for you, I have an appointment coming up at 10 and then and I might be free after 2pm, but I'll have to check my schedule and get back to you when I know for sure."

"OK, I would really appreciate it." Steve sounded more sad than appreciative.

"Steve," Sydny responded, "You said you are dreaming *again*? Did the dreams stop and then start up again?"

"Yes, well actually I had an old Ambien prescription that I have been taking and I was going to ask if you can prescribe me a refill, but now even that isn't working very well."

"What do you mean?" Asked Sydny

"Well it was great for a couple of nights but then last night I had another dream. I can't really remember much, but a few pieces came through and it has been enough to keep me from focusing at work. That's why I called you."

"Can you tell me more?"

"I don't really remember *doing* anything, like in the other dreams, but there were pieces like a dark room and flashes of candlelight. And the smells, not a musty basement this time but lavender, which reminded me of my Grandmother's house. And the other thing that was different was the hair, this time it wasn't blond or dark, this time it was dark red and curly."

The line was quiet and Steve waited. "Ms. Samuels? Sydny?"

"I'm sorry! I dropped the phone." Sydny replied. "Um, I need to get ready for my appointment, but can I call you back as soon as I verify a time?"

"Yes, of course. I know you are busy, and I really do appreciate it. Thank you." Steve ended the call.

Monday 9:58am

Sydny fumbled with her phone trying to find Detective Howard's number. The adrenaline raced through her entire body causing her hands to shake. It couldn't be a coincidence! Dark red, curly hair and the smell of lavender! That was Shannon. She used a lavender shampoo and Sydny had asked her where she bought it at some point but she couldn't remember exactly when.

She found the number and looked at the time. Her appointment would be here any second, but she had to make this call. She initiated the call and then walked to the window to watch for her 10 O'clock. The mother and daughter were walking up the sidewalk to her outer door. Sydny turned toward her front door and Detective Howard answered his phone,

"Detective Howard."

"Detective Howard, please hold on for one second, it's important!" She opened her outer door and screen door to greet her appointment with the phone smashed against her stomach.

"Hello, I'm terribly sorry but can you please give me a moment to finish this call? I promise to be brief. You can sit here on the bench." She gestured the bench with her left hand and then went back inside the office-living room area and closed the inner door behind her.

"Detective Howard, thank you so much for holding. I have to tell you something very important and I don't know but I may be making a big mistake, one that could cost me my license, but then again I could lose my friend if I don't and..."

She was cut off by Detective Howard's voice,

"Ms. Samuels, Sydny, Sydny, I need you to calm down. Just tell me what's the matter."

Sydny took in a breath and then began.

"OK, I have another appointment but I need to tell you that Steve Waters called me this morning asking if he could see me today."

Derrick cut her off,

"And you are afraid to see him? I told you I would come and arrest him if he pushed you for another appointment."

"No," Sydny responded, "I mean, yes, I mean I wasn't worried about seeing him again because I really thought I made a mistake. I was going to call you today and tell you that, but now I'm not so sure. He asked to see me today because he is having dreams again.

Apparently, he stopped having dreams for a day or two and now he is having them again, well last night he had one again."

"Sydny, I don't understand, what is your concern?"

"He told me that last night he took a sleeping pill but still dreamed. He said he couldn't remember much, but he did remember the smell of lavender and dark red hair. Not blond hair! Not dark brown hair, *auburn, curly* hair!" Sydny's voice was rising as she specifically enunciated the words. "Shannon has *auburn, curly, hair* that smells of *lavender!"*

"Oh my god," Derrick said slowly. "OK, here is what you are going to do. You need to find some time on your calendar or free up a spot for him and call back to let him know the time. Then you are going to call me right back and tell me the time so I can be there in advance. I don't know what this guy's deal is, maybe he knows what he is doing and he is just toying with you, or maybe he has some kind of mental disorder and has no clue, but we are going to arrest him and figure out how to get him to tell us where Shannon is! Call him now and call me right back!"

"OK." Sydny ended the call, put the phone down and walked out to the foyer. "I am terribly sorry but I have to reschedule your time. A woman has been abducted and I may be able to help find her." Sydny pleaded with the mother, who she remembered to be Tina Blackwell.

Mrs. Blackwell looked concerned and responded,

"Why of course, don't even worry about it. Just call us and we can reschedule." The teenage daughter with the drug problem responded with an annoyed "Whatever!" and stomped out the front door. Mrs. Blackwell said,

"I'm sorry. You do what you need to do and I hope you find the woman safe and sound." And then she followed her daughter out the front door.

Sydny closed and locked the front door. She went immediately to the patio door off of the kitchen and made sure it was locked too. Then she went to her printed copy of today's schedule and checked for at time slot. After her 1 O'clock she was open the remainder of the day. She decided she would cancel the 1 O'clock as well and then tell Steve to come by at 2pm. That would give her time to check on Andrew and then come back and let Detective Howard in well before 2pm.

She found Steve's number and took several slow, deep breaths in an effort to calm her nerves and her voice. Not sure if it would work, she made the call to Steve. He picked up on the first ring,

"Hello?" He sounded hopeful.

"Hi, Mr. Waters," Sydny was amazed at how normal she sounded, "I just wanted to call and let you know I can see you at 2pm today if that works for you?" She held her breath and silently wished for him to take the time slot and not request something later.

"Great!" Steve responded and let out a sigh of relief. "Thank you so much, you're a life saver!" He sounded so appreciative and a sharp feeling of guilt went through Sydny.

"OK, I'll see you then." She ended the call and sank down in one of her large arm chairs. Sydny felt horrible. What had she done? But then she thought about Shannon and the idea of her body being found somewhere, lifeless and cut up, eased her conscious, and the guilt was replaced by fear.

Alex would be there at 11 and she wasn't going to cancel on him, but she did need to call her 1 O'clock appointment and hope it was enough advanced notice to catch...who? She picked up the schedule and looked, Theresa Bronson, enough time to catch Theresa Bronson before she left her home.

Monday 10:14am

Detective Howard hit the Bluetooth answer button in his car to take the call from Ms. Samuels. She let him know Steve Waters had confirmed for the 2pm appointment. Derrick informed her that he and another officer would be at her home at 1:30pm sharp to get set up.

As he ended the call, he felt bad, just a little, for putting Ms. Samuels in this situation. But he also felt a small surge of electricity go through him at the idea of finally catching the person he believed had been killing and dumping the bodies of young women for years.

It sickened him that no one missed these women as they were all likely run-aways or kids who grew up in the system. It was the very same reason that Jane Doe was sitting in the hospital with no one to identify her. This perpetrator had selected his victims wisely over the years and dumped the bodies very carefully in random places. His mistake had been abducting a local college girl and dumping her body in the park.

Derrick believed the perp had acted rashly after Jane Doe had escaped; not waiting and finding the next unknown victim but snatching another young girl within what? One or two days after Jane escaped? But then he wondered if the park wasn't a deliberate dumping sight. Was it meant to be a message to Jane if she was hiding out there somewhere in the world? Was it a way to scare her into silence?

And the horrific, million-dollar question now was, did he have Shannon Medford as his next victim? Had she gone snooping around somewhere and drawn attention to herself?

Derrick had his team canvassing the coffee shop, the park and the homes around the park, but if this serial killer lived in the area, he wasn't exactly going to open the door to a cop and say 'OK, ya caught me! I've got the girl locked away in my basement.'

And that was the one piece that didn't make sense, he knew where Mr. Waters lived, and he had only lived there for just over four months. Was it possible that Mr. Waters had a house somewhere and used the apartment as cover? Did he move from time to time in order to create some kind of alibi? But he had only worked at the law firm for that same amount of time. Derrick realize he had not checked into where Mr. Waters had come from and where he worked before. What if he was using a false identity? There were too many holes, but he felt strongly he would get his man this afternoon.

His thoughts were interrupted by another call. The screen and Bluetooth announced the call was from the station.

Monday 10:55am

Alex rang the doorbell and hoped he wasn't interrupting anything by arriving early, but Sydny opened the door and invited him in.

She had spent the past 40 minutes mentally preparing herself for his visit and trying to take her mind off of Shannon and Steve. She actually had felt a little nauseated but some peppermint tea had settled her stomach.

"Alex, have a seat. How are you doing?"

"Thank you. And thank you for making time for me today. I just don't think I could face work without getting this off of my chest."

"Well, that is what I'm here for, so I'll just let you do the talking."

Alex inhaled and blew out a deliberate breath as he rubbed his hands back and forth on his knees.

"OK. Well I guess I'll just tell you the dream as best I can." He breathed again and continued. "Well, I am in the ambulance with Jay, he's my paramedic partner, and he is driving, only he is driving like a crazy person. I try telling him to slow down but he says he can't hear me over the siren and then he tells me we have to hurry or it will be too late.

We drive into the park, and by the way, it's night time. We go into the park, from the south end, and Jay keeps driving like he is trying to win a race or something. He drives over that hill and I think for sure we are going to roll the ambulance but we don't. In fact, when I go flying around in my seat, it's like I'm floating and I don't slam into the dash or the door or anything.

But I hear something and that's when I realize there is a patient on our gurney in the back bay. It's the girl from the accident. I guess it all makes sense, right? The park, the ambulance, the patient we attended to just a week ago? I mean the dream was last night, Sunday, one week exactly."

Alex paused and looked at Sydny for reassurance of his theory.

"Yes, that could be it. Was that the end of the dream?"

"No, there's more. The girl is on the gurney, and she's strapped in but she is only wearing her under wear, like the night we were called to the accident. And Jay keeps driving like a mad man across the park toward Seventh east and he is swerving around trees and I am sure he is going to plow us into one.

And then the girl in the back sits up and she's bleeding from the cut across her stomach and she reaches out and points out the front window and says 'hurry'.

And then I look out the window and we are speeding across the street and into the yard of some old brick house on Seventh, and we are about to crash right into the house and I wake up screaming. And Victoria is shaking me to wake me up." He finished and looked at Sydny who was staring at him with a serious look of concern. Of course she was, it was a shitty nightmare.

Sydny felt more than concern for Alex and his nightmare as she pondered the reasons. On the one hand, it made sense for him to have the nightmare after what he had been through, but then again, he handled accidents all the time. But he had said things were different now that he had a serious girlfriend. And perhaps he had never handled a victim of a murder or sick predator before. But why the dreams now and not right after the accident? Maybe because it *was* one week later and his mind was processing through that.

"Ms. Samuels?" Alex asked as Sydny realized she had just been staring at him.

"I'm sorry. And please, call me Sydny."

"OK, Sydny, are you alright?"

"Yes, sorry, I was just thinking and I am sorry that you are having these dreams. It really is a scary situation that you came across and I'm sure you are still concerned, not knowing whether the girl is ok. You don't have any closure so you can't really put the whole thing to bed. And no one has been caught for doing that to her, so again, no closure.

"Ya, I guess that makes sense." Alex agreed.

"I do have a few questions though. Why do you think that the girl in your dreams told you to hurry?"

Alex tilted his head slightly to the right and looked at Sydny with furrowed brows.

"I'm not quite sure." He pondered some more. "Do you think another girl has been abducted? Jay and I found Laura Roundsley in the park, and she had the same cuts on her body, only her throat was slit and she was dead." Alex looked at Sydny and watched as her face turned completely ashen.

"Are you OK?"

Sydny shook her head, "No, I'm fine, I just have had a bit of a stomach bug today." She couldn't get the image of Shannon laying on the ground with her throat slit out of her head. She began to breath more quickly and her ears started to ring.

"Sydny, you're not OK, you look like you are in a state of shock." Alex stood up and grabbed Sydny's wrist and took her pulse. "You are hyperventilating. Is there a place where you can lay down?"

Sydny looked around and realized he was right. "I don't have a couch." She responded breathlessly.

"OK, I want you to lean forward and put your head down over your knees. Do you have tea towels in your kitchen?"

Sydny leaned forward and answered in a muffled tone, her head in her hands, "The first drawer on the left side."

Alex went to the kitchen and took a towel from the drawer, then he wet it in the sink and rung it out. He returned and placed the cool, wet towel across the back of Sydny's neck. Then he went around and sat on the coffee table in front of Sydny and felt her wrist again.

"Breath slowly, he gently commanded, "in through your nose and out through your mouth. He modeled the breathing for her so that she began to breath along with him.

"That's good." He coached her. He continued to feel her pulse and it began to slow.

After a couple of minutes, Sydny looked up and then sat back in her chair. She grabbed the wet towel before it could fall and brought it around and placed it over her eyes and forehead.

Alex got up and went back to the chair across from her. "Are you feeling any better?"

"Yes, thank you." Sydny removed the towel from her face. "I'm so sorry, I guess my stomach isn't done being upset today."

"Are you sure that's what it is? I'm mean, you really seemed to have a reaction to my dream, and even more so to my answer to your question." Alex leaned forward and looked at her with kind eyes.

Sydny looked at him for a minute and there was only silence in the room. Then she sat up straight in her chair and looked at Alex. She breathed in through her nose and slowly exhaled a couple more times and then said,

"There is another woman missing, and I know her, personally. I just pictured her in that awful state, as a victim..." She trailed off, being unable to say the awful things consuming her mind.

"I'm so sorry." Alex apologized. "Is there anything I can do?"

"No, you have been so kind and this is supposed to be *your* session. I appreciate you helping me though, I did kind of have a panic attack. Again, I am so sorry. I think you are right, though, the dream makes sense. Last night was one week from the date of the accident and your treatment of the victim. And like I said before, you haven't received closure, you don't know the state of the victim, and you are worried about future victims, which is made worse by the fact that you have someone special in your life and you don't ever want her to be the victim of any kind of accident or tragedy."

"Ya, you're right." Alex agreed. "The last time we spoke things seemed to get better for a while. Perhaps just talking about it today will help me get back on track."

"Will you call me if you have another dream or day time vision?"

"Sure, and will you lay down and rest for a bit? I bet your friend will be OK."

"Thank you. I'll lay down for a minute after I walk you out and lock the door." Sydny walked with Alex to the door and thanked him one more time. As she closed the door, she looked at her watch and saw that it was 11:52am. She owed a visit to Andrew and wanted to take him some lunch. He probably wasn't eating.

Monday 12:08pm

Andrew reined Molly and Murphy in by wrapping the leash around his hand several times as they came to Ninth south. The dogs were only half excited about the walk and Andrew thought it might be because they wanted to find their mom. He instructed the dogs to sit as he waited for the traffic to clear so they could cross the street into the park. He wondered if the police officers sent out to canvas the area this morning had found anything that would help bring his wife home. He was going crazy sitting in the living room, holding his cell phone and waiting for someone to call, so he had decided to take the dogs and go check out the park himself.

The street was clear so he told the dogs, "let's go" and they crossed into the northern entrance of the park. Molly and Murphy weaved back and forth in front of him on their duel leash, sniffing and exploring as they went along. He walked to the east, heading toward Seventh, and the area where Shannon had given CPR to the accident victim until the paramedics arrived.

His stomach lurched as he remembered her fear the other evening when she told him someone was following her around the block. Why hadn't he believed her? He stopped and sat down on the grass. Molly and Murphy came over to him and Molly comforted him with a wet kiss. Andrew wrapped an arm around each of the dogs and pulled them to him as the tears welled up in his eyes.

His cell phone rang and he jumped to his feet to get it out of his back pocket. The screen showed a familiar number but it wasn't programed into his phone. "Hello?" Andrew held his breath.

"Andrew, it's Sydny, I'm at your house, are you home?"

Andrew slumped back down onto the grass. "No, I'm just at the park with the dogs. I'll head that way now." His heart sank again.

"OK, I'll just wait in my car, unless you just want me to come back at another time?"

"No! Stay there, please." Andrew pleaded, "I'll be there in less than 5 minutes, don't leave!" Andrew ended the call and got back up. He encouraged the dogs, "Let's go home babies." The dogs reacted with excitement. No doubt they thought they would discover their mom at the house. If only that were true.

When they reached Ninth South, they had to wait for a police cruiser to pass before they could cross. The cruiser slowed at the corner and turned right along the east side of the park. He hoped it was one of the police officers on the task force Detective Howard had sent out in search of clues to find Shannon.

He and the dogs crossed the street and then ran the two and a half blocks back home. Normally the dogs would run out of steam as they neared the house, but they were fueled by both Andrew's energy and the idea of mom, whose very existence was tied to the house. Andrew opened the gate and could barely contain them as they ran through and toward the front door. He let go of their leash and they ran up to the door together. Only then did they look back for Andrew to open it for them.

Andrew was still at the gate, holding it for Sydny. He closed it behind her and turned as Sydny gave him a hug with one arm, the other holding a bag of take-out food. Andrew was surprised by the hug but realized that she was also upset by the fact that Shannon was missing. He hugged her back, very gently and then said, "Come on into the house."

Andrew had to ask the dogs to get back from the door several times in order to get close enough to unlock it. He opened it and both dogs tore into the house on their double leash jerking and tripping each other as they tried to go in search of their mom.

"Molly! Murphy! Come!" Andrew called and ran after them. He caught them in the entrance to the kitchen where he untangled and set them free of the leash. They continued to run back and forth throughout the house for another couple of minutes with Molly giving a quick bark every so often.

Andrew went back to the living room and found Sydny unpacking Mexican food on the small dining table that was in the back corner, against the wall separating Andrew's office from the living room.

Someday soon Shannon planned to rip out the walls of his office and open up one big space from the living room to the kitchen. They would remodel one of the rooms in the back to make a new office. A cold feeling seized his heart as he considered the fact that Shannon might never come home again.

"Andrew, are you OK? You face is completely white! You should sit down." Sydny stopped unpacking food and led Andrew to the couch. As he sat, Molly and Murphy climbed up on either side of him.

"I don't know what I'm going to do?" the tears welled up in Andrew's eyes again and he buried his face in Molly's neck.

Sydny went back to the food and gave Andrew a minute. Then she went over to the couch and pushed in next to Murphy. She considered carefully and cautiously before beginning,

"I think Detective Howard may have a very strong lead on how to find Shannon."

"What?" Andrew sat up straight and looked intently into her eyes with a pleading emotion so strong, it nearly made her cry too.

"I'm meeting him at my house at 1:30 and he should have his answer shortly after that. I'm so sorry I can't tell you more, but I need you not to give up hope." Sydny finished.

"Who? Why hasn't Detective Howard called me? How do you know? Why *your* house?" The questions shot out of Andrew. "Is it someone you know? Is it someone Shannon knows?"

Sydny put her hand on his and cut him off, "Andrew, I honestly cannot tell you anymore. I wish I could, but I'm not one hundred percent sure and neither is Detective Howard. I just wanted you to know that it isn't hopeless, that there is a possibility we could bring Shannon home today."

"I need to be there! I need to come with you!"

"Andrew, you need to be here in case something else happens. What if Shannon comes home and you aren't here?"

Andrew felt a burning sensation in his gut as he struggled with the idea of leaving and then not being here for Shannon.

"What am I supposed to do? I can't just sit here all day! I need to do something. I need to find her!"

"Andrew, I'm sorry. I think I made things worse by telling you when I only wanted to make things better." Sydny squeezed his hand and then looked at her watch. It was 12:37 and she had to get back home within the next half an hour.

"Will you sit with me and try to eat a couple of bites?"

"I'll sit with you but I'm not sure I can eat anything." They both moved to the table and the dogs stretched out on the couch overlapping each other in their typical fashion.

Sydny handed a drink across the table to Andrew, "It's Sprite, it shouldn't upset your stomach. When was the last time you ate?"

"Um," Andrew thought for a moment, "I guess the coffee and bagel I had yesterday morning."

"OK, so please, drink some Sprite and then take a few bites. Just so I know you have something in your system."

Andrew took a sip of the Sprite and then realized how thirsty he was. He drank half of it and then picked up a small bean burrito and took a bite. Sydny went to the kitchen and found a glass that she filled with water from the spigot in the refrigerator. She took it back out to him and set it down next to his Sprite.

"You must be dehydrated. Drink this water too, it'll make you feel better."

They both sat in silence picking at their food and sipping their drinks. Sydny also hadn't eaten or drank much. After some time, Sydny looked at her watch again and told Andrew she had to get home. She promised to call him as soon as she had any news and again pleaded with him to stay home and wait for Shannon. Andrew agreed and then walked her to the gate. The dogs milled about in the yard and she reassured him one more time and then got into her Land Rover and left.

Monday 1:25pm

Sydny parked in the back and walked around the side of the long building to the front. As she opened her door, she wondered why these town houses hadn't been designed with a regular back door instead of a sliding, patio door. That would be safer at night with residents parking in the back, they would be able to just enter their homes with a key and not have to walk around in the dark, to the front. She wondered if there was any way to convert her patio door to lock and open with a key. She made a mental note to look into it. She used to think this neighborhood was safe, but now she didn't think any neighborhood was safe.

She locked the outer door behind her and considered that she might not continue the practice of leaving the front door open for clients and allowing them to sit in the foyer while she finished with another client. She would have to put a 10-minute buffer in between appointments as she scheduled them in the future. Had she really just been so naive all of these years?

She put her purse and sweater upstairs and then came back down to wait for the detective. She just wanted this entire experience to be over. She still felt horribly conflicted; guilty for betraying Steve and hopeful at the idea that they could bring Shannon home today. Her thoughts were interrupted by the doorbell. She looked through the peephole to confirm before opening it.

Detective Howard had brought another uniformed officer with him. "Ms. Samuels, this is officer Barkley." They entered the foyer and the tall, mocha-skinned officer Barkley shook Sydny's hand. She led them into the living-office area and invited them to have a seat.

"Mr. Waters won't be here until just before two so tell me how you plan to do this, and let's get it over with quickly, please." Sydny sounded nervous. "Do you want a drink of water or anything while we wait?"

"Actually, Detective Howard replied, "This will take some time. We really need you to hold your normal session with Mr. Waters before we arrest him."

"But that is violating confidentiality!" Sydny replied.

"Ms. Samuels, you have already violated the confidentiality, legally, I might add, by informing me that you believe this man has committed a crime. And the risk we take by arresting him is that he either won't be willing or able to give us more information regarding Mrs. Medford's where-abouts. We need to hear everything he has to say in the hopes of finding her as quickly as possible." Derrick looked at Sydny.

"I," Sydny wanted to argue but really understood the logic, "I'm not sure. What if I can't pull it off? What if he thinks something is wrong?"

"Then we will intervene. We just need to figure out where you want us and get set up. I parked out back and officer Barkley rode with me so there is no police vehicle on the street, and my unmarked car should just blend in. Is there a place upstairs that we can sit while you hold the session?"

"You won't be able to hear me upstairs." Sydny stated with concern.

"We have a microphone that we will place here in this room and then we can listen via headsets from upstairs. At the first sign of anything wrong we'll come down. Will that make you feel better?"

"Well, I guess, can I leave the hallway door open?"

"Yes, that's fine, just show us upstairs so we can get settled so we don't make any noise. It's 1:40 and I think we are about out of prep time."

Sydny watched as Detective Howard placed a small, wireless microphone between 2 books on the wall book shelf. Then she led them up the stairs to the landing area office. She indicated her office chair and then went in to the spare bedroom and brought a small vanity chair out into the hall.

"What if he asks to use the restroom?" Sydny asked with a start.

"If it comes to that, just let him come up and we will arrest him. No matter what, we are arresting him, the best-case scenario is getting some extra information out of him. The worst-case scenario is just arresting him, either way it is a good thing."

"OK. Do you want some water or anything?"

"No, we will be fine. Please go downstairs and take a minute to catch your breath."

As Sydny walked past the two officers to descend the stairs, officer Barkley put his hand on her shoulder and told her, "You're going to do just fine."

Monday 1:58pm

Steve parked next to the line of trees and bushes buffering the beautiful town houses from the street. They were losing more leaves and the roses that had bloomed during the last warm spell were dying and dropping withered petals to mix with the orange and brown leaves on the sidewalk. He imagined how lush they would look in the spring and summer. For a moment, he felt peaceful, but then he remembered why he was here. He actually felt guilty for subjecting Ms. Samuels to his disgusting night mares. Was he the only one? Or were there others who shared equally nasty problems with her? She was a saint for working in this profession.

Steve reached the door and tried the handle. It was locked so he rang the bell. Maybe she had just come back from lunch and hadn't had time to unlock the door yet. He waited patiently until she opened the door and stood in the foyer looking at him. "Thank you again for seeing me today. I don't think I can thank you enough."

Sydny stared for a second and then self-consciously said, "Oh, you're fine. Please, come in." She indicated the sitting area and allowed him to enter the room first. She did not want him to be walking behind her.

Steve walked through the foyer to one of the big chairs triangulated around the coffee table. As he sat down, he remembered the woman from the accident had also been here. Perhaps she was also seeing Ms. Samuels. He wondered if she was wracked by nightmares too. "You know, I saw the other woman who helped with the accident yesterday.

"You saw her? What time was that" Sydny asked too eagerly and hoped she didn't spook Steve.

"Yes, it was sometime shortly before noon. I went out for a late breakfast and then grocery shopping. Like I said, I actually got some sleep for a couple of nights, and I took advantage by sleeping in yesterday."

Sydny wondered if he was toying with her and probed deeper. "Where did you see her?"

She was crossing the street from the park on Seventh East. I would guess that she lives in that area east of the park and probably walks her dogs there a lot." Steve breathed in, "You know, I really don't mean to pry, but I realize I saw her here once too. Is she having nightmares like me?"

Sydny sat back in her chair and considered for a moment. She wondered if Detective Howard and officer Barkley were hearing all of this upstairs.

"I'm sorry, I know you can't ask you things like that." Steve said genuinely apologetic. "I guess it would be nice to know I'm not the only freak who has been impacted in such a crazy way by this accident." He looked down at his shoes.

Sydny felt bad for him for a moment. Was he a sociopath? Was he good at playing this game with her? She wasn't a hundred percent convinced yet.

"Well, I guess I should tell you about my latest dream, or remnants of a dream so you can tell me I going to be fine, *eventually* and that I just need to be patient."

"Yes, please do." Sydny clasped her nervous hands in her lap so he couldn't see them shaking.

"This morning, I woke up and I was dog-tired. I took my last Ambien last night and I know I slept because my alarm drug me out of what felt like a deep sleep. Only I wasn't refreshed at all like the other mornings." He looked at Sydny and she just nodded.

"Well I did my usual morning coffee, shower, etc. and left for work. As I was driving, I was using the seek function to find a good radio station. One of the stations hit on some old music that reminded me of some old memory but I couldn't place it. I tried turning the music off and still couldn't get it.

Then later, when I was at work, I couldn't concentrate so I tried to close my eyes and just focus on my breathing. That's when the memory of the dream came flooding back. I could literally *smell* the scent of lavender and it reminded me of my grandmother's lavender bush that grew in her front yard. Then I remembered the candle light and the dark curly hair. It was dark reddish brown, you know, um what's that called?"

"Auburn." The word came as more of a whisper from Sydny and Steve stopped and looked at her.

"Oh my god." Steve responded in a whisper softer than Sydny's.

Sydny looked toward the open door leading to the foyer and watched for the detective and police officer to come charging into the room. They didn't. She looked over toward the book shelf and wondered if the microphone was working. She looked back at Steve and knew he could read the terror in her face.

"Sydny," he said this with real concern and she thought it was strange for him to revert to her first name now.

"That woman is one of your clients." Steve looked intently across at Sydny. "Is she missing?" Steve shook his head, "No, no, no, no!" Each rendition getting louder, "Oh my god! You don't think it was me, do you?" Steve leaned forward in his seat and reached out to her but she pushed back practically becoming part of the chair.

Just then he heard footsteps barreling down the stairs and into the room. Steve turned and saw two men with guns pointed in his direction. He recognized Detective Howard as the man who had come to his office to interview him about the accident. The other officer was wearing a uniform and he spoke, "Ms. Samuels, please move to the kitchen."

Sydny jumped up and backed out of the room with a horrible look of both fear and guilt on her face.

"I didn't do anything!" Steve pleaded as Detective Howard ordered him to stand and then the uniformed officer placed not hand cuffs, but a large white plastic zip tie around his wrists, after wrenching his arms behind his back. Steve's head was spinning with a hundred different thoughts. How could she think he had done anything like this? How could she betray him? Was the other woman really missing? How could he be dreaming about something he had nothing to do with? He had dreamed of a dark-haired girl and then the missing college girl from the TV had been found in the park, *dead*. And now he was dreaming of someone with curly, auburn hair. The woman who helped him give CPR to the girl he hit had auburn hair! And he had admitted he had seen her near the park on Sunday.

"I didn't do it, Sydny! Is she really missing? The red head, is she missing? I swear, I didn't do anything!"

"Steve Waters, you are under arrest. You have the right to remain silent. Anything you say can and will be used against you in a court of law. You have the right to an attorney. If you cannot afford an attorney, one will be provided for you. Do you understand the rights I have just read to you? With these rights in mind, do you wish speak to me?" The tall, dark officer recited his well-practiced line.

"I didn't do it! Please, you have to believe me." No one was listening to him as the uniformed officer placed his gun back in his holster, placed on hand on Steve's elbow, led him out of the town house and into the back seat of a police cruiser that pulled up just in time. How had this happened to him?

Monday 2:40pm

Detective Howard led Sydny to one of the big chairs in her front room and gently pushed her to sit down. She put her head in her hands again like Alex had instructed her to do earlier in the day. Then she practiced the breathing exercise he had taught her; in through the nose and out slowly through the mouth. This helped and after a minute she sat up and looked at Detective Howard sitting across from her.

"I'm not sure I did the right thing today." She searched the detective's eyes for confirmation. "What if he didn't do it? He doesn't seem like he is aware he has done anything? What if he can't tell you anything? What if we are *wrong*?"

Derrick did his best to sooth her,

"It has to be him. How could he dream about each of the victims? The first victim is blond and sitting in the hospital after he ran her down. The second was brunette and she happened to turn up dead in the very same park where Jane Doe appeared to be headed when she was run down. And now Mrs. Medford is missing and she has auburn, curly hair, and according to your statement, she uses lavender shampoo.

There is no way this is all a coincident. Plus, we have footage of him leaving the grocery store on Saturday a week ago. And not long after he leaves the store, the Jane Doe laying in the hospital right now, the girl Steve Waters hit with his SUV, walks out of the very same grocery store."

Sydny's fear for Shannon came back stronger than ever and her entire body shuddered. She was almost convinced and then she remembered Alex. "What if I tell you that one other person who was also at the accident scene is having nightmares too?"

"What do you mean? You think he has an accomplice?"

"No, I mean someone else is also suffering from post-traumatic stress manifested by daytime hallucinations and night mares."

"Can you tell me? Would that be violating your oath of confidentiality? Or would it also fall under the duty to report a potential crime?"

"Hell, at this point I don't even care!" Sydny responded. "I won't tell you his name right now, but he was one of the Paramedics that responded to the accident. He's had several episodes of what you might call day mares. He imagined the same types of cuts on other patients he treated and even on his girlfriend, who recently moved in with him."

"That sounds more like regular post-traumatic stress." Derrick responded.

"Yes, but then he called this morning and asked if he could see me because last night he had a nightmare for the first time. It could have been because it was Sunday and one week after the accident, but then again, maybe not. Anyway, he dreamed he was in his ambulance with his partner and they were driving the Jane Doe patient through the park. His partner was driving like crazy and told him they had to hurry before it was too late and then Jane Doe sat up and pointed at the house they were about to crash into on Seventh, just east of the park. She also told him to hurry."

Derrick looked at her and tilted his head to one side, "The patient, the Jane Doe victim told him to hurry?"

"Yes. According to him, she sat up, pointed out the window and said 'hurry'. That's when he realized they were about to crash into some old house and then his girlfriend woke him up."

"Again, that sounds more like his dreams are limited to his own experiences. Nothing about Laura Roundsley or Shannon Medford." Derrick wanted to reassure her and get back to the station and question Steve Waters. He also wanted to call Katrina Dempsey back and ask her to tell him the story about Jane Doe waking up and speaking to her last night.

"Sydny, I really need to get to the station and question Mr. Waters so we can get Shannon back home to her husband safely. Are you going to be alright here? Do you want me to send an officer by to check on you later?"

"No, I'm going to be fine. Plus, I promised Andrew I would go by and check on him again. Can I tell him that you have arrested someone? That might help him to feel better."

"Yes, that will be fine, and I will head over there as soon as I have anything new to tell him." Derrick stood and Sydny stood too. They walked to the door where Derrick clasped her right hand with both of his and told her everything would be fine and to lock the door behind him.

Monday 3:08pm

Sydny checked her cell phone and saw that she had five missed calls from Andrew. She dialed him back and let him know she had some information for him but would rather tell him in person. She grabbed her purse and a leather jacket from upstairs in case she didn't make it back home before it really cooled off this evening. She locked up and walked around to her Land Rover parked in back. She almost felt stupid driving around the block she could so easily walk, but she also found herself realizing again that the neighborhood no longer felt safe.

Sydny pulled out of the driveway and headed left toward Sixth South. With two right turns she was on Sixth East. Half way down the block she pulled to a stop in front of the red, brick Victorian that Shannon shared with Andrew. He was already standing in the yard with the dogs anticipating her arrival. Both dogs came excitedly to the fence as Sydny approached. Molly stood on her hind legs and put both of her big paws on the fence and reached out to attempt a kiss. Sydny patted her on the head as Andrew opened the gate.

They all went inside and settled; Andrew took the big chair so he had a view of the street out front through the picture window, and Sydny sat on one end of the couch. Molly jumped up beside her and placed her paws and head on Sydny's lap. Murphy curled into a peculiarly small ball for such a large dog on the other end of the couch. As Sydny scratched Molly's head Andrew broke the silence,

"I can't handle this! What's going on?"

"Well, Detective Howard said I could fill you in and he will be on his way over in a bit to give us more information."

"What?!?" Andrew was on the edge of his seat and Sydny could only imagine how tortured he felt. She was feeling somewhat tortured herself.

"OK." She stated calmly and drew in a breath, "I have been counseling a client suffering from some post-traumatic stress and each time I have met with this person, he has had a slightly different bad dream that seems related to the initial event causing the stress."

"What are you talking about? I don't understand what this has to do with Shannon and how to find her!" Andrew was frustrated and losing hope. Sydny didn't want him to lose hope.

"OK, the short version. Steve Waters was the man who hit the girl running across the street, the girl that Shannon performed CPR on after the accident that Sunday evening." Andrew watched her with confusion while Sydny continued.

"First, he dreamed of a blond girl in a basement, the girl he hit who is now in the hospital. Then he dreamed of a brunette girl and I thought it was just because he had seen pictures of Laura Roundsley on the news. And now he came today and told me he dreamed of the dark basement again." She paused and Steve looked ready to lunge at her from across the room. "He dreamed of a girl with auburn hair," she paused, "that smelled of Lavender." Sydny stopped and looked down at her hands.

"Shannon?" He asked. "You think he is the man who has been hurting these women and you think *he* has Shannon?" Andrews eyes were wild.

"Detective Howard thinks it is too much of a coincidence and that perhaps he has just been toying with me this entire time. Or maybe even that he has some kind of mental disorder and doesn't actually realize he isn't dreaming, but actually committing these terrible acts."

"He thinks he's dreaming of killing women?" Andrew's voice came louder now. "What do you think?"

Sydny looked across at Andrew and chose her words carefully. "I am not a hundred percent convinced either way. It's obvious that he would dream about the first victim since he hit her as she ran across the street. And if he saw Laura Roundsley on the news, he could have easily swapped out her face for the first girl's. And he did go through the traumatic event of hitting *and* helping the accident victim *with* Shannon, so he would know her face too. And I could argue that having seen the cuts on the girl's body would trigger his dreams of abducting and torturing the girl in some dark musty basement somewhere. And many of the houses in this area have..."

Andrew cut her off, "What? He dreamed of torturing the girl in a basement?"

"Yes, but don't think about that. Detective Howard thinks he can get Steve to tell him where he has taken Shannon. You need to concentrate on that."

"Sydny, did Shannon ever tell you about her dreams?" Andrew was angry now.

"She told me that she dreamed about the girl from the accident, that she *was* the girl from the accident; essentially dreaming through the girl's eyes. She figured out that in the dream she was in some old basement and she had cuts on her arms and legs like the victim she helped that day."

"Right," Andrew confirmed, "and she dreamed she was strapped to a metal table, like the kind they use to do autopsies and that she got one hand lose so she was able to escape."

"A metal autopsy table? With straps?" Sydny looked at Andrew. "That's exactly the same way Mr. Waters described it. And candle light, did Shannon mention candle light?"

"No, in her dream it was always dark except the light she could see coming in under a door at the top of the stairs."

"Andrew, it doesn't make sense for both of them to dream the same thing. Yes, it makes sense if Steve Waters is actually the one abducting and torturing women, but how would Shannon have dreamed so many similar details?"

They both sat in silence, staring across the room at each other. The dogs could sense the tension in the air. Molly whined and looked up at Sydny.

"Andrew," Sydny broke the silence, "on Sunday, Shannon said she dreamed of escaping the house in her dreams and that she wanted to go look for the street from her dream so she could prove to herself it wasn't real."

"And you think Steve Waters saw her nosing around and abducted her?"

"Maybe, maybe not. He did tell me today that he saw her crossing Seventh, heading east and he thought she likely lived in that neighborhood. But can I tell you one more thing?" Andrew nodded. "There is another young man who attended to the girl in the hospital. He's a paramedic and he has been seeing me as well for PTSD." Andrew looked at her and didn't say anything. He wanted Sydny to continue.

"Well he told me he had a dream last night about the girl from the accident being in his ambulance and she sat up and pointed and said 'hurry', and just then he looked out the window and the ambulance was about to crash into a house on Seventh East."

"Is it possible that these people are all having dreams about this same thing?" Andrew asked and almost sounded hopeful.

"Well of course, I mean, they all experienced the same traumatic event. But on the other hand, they all are experiencing details that are shared, but not from the actual accident itself." Sydny was beginning to share the hopeful vibe filling the room. Even the dogs perked up their ears, like they'd heard someone offer a treat far off in the distance.

Monday 5:15pm

Derrick was on his way from the station house to the home of Andrew and Shannon Medford. Steve Waters had given up nothing. He seemed genuinely confused as to why he had been arrested, and to make matters worse, he worked for an attorney firm and lawyered up instantly. His lawyer was trying to convince some judge he knew to arrange for a quick bail hearing and get Steve in front of a night court judge if possible.

Derrick tried the house phone of Katrina Dempsey one more time and once again got her voice mail. Perhaps she was running errands. Perhaps she was sleeping before her night shift. Perhaps she had gone to work early. He wished he had her cell phone number. He would check with the hospital after meeting with Andrew Medford. He knew it was only a coincident, but he wanted to confirm the story again about Jane Doe reaching out and saying, 'hurry' from her hospital bed.

It still made him feel creepy knowing that the paramedic had dreamed a similar thing. It was probably just the fact that he knew their time was limited and whether Steve Waters was the serial killer and had left Shannon Medford to bleed out, or worse, he wasn't, and some other perp had her right now; torturing her right now, things were likely not to end well if they didn't find her soon.

He pulled up behind Sydny Samuels vehicle and parked. It made sense that she was here, and probably for the best that she was comforting Mr. Medford, and *not* home alone.

As he approached the gate, Andrew came out of the house, *sans* dogs. That made things easier. He reached over and unhooked the carabiner and unlatched the gate, walked through and closed everything up again. "Good evening, Mr. Medford." He shook Andrew's hand.

"Andrew, Detective Howard, call me Andrew."

"OK and then it's Derrick for me."

"Sure, come on in and *please* tell me have some good news."

Inside the house, Andrew gestured to the couch where Sydny was sitting as he took a seat in the single over-stuffed chair that matched the couch. Derrick shook Sydny's hand and again clasped it with both of his and thanked her for her participation this afternoon.

"You were great!" Then he sat at the opposite end of her on the couch. He could hear one of the dogs barking in the room across the front foyer. Andrew sent a serious order to stop and the dog did.

"Sorry." Andrew stated. "Please, have you located Shannon? Do you at least have an idea of where she is?"

"We have a man in custody that we believe is responsible for the disappearance of your wife and ..."

"I know all that." Andrew interrupted. "Sydny has explained all of that to me, but how do you know you have the right guy?"

"Mr. Medford, I just don't believe in the coincidences that tie Mr. Water's dreams to the reality of each of our victims, and to your wife. I know it's difficult to hear and certainly scary, but the simplest explanation is usually the right one."

"But what about the dreams? How do you explain that?" Andrew's frustration was coming through again.

"All of his dreams are based on facts about his victims, including hair color." Derrick felt bad making this statement.

"No," Andrew shot back, "How do you explain my wife and this man, Steve, having basically the same dream?"

Derrick looked from Andrew to Sydny,

"I'm afraid I don't understand." He said looking to Sydny for an explanation. "I wasn't aware that Mrs. Medford was having dreams. Were you also counseling her?"

"No," Sydny filled in the blanks, "We're friends, we have coffee from time to time. I first met Shannon walking her dogs on my street. We just sort of got close after that. She had mentioned the dreams to me before, but not in a lot of detail.

I did spend some time considering what I knew of her dreams and the vague similarities to Steve's, but everything made logical sense based on the trauma they had both experienced." She looked at Andrew, "But today as Andrew and I have been talking, we realized there were more than vague similarities."

"And what about the paramedic who responded with the ambulance? Andrew broke in, "He dreamed about the girl in the hospital too. The girl in his dream told him to hurry. What if it's a clue or something and we need to figure this out right now! Shannon's been missing for over twenty-four hours and doesn't that make it statistically worse?" Andrew was getting more frustrated by the minute.

Derrick sat and pondered whether to mention the one thing that was nagging him in the back of his mind. He looked from Sydny to Andrew again, and one of the dogs gave a quick bark and a growl from the other room. He imagined they could sense Andrew's anxiety, and Andrew sent the order to stop barking again, never taking his eyes off of Derrick.

"I want to share something with you both, but you must promise me you will listen and not jump to any conclusions." Both Sydny and Andrew nodded and waited. Derrick remained quiet for a few seconds longer and then started.

"The young lady that was hit, pedestrian verses vehicle, by Steve Waters is in a coma under the name of Jane Doe. She is likely a run-away, which makes sense. I think this perpetrator has been at it for several years, only abducting women that no one will miss.

I think that when this girl, Jane Doe, escaped, he panicked and abducted a local college girl. Off the record, we all know that girl was Laura Roundsley. We don't have any evidence supporting the idea that your wife, Shannon, was taken by the same man, other than Steve Water's dream, which is loose at best.

The Auburn hair and lavender scent could really be any number of different women. However, I do admit that I feel better knowing Mr. Waters is currently in police custody. But Andrew, you are right, the more time that goes by, the worse the odds are of finding her. I'm not trying to upset you, but I need to be honest."

"I understand all of that, but why would we jump to conclusions? We already know most of that."

"You're right. So here is the piece I want you to be careful with. Jane Doe has been under the care of a night nurse at the hospital. I'm not comfortable disclosing her name now, but I've obviously been in close communication with her *and* the hospital staff because I want to know the minute Jane Doe is awake. If I can question her, it is much more likely that I can catch this perpetrator."

"I still don't see anything to jump to conclusions about." Andrew impatiently butt in.

"You will." Started Derrick again, "The nurse has reported to me that on two separate occasions, Jane Doe has spoken. And let me clarify, she isn't awake yet, that I know of. I was trying to reach this nurse on my way here. You see, I wanted to clarify the specifics regarding the second time she witnessed Jane Doe speaking, which was last night."

Andrew was already on the edge of his seat, and Sydny now leaned closer to Derrick sitting opposite her on the couch.

"The nurse was not on duty, but was at the hospital last night retrieving some personal item she had left and she decided to checked on Jane. She told me today that last night, Jane Doe lifted her arm and reached toward her and said one word. That word was 'hurry'.

"Hurry? She said hurry? The same as the paramedic in his dream? But she said it? She actually said it? This nurse didn't dream it?" Andrew fired the questions at Derrick. "But she isn't awake? Has anyone tried talking to her? Are you sure she isn't awake?"

"Andrew, I need you to take a breath. If Jane Doe awakens, the hospital will call me immediately. They know how important it is. And yes, I do think it's strange that your wife and Steve Waters were having similar dreams, just like I think it is strange that the paramedic and the nurse on night duty basically dreamed and experienced the same event as well."

"What are we going to do with this information?" asked Sydny.

"Well, *I* am going over to the hospital as soon as we are finished here and see what more I can find out. I'm hoping to confirm the information provided by the nurse." Derrick stopped and thought for a moment and then resumed, "Sydny, can you help me get in touch with your paramedic client? I would really like to hear his account of his dream."

"Absolutely. Will you call us as soon as you talk to the nurse and to Alex?" She turned to Andrew, "Can I stay here with you until then?"

Both men answered in stereo, "Yes, of course." Sydny pulled her cell phone from her purse and scrolled through her contacts. "I'm texting you the contact file now."

Derrick saved the contact to his phone, walked over and placed his hand on Andrew's shoulder,

"Hang in there, I need you to be strong for your wife's sake." And with that, he left.

Monday 5:26pm

Alex had been playing HORSE with Jay and a couple of the other guys when the alarm had sounded. They were all well trained and each had gotten into their own appropriate gear and vehicles within less than two minutes. Alex had insisted that Jay drive, not feeling comfortable behind the wheel; still a bit shaken by his dream.

The call was for a house fire just north of the downtown area. The houses were old and made mostly of brick, so the chances of saving the structure were pretty good, but if there was still old insulation in the house, that was actually a bad thing. According to the call details, the neighbors had called when they noticed the smoke coming from the garage. They didn't think the house was on fire yet, but there was an elderly couple living in the home. The neighbor had knocked but no one had answered.

Jay pulled the ambulance up parallel to the fire truck on the opposite side of the street. The ambulance was never to block access to the home in case another fire truck was needed. The flames had engulfed the garage and smoke was coming from the left side of the home where it attached to the garage. Small flames were playing at the front room window.

Two of the firemen were busy uncoiling the hose from its internal storage while others suited up for entry of the home. Another triggered the water supply by connecting to the fire hydrant on the street just left of the small brick house. The hose had to be manned by two firemen in order to control the brute force of it and as they aimed it at the house, the front window exploded, pummeling the house and the interior.

The two assigned for rescue kicked the front door open and proceeded inside wearing full respirators. After only thirty seconds, the first fireman came out with an elderly man at his side. He looked like some kind of rag doll tied to the fireman's side, half walking, half dragging with most of his weight being carried by his rescuer. Just as the fireman was placing the gentleman on one of the two blankets laid out by Jay and Alex, his teammate exited the house with a tiny, elderly woman in his arms. She was placed onto the other blanket. Alex and Jay began their first aid routine consisting of oxygen mask, IV, checking pupils and pulse, and asking a set of routine questions to determine level of consciousness and state of mind.

Having been given the couple's name by the dispatcher, Alex spoke gently to the woman, "Mrs. Peterson, do you know what day it is?"

A cough from under the oxygen mask was followed by a feeble, raspy voice, "Monday".

"Great, can you tell me your address?" Alex followed up. This was met by a coughing spell and then Mrs. Peterson closed her eyes. Her body became limp and the wrist Alex was gently gripping to measure her pulse became dead weight. Alex switched to the pulse in her neck, which was thready and weak. He positioned his stethoscope on the woman's chest to confirm and then pushed a dose of epinephrine into her IV line to prevent cardiogenic shock. Continuing to call her name, Alex rubbed his knuckles heavily on Mrs. Peterson's sternum to test for consciousness. He paused when she lifted her arm and clasped her hand on his shoulder and said,

"Hurry, you must hurry." The she opened her eyes and dropped her arm back to her side.

"Mrs. Peterson, we have already gotten your husband out of the house. Is there someone else in the house?"

"Ralph!" Mrs. Peterson croaked out with a level of fear.

"He is right here, next to us, right behind me." And Alex leaned to one side so that Mrs. Peterson could peek around him and see her husband.

"Mrs. Peterson, is there anyone else in the house?" Alex prodded her sternly.

"No, just us." She said looking up into his blue eyes.

"OK, just confirming, you asked me to hurry, so I thought perhaps there was still another person in the house. Or perhaps you just didn't realize your husband was already out here with us."

"Did I?" She asked and looked somewhat confused.

"Don't worry, Mrs. Peterson, the other ambulance just got here and we will be taking both of you to the hospital now."

Monday 6:10pm

Once in his car, Derrick commanded his Bluetooth to call Katrina Dempsey. The call connected through to her home number and rang until the voice mail picked up. He didn't bother with another message, but instead redirected his Bluetooth to call the hospital number, which was also programmed in to his phone. A young woman answered the main, switchboard number and asked how she could direct his call. He identified himself and asked for the nurse's station in the women's ward. The call was answered after only two rings and the nurse on duty only confirmed that Nurse Dempsey was not on shift. It was against hospital policy to give out employee or patient information by phone, and Derrick knew this so he thanked her and hung up. He would just drive over to the hospital and have them call Ms. Dempsey on her cell. In person, he could demonstrate he was acting in an official police capacity.

Derrick gave another command to his Bluetooth system, this time to call the recently saved contact for Alex Jones. He wondered if Alex could even take a personal call while on duty with the Fire Department. There was no answer so he left a message identifying himself and stating that he had a few questions regarding an accident he had responded to just over a week ago. Derrick indicated the critical nature of his call and requested a call back as soon as possible. He figured this would give Mr. Jones permission to make a personal call while on duty because it really wasn't a personal call at all.

Soon Derick was pulling into the visitor parking at the hospital. He found an open spot and parked just as his phone rang. The caller ID and the Bluetooth announced that it was Alex Jones. Perfect, he thought and hit the green phone button on his steering wheel to answer the call.

"Detective Howard." He stated

"Hello, Detective Howard, this is Alex Jones returning your call."

"Thank you for calling me back so quickly. I wasn't sure if you were even able to take a call while on shift."

"Well, I'm really not supposed to take personal calls when I'm on a run, but I didn't recognize the number and I wanted to make sure it wasn't an emergency, you know, my girlfriend, or something like that. Anyway, I checked the message and I am just riding in the ambulance with my partner. My patient is stable and I figured I'd call you back really quickly."

"Well thank you, again. Perhaps you can call me back when you have a minute. I actually wanted to speak to you specifically about a dream you recently had. I know it sounds strange, and I want you to know that Ms. Samuels only disclosed it to me because she is helping me with a missing person's case and your dream seems to tie in with some other important information. I apologize for any breach of confidentiality."

"My dream? Oh, I don't mind." He paused and the dream came back to him; ..."*Hurry*." And then as he looked at Mrs. Peterson and remembered her words, "*Hurry, you must hurry*." Alex realized he was still on the phone, "Yes, I'll call you back. I'll be at the hospital in the next ten minutes so give me about twenty total."

"I'm actually at the hospital now and I'll be in the Women's ward if you want to come and find me there."

"OK, sounds good."

Derrick ended the call and switched off his engine. He hit the button on the key fob and the horn announced loudly that the vehicle was secure as he ran over to the entrance of the hospital. He knew his way around this hospital like any employee would; too many times, his line of work had brought him here. He caught the elevator to the third floor and proceeded to the nurse's station where he pulled out his badge and introduced himself.

"How are you this evening?" He looked at the badge pinned to her pink scrubs to find her name embossed there as Tammy.

"I'm fine Detective Howard, how can I help you?"

"I actually hoping you can help me track down a co-worker of yours, Katrina Dempsey. I know she will be on shift later tonight as she indicated this to me earlier today. But I've called her house several times without any luck. I thought perhaps she might have come to the hospital early, or she might be running errands. You do have her cell phone on file, right?"

"She is likely just sleeping before her shift, but I can give her cell a try." As Tammy consulted a phone list and then dialed a number on the desk phone she added, "You're right, she will be in later this evening, so you might have to come back then."

Apparently, someone answered because Tammy responded, "Katrina, there is a Detective Howard here at the hospital hoping to speak with you. Do you have a minute to talk to him?" Tammy listened and nodded. "OK, I'll let him know." And then she placed the hand set back into the receiver.

Derrick was about to express his frustration at not being handed the phone when Tammy looked at him with a bit of surprise and stated, "She's here, in the hospital. She's in the cafeteria reading and waiting for her shift to start. She said to tell you she will be right up."

"Great." Derrick responded, and released the pent-up frustration he was about to unload on Tammy.

"You can have a seat in one of the chairs over there while you wait. Can I get you a Pepsi or 7up?"

"A Pepsi would be great, I think it's going to be a long night." Derrick walked over to the small waiting area and sat in one of the four chairs. He figured most patients had their visitors sit in their rooms, and very few waited outside at the nurse's station. As he sat, he peeked down to the end of the hall and could see the officer on duty, so he got back up and headed in that direction. Passing the nurse's station, Tammy handed him the small Pepsi she had gotten from the kitchenette area.

Derrick approached the officer who looked up from his cell phone. "Excuse me, sir, but this area is off limits." He immediately changed his tone after noticing the badge Derrick had on display. "Oh, Detective Howard, you're the one in charge of this case, right?"

"Yes, I am, and thank you for doing your job so diligently. I really appreciate it."

"Thanks." The young officer with bright orange hair and a face full of freckles turned beet red."

"Is the patient still unconscious?"

"Yes sir. No change, I would immediately call you. I have your number." He shot the statements at Derrick like bullets, each one intended to demonstrate he was a dutiful officer who would never let a detective down.

"OK, thank you. You're doing a great job." Derrick tried to calm the guy down. "This is important work and I really appreciate you being here for the victim." The officer relaxed in his seat. "I'm just here to speak with one of the nurses tonight, so if you notice or hear anything, give a shout to nurse at the station." Derrick stepped around the officer and looked into the room. Dusk was coming on and the room was barely lit by the waning light from outside. Everything was quiet.

He turned and went back to the seating area where he was greeted by Katrina. "Detective Howard. What brings you here tonight?"

"Derrick." He corrected. "Thank you for speaking with me. I hope I wasn't interrupting anything?"

"Oh no, I just couldn't sleep, last night or this afternoon, so I decided to come to the hospital, check on our Jane, and then read a book. I was having a coffee as well, because it will be a long night."

"I agree." He confirmed. "Ms. Dempsey, Katrina, is there a place that we can chat for a few minutes?"

"Yes, over here, we have a small physician's room."

As they both turned the elevator indicated its arrival and the doors opened for Alex Jones to step out. "Are you Detective Howard?"

Derrick stopped and took in the young man with sandy blond hair and blue eyes, dressed in the uniform of a paramedic. "Yes, and you must be Alex Jones."

"I am, is this a good time? My partner is downstairs having a coffee break, but I can try to meet you another time." Alex was very cooperative.

"No, please, Alex, this is the perfect time. I would actually like to speak with both of you, if that's OK with you, Katrina?"

"Yes, anything we can do to help that poor girl. Right here." She gestured to the room.

"Can I ask you a favor?" Derrick turned to Katrina, "Would you be willing to wait for just a minute so I can ask Alex a few questions?"

"Of course, I can wait at the nurse's station. Take your time, I'm not going anywhere."

"Thank you." Derrick and Alex entered the physician's room with Derrick closing the door behind him. The room was small and plain with a simple desk, chair and computer on either side. It appeared that two doctors could work in the space at the same time. Derrick took one seat and Alex followed suite, turning the other chair around and facing Detective Howard.

"Alex, I don't have a lot of time." He began, "I believe that another woman has been abducted. I know you were on scene for the female victim who was found in the park recently."

"Yes," Alex looked down at his hands and then continued, "that one has been haunting me for a while now."

"I'm sorry to hear that, and I want to ask you about something related."

"My dream?"

"Yes. I know this may sound unorthodox, but can you tell me about your dream, the one you had last night, and don't leave anything out."

"OK."

Alex relayed his dream in detail, very similarly to that morning when he did the same thing for Ms. Samuels. The same eerie feelings came back to him as he explained the final moments before waking. He could see the blond girl vividly, even now in his mind, sitting up, reaching out, pointing and speaking the single word, *'hurry'*. And then turning to see the old brick house as they were about to slam full force into the porch. Alex looked pale as he finished his story.

"Thank you for walking me through your dream." Derrick stated with appreciation. "Now I want to ask you another favor." Alex nodded and Derrick continued, "I am going to invite Ms. Dempsey in to speak with us. She has been caring for the victim, the one you responded to last Sunday. She is still here in the hospital, unidentified and in a coma. But the most important thing I need to ask of you, is not to say *anything* unless I ask. Can you do that? No matter what, don't speak."

Alex nodded and said, "Sure." with a look of confusion plastered across his face.

Derrick got up and opened the door. He smiled at Katrina and asked if there might be another chair she could bring into the room. She rolled one in from the nurse's station, closed the door and took a seat.

"Thank you, Katrina. I apologize for all of the secrecy, really, I just need to make sure neither of you is influenced by the other."

"I understand." Replied Katrina, and Alex sat patiently watching Detective Howard.

"Thank you, now Katrina, can you tell me specifically what happened last night when you came here to the hospital?"

"Sure. Well, like I said earlier, I came by to pick up some personal items and decided to check on our Jane. I noticed that you had made arrangements for an officer to sit outside her door to keep anyone form harming her, you know, that might want to. I didn't expect that he would be so protective, but I guess I am glad that he was. He wouldn't let me pass to go into Jane's room, even after I saw her move. I tried to go to her side, be he stopped me, and while he was holding me against the wall, I saw her. She reached out to me and tried to talk, but she only got one word out."

"You are sure it was only one word?" Detective Howard prompted.

"Yes, she only said '*hurry*'.

Alex opened his mouth and then looked at Detective Howard and closed it again.

"You're sure she didn't say anything else." It was more of a statement than a question. "You're confident you didn't imagine her speaking? Or reaching out to you?"

"No, I didn't. I mean, yes, I am sure I didn't imagine it."

"Thank you, Katrina. As you may have noticed, Alex here looks like he might have a few thoughts that he wants to share, but before we do that, let me tell you why I wanted to speak with you both. Alex had a dream last night that basically consisted of your Jane Doe in his ambulance. She sat up, pointed, and said the word, *hurry*.

Katrina and Alex exchanged looks. Derrick went on.

"There is another woman missing, and I have someone in custody who seems, very clearly to be our guy. All of the evidence points to him, only he is playing at some game like he doesn't know anything about it. I'm trying to get any details or information from anyone involved in this messy business that might help us to locate the missing woman."

"Katrina turned to Alex and asked, "You dreamed about Jane?"

"Yes, just once, but I've seen things."

"What have you seen?"

"Mostly I've imagined the same kinds of incisions that were on the victim, on Jane," Alex corrected himself, "on other patients I have attended to. And I was on the call for the latest victim, Laura Roundsley, where she was found deceased in the park. I saw the cuts on her body, only they turned out to be real."

Katrina looked at Derrick and then back at Alex.

"I have dreamed about Jane too. And I have seen a few things, well I thought I saw something, but then it always turned out to be something very different."

"Like what? Alex prompted.

"Well, one night I saw someone pass by her door while I sat in her room. But when I asked, no one had been on our floor. Then the next day, a man came into her room before it was dawn. He had a scalpel in his hand, at least I thought he did. He turned out to be the phlebotomist there for a blood draw."

"Wow." Said Alex. "I mean it kind of makes sense, our minds can play tricks on us when we are under stress. But on the other hand, it is really weird, don't ya think?"

"Yes, I do."

Monday 6:12pm

Steve shook his attorney's hand who in turn clapped Steve on the back, "What kind of a mess have these people mixed you up into?" James Smith, one of the firm's partners asked Steve.

"I really don't know, and I don't understand. Do you remember the horrible accident just over a week ago?"

James nodded, "They aren't charging you with negligence or reckless driving, are they?"

"No, not at all, but there was a by-stander who helped me take care of the girl until the ambulance arrived," Steve paused and looked at James with a strained look, "and she is missing (deep breath) and for some strange reason, they think I'm responsible!"

Steve sat with his attorney in the small room where interrogations took place and where the accused consulted with legal representation. He explained the events of the day, beginning with his visit to Sydny and ending with his arrest. He was careful not to give too much detail about *why* he was seeing Sydny, just that the accident had been traumatizing and he was having nightmares about it. James indicated understanding and asked if there was any real evidence against him other than the connection to the woman the day of the accident.

"There is zero evidence against me. They haven't even formally charged me. I just insisted on my phone call and right to an attorney so they finally let me call you."

"They can hold you for twenty-four hours without charging you, and easily thirty-six or longer if they suspect you of murder. But you said the woman is only missing? No evidence of abduction?" James queried.

"The hell if I know!" Shouted Steve "I only know that she is missing and they grilled me for several hours as to where I took her. They said they knew I was hiding her in a basement somewhere in town. It's insane!" Steve pounded his clenched fists on the table.

"OK," James said in a calm voice, "it's OK. I'll have you out of here in fifteen minutes. They will have to formally charge you or let you go right now. And they aren't going to charge you, they know the connection I have to Judge Thomas. If they had any real evidence, they would have charged you immediately."

James rose and knocked on the door. It was answered by a young, dark-skinned woman with striking green eyes. She allowed attorney James Smith to exit the room and then closed the door behind her.

Steve folded his arms across the table and rested his forehead. He thought about Sydny, how attractive she was. He remembered thinking if he wasn't her client, he would ask her out. He had trusted her. Then he remembered the young lady with the curly dark red hair. She had been a client too. But the two had seemed more like friends. What a strange, and unlikely circle of connections the three of them had. The accident and then Sydny, counseling them both, or at least knowing them both. Also strange was the fact that Sydny and the red-head lived so close to the park. He wondered why on earth he didn't know her name! He should have gotten it from her the day of the accident. He felt like he was drowning in a pool of confusion.

"Steve, are you OK?" James interrupted his thoughts and Steve sat up.

"Yes." He turned to look at James.

"I called your name three times."

"Sorry, I was thinking." Steve said feebly.

"Let's get out of here. They have no case against you." Steve stood in the door way and the young police woman was gone. I'm taking you out for dinner and then we will go retrieve your car.

Monday 6:37pm

Sydny stayed with Andrew for the afternoon, not knowing what else to do with herself. She'd asked about feeding the dogs and received some minimal instructions so after watching them mill around the front yard, sniffing and searching for who knows what, and then doing their business, she brought them back into the house and fed them. Then she searched the kitchen for something she might cook for Andrew. She knew the importance of eating and wondered how much he had eaten in the past two days. She was sure the answer was, not much.

She found a head of lettuce in the vegetable drawer and some sliced ham in the meat drawer. She set four eggs to boil and began slicing up a tomato-half she found, along with the ham and some newly discovered cheddar cheese. Lastly, she cooled the eggs, peeled and sliced them. She felt pretty good about the chef's salad as she threw it together and then searched for dressing. She found both Italian and ranch in the door of the refrigerator.

Sydny took everything, including some plates and forks out to the dining table. She went back for drinks and found a beer for Andrew, but made a glass of ice water for herself. Returning to the living room, she looked at Andrew who had not moved from the big arm chair in the corner. He just stared out the front window, where the real-life movie screen was slowly transforming to show only the reflection of the room as dusk settled outside.

Sydny sat at the table and used her best attempt at psychological guilt, "Andrew, I made this salad and I really think you would benefit from eating a couple of bites. I got you a beer too, maybe it'll help calm your nerves." She looked at him and eventually he turned his face and met her eyes with his. He stared at her for a minute and then got up to join her at the table.

"What are we supposed to do? How can we just sit here?" Andrew pleaded with her for an answer.

"I'm not sure. Why don't you eat something and then we can call Detective Howard and see what progress he has made?" Sydny encouraged.

So they sat, and ate, sort of. Andrew picked at his food, but managed to consume a few bites. He sipped at the beer and Sydny felt stupid about giving it to him in the first place. She went back to the kitchen and retrieved a glass of ice water for him too. She felt relieved when he drank half of it and then picked at his salad again.

"I don't understand why he hasn't called us. If that man took Shannon, wouldn't he have confessed by now?" Andrew spoke more to himself than to Sydny. He took another bite and then dropped his fork on the plate with a clatter. Andrew pushed back from the table,

"This is ridiculous! I'm sitting here like a helpless idiot while my wife is out there somewhere in the cold enduring God knows what!"

"You're right," Sydny said gently putting her fork down, "let's call Detective Howard and find out what what's going on." She retrieved her cell phone from her purse and resent the last number called.

"Put it on speaker." Demanded Andrew and she obliged with understanding.

"Detective Howard." Came the strong voice.

"Hello, it's Sydny and Andrew. Do you have any news for us?" Her voice was hopeful.

"Unfortunately, I don't have anything new to tell you. We didn't get anything out of Mr. Waters and his attorney was on the way last I heard."

"Oh." Sydny responded softly and Andrew turned to pace the living room. Molly and Murphy looked up from the couch where they were silently cuddled together.

"I'm at the hospital now, cross referencing some information that could be helpful."

"Did you find the nurse? Or have you spoken with Alex Jones?" Sydny asked with hope renewing in her tone. Andrew came back to her side to listen more closely.

"Yes, actually I was speaking with them when you called. Can I call you back? No more than thirty minutes, maybe quarter of an hour."

"Yes, absolutely, and thank you for the update." Sydny ended the call and looked up at Andrew. "That's at least something, right? And we can finish eating and clear up while we wait for his call."

"No. I can't sit here and do nothing any longer. If he thinks those people know something, then I want to go to the hospital and hear what they have to say." Andrew grabbed both plates and marched to the kitchen where he deposited them into the sink.

"I'm sorry." He called as he walked back from the kitchen. "I appreciate you making me dinner, and I feel bad if you are still hungry but I have to go." He walked to the foyer and opened the front door for Sydny.

"No, I'll come with you." She responded and gathered up her purse and coat.

Andrew closed and locked the front door. He walked over and patted each dog on the head saying, "I'm gonna find mom, I promise." Murphy's ears perked up and Molly let out a soft whine. He headed down the hall to the back door and Sydny followed, throwing on her coat. Andrew grabbed a leather jacket off of the wall rack as he passed and they both went out to Shannon's Jeep.

As they pulled out of the driveway, Sydny asked, "How are we going to find Detective Howard and the others? What if they won't allow us access to wherever they are meeting?"

"The nurse," he responded making the connection, "doesn't she work on the floor where they're keeping the girl in a coma? We just have to figure out which floor that is." Andrew sounded positive for the first time in a long time.

"There's a women's ward, I think it's on the third floor. Maybe that's where they are, and it's not restricted, I visited a friend there once. You just check in at the nurse's station."

Andrew responded by pressing on the gas. He was driving with a purpose now and Sydny wondered if that was good because it gave him a positive focus, or bad because it would be a huge disappointment when they weren't able to find Detective Derrick Howard and Alex Jones. Worse yet, they would find them and Detective Howard would prevent them from speaking to his witnesses.

They rode in silence until Andrew pulled into the parking structure marked for visitors. Finding an open spot, he pulled in and put the Jeep into the park position. He was out of the vehicle and hitting the lock button on the key fob before Sydny could get one foot out the door. She barely caught up to him as the garage elevator doors opened. They stepped in and Andrew hit the ground level button over and over until the doors finally closed. She thought about saying something but knew it would only make things worse. Telling a person to act rationally when they were distraught was the very definition of irrational behavior.

The elevator landed and she followed Andrew out and across the wide drive to the main hospital doors. She realized how long his legs were as she doubled her pace to keep up.

The main foyer of the hospital was wide and a security officer sat behind a desk to the left. Sydny smiled at the officer as they passed. She hoped he didn't catch on to the crazed purpose that was now Andrew's sole focus. The bank of elevators was straight ahead, housed in hallway that lead to other parts of the hospital. Those areas were protected behind double doors that could only be activated by a badge or an alarm.

Andrew hit the button indicating his desire to go up. He stood in the middle, between all four like a kid ready to compete with his siblings to get into the arriving elevator first.

He visibly jumped when the elevator chimed indicating the arrival of the far-left car. They stepped in and as the doors closed Sydny placed her hand on Andrew's shoulder and stated gently, "Please, let me do the talking. If you sound too anxious or demanding, they may just have security kick us out right away. Please, trust me and let me help you."

His eyes met hers and she saw the cyclone of emotions tearing him up inside, but she also saw the understanding that registered on his face. The elevator stopped and the doors opened. Andrew waited and let her exit first.

On this floor, the hallway was not blocked by double doors but instead stretched out in front of them with a few chairs along the wall on the right and a nurse's station on the left. The remainder of the hallway was lit by soft, evening lighting and lined with doors to patient rooms. The nurse behind the station looked up at them and smiled,

"Can I help you?"

Sydny stepped up to the counter and introduced herself.

"Yes, I'm Sydny Samuels and this is Andrew Medford. We recently spoke with Detective Howard and he indicated that he was here speaking with one of the nurses who works here."

The nurse, who's badge identified her as Tammy, just looked at Sydny waiting for more.

"Mr. Medford and I are actually part of an investigation to find a woman who has gone missing and we came here to meet with Detective Howard."

"Oh," Tammy responded, "I'm sorry. That's terrible. Can you have a seat? I'll let you know when he is available. He is meeting with some other people right now."

Sydny nodded and looked at Andrew, continuing to nod so that he would understand it was OK to sit down.

Monday 7:22pm

Steve had protested the offer for dinner. He was humiliated and tired. He was even scared and had argued most of these points to convince James to take him promptly back to his vehicle, which was embarrassingly, still parked in front of Sydny's home. He had prayed she wasn't there and upon arriving, saw that her windows were dark. That was the only thing that had gone his way all day.

Steve thanked James and awkwardly shook his hand before exiting the vehicle and climbing into his own. He started the engine and turned on the heater. The evening air was chilly.

He waited long enough for James to drive off, and then pulled out behind him. The small side street was quiet and dark, lit only by the occasional street lamp. The half-naked trees and bushes lining the sidewalk in front of the town homes looked eerie and reminded him that Halloween wasn't far away.

In that moment, Steve realized his dreams of buying a house and settling into some nice, historic neighborhood here were completely unrealistic. He would have to move, and that would require finding a new job. And *that* couldn't happen until the police figured out he was not a criminal.

He wondered if he could even show his face at the office in the morning. He would have to call in sick and then, like James had insisted, he would make an appointment so the two of them could realistically evaluate what the police were thinking and planning. The two of them would have to figure out what alibis he had for any of the days or nights that would be in question, based on the stupidity of current or new police theories.

Reality came crushing in on Steve as he turned out of the small neighborhood and onto Ninth South at the north end of the park.

How had everything turned upside down in a matter of hours? He pulled into the right lane and flipped on his blinker. The light was red but the traffic was light; only one car coming in the direction he wanted to go, but it was in the far lane. He made the right turn and noticed the park seemed empty.

Why had he come this way? It was force of habit, Seventh East was three lanes wide on each side and allowed for better travel times with traffic lights at the major intersections, instead of a stop sign at every intersection on the smaller streets. The speed limit was higher too. He just wanted to get home, and made a mental note to avoid this area of town from here on.

The other car had passed by quickly and was now some distance ahead of his vehicle. He accelerated slowly, having that spooky feeling of Deja vu, only it wasn't Deja vu, he *had* been here before. He cursed himself for accelerating so quickly a week ago. Why had he been in such a hurry to get home? If he hadn't done so, he wouldn't have hit the girl. She would have made it across the street and into the park. She could have gotten help. Hell, she would probably have gotten help from the red-head. And he wouldn't have had any involvement. No dreams, no counseling, no connection to any of this. His life would be blissfully boring.

As he accelerated, Steve looked to the left. The houses that faced the street and the park were mostly dark. And then he saw her as she bounded off of the median into the first, empty lane of traffic. Her skin was sickly white except for the angry dark lines down her arms and legs and across her stomach. The whole thing felt like slow motion as her next stride brought her into the middle lane.

Her bra and panties looked to have originally been white, but now were darkened with fear, sweat and possibly dried blood. Her eyes met his; glowing immensely blue in his headlights. And then she was in front of his vehicle.

He slammed the brakes as hard as humanly possible, but never took his eyes off of her. He knew the grill of his SUV was going to connect with her chest as she flung her right arm out behind her, in the direction she had come. The fingers of her right hand clenched into a fist with only the index finger pointing stiffly at the houses behind her. She opened her mouth and formed a word, which Steve heard as plain as day, "Hurry." And then she was gone.

The impact Steve had braced for never happened. He heard his tires squealing in spite of his disc brakes pumping at the same speed of his racing heart. The vehicle came to a stop and the seat belt bit into his shoulder. He looked up expecting someone to rear-end him, but the street was empty.

He sat and shook for a few seconds and then jumped out of his SUV to confirm no body lay on the street in front of him. He left the door open and walked around to the front of his vehicle. The only sound was his engine. He continued over to the sidewalk and looked around in every direction. A blaring car horn made him jump as a dark sedan skirted around his parked vehicle with door flung wide into the next lane.

He was still shaky but walked around to the back of his SUV to double check he hadn't run over anything. Before stepping off the sidewalk, he bent low and peered anxiously under his vehicle. Nothing. He walked back to the open door, got in and closed it.

Steve drove to the southern end of the park and turned right and then into the park. He pulled over into the first parking spot. He only saw one other car parked about half way down the road. It was starting to get too dark and too cold for running.

He killed the engine and folded his arms over the steering wheel. He rested his forehead against the wheel and the interior light went off, plunging him into shadows and the sickening feeling of sadness and fear. The adrenaline was wearing off and he felt nauseated. He opened his door and wretched three times before finally vomiting up what little fluid was in his stomach. He sat there, turned sideways in the doorway with his feet on the running board and his head in hands, balanced by elbows on knees. The cool air swept around the back of his sweaty neck and he shivered.

He swiveled back into his seat, facing forward and closed the door. He hit the lock button and reclined his seat. He took a few deep breaths and slowly exhaled. He wondered what had just happened to him. Was that a day mare? Was he graduating from night mares to day mares? Well technically it *was* night, but he wasn't asleep. He'd obviously imagined it, being so worked up over the events of the afternoon and then feeling anxious about driving by the park. It was just a bad memory. Or was it? He didn't remember the girl pointing *or* speaking. He had definitely imagined that because there was no way he would have heard her say the word *'hurry'* from inside his SUV. He replayed the scene over and over in his mind.

"Hurry"

"Hurry"

The word sounded hauntingly in his mind. "Why hurry?" Steve asked himself out loud. "Why not *stop*? Why not *help*? Why not just a scream?" he asked the empty space surrounding him.

"Hurry"

"Hurry what!" Steve shouted.

"Hurry"

"Hurry"

"Hurry"

The word wouldn't stop repeating softly but urgently inside his head. He didn't understand what was wrong with him. He needed to talk to someone, to have a conversation that would wipe this memory out of his mind. But there was no one to talk to. Sydny, he could talk to Sydny. The only problem with that was she thought he was a murderer and a kidnapper. James? He couldn't very well call his lawyer and tell him that he was having a nervous breakdown and was quite possibly, just crazy.

"Hurry"

Sydny! He *could* talk to Sydny, he could call her. He didn't need to see her face to face to talk to her. But would she answer her phone? She probably knew his number.

"Hurry"

Steve wanted to dig into his brain and claw the memory out of his mind! He fumbled for the clear, plastic bag of personal items that the police had taken away and then given back upon his departure from the police station. He held the power button and waited for the phone to come to life. The police had searched through his phone looking for some kind of evidence, perhaps pictures or texts, but finding nothing they had powered it off. The cabin of his vehicle was suddenly lit by the dancing colors of his phone connecting to the network.

"Hurry"

He was going to officially lose his mind before he could even dial Sydny's number. He watched the screen and then finally the phone settled so that he could scroll through the contacts and select Ms. Sydny Samuels number. The connection was made and he sat holding his breath, counting the rings, and praying she would pick up.

"Hurry"

Monday 7:40pm

Sydny and Andrew had been sitting for about five minutes when her phone rang. Andrew's impatiently tapping foot froze and he looked at her like whoever was calling would definitely have all the answers. Sydny dug her phone out of her purse and saw the name on the screen and found herself frozen in place.

"What?!" Andrew asked.

"It's Mr. Waters." Sydny responded with a nervous voice.

Before she could even think, Andrew grabbed the phone out of her hand and answered the call, "Do you know where my wife is?" He heard nothing but breathing before Sydny grabbed it back from him.

"Mr. Waters, why are you calling me?" Sydny had found her sense of authority, brought on by Andrew's rash behavior.

"Ms. Samuels, Sydny, please don't hang up on me. Something is terribly wrong." Steve pleaded.

"I won't hang up, are you OK? Do you need to call 911?"

"No, and no. I'm not OK, but I'm not hurt either. I just need to talk to you." Steve's pleading continued.

"Mr. Waters, now really isn't a good time."

"No, please, please don't hang up. Please, just two minutes?"

Sydny could hear the desperation in his voice but didn't know if it was from guilt or fear or even brought on by a mental disorder. She felt the deep stabbing guilt of her betrayal again. But his sessions had been about dreams that were too close to reality so she had done what was ethically expected of her.

As she justified her actions she considered, what about the others? Shannon and Alex were excused from their dreams by the trauma caused by the accident. Steve's dreams were *supposedly* caused by that same trauma.

"Are you there?" Steve's voice was gravelly with emotion.

"Yes, I'm here. What do you need to talk to me about?"

"Thank you!" Steve let out a sigh of relief, "Sydny, I know you think I had something to do with that woman's disappearance, but I didn't."

"Mr. Waters." Sydny interrupted him.

"OK, OK, I'll get to it." Steve took a deep breath, "I was driving home tonight and I went by the park. I don't know why, habit I guess. Anyway, I was at the same intersection as right before the accident, only I was turning right on to Seventh instead of heading straight south. Well, I realized where I was and I made a mental note never to drive that way again. Anyway, the street was empty and I wasn't driving very fast and it happened again!"

"What? Did you hit someone? You need to call 911, Steve!"

Andrew had turned in his seat, watching Sydny and trying to fill in the missing pieces of the phone call he was only witnessing from one side.

"No! I didn't hit anyone, but I *saw* her. She ran out in front of me again, the girl I hit. I saw her! But I hit my brakes and stopped and jumped out. There was no one there! I looked everywhere, I even looked under my SUV."

"Steve, I'm sorry, that must have been tough, imagining it all over again. You're right to avoid driving that way for a while. You need to let your mind heal."

"But I didn't imagine it. It was as real as the night it happened, only it was different."

"How was it different?" Sydny encouraged.

"The girl looked at me. I think she must have looked at me before because she had to have seen me about to hit her. But this time she looked at me and *spoke* to me. And I *heard* it, I actually heard what she said." Steve's voice was strained.

"What did you hear her say?"

"But there's one more thing." Steve paused, "She pointed too, and she said 'hurry', and I heard it as plain as I hear you on the phone right now."

"She pointed? At you?" Sydny asked trying to keep the emotion in her voice at bay.

"No, she pointed back behind her, across the street, back at the houses."

"Steve! Do NOT hang up the phone." Sydny demanded and jumped out of her seat. Andrew was right behind her as she pressed the phone to her chest and leaned against the counter at the nurse's station. "Tammy, I need to speak with Detective Howard right now. It's an emergency!"

Tammy stared back at Sydny with a look of confusion. As far as she could see, no one was injured or life-threateningly sick. In her world, that was the definition of emergency.

Sydny stared back at Tammy wondering why the young lady sat there looking confused and then they both turned their heads as a door to the left opened up and Derrick stepped out.

"What's going on?" The noise had obviously drawn him out.

"Detective Howard, I have Mr. Waters on the phone and I need you to listen to him."

Derrick stepped out of the physician's room with Alex and Katrina on his heels. Sydny put the phone back to her hear and instructed Steve,

"I want you to repeat everything you just told me, to Detective Howard." She listened and then, "Please, Steve, please just trust me." She handed the phone across the counter to Detective Howard who answered and then listened for what seemed like an eternity.

"Mr. Waters, I need to ask you a favor and I know you probably don't trust me, but I'm going to ask you to, this one time, and here's why, I believe you." He listened and then continued, "I need you to come to the hospital and share what you just told me with two other people. And I need you and the others to help me find Mrs. Medford." Derrick listened and nodded. "Yes, I give you my word, I'm not trying trick you or arrest you. I really need your help."

Sydny felt relief as it appeared that Steve had agreed. Derrick closed the call by letting him know they were waiting on the third floor of the hospital in the women's ward. Then he handed the phone back to Sydny and turned to Alex,

"Are you OK to stay here longer?"

Alex eagerly replied, "Yes, let me call my captain and tell him I'm going to stay and help for a few hours. That way he can contact someone to come in and cover. I need to let Jay know too so he can get back to the station."

Derrick confirmed that everyone else was able to stay. They all agreed and Sydny offered to go to the cafeteria to get coffee and a snack for everyone. She knew Andrew was on pins and needles and wouldn't last much longer just waiting, so she insisted he go with her to help carry everything back. They had at least fifteen minutes to wait for Steve to arrive.

Monday 8:00pm

Shannon shivered and dreamed of a dark, musty place that she could not escape. Someone was in the darkness and she could feel his presence even though he didn't speak. There was scratchy music accompanied by a strange old voice singing about Daisy Bell. Candlelight danced around in the darkness and then he was there beside her with something shiny and metal in his hand.

She jerked awake and felt her heart racing in her chest. "It was a nightmare." She told herself. She lay in silence, breathing in slow, deep breaths to calm her heart and allow her head to clear. Her eyes were trying to adjust to the darkness of the room and then the musty smell of dirt jolted her back to reality.

She jerked against the handcuffs that held her wrists and yanked at the leather straps on her ankles. The strap across her mid-section kept her from sitting up. She thrashed and cried and then stopped abruptly when she heard the creak on the stairs.

"Ah, my dear, you're awake." The raspy voice crooned in the darkness and she heard the familiar scratch of a wooden match against the flint side of its box. A candle flickered to life on the bench near her feet and the dark figure turned to face her.

The sting of her bicep brought the memory crashing back.

"NO! Please!" She begged. Her focus went wildly from his dark eyes to the cut along her upper arm. A small trickle of blood was oozing from the wound, freshly opened by her panicked movements.

"Now my dear, look what you have gone and done." He crept closer, moving along side of her. His face was difficult to see with the candle light to his back, but his eyes glimmered with excitement.

"And I don't have the time right now to enjoy this." He reached with his index finger and gently smeared the fresh blood along her skin and then sucked the remainder from his finger like a child licks the cake batter from the bowl.

He bent slowly over her and Shannon willed herself to shrink down in to the table. He took a long deep breath as he hovered over her chest, face and hair.

"Lavender." He slowly exhaled the word and stood up straight. "The deep crimson of your blood against your creamy skin is only topped by your fiery locks." He said the words as if he was seducing her on a date. "Oh, my dear, you make me hard." He placed his hand over his crotch and continued, "but you will just have to wait until we both have the time to enjoy. I have an errand to run, but don't worry, I'll be back."

He laced the fingers of his left hand through the thick curls of her hair and then made a fist and yanked her head toward him. He lowered his face again and his dark eyes stared into hers as the tears welled up. One single tear escaped down her cheek and he whispered, "Lavender." And then flicked his tongue out to catch the tear.

Shannon held her breath and he finally let her go. He walked back around the foot of the table and blew out the candle. "I wouldn't want you to accidentally burn down the house, my dear." And he ascended the stairs.

Monday 8:15pm

Steve pulled into a spot in the hospital parking garage and turned off the engine. He sat and contemplated what he was about to do. He was walking right back into the hands of the very people who had betrayed him earlier today. He should've called James. James would have forbidden him to come here, he would have insisted that any interviews take place during the day, at the law offices, with him present to represent Steve.

Steve took another breath. Was he really going to do this? Was Detective Howard lying? Was this a trick?

"Hurry" The word and the girl returned to his mind. He had gotten rid of them temporarily by talking to Sydny and driving to the hospital. Now they were back.

"Hurry"

"Hurry"

"OK!" Steve shouted out loud to his steering wheel and then pounded his fist, "OK, I'm going".

Steve entered the hospital through the main sliding doors and looked nervously over at the security guard. "I'm acting like a guilty person." He mumbled, chastising himself. He continued on and didn't look back because he knew he *did* look guilty even though he wasn't.

One of the elevators opened as he approached and a young couple exited holding hands. *'They have no idea.'* He thought to himself as he entered and pressed the button for the third floor.

"This is it buddy, no turning back now."

The doors closed. He stood in the middle of the elevator as it rose, feeling like a man going to his own execution. And I've done nothing wrong other than driving on the wrong street at the wrong time, he thought.

The elevator settled and the door slid back. He stepped out into the hallway and saw the group of people waiting for him. They must have been in the middle of some conversation, but the ding of the arriving elevator had drawn everyone's attention to him. He felt like a complete fool and the cold grip of fear made the hair on the back of his neck stand on end.

Detective Howard was in front of him so quickly that he braced himself for another arrest. Instead he shoved his hand at Steve and said,

"Mr. Waters, Steve, thank you for coming. Especially under the circumstances."

Steve tried to grip the strong hand pumping his but he wasn't feeling all that strong.

"Sure." Was all he managed to get out.

Detective Howard directed him to a small room behind the nurse's station with a desk and computer on each of two opposite walls. There were three office chairs in the room and the detective asked the nurse on duty for three more. Steve watched in confusion as Sydny followed the nurse. They came quickly back with an office chair and two stools; the kind you find in a patient's room for the doctor to sit and roll around on. A woman in scrubs took one of the stools and pushed into the office followed by Sydny.

"Please, have a seat in here." Detective Howard indicated to Steve.

That feeling of being ambushed came back to him, as they all filed into the room and the detective stood indicating the door, patiently looking at him with sincerity.

Steve finally went in and sat in one of the office chairs. Detective Howard rolled the last chair in and closed the door as well as the circle.

"I know this is very strange and even disconcerting after your experience this afternoon, but I really do think you can help us."

"I told you I have no idea where Mrs. Medford is. I had nothing to do with it." Steve's voice rose slightly and became shaky as he spoke.

Sydny was seated to his left and gently placed her hand on his.

"I actually believe you." Derrick stated and looked genuine. "I don't understand why, but I think somehow each of you has been experiencing or," he paused for a second, "or dreaming some kind of connection to Mrs. Medford and I am hoping if we put it all together it will help us to find her."

A dark-haired man who looked to be in his early thirties with dark circles under his eyes sat next to Sydny and leaned forward and spoke with desperation,

"Mr. Waters, I'm Shannon's husband, Andrew. Please, just listen to the detective. Anything you can tell us, I promise, I just want to find my wife."

Steve looked around the tiny room which was warming from the heat of six bodies crammed into such a small space. He knew Sydny to his left and the man to her left was obviously Mr. Medford. He knew

Detective Howard across from him but the older nurse and the young paramedic were people he had never seen before.

As if on cue, Detective Howard introduced each person in the room.

"Mr. Waters, as you have no doubt figured out, this is Mr. Andrew Medford and you already know Ms. Sydny Samuels." Indicating to his left, "This is Ms. Katrina Dempsey, she works the night shift and has been caring for the young woman you hit just over a week ago."

Steve flinched at the words and Derrick continued,

"Lastly, this is Mr. Alex Jones and I thought you might remember him since he was one of the paramedics who responded to the accident last Sunday." Detective Howard looked closely at Steve.

Steve looked closely at Alex and then slowly nodded his recognition.

"Yes, I remember you now. You took over after we did CPR on the girl."

"Yes, I did." Alex answered. "And I've been having strange experiences and dreams too."

"Steve," Derrick coaxed, "both Ms. Dempsey and Alex have been experiencing something similar to you. If you don't mind, we would like to hear what you experienced tonight."

Steve looked around the room again and landed his gaze on Sydny's. She nodded and squeezed his hand.

"OK, well, OK. After I was released from the jail, my attorney, James Smith, gave me a ride to your house." He looked at Sydny again, then back at the detective. "I had to get my SUV so I could go home."

He both looked and felt ashamed and embarrassed but no one said anything. "I headed home without thinking, kind of on auto pilot. Anyway, I found myself turning right onto Seven Hundred East and realized where I was. I was mad at myself for going that way and I never wanted to drive past that park ever again. That's probably what did it. You know? Made me recall the whole thing." Again, he looked around the room. No judgment, just patient understanding in all of their eyes. "Well, it seemed like I was remembering that night when I hit the girl, only it was actually different."

"How was it different?" Detective Howard asked.

"The young lady ran out in front of me, that part was the same, but there were no other cars on the road, and it was a little darker. But what was really different was that this time, she looked at me and spoke to me, and she pointed."

Both Alex and Katrina leaned slightly closer to him and watched intently.

"What did she say?" Detective Howard prompted.

"She said *'hurry'*, that's all, just *'hurry'*. And now I can't get it out of my head.

Everyone in the room let out a breath, and Steve was more confused now than ever.

"OK, I need everyone to listen carefully. Steve, you, Ms. Dempsey and Alex have all dreamed or experienced, the same three elements."

Steve looked at the nurse and paramedic and they both nodded at him in confirmation.

"Everyone can call me Katrina." The nurse responded.

Detective Howard continued, "All three of you saw the victim, Jane Doe, point, look at you and say the word *'hurry'*. Now what I need from each of you is to think about what she pointed at." Derrick paused to give them time to conjure up the memory of that moment.

"I want to start with you, Steve. Think about where you were and what she pointed at."

The entire group now leaned closer to Steve sitting in the office chair with his back to the wall. He felt claustrophobic. He took a deep breath and pictured it in his head.

"I was just a short distance south of the intersection with the park on my right and the median on my left."

"What else." Prompted Derrick.

"The girl pointed at the median and the new trees growing there. No, wait, there wasn't a tree in that spot. She had run across between two trees. She pointed across the street at the houses."

"Do you remember which house?"

"No, just one of those old brick houses lining Seventh."

"Ok, Steve. Thank you. Alex, what about you?"

Alex nodded and began. "Well in my dream we were driving across Seven Hundred toward those houses. It was the same spot where we responded to the accident. I know the house was a farm-style, brick with the porch running across the front of the house. It was pretty close to Beckford Avenue."

"Yes!" Steve chimed in, "It was a brick house with a long porch in the front."

"What about you Katrina?" asked Andrew with renewed hope.

"I didn't dream anything like that, but Jane did reach out from her bed and point at me. She said *'hurry'* just like the rest of you experienced.

"Oh!" Alex jumped in, "And I responded to a fire today and one of the victims told me to hurry as well. Until now I thought she meant someone else was in the house, but no one else was."

"OK, I know we don't have a lot of time, so here is my next question. Do any of you think you might recognize the house if we went there now?" Detective Howard asked.

"Ya!" "Yes" Steve and Alex chimed in at the same time.

Andrew was the first out of his chair. "Let's go!"

"Andrew, I really think you should go home and let the police take care of this. I'll call for back up right away and let you know the minute we find her."

"Screw that!" Andrew stated, "I'm going and you can't stop me."

Steve watched the momentary power struggle that took place as the two men considered each other. He saw the wisdom in Detective Howard's eyes as they softened.

"OK, but you have to promise to stay back and let us work, no matter what we find. Alex, do you think you can get your unit to meet us there?"

"Absolutely!"

"Katrina, I need you to stay here and cover your shift, *and* If Jane wakes up, I need you to be ready to call me and ask her if she remembers anything that might help us." Katrina nodded with understanding as Detective Howard got up and opened the door. He pushed his chair out of the office and then turned to Steve, Sydny and Andrew.

"I would like the three of you to ride with me."

Steve agreed along with the other two. He wondered to himself if this was Detective Howard's way to make sure he didn't run off, and also to keep Andrew and Sydny under control. Whatever the reason, he was beginning to feel like he was no longer a suspect.

Monday 8:47pm

Steve, Sydny and Andrew rode along with Detective Howard with Sydny in the front passenger seat. All three men had insisted she rode in the front and since it was not an official police vehicle she felt less guilty about riding in the front.

Alex had found Jay in the cafeteria before he left the hospital and the two of them followed Detective Howard with their bus. Upon arriving on the east side of the park they were met by another squad car and fire truck that had been dispatched before they even left the hospital. The Fire Engine was idling on the inner road of park awaiting instructions.

Derrick parked the car on Seventh, in nearly the exact same place where the vehicle versus pedestrian accident had taken place just one week and one night ago. All three exited the car and assembled on the sidewalk where they were joined by Alex and Jay.

The first officer on the scene reported to Detective Howard, who instructed him to direct the other arriving squad cars. He wanted the street blocked off from the north and south ends of the park to prevent through traffic. The officers could direct the traffic one block in either direction. He would further deploy them once they identified the house he was *hoping* they could identify.

All of the emergency response vehicles had arrived without sirens. The situation was critical, but Detective Howard was hoping to avoid both a neighborhood panic and spooking the perpetrator in the house. This type of guy sometimes made rash decisions in the heat of the moment and it didn't always end so well for the victim.

Detective Howard gathered Steve and Alex, who was busy filling in the fire truck driver, and then asked them both to stand on the sidewalk and look across the street. He had ensured no vehicles other than his own, were within three car-lengths of where the accident had occurred.

"I need each of you to take a minute and look around. You can walk around, stand in the street, do whatever it takes to bring back, as clearly as possible, the memory of your experience. I need to know exactly which house."

Hospital 9:21pm

Katrina sat in room 302 holding the hand of hospital-identified victim, Jane Doe Seventeen. Her shift hadn't started yet, and compliments of Detective Derrick Howard, Tammy was planning to stay and cover while another on-call night nurse was contacted. Her regular shift partner, Brenda would be there soon as well. Her instructions were to remain in the room with Jane, in case she did or said anything else.

A new officer was on guard outside the door but the feelings she was experiencing were everything *but* safe. She felt helpless and cold even though the room was a pleasant temperature. She felt lost and a little bit excited at the prospect of finding the horrible man who did this to Jane. But most of all she felt sick at the idea that another sweet young woman was within the monster's control.

Jane's hand squeezed around Katrina's and her eyes began to move under the closed lids. Jane leaned over the girl and called her sweetie. A quiet moan came from Janes lips but her grip never loosened. Katrina grabbed the remote unit from the night stand and pressed the call button.

Basement 9:24pm

Shannon was so cold that metal the hand cuffs at her wrists jingled in tune with her chattering teeth. Her entire body was shivering. She wanted to cry but there were no more tears due to her severely dehydrated state. To make matters worse, she could smell the aging urine that had dried to her underwear and skin on the backs of her legs. She had held her bladder as long as humanly possible, at least a full twenty-four hours she believed.

At one point, she'd begged the man to let her use the bathroom, not just because she needed it, but because it might lead to the ability to escape or call for help. He hadn't even told her no, just reassured her that the table was set up to drain and everything would be fine. Having to lay there and urinate on herself was horrible. Knowing she was strapped to a table designed for autopsies was even more horrible, but not the worst. The frightening, sickening feeling that had caused her to cry until there were no more tears, was knowing that urine was not the only liquid the table was designed to collect and dispatch of; the precious blood that flowed from the cuts he inflicted would also collect and silently drain away, stealing her life as it went.

She heard the footsteps above and froze for a couple of seconds. Her body stopped shivering and the basement became silent. She held her breath and prayed the footsteps didn't cross in the direction of the door. Her prayers were not answered, and as she heard the door open and the first step on the wooden plank of the stairs, her body did more than shiver. She was racked with the violent sobs that normally accompany an all-out crying fit. Only there were no tears.

Seven Hundred East 9:28pm

Steve stood in the southbound lane closest to the park and looked ahead. He tried to envision himself in his SUV with the girl in front of him. He pictured her long white arm stretched out to her right, pointing in the direction from which she had come. *'Hurry'* *'Hurry'* *'Hurry'* The words echoed in his head and he closed his eyes.

Alex had walked into the park and turned south for quite a distance. He was now traveling back trying to recreate the path of the ambulance from his dreams.

Andrew paced back and forth blurting out,

"C'mon! What are we waiting for? Let's just knock on every door! The Police should be checking every basement on this street!"

Sydny stepped in front of him and placed both hands on his shoulders,

"Andrew, please, just give them five more minutes. Let Detective Howard get the right house and then we go in and get her."

"And what if it's not the right house?! What if it's too late?!" Andrew's voice was becoming shrill.

Sydny shook him as hard as she could,

"It won't be too late, I promise!" She felt horrible for lying to him but she wanted him to settle down so that Detective Howard, Alex and Steve would not get distracted.

Steve opened his eyes and pictured the girl again. He saw the pained look on her pale face. He followed the line of her ghostly, thin right arm and slowly looked left across the street.

Alex stepped gingerly into the street in front of Steve as if he were in a trance.

"There!" both men shouted in unison.

Hospital 9:30pm

Jane's eyes flew open and she gasped, barely audible, "Hurry! Please Hurry! You have to save her!"

"It's OK, sweetie. You're OK. You're safe, you're in the hospital." Katrina stood over Jane trying to sooth her. Jane tried to sit up and Katrina gently pushed her back down by the shoulders.

"Who are you? He's going to kill her! You have to hurry! Where am I?" Janes voice was scratchy and hoarse.

"You're in the hospital. My name is Katrina Dempsey. I'm the night shift nurse assigned to care for you." Katrina watched the girl as the confusion played in her eyes. She looked around the room lit only by soft lamplight.

"Where am I?"

"You are in the hospital. You are safe." Katrina stated each sentence carefully. "Sweet heart, I need to ask you some questions, do you think you can answer them for me?" Jane stared at Katrina. The confusion was still prevalent in her eyes. "Sweetheart, can you tell me your name?"

Basement 9:31pm

The match scratched against the box and the candle near her feet came to life. With each candle, he came closer to her. Shannon's stomach lurched inside of her and her tongue became thick in her throat. He was next to her now and he touched his knuckles against her cheek. She jerked her head away and heaved but nothing came. She dry wretched again and coughed, gasping for air.

The Victrola came to life and the eerie music filled the room. Shannon's heart raced in her chest. She couldn't see him, where had he gone? She strained to hear him beyond the music and the crackle of the candles.

The flash of metal in front of her face made her jump and her body tried to expel the fear by dry vomiting again.

Seven Hundred East 9:32pm

Detective Howard was instructing both Alex and Steve to stop and speak one at time.

"There it is!"

"It's that one there!"

"The house with the porch!"

"That house there, with only the one light!"

"The second one in from Beckford, that one!"

Alex and Steve spoke over the top of each other, both crossing the street as they spoke. Derrick followed after them and put a hand to each of their shoulders to stop them. One of the other officers came over to help. Andrew came up between the two of them and asked in a frenzied tone, "That one there?" He began to push through and Detective Howard grabbed him.

"Everyone just stop!"

Sydny was there asking Andrew to please let the police do their job. A third officer came over and escorted Andrew, Sydny, Alex and Steve back to the park.

Detective Howard circled his hand above his head and all of the officers came to meet him in the street. He indicated the house and assigned the officers to park one vehicle out front, take one down Beckford Avenue and park in the alleyway behind the houses, and park a third on Beckford.

He assigned two men to the back of the house and two more to stay with him. The he waved Alex over and instructed him to bring the ambulance around and park it in the street out front with some safe distance, but close enough to be ready to provide medical attention.

Alex ran back over to his teammates as Detective Howard and his men approached the house.

Hospital 9:33pm

"What?"

"Your name, sweet heart, can you tell me your name?" Katrina asked as Brenda came into the room.

"My name?" She looked puzzled. "My name." She finally stated as the two nurses looked at her. "My name is Rebecca, Rebecca Stone."

"Thank you, Rebecca." Katrina cooed. "Now I have a more difficult question for you. Do you remember where you were before you came here to the hospital?" It pained Katrina to ask her this question, knowing it would likely conjure up the most horrible memories.

Tears welled up in Rebecca's eyes,

"I was," she sobbed, "I was in a house. In a basement."

The tears streamed down her cheeks and she struggled not to choke. Katrina pressed the button on the large remote to raise the bed and Rebecca's coughing subsided but the tears did not. She continued,

"There was a man! He..." she stopped and looked at her arms wrapped carefully in hospital gauze and then she spoke no more. She cried hysterically and Katrina folded her arms around her.

"We have to call the detective." Brenda stated and Katrina nodded in agreement.

Basement 9:34pm

"Do you have any idea how beautiful you are?" the deep, raspy voice asked, but Shannon could not answer. "You have the most amazing creamy, white skin and your hair is the color of blood in the moonlight. But what really gets me off, what really shows me how much you love me, is the thick, sweet crimson of your blood against that creamy, white skin. When you bleed for me, baby, I know how much you love me. Baby, you're gonna bleed for me now."

Shannon whispered, "Please, no!" Her throat was dry and she tried harder, "Please!" She half screamed.

Before she could speak another word, he clamped his hand over her mouth and held the scalpel to her neck. Neither of them breathed as he cocked his head to one side and listened.

A far-off thudding on the front door of the house carried down to the basement. He leaned over her and she felt his hot breath against her ear and neck. His voice was cold and threatening now,

"Make a sound and I will slit your pretty, white throat." And then he was gone.

Shannon gulped in a breath through her mouth and then held it. She strained to hear him in the room. Where had he gone? She considered screaming for help but knew he would be at her side slicing the blade across her throat. She shivered and her breath came raggedly out of her mouth. She heard the pounding again only this time it was closer. She remembered the back door from her dreams.

Again, she wanted to scream for help but instead she listened and scanned the darkness, broken intermittently by candle light, for his presence. She heard only the creepy music of the Victrola.

Time stood still in her dank, dark basement world and she prayed again. This time her prayer was answered by the crashing of a far-off door. It was quickly followed by the crashing of the back door not far beyond the reach of the basement.

As the words left her lips, she continued to pray softly,

"Help me please! I'm down here!" The basement door slammed open and beams of flash lights bounced against the walls of the stair way. She braced herself for the scalpel at her throat but it never came.

"Help me, please!" The flash lights bobbed and loomed, coming down the stairs and she could hear an army of footsteps both above hear and coming toward her.

The room was suddenly and painfully bright and a tall man in street clothes was at her side. He was followed by several more police officers in uniform.

"You have to find him! He is still down here!"

"OK, we'll find him, don't worry. I'm Detective Howard, do you remember me?" Shannon nodded and he continued,

"Are you hurt? Is anything broken? I want to get you out of here if I can."

Shannon looked in disbelief as the other officers scanned the basement with their flashlights, finding nothing and no one. The Victrola music stopped and she jerked. Several of the officers call out an all-clear and Detective Howard asked her again if she was OK. She looked at him, nodded and cried. One last tear moistened her right eye and she wailed softly,

"Please, get me out of here."

"OK, we will. Don't worry, we're gonna get you out of here."

Detective Howard removed the straps from her feet and chest. He called to one of the officers to unlock the handcuffs with his key. Just as he was helping her to sit up a young, blond paramedic came down the stairs and brought a blanket to wrap around her. She shivered and pulled the blanket to her chest and then heard shouting from above. Detective Howard called up the stairs,

"It's OK, let him come down."

Andrew's voice reached her before he did, "Shannon! Shannon!" She was just trying to stand with the help of Detective Howard and the paramedic when Andrew came crashing into her. She collapsed into his arms as he pulled her tightly to him.

"C'mon, she needs medical attention, let's get her out to the ambulance." Detective Howard gently counseled and Andrew swept her up in his arms and carried her sideways, head first up the stairs.

The bright lights seared her eyes and she closed them tightly as Andrew carried her through the house. Two firemen and another paramedic met them inside the front door with a gurney and Andrew gently placed her on the padded surface. Another blanket was placed over her and the men went to work starting an IV, placing an oxygen mask over her face and checking her vital signs. After a moment, they wheeled her out onto the front porch and then carefully maneuvered the gurney down the stairs and into the waiting ambulance.

Andrew, who had never left her side, climbed in to ride with her to the hospital.

"Molly and Murphy are going to be so happy to see their mom." he kissed her on the forehead.

Seven Hundred East 9:47pm

Detective Howard stood in the light of the street lamps surrounded by officers. His phone rang. As he answered he heard Katrina's worried voice,

"Detective Howard? Are you there?"

"I'm here, is everything OK at the hospital?"

"Yes! Jane has awakened! I mean Rebecca. Have you found the other poor woman?"

"Yes, we found her and she is on her way to the hospital. Everything is going to be OK."

"But Detective Howard! Did you catch the man?" There was understandable concern in Katrina's voice.

"No, unfortunately, I think he was gone by the time we arrived."

"Detective Howard! You have to look carefully! Rebecca said he has a door in the basement; a place to hide or get away!"

Derrick didn't respond. He shoved the phone into his pocket and yelled for the officers to follow. He got on his radio and called for all of the officers to surround the house, stating that the perpetrator was likely still inside and to proceed with caution.

The men carefully cleared the upper floor of the house again while Detective Howard and Officer Thompson focused on the basement. They felt along the walls as they went. The cold, stone foundation walls prohibited any kind of escape route and there was no other room except for the small wooden doors that led to an old-fashioned fruit room lined with wooden shelves and cobwebs.

Derrick shined his flashlight around the small space that was designed to keep fruits and vegetables canned in mason jars fresh for months. The cob webs were missing from the back wall. He looked closer and called to Officer Thompson to shine his light along with his own. Detective Howard pushed on the shelf-bearing wall and it bounced back leaving a two-inch space of darkness. He grasped the edge and swung the hidden door open revealing an old coal shoot. Both men shined their flashlights up the shoot and saw the cellar style doors that covered the exterior at just above ground level.

"Damn!" Derrick growled and grabbed his radio. "I need an officer in the back yard!" He turned to Officer Thompson, "You stay here. I'll send another officer down." And he ran to the stairs taking them two at a time.

Passing Officer Clark, he ordered him down to the basement to secure the fruit room at the back end of the basement and then lunged out the back door. He nearly collided with the officer waiting for him in the back yard.

"Cellar doors! North side of the lot" Derrick ordered and the officer followed him to the far end of the back yard. The cellar doors lay closed and the two men pulled them open. A single padlock hung from a metal loop on the inside of the right door. Derrick looked at the fence line where it came close to the side of the house and with his flashlight he could see a narrow gate still slightly ajar.

"Damn! Damn! Son of a bitch!" Derrick yelled and then got back on his radio to organize a manhunt.

Monday 9:52pm

The moon was full as he drove south on State Street toward the freeway entrance. The traffic was light. Most people were home tucked safely and soundly in bed at this hour. He was grateful that he had taken precautionary measures after that last homeless girl escaped. Keeping a car and go-bag in the storage unit three blocks from his house was his saving grace this evening.

He wasn't exactly sure where he would go. He felt a sense of melancholy. He would miss this city. It has served him well for over nine years.

He wasn't worried about the house, it had belonged to an elderly man with no family and when he landed on his autopsy table it was the perfect opportunity. All he had to do was keep paying the utilities and the annual taxes. He'd released the body to a fabricated family member who had requested transfer to the mortuary for cremation. The cost was only a drop in the bucket and the poor bastard still sat above the fireplace on his own mantle.

No, the real problem would be when he didn't show up for work. A missing medical examiner was pretty obvious, and then there was the small issue of Detective Derrick Howard knowing his identity. How long would it take for Derrick to at least become suspicious? He didn't think the fiery red-head could identify him and the other girl was still safely in a coma at the hospital. With any luck the hospital would eventually pull the plug.

Regardless, if ole Derrick did go nosing around his house and financials, he wouldn't find anything. The majority of his money was in a bank located in the Cayman Islands under an alias.

Well he had at least two days of travel ahead of him, plenty of time to come up with a new career and a new identity. Yep, he would miss this city.

Tuesday 3:48pm

Andrew turned his Audi into the driveway to see Molly and Murphy at the large picture window barking like the world was about to explode. He squeezed Shannon's hand.

"I think I had better lock them up before you go into the house. They're going to freak when they see you. I think they were as worried about you as I was."

"No, let's just get out here and go in through the front. You can let them out into the yard and I'll be OK."

"How about if I let them out into the front yard and *then* come and get you. They can get all excited and love you through the fence until they settle down." With that Andrew put the car in park and got out.

Shannon watched as the dogs left the window to go wait at the front door. Soon, both dogs appeared in the yard. Molly was barking and announcing to the world that she was large and in charge, so don't get in her way. Both dogs came to the fence and put their big paws on the top rail. Molly continued to bark and Murphy shivered and whined. One would think they hadn't seen Shannon in a month!

Andrew had secured the gate and was back at her door. He helped her from the car, careful not to grab her arm where it had been bandaged. The cut underneath had been cleaned and sealed with a special type of super glue for cuts. Apparently, this process made for less scars.

Both dogs were shivering and whining now, jumping up and down along the fence line as Andrew escorted Shannon to the gate. Some of the color had returned to her face and skin after a night of IV fluids and electrolyte-filled drinks. She had even managed some crackers and apple sauce. Tonight, Andrew would make her the chicken noodle soup recommended by the doctor and he would pay for the delivery service to get additional groceries and Gatorade for her to drink.

As Shannon stood at the gate, gently cooing to the dogs while they jumped and licked and cried, he thought about the fact that he might never be able to leave her alone again. He didn't even want to talk to her about being alone for fear it would upset her beyond anything he could imagine.

The two stood at the gate for what seemed like an eternity and he could tell that she was getting tired of standing. Finally, Andrew addressed the dogs in a stern tone and told them to get back. They half-way complied, sniffing and dancing around Shannon as he helped her through the yard toward the house.

At the porch, she dropped to her knees and wrapped her arms around the necks of both dogs. She buried her face between the two and sobbed. Andrew knelt down behind her and thought about pushing the dogs back but changed his mind. He too began to cry as Molly and Murphy covered Shannon's neck and ears with doggy kisses infused with whines and howls of joy.

Tuesday 5:28pm
One Week Later

Derrick closed the murder book and placed it on the shelf behind his desk. The perpetrator had obviously gotten away and they had given him the ten-minute head start. The house had belonged to an elderly bachelor who had passed away nearly seven years ago. The taxes and utilities were paid by money order, consistently on time. Those had been purchased with cash at the local supermarket.

All of the furnishings and clothing in the house seemed to be from the previous occupant. There had been some food items in the refrigerator along with a six pack of bottled beer. None of the bottles had been touched, so no usable prints were found. The refrigerator handle and door knob to the basement had smeared prints that were also unusable. Everything from the basement had been brought to the station for closer examination and a tiny sliver of a print had been recovered from the scalpel. If they had a clear print to run it against, they might be able to convince a jury it was a match. For now, they would collect and catalog everything and in preparation for the day this guy resurfaced.

Derrick had an appointment with the local FBI office to review his theory that this was a serial murderer and officially link the victims he had personally tied to the case. Once that was done, they could utilize Federal resources and look nationally for this perp. The unfortunate piece was that he would likely have to kill again in order to get caught. This guy either had dumb luck, or he operated with knowledge of forensic science.

Derrick looked at the clock. If he didn't leave now, he would be late. Sydny had convinced all parties involved to do a group counseling session and the first one was scheduled for tonight. He wasn't included in the counseling services, but she thought it might be useful for him to attend the first session and kick the meeting off with commitment to finding the man responsible, as well as ask if they were OK with Sydny sharing any important details with him that might help him solve the case.

He grabbed his leather jacket from the hook by the door and headed out. In the hallway, Captain Rhodes stopped him. "Hey Derrick, have you heard from Dr. Rutherford this week?"

"No, the last time I talked to him was over a week ago, when the Roundsley girl was brought in."

"OK, thanks. You look late for something, we'll chat later."

"I'm about to be, so thanks." Derrick continued down the hallway toward the back door and the parking lot. He looked back at the captain, "Why do you ask?"

The captain was in the doorway of his own office and turned his head toward Derrick, "He hasn't been to work for a week, and I guess he hasn't called in either, so his boss has started asking around."

"That's weird." Derrick said. "I hope he didn't get lost up hiking in the canyon. He goes just about every weekend. Someone should send a patrol up to look for his car."

"That's good info, thanks, Derrick."

* * * * * * * *

Derrick joined the group already seated in the front room of Sydny's townhouse. She had expanded the triangle made by the three large chairs and brought in folding chairs to create a large circle. One folding chair waited, empty for him. Several bottles of water were placed on the coffee table and Sydny indicated an unopened bottle to him.

"Sorry I'm late and thank you for allowing me to be here." Derrick took his seat.

"You're actually right on time." Sydny said as she went to the front door and locked it. She closed the foyer door behind her and rejoined the group.

"I am so happy that all of you have agreed to this group counseling plan. It's important that we establish some rules of engagement before we begin, especially since our group is made up of people with different experiences. We must be sensitive of Rebecca and Shannon, who lived through an awful nightmare, but at the same time we must not down play the feelings of fear and helplessness experienced by those whose loved ones went through a traumatic situation as well.

Every one of you experienced trauma and every one of you felt helpless to do much about it. Many of you experienced some sense of guilt as well. All of this is normal, but what I really want everyone to understand is that the level of sharing in this group is limited, and the purpose is to help each other work through fears and feelings that keep us from living our everyday lives." Sydny looked around the room and made eye contact with each person as she spoke. "Before we start, I want Detective Howard to share the reason for his visit today."

"Thank you, and please, everyone, call me Derrick, I'll use your first names if that's OK as well. I feel like we have earned that standing with each other." He looked around the group and was met with understanding and agreement.

"I'm not here to pry into your business, so I won't stay. I just wanted to first, tell you all that I am committed to finding and convicting the perpetrator responsible for all of this. I'm meeting with the FBI later this week and I believe they will be joining in on the investigation." Again, looks of agreement and support from the group.

"That leads me to the second reason I am here. I would like to ask that as you share in your group, you allow Sydny to capture any details she thinks could help us in the investigation. I'm talking about descriptions, smells, details of places or things, that not only help us to find this person, but also might help us to convict this person once found.

Lastly, I wanted you all to know that even though we are going to maintain surveillance of your homes, we believe the perpetrator has left the state. That probably won't help you to sleep any better, but I thought you should know. Are there any questions before I go?"

The room was quiet but Derrick gave everyone a minute to think. They were all probably tired of speaking with him already, as he had interviewed each of them at least twice during the past week.

Rebecca, who had no family and had hitch-hiked her way into town almost a month ago, was staying with Sydny, who insisted on taking her in.

The girl was barely eighteen, and had been raised in one bad foster environment after another. Once she hit the legal age, she was on the streets. She would likely regret coming to this valley for the rest of her life, but the bond that was forging between her and Sydny was obvious, so Derrick thought perhaps this girl could have a normal life someday. It was Rebecca, who was the most damaged, was the first to speak up,

"Why can't you stay? I mean, wouldn't it be better to hear the information straight from us, and not risk losing some piece of the puzzle by having it retold to you by another person? I mean," she looked around the room at the others, "I don't mind if everyone else is

OK with it." Her eyes landed on Shannon, her kindred soul mate in this nightmare.

"I don't mind at all, in fact, I agree, anything we can do the help you find this horrible man. I'm not sure I'll ever sleep through the night until you do." Shannon looked at Andrew who nodded in agreement.

"I'm good." Said Steve

Alex held Victoria's hand and stated matter-of-factly, "It really isn't up to us, it's all up to Rebecca and Shannon, so if they are OK, I'm OK." Victoria nodded alongside of him. Katrina was agreeing as well and they all looked to Sydny for her approval.

"It's your group and it's your rules. If at any time someone changes their mind, we must all agree to honor that request." Again, there was agreement from the room. "OK then, why don't we get started on the ground rules. Any suggestions?"

Rebecca spoke up again with the courage that must have been formed over years of having no one to take care of her,

"I say that everyone should share whatever they are comfortable with and nothing more. And if someone is uncomfortable with what is being shared, they can step out of the room."

"I agree," said Shannon, "and we have to agree not to judge."

"Definitely." Said Steve. "Definitely."

Some nodded and some agreed verbally, but no one offered up any additional rules, so Sydny looked at Derrick and asked, "*Can* you stay?"

"I can, and thank you, I really do appreciate you allowing me to be here. I hope I can use what you share to close these cases."

OK then, let's begin, but remember, anything you are not comfortable sharing with this group can be saved for private sessions. Why don't we go around the room and each of you tell me how you've been doing over the past week. Rebecca, are you comfortable starting?

"Ya, sure. Well some of you know that I only got out of the hospital last Thursday, so I've mostly been getting settled her with Sydny. I've had a few doctor appointments too and I'm tired of getting poked, but is sure beats being cut." She tried to chuckle but the tears welled up in her eyes and what she hoped could be a joke only caused the others to look down or away.

Shannon's eyes met hers, equally filled with tears, "No, you're right, after that I don't think getting my blood drawn will ever bother me again." She smiled and a tear escaped down her cheek.

Sydny picked up the tissue box that had also been strategically placed and offered it first to Rebecca and then to Shannon. Both took a few tissues and Sydny replaced it asking Katrina,

"How has your week been?"

"I've been good. They didn't let me work at all last week so I spent a lot of time with my sister. We saw every PG or G rated movie that is out right now and I helped her do her grocery shopping for the week. I don't really think I *needed* a break from work, but I definitely need one from my sister now."

Everyone grinned and light laughter filled the room. "I went back to work last night and I napped on and off today. I'm happy to be getting back to normal, well, at least trying." Katrina let the group know she was finished sharing by looking at Alex to her left.

"I'm like Katrina, they sent me home for a few days and I just puttered around the house getting things ready for the snow. But I got back to work before the weekend. I'm happy to be back on shift, and the hallucinations have stopped, but every once in a while, I wake up in a cold sweat and I can't remember why."

Victoria jumped in, "You have nightmares, that's why." She looked at him with concern.

"And how are you doing, Victoria?" asked Sydny.

"I'm OK. Nothing happened to me. I have no room to complain."

"Nothing may have happened to you *per se*, but you have the burden of watching something scary happen to the person you love. And that gives you the right to tell us how you feel." Sydny encouraged.

"I'm just glad it's all over. I just want Alex to stop having nightmares."

"That's understandable. Unfortunately, nightmares are our brains way of dealing with information that is difficult to process. Eventually they'll go away. Andrew, are you experiencing some of the same emotions as Victoria?"

"Ya, we don't sleep very well. Shannon has nightmares every night and somehow our dogs have now become a part of our sleeping party." Andrew smiled and squeezed Shannon's hand. The two exchanged a knowing look.

"I just don't feel safe without Andrew and my dogs in the bed with me. Well, the dogs aren't *in* the bed, they sleep on a blanket on top."

"Don't lie, sweetie, they eventually make their way under the covers." A little more anxiety was released within the room as laughter pushed back the ominous feeling that hung in the air.

And so, the session went, with each member of the group becoming more comfortable at sharing a thought or a feeling about their current situation. Detective Derrick Howard patiently listened and observed. *'What an amazing group of individuals.* He thought to himself. He was still at a loss as to how they were each somehow connected to this young girl, Rebecca, who had lay silently in the hospital for over a week, and yet somehow brought them all together to solve a mystery; part of one, anyway. The rest was yet to be solved and he had an uncanny feeling that if it could be solved, this group would help to do it.

Epilogue
Spring - 2:27am

Steve could smell the fresh mountain air laced with the scent of pine and recent rain. He stepped carefully to minimize the noise, which came naturally to him. He knew the cabins were at least two miles behind him, but sound carried easily through the sparse trees. The walking path was off to his left, not where he could see it, but where he knew from experience it would be.

The sun was beginning to set, elongating the shadows of the trees. A small wind picked up and he caught the scent of her hair. He breathed in the soft coconut and sparks of anticipation shot through his body.

He continued on until he was ahead of her and then stepped out onto the path,

"Oh, thank goodness! Is that the way back to the cabins?" He asked, feigning concern.

She smiled at him and nodded as she turned to point in the direction she had come.

"Yes, just follow this path all the way back."

As he listened to her voice and noticed the way her dark hair framed her delicate skin, he pulled the plastic bag from his back pocket and removed the damp cloth. She finished and turned back to look at him.

He had already closed the distance and the fear registered in her eyes as he pushed the cloth to her mouth and nose, and cupped the back of her head with his left hand. He moved quickly behind her as she struggled to push free. He pulled her head against his chest and wrapped his left arm around hers, still holding the cloth soaked in chloroform to her face. She clawed at his arms briefly and then went limp.

He readjusted to take on the weight of her body, and then she jerked up and slammed the back of her head into his face. The pain exploded through his nose and he jerked awake in the darkness.

The End